The Cupid Effect

ALSO BY DOROTHY KOOMSON
FROM CLIPPER LARGE PRINT

Marshmallows For Breakfast
My Best Friend's Girl

The Cupid Effect

Dorothy Koomson

W F HOWES LTD

This large print edition published in 2007 by
W F Howes Ltd
Unit 4, Rearsby Business Park, Gaddesby Lane,
Rearsby, Leicester LE7 4YH

1 3 5 7 9 10 8 6 4 2

First published in the United Kingdom in 2003
by Judy Piatkus (Publishers) Ltd

A CIP catalogue record for this book is available
from the British Library

ISBN 978 1 40740 933 7

Typeset by Palimpsest Book Production Limited,
Grangemouth, Stirlingshire
Printed and bound in Great Britain
by Antony Rowe Ltd, Chippenham, Wilts.

For
my twelve little samurai
(you know who you are)

THE LUVVIE BIT . . .

Heartfelt thanks to:
Colette Harris; Sharon Wright and David Jacobson; Marian and Gordon Ndumbe; Graeme Delap; Ginny and Paul Baillie; Sharon Percival; Maria Owen; Stella Eleftheriades; Rhian Clugston; Mark Barrowcliffe; Martin and Sachiko O'Neill; Christian Lewis; Tracy Jurd; Selina Bromley; Tasha Harrison; the Cunniffs; and lovely Janet, for inspiring this story.

Also:
Thank you to my parents, Agnes and Samuel; my sibs, Sameer, Kathleen and David; Maryam, Dawood, Maraam, Muneerah, Yusuf, Ahmad and Ameerah; Liah, Skye, Aysah and Joshua; Luc; Jonathan and Rachel; Connor; and Habiba, David and Jade. Your love and support has kept me going.

PROLOGUE

GOOD INTENTIONS

1. Thou shalt sort out thy cardiovascular system
2. Thou shalt NOT get involved in other people's lives
3. Even if they're really, really nice thou shalt remember Commandment 2
4. Thou shalt think before thy speaks
5. Thou shalt think again before thy speaks
6. Thou shalt watch less *Angel*
7. Thou shalt remember that Angel is a 250-year-old vampire who dated Buffy The Vampire Slayer, not the man you're going to be with for ever and ever.

Simple. No? Easy. No? And I've broken two of them within, oooh, four hours.

CHAPTER 1

HEART'S DESIRE

I blame Oprah.

This is all her fault.

I mean, if it wasn't for her, I'd be waking up to 'just' another weekend, right about now. The usual: Saturday morning telly, wander round Bromley shopping centre, battle for food in the Savacentre.

Instead, I'm stood at Leeds train station with my worldly goods at my feet.

I've *really* done it this time, haven't I? I've done some stupid things in my life, most of them either involving sex or money or shoes, but this time I've truly surpassed myself. And it's all down to Oprah Winfrey.

Oh, it started innocently enough. I woke up one morning and I couldn't *get*.

I couldn't get up, get showered, get dressed, get to the station, get on a train, get to work. I couldn't get, so I pulled a sickie and I saw *Oprah*. My life went pear-shaped right after that.

Up to that point, any doubts I had about my life were formless. Just floating around at the back of my consciousness. After my sickie, though, these doubts and insecurities had a voice. An American talk show host's voice.

First, I was taping Oprah's show. *Every day*. Next, terms like 'heart's desire' and 'you can't change what you don't acknowledge' were never far from my lips. Then came the books. I became the Noah of self-help manuals. I was hoarding them two by two as though, instead of a flood, there was a predicted self-help drought coming and yea, verily, it was almost upon us. A few moments after that – or maybe it was months – I was headed for Leeds clutching a one-way ticket. Because that's where my heart's desire was. Supposedly. Two hundred miles away from everything I knew and loved.

I glanced down at my suitcase and holdall.

WHAT THE HELL HAVE I DONE?

I've given up everything to go back to college, that's what.

Two hundred miles away, in London, I had a life. I had my own flat. Two televisions, a sofa, a wardrobe, bookcases, video shelves, a bed made from reclaimed antique wood. Not some cheapo self-assembly job. It was actually made for me from antique wood. How many people could say that? Not many, that's how many.

And, down south, I had friends. Hoards of them. I couldn't go down the end of my street without tripping over them. Up here, I had my best mate Jessica and . . . and . . .

The breath caught in my chest, my heart started flinging itself against my rib cage. *Oh God. I'm*

4

insane. I'm actually insane. (That revelation was on a par with finding out I was never going to marry Arnold Schwarzenegger. Except I'd cried quite a lot then.)

This was what everyone said. My family, my friends, my colleagues. They'd all reminded me how I'd struggled to pay off my student debts and buy a flat and decorate it and become respected in my career. 'And you're giving it all up to go back to living out of one room? Why exactly?'

'Because Oprah told me to,' would've been the short answer.

I explained, though, that I was leaving because life is too long, not too short. What if I get to ninety with my memory intact? Wouldn't I be *more* pissed off if I got to that ripe old age and realised I'd not had the courage to follow my true heart's desire and do what I really wanted with my life instead of carrying on with the day to day because it was easier not to rock the boat? Life's too long not to do it; not to be true to myself. Most people understood when I spelt it out like that. Either that, or they lost interest halfway through and agreed with me to shut me up.

But why didn't anyone stop me? If I really thought someone was going to do what I'd done on the strength of an American chat show and a few self-help tomes, I'd have gone in for a spot of kidnapping and self-help deprogramming. But that's just me, obviously.

Anyway, it's too late now, isn't it, Ceri D'Altroy?

You're here now, they're expecting you on Monday, and someone else is living in your flat. Might as well get on with it. Start dealing with the now. (Dealing with the now? Dealing with the now?! I was even thinking like an Oprah guest. The pre-Oprah me would've said, 'Right Ceri, move your bloomin' arse.')

I hoisted my holdall onto my shoulder, gripped my suitcase handle with renewed purpose and vigour then headed for the taxi rank outside.

As I staggered towards the station exit, I kept my line of sight firmly lowered, with my head down, my chin-length black hair hiding my face. I often walked like this, as though I had the weight of the world, as well as half my flat, on my shoulders. I wasn't a miserable old cow, I'd actually trained myself to not look up. To not look anyone in the face or initiate eye contact. The last thing I needed at this stage of the game, when I was already fragile, was to make eye contact with a stranger. Catch someone's eye and you soon found yourself signing up for a credit card, giving some freak a fake phone number or hearing about some old dear's gall bladder operation. At least, that's what happened to me. Regularly. More regularly than should've been statistically possible. Most people didn't get on a bus and get off fifteen minutes later knowing the entire life story of the woman next to them. I did. There were whole bus routes where I knew most of the passengers by their ailments, not their names.

This was my talent; my gift. Unintentionally eliciting personal info from perfect strangers. I never did have the brass front to tell these people to get lost or even ignore them. The best I could do was not make eye contact in the first place. And I'd found it perfectly feasible to go about ninety-two per cent of my daily business without looking anyone in the eye.

I wrestled my slipping holdall back onto my left shoulder, ignoring how my rucksack lacerated that soft, fleshy bit between my neck and shoulders. *I can do this. I can do this*, I repeated in my head.

I hadn't got past the entrance of Menzies when a body stepped into my path. Shite. This happened sometimes. The 'no eye contact' thing didn't work. People approached me anyway. But, I could still get out of this if I kept my head down and moved on.

'Sorry,' I mumbled, and stepped to my left without looking up.

The body stepped with me.

I stepped to the right, the body stepped to the right.

Left, the body went left. We danced on – right and left, left and right – like this for a few more seconds, then I attempted a double-bluff, left step, but actually went to the right.

But my escape plan was foiled by a fiendish body block. This person had me bang to rights. And I was going to be signing up to be a Jehovah's Witness in, oooh, three minutes.

With a silent sigh, I looked up.

I wasn't greeted by a magazine promising to save my soul (but let me die if I needed a blood transfusion), instead, a cardboard sign with:

Kerry Dalboy

was thrust in my face.

My eyes shot to above the sign. Jess grinned back at me so wide I could hardly see her face.

'Welcome home sweetie,' Jess cried and threw her arms around my neck. As she did so, our combined weight tipped back onto my overstuffed rucksack and before either of us could do anything, we both went tumbling to the ground.

CHAPTER 2

STUDENT COUNTRY

In the short-stay car park across from the station, Jess stood behind me as I struggled out of my black rucksack. Her legs buckled as she took the strain. We both then huffed and puffed as we pushed the rucksack onto the back seat of the car. We'd silently agreed never to mention again what had just happened in the station. Ever.

'OK, one, two, three . . . hnnnugh!' We both heaved my suitcase into the boot. I had, of course, managed to travel across London and nigh on two hundred miles with this stuff on my own, but the grunting and straining made my efforts seem all the more heroic.

'I thought you'd be bringing more stuff,' Jess said as she squashed my holdall on top of the suitcase. She knew I couldn't pack light if my house was on fire. And I'd *never* packed a two bedroom flat into three luggage items before. Which is why I'd been up half the night packing and repacking and repacking. I'd finally fallen asleep at about three a.m., still wondering if I should take everything out and start again. I'd never had to pack for twelve months before. Not even when I was in college – it'd always been packing for a few months until I went back to London.

I haven't brought that much with me, have I? Maybe I'd been a bit too ruthless in deciding what I couldn't live without. Clothes, shoes, books, videos, my photo albums, my beloved iBook, toothbrush, beauty shelf or two. But not enough for twelve months away from home. 'I'll probably go back next weekend for more,' I said.

'Oh Ceri,' Jess said, she paused in the driver's open doorway, 'that'll cost you a fortune.'

'It won't cost *that* much, I'll get an Apex,' I said.

'You'll be knackered though.'

'Yes, Mum.'

'Oi, watch it, Cockney.'

'That's the sort of thing you'd say to your kids, isn't it? "You'll be knackered."'

'I don't know, you show a person a bit of concern and she just flings it back in your face.' Jess sounded hurt. 'Well, if you don't want my concern . . .'

'I'm surprised you ain't got fake tears to go with that fake upset.'

She laughed and started the car. 'You're all heart, you.'

'I learnt it from you, Teach.'

My life path had crossed with Jessica Breakfield's life path when I was a first year psychology and media student at college in Leeds and she was a psychology lecturer. So that should be, *Dr* Jessica

10

Breakfield. She hated me calling her that, though. 'You use it like mothers use middle names,' she'd once said. 'It always sounds vaguely insulting or like I'm in trouble.'

She terrified me when I first met her. Jessica was the first woman doctor of psychology I met who looked and was under thirty-five. She had theories to her name, she was young and she made lectures interesting.

Jess remembered me as prone to hiding behind my waist-length hair and not talking very much. Probably something to do with me staring at her in wide-eyed, nineteen-year-old awe.

I'd done a comedy gulp when she was assigned as my personal tutor, but as I got to know her and began to relax around her, she began to see my face because my veil-like hair got shorter and shorter. (The shortest being the crop, and cleanly shaved at the back, which resulted in my parents not speaking to me till it grew back.)

It was at the end of college, though, when I decided to do a PhD that Jess and I became proper mates. She helped with my PhD proposal and the more time we spent together, the more we found that we had loads in common: a love of television, a worship of chocolate and an almost fanatical obsession with not getting out of our pyjamas on a Sunday unless we really, *really* needed to buy food. But these were only the tips of the icebergs floating in our sea of similarity.

Our connection went far deeper than was first

11

visible to the naked eye. It was as if Jess and I were separated at birth – twelve years apart. She had a husband – Fred, teenage twin daughters Sharon and Colette – and grew up in Harrogate. I didn't. She was five foot ten, slenderish with waves and waves of auburn hair and a Yorkshire accent. I was five foot four-and-a-bit, nearly five foot five, actually, curvyish, with a shiny black bob and a posh Sarf London drawl. (Yes, that sounded like an oxymoron, but there I was, saying 'scowns' (scones) and 'cheeky caaa' (cheeky cow) in the same sentence. Well, I'm pretty sure I've said them in the same sentence.) We were definitely the odd couple on the outside. Had you to pick out the two partners in crime in a line-up you'd never put the two of us together. Age, height, looks, background, nothing went together. But when Jess and I were together we were one person. We thought alike, we argued alike, we were scathing on demand. Under it, though, was a deep understanding. Jess was the only person who hadn't said. 'You're mad you' when I told her what I was doing. She'd been extremely supportive. Actually, what she said was, 'Awww, honey, that's fantastic! I knew you could do it. But you can't live with me. And you can't live within walking distance of me. I'll never sleep if you do.'

I never did get on that PhD course, but I did get the most honest, caring, strangest best mate known to womankind.

★   ★   ★

Jessica parked Fred's metallic blue Mondeo outside the orange-brick house, slap bang in the middle of Stanmore Vale, Burley Park. I'd lived near here, in Burley Park, when I was a Leeds student the first time. This area was unofficially Student Country.

You had to leave your maturity, dress sense and need to keep regular hours at the various border checkpoints around here. Student Country was made up of Hyde Park, Headingley, Burley Park and Kirkstall; it was where most of the students who went to Leeds Uni, Leeds Met, All Souls and the other colleges in Leeds lived, loved and drank. It'd occurred to me more than once that you could wipe out at least seventy per cent of the student population by napalming that relatively small area of West Yorkshire.

Three streets over was the last student house I'd lived in. Now *that* was a student house. 98 Stanmore Avenue. I'd never forget that address. So much had happened to me in the year I lived in that house it was hard to believe it was only a year. I'd got pneumonia in that house. I'd met the love of my life when I lived in that house. I was dumped by the love of my life *in* that house. I had what turned out to be my last shag in Leeds in that house (and hadn't had another one for about two years after that). I got my finals results in that house. It was a very momentous house. I was hoping that 17 Stanmore Vale, the house I was about to move into, would be far less dramatic. I'd grown out of student dramatics.

★　　★　　★

I'd been clutching my *Leeds A to Z* and a borrowed copy of *The Itchy Guide To Leeds* when I first knocked on 17 Stanmore Vale. It was the first time I'd been back round these parts in well over six years and I'd needed a little help in finding my way around.

Jess, who taught at Leeds Metropolitan University ('The Met' to most people), had seen the advert for a double room and thought it'd be perfect for me: I knew the area (ish) and it was living with two post-graduate students as averse to first-time-away-from-home, freedom-insane undergraduates who'd want to party all night and slob all day as I was. And it was a good twenty-minute drive from her home. So, she'd noted the details then went round taking down all the flyers she could find so I'd have a chance to look at it before anyone else did.

The front door had been opened about two seconds after my knock by a lad with messy, rust-coloured hair and a pierced eyebrow. He was casually clothed in baggy jeans and a plain white T-shirt. I say lad, he was more a bloke. But could pass for a lad because he was younger than me. (Not that I was old. He was twenty-five, twenty-six and I'd almost left my twenties. But only almost.) His light eyes sparkled as he said, 'Hi, you must be Ceri,' and grinned. His whole face relaxed into that grin and I fell instantly in like with him. I was a relatively simple creature like that. You were nice to me,

I liked you. Hell, I'd been out with blokes on the strength of them being nice to me as opposed to any kind of attraction.

'And you're Jake?' I replied, grinning back.

'Yup, that's me. You're right on time. Come in. Have you just come up from London?'

Is it that obvious? I wondered. I glanced down at myself. I did indeed look like I'd just crawled away from a three-hour train journey. My jacket and jeans were travel-creased, my Walkman, crisp packets, spare jumper, notebook and reading material all bulged in my bag. 'Yeah. I'm going back straight away as well,' I said, looking back up at Jake. 'I could only get the afternoon off work. They're not too happy about me leaving so want to get every second out of me.'

'Oh, right, better get on then. This way.'

My feet bounced slightly on the ruby red carpet of the hallway. Quality carpet, and from the cushioning effect, it probably had underlay. *Clever colour choice*, I thought, as I followed Jake. Subconsciously you felt important, like VIP material, because you'd come into a place where they'd laid out the red carpet, literally. Or it could be a way to get a murdered body out of the house without the worry of blood stains on the carpet (but that was the kind of thought that plagued my mind).

Opposite the stairs lay the living room. I stepped in after Jake and my mouth fell open. It was straight out of a homes magazine: porridge-coloured carpet, cream walls and two squashy, tan leather sofas. Standing guard over the fireplace was a professionally-framed Dali print – *The Metamorphosis of Narcissus*. At the other end of the room were two huge bay windows with net curtains and everything. This was a proper sitting room, not a hashed together, student job. I'd steeled myself when I knocked on the front door for threadbare carpets, limescale plumbing and tales of a nightmare landlord.

Jake explained that he was in fact that nightmare landlord, that he owned the house, as he showed me round. 'My parents lent me the money for a deposit on this place and acted as guarantors when I first came to college here just over four years ago. I was a mature student, I mean, not that mature, but I couldn't stand the thought of a normal student house, so I talked them into it. They also lent me the cash to do it up properly. That's why I rent out the other two rooms, it covers the mortgage and pays back my parents.'

I was only half listening to him; I was far too busy falling in love. The red carpet and living room were like passing someone attractive in the street and glancing back to get a second look. The rest of the house was like getting to know someone, dating them, sharing with them and finding out that everything about them is wonderful. Finding no reason *not* to fall in love with them.

We wandered down the narrow corridor to the kitchen and my heart fluttered. It was another large space, this time with real wood flooring.

A chrome and beechwood dream, white cabinets with real wood worktops that, Jake explained, needed special oil rubbing into them – 'we take that in turns'. A breakfast bar divided the room, and around it stood four high, padded stools. The kitchen had stainless steel appliances, a blender, a real coffee machine, canisters that had 'tea', 'sugar', 'coffee' and 'biscuits' on them. (I had a sneaking suspicion that each jar was filled with what was written on the outside of it.)

'There's a little bit of a garden-patio area that we sometimes sit on, but me and Ed don't use it that much,' Jake added as he nodded to the back door. 'Do you want to see upstairs now?'

'Oh yes,' I whispered.

The soft-pile redness of the corridor went all the way up the stairs, both flights of them. The room on offer was right at the top of the house.

I trailed behind Jake as he swung open the white painted door to the attic room, my heart pounding hard in my chest, my breath short with anticipation. I fell completely head over heels as the door revealed the mysteries of the attic.

Part of the ceiling was slanted, with two skylights set in it. The cream walls made the room seem even larger. It had a double bed, a grey metal-framed desk, an oak wardrobe, and rather thoughtfully, a window had been installed in one of the walls so you could look out at the treetops and into bedrooms of the opposite houses when you lay on the bed.

I was speechless with lust as I turned to Jake and said, 'And you don't want to move in here now that it's free?'

Jake shrugged and shook his head. 'It's too far to stumble if I come home drunk or stoned or both. Bill, that's the lad who lived in this room before, would often sleep on one of the sofas downstairs cos he couldn't make it up here when he was pissed. It's a long way.'

'And what about the other lad?' I added, just as breathlessly. 'Doesn't he want a bigger room?'

'All the rooms are quite big. But Ed? Nah, he doesn't want it. He's a boy, and to him more space equals more to clean.'

'I see,' I said in a small, small voice. *If I don't get this room, if I end up in a hovel in Hyde Park with bars on the windows and doors, then I was Attila the Hun in a former life.* 'So, do you need references or something if I want to take it?'

'Um, no. I mean, there's a standard six-month contract and I'd need a month's deposit and a month's rent in advance, but no references,' Jake said. 'But you'd be interested in moving in?'

I almost nodded my head off. 'Oh yes.'

'Right. Well, there's no one else waiting to see it. It's weird, actually, no one else has rung up about it. I don't know why . . .' Jake went off into a stare. 'I put up loads of flyers and no one's called.'

'Really?' I replied, sympathetically. *It'll have absolutely nothing to do with Jess taking down the*

18

posters all round the college campus, I'm sure. 'That *is* weird.'

I reached into my bag, pulled out my cheque book, rummaged around for a pen. 'So, that's £600, is it?'

'What?' Jake said. 'Oh, yeah. You can make the cheque out to Jake Halder. We can set up a standing order after that.'

I was already writing at the speed of light, just in case he changed his mind and decided to investigate the case of the disappearing flyers more closely.

'You're not a psycho, are you?' he asked as he led the way back down to the ground floor, my HSBC cheque peeking out of the top of his jeans back pocket. 'The lad who lived here before, Bill, turned out to be a bit of a nutter. Me and Ed were well pleased when he got chucked off his course and had to move. You're not one, are you?'

'I've been told I'm a bit strange sometimes, but not a nutter.'

'Cool,' Jake said. And there was me thinking *I* was easily pleased. 'Anyway, let me know when you want to move in and either Ed or I will be here. Then I'll give you your own set of keys and you can sign the contract. Do you want a cup of tea before you go?'

And that was it. I'd got myself a place to live. The only bind I could see would be trailing down to the second floor to the bathroom or to use the loo. But that bathroom had floor-to-ceiling blue

19

and white mosaic tiles, a power shower and squashy rubber floor tiles – it was the kind of suffering I could handle.

'Hi,' I said to the stringy lad who answered the door of 17 Stanmore Vale this time around. He was about twenty-two, looked like he'd been elongated on a rack, had long blond hair and wasn't there when I'd looked around the house. And there ended the list of things I knew about him. I couldn't even remember his name. Eric or something.

He in return cast an eye over me, my luggage, the woman technically old enough to be his mother behind me. Then he made no secret of his confusion: his forehead knitted together, his green eyes tried to calculate what was going on. 'You all right?' he asked, vague flirtations with a non-Yorkshire accent lilted in his voice.

'I'm Ceri D'Altroy. I'm moving into the room? Upstairs?'

'Ah, right,' he replied. 'I'm Ed.'

Ed. That was it. 'Hi, Ed. This,' I indicated to Jess with a slight nod of my head over my shoulder, 'is my best mate Jessica.'

'Hi?' Ed offered cautiously, his face blanking out completely. He made no move to let us in. He stood guarding the doorway like one of the guards outside Buckingham Palace; we were one moment away from him putting on his bearskin hat, picking up his rifle and totally ignoring us until his shift was over.

'OK Ed,' Jess said, 'are you going to let us in, or do we have to break in round the back?'

Ed, blankness aside, was polite and friendly. He made Jess and me a cuppa, even though I rarely drank proper tea. I'd been hoping he had herbal, but when I mentioned it he'd got that glazed-over expression he'd got when I introduced Jess as my best mate so 'Ordinary's fine,' I'd said, quickly.

Jess gulped hers down the second he set it down on the coffee table. While gulping, she twiddled locks of her auburn hair around her fingers. She was gagging for a cigarette. She'd abstained all the way from the station (Fred, her husband, didn't allow smoking in his car) and she didn't want to light up in what was so blatantly a smoke-free environment. It was painful to watch; I twisted in my seat so I wouldn't have to. Watch, that is.

After making the tea, Ed said he'd take my stuff up to my room.

'You don't have to, I'll do it later,' I'd said.

'It's no trouble,' Ed replied. 'I'm going upstairs anyway. Getting ready to go out later.'

'If you're sure . . .'

Ed shrugged his whole body. 'Course.'

'Thanks,' I said. 'I'll make you dinner one day as a thank you.'

'Yeah, she does a fantastic Pot Noodle,' Jessica chimed in.

I elbowed her, hard.

Despite his slender frame, Ed picked up the

21

rucksack, suitcase and holdall effortlessly. We watched his progress up the stairs with admiration. He must've been muscle and bone, rather than skin and bone as he looked.

Jess hopped up on the sill of the left bay window the second he'd gone, swept back the net curtain and opened the window. One cigarette went down in frantic silence – with each puff she visibly relaxed. The second cigarette was smoked slower, she could even talk. And, 'I'm glad you've got a nice place,' she said. 'Ed seems all right. I hope you'll be happy here.' Most best-est friends in the whole world would've been reassuring, possibly offered a hug, not Jessica. She called it like she saw it, even if I was falling apart.

Those words sparked my anxieties again. 'Do you think I'm mad?' I asked urgently.

'In general, yes. In doing this, no.' Jess's eyes studied me, her cigarette burning away as she hung it out the window. 'Well it's too bloody late to have doubts now, isn't it? You've chucked it all in down south and made a commitment up here.' (Most best-est friends in the whole world would've been reassuring, possibly offered a hug, not Jessica. She called it like she saw it, even if I was falling apart.)

I nodded in understanding. She was right of course. It really was too late. Sudden, violent nausea surged through my veins. Every heartbeat made me feel sicker. Less sure of what I'd done. Sure, it was all sane and rational and 'woo-hoo,

22

life affirming' in theory. Even on paper. In reality, I'd jacked in a life. My job was gone. My flat was rented out. My friends had thrown me a leaving do. Most people, when they had a life crisis, bleached their hair or shagged someone unsuitable. I jacked in a life and moved two hundred miles.

I chewed on my inner cheek and stared beyond Jess. It really was too late now.

'When I finish this,' Jess said, nodding at her cigarette, 'we'll go get you some food in Morrison's in town and then, if you're very good, I'll buy you a video recorder as a welcome home pressie.'

This was how Jess was supportive. Platitudes and empty reassurances in times of need weren't her thing; acts of true love – like buying me a video – were.

'Don't grin too soon D'Altroy, a video's no good without a telly.'

CHAPTER 3

THOU SHALT NOT . . .

Where the hell am I?
   I know I'm in a college. But, beyond that, I'm lost.

I was stood at the bottom of a winding stone staircase with wooden handrails, wondering if I should go up it or stay where I was, stuck in that first day at school nightmare where I don't know where I'm going and don't know anybody. I'd had that nightmare quite a lot over the weekend because it was my first day back at school, kind of. Except I'd be lecturing as well as learning. But still, I'd had the same dream over and over. I was wearing my hideous blue school uniform and I couldn't find out where I needed to be. When I eventually got there, all the students were older than me and laughed at me because I was wearing a school uniform. It didn't take a psychologist to work it out. I was scared. On every level of consciousness I was scared. And now the nightmare was coming true. I couldn't find where I needed to be.

I glanced around me, wondering how to get help. It probably had something to do with initiating eye contact.

All Souls University College, the institution who'd agreed to employ me for a year of teaching and researching, was only small. So small it'd been merely affiliated to Leeds University for years and years and had only become a college of the University in the last two years. There was a distinction between being a college affiliated to the University and being an actual college of the University, and that distinction was probably something to do with money. Most things were something to do with money. All Souls was a picturesque little college in its own way, surrounded by green playing fields. Most of it was sandstone-coloured because it'd been built during the sixties and that was the colour that was *en vogue* then. It was small. There were, what, 3000 students here? Small, intimate, part of the reason I'd applied here. Not as many people, not such a big pond to be a small fish in.

So why was I being belittled and looked down upon by the architecture?

I glanced up. The ceilings were so high, they were almost sky level. I took a peek at the ground. The parquet floors were made from king-size blocks, the windows went on for ever.

Scariest and biggest of all, though, were the students. I *wasn't that big when I was a student*, I thought as I side-stepped a gaggle of under-graduates. Most of them had been born in 1981 for goodness' sake, how could they be so huge? Was there some Thatcherite plot to make the voters of the future so big and brainwashed they'd scare off anyone who didn't think like she did? (I always knew that woman planned to stay in power for ever – Dr Evil was slightly naughty compared to her.) Were those hormones pumped into meat to make cows bigger and yield more meat, finally being shown in the youf of today? Or, horror of horrors, was I actually shrinking? Was I now shorter than the five foot four-and-a-bit, I'd left the house as this morning? Was it finally happening? My nightmare. The only age-related thing I was truly, TRULY frightened of. Getting shor—

'You look lost,' a male voice said behind me.

I spun to him. He had kind eyes and a soft face. He was wearing a white, long-sleeved T-shirt and blue Levi's. Most importantly, he wasn't as giant as everyone else. He was a lecturer.

'Yes! Yes, yes, I am.' *Could you please try to sound more desperate there, Ceri, he is after all the Pope and he did just ask you if you wanted sex before marriage sanctioned by the Catholic Church.* I cleared my throat. 'I mean, a little.'

'I'm Mel,' he said, 'I'm a sociology lecturer. You're about to start work in the psychology department, aren't you? I remember you being shown around last month.'

I nodded. 'That's me.'

'What's your name?' he asked and smiled. He had good teeth: white, straight, brushed and flossed twice a day. He was probably on first name terms with his dentist.

'Ceri. Ceri D'Altroy.'

'OK Ceri, where do you want to be?'

At home, in London, watching *Trisha*, eating bananas on toast in bed. 'The place where the secretaries are.'

'The department office?' he said.

That'll be it. 'Er, yeah. Just forgot the name of it for a second.'

Mel laughed, he thought I was joking. I was so scared, so panicked, I barely remembered my own name.

'It's this way.' He started up the stairs.

The canteen was, like everything else in this college, huge. Long, with regulation parquet floors and round tables with room for eight (maybe ten people, if everyone ate with their elbows tucked in). The right wall was floor to ceiling glass, giving you an unhindered view of the various halls of residence that were dotted around the campus. All the halls of residence looked like slightly narrower and shorter versions of sixties tower blocks, they were the same colour, probably designed by the same architect. As you entered the canteen through big wooden swing doors, you headed left for the service line: a long counter with glass protecting us from the food; behind it stood women and men in white kitchen overalls and white net caps ready to dish up.

I ordered fisherman's pie with a double side order of peas and a bottle of water. I paid, stepped

27

away from the cashier, then went into new girl free fall. I was all alone here.

The canteen instantly doubled in size. Then tripled. Then tripled again. It went on tripling in length and width until the far wall was nothing but a blip on the very distant horizon. I was suddenly the smallest girl in the world standing in the biggest room in the world.

I'd just come from the longest, most tedious briefing in the history of job briefings, there was nothing in my job description I didn't now know. The horror of it was going to live for ever in my mind. I did not need to eat by myself on top of that.

The room buzzed with chatter and eating and drinking and cutlery hitting crockery. And bonding. I couldn't see anyone sat alone. My footsteps would probably echo and echo and echo as I headed for a solitary table. Everyone would make 'look at saddo' eyes at each other about me as I took up a seat alone and ate alone. Gwen, the head of department, had sent me off to lunch on my tod, saying, 'I have lots of important things to do. I've scheduled your meetings with the three other lecturers you'll be working with for later this afternoon. Bye.' It didn't occur to her that me being new, this being my first day, I'd need someone to lunch with. Or, failing that, directions to the canteen.

Across the canteen, someone waved, and the room returned to normal size. I wasn't wearing

28

my glasses so I couldn't tell who it was from their face. They were a blue and white fuzz amongst the general colours and shapes in the canteen. Maybe they weren't waving at me at all. The room swelled again. I glanced over my shoulder, no one but the cashier behind me and she had her back to the waver. I peered forward, craning my neck and narrowing my eyes; the shape seemed familiar, as were the clothes. A white, long-sleeved top and blue jeans. Mel? He got up, beckoned, pointed to the plastic orange seat opposite him. My body sagged with relief. *Thank you, God! I will try very hard to get to church some time very soon.*

'Hi,' he said as I approached.

'Hi,' I grinned. Mel probably thought I spent my entire life in a constant state of relief and desperation.

'This is Claudine,' Mel said, indicating to the serene woman on his right. She was make-you-jealous gorgeous. Cropped, raven-black hair, Mediterranean skin, plump lips. This woman, this Claudine, had eyes that actually smouldered as she looked at you. 'Claudine, this is Ceri, she's the new person I was telling you about.'

Claudine's face broke into a friendly grin. 'Hi ya,' she said, 'how's it going?'

'Not bad, so far,' I said and reached for my fork – only to find it wasn't there. No cutlery. Great. I'd have to do the walk of shame back to the cashier. I'd feel a 24ct fool, sidling up to her, smiling, nicking a fork then running away again.

Those were moments I had nightmares about. I'd already relived a million and one times flailing about with another woman on Leeds station concourse. Each reliving brought a new and deeper horror. Sophistication was all about *not* doing those sorts of things. Bet women like Claudine didn't do those things.

'Here,' Mel said, giving me the second fork on his tray. 'I got this for Clau, cos she always forgets her cutlery, but for the first time ever, she remembered.'

Claudine rolled her smouldery eyes. 'Just give her the damn fork Melvin. All Ceri needs to know is that it's clean, and your lips haven't been anywhere near it.'

'Thanks,' I said, taking the fork, digging into the creamy sauce, hitting the white flesh of the fish with gusto. I was hungry. The kind of hunger that came from being so nervous I couldn't eat on Sunday and I couldn't even force water down my neck this morning.

'What's your PhD on?' Claudine asked after they'd watched me wolf down a couple of mouthfuls. I was that hungry the food didn't even touch the sides.

I swallowed a full mouthful, not wanting to talk with my mouth full – I was well brought up like that. In fact, I was constantly horrified that people sat happily chewing away while telling you some convoluted tale. 'I'm not actually doing a PhD,' I said to Claudine. 'I'm not technically studying either. I'm doing a year's research in the psychology department. I've had this idea in my head for years and I'm actually following it up. I'll also be lecturing first year, a bit of second year psychology, and taking tutorials. If it works out, I might be allowed to apply for a PhD course, though.'

'I didn't realise All Souls did that,' Claudine replied.

'They don't, usually. I happened to write to them about it around the same time that woman from the psychology department left.'

Claudine turned to Mel, 'Is that Eva?'

Mel nodded.

'Yeah, I think her name was Eva. They were desperate cos she left so late in the year,' I continued. 'I've taken over most of her teaching duties, well, I will be from tomorrow.'

'I guess from your accent you're from London?' Claudine asked.

I nodded. 'Although I did my first degree up here in Leeds. I lived up here for five years altogether.'

'Do you lecture in London?' Mel asked.

I shook my head. Braced myself to tell them what I did. 'No. I'm . . . I was . . . I am, I suppose, a journalist.'

I was terrified of not sounding qualified or experienced enough for my current teaching position. Journalist to psychology lecturer did not sound experienced or qualified a leap. Even I wasn't convinced about the leap and that leaping was being done by me.

'I've got a masters in journalism, I did that in London, and I have taught and lectured in psychology,' I added quickly. 'I mean, I taught psychology A-level for a bit before I went back to London, and I did a bit of psychology lecturing in London, on the subject I'm researching. I also lectured a bit in journalism. You se—'

'Whoa, calm down,' Mel said.

'This isn't an interview,' Claudine finished.

I relaxed against the uncomfortable orange seat, an interview was exactly how this felt. How everything felt. A gigantic test. Because I couldn't help thinking there'd been some kind of mistake. I'd written to the college on spec, on the off chance that they had an opening in the psychology department for someone who wasn't very experienced but who could take seminars while doing research. And All Souls took me seriously. Suddenly they were inviting me to an interview, then another interview, then a written test. Then a test lecture followed by another interview and, WHAM-BAM! I'd got this made-up position. My sister wouldn't trust me with her goldfish when she went on holiday, and this college was entrusting some ninety or so formative minds to me. How was that going to work?

'Do you two always have lunch together?' I asked them to deflect the attention firmly away from me.

Claudine and Mel looked at each other, then returned their joint gaze to me. 'Yeah, pretty much,' they said together.

Awww, bless. I got a kick out of seeing couples in love. It gave me hope: if other people could find that sort of closeness, then so could I. It could be done, so I could do it. Besides, the bitter, twisted jealous route had got me a bad rep and wrinkles.

'That's really good that you two can work together and lunch together every day and not have it damage your relationship. How long have you been going out?'

'Sorry?' Claudine replied.

'Excuse me?' Mel asked.

'You two, how long have you been going out together?' I repeated.

Silence hacked into the good humour like a machete into plywood.

Oh, good God. I've done it again.

I was infamous for wading into situations, mouth first. I tried not to, I just couldn't help myself. A question formed in my head, it came out of my mouth a microsecond later. There was no time for the thought to drop by the 'how's that going to sound out loud?' centre of my brain, in fact, it bolted right past it, wearing a disguise so good no one recognised it.

It was my total lack of fear in asking the questions other people pussyfooted around that made me a good journalist. And a nightmare dinner party guest. I'd once asked someone across a dinner table, 'So, did you finally end your four-year celibacy with that blind date last weekend?' Everyone else was thinking it, I'd said it. Silence was the reply, then, too.

I stopped eating as the current silence lengthened. I couldn't fit any more food into my mouth anyway, what with there being a size eight trainer rammed in my gob.

'I live with my boyfriend, Kevin,' only thin veins of ice laced Claudine's previously warm voice. 'Have done for two years.'

Mel's tone had evened out as he said: 'I'm not seeing anyone special.'

But, but . . . I looked from her face to his face to her face . . . two seconds with them and you knew, you just knew they were together, emotionally linked, *COUPLED*, dammit. It radiated from them like heat from a flame. Their emotion, their adoration, their affection, their attraction. Felt and reciprocated.

'Oh, sorry, I was doing that thing again,' I launched myself into an apology. 'You know that perception thing?' Blank faces greeted me. 'There's this theory in psychology about perception and how people often fill in the missing information in stuff like pictures and sentences with what they expect to be there. That's what I was doing, filling in the missing information with something, anything, the first thing that came to mind. Sorry.'

They both looked at me.

NOOOOOOOOO! Not The Look. Not The Silence. If you've messed up, and are trying to explain, the worst thing – other than being told you've disappointed someone – is to get The Look back. Hostility, disgust and hurt all balled up in one expression. Coupled with The Silence, it's unbearable.

I could now either shut up and let The Silence take its course, or keep talking until my voice ran dry/someone told me to shut up.

I'm not good at silences.

'Thing is, at our age, I kind of expect most people to be coupled up,' I explained. 'That's not to say that everyone should be coupled, I just expect them to be. Even though I'm not. And when I see two people getting on so well, I kind of . . . That's not to mean . . . Just cos you're friendly with someone you're automatically going out together, I suppose I wasn't thinking and it j—'

'It's all right,' Mel said, or maybe it was Claudine. Who could tell the difference?

'We get that sort of thing all the time,' Claudine said.

'Yeah, most people just hint at it though,' Mel added.

'No one has actually come out and said it before,' Claudine continued.

'Not directly,' Mel finished.

See? *SEE?!* They didn't simply finish each other's sentences, they knew what the other one was thinking; they actually voiced each other's train of

35

thought. That's not normal. That's not 'living with a boyfriend for two years'; that's not 'seeing no one special'. That's, 'I'm involved with the person I'm sitting next to'.

'Sorry, I'm a bit too direct. People tell me I'm like Cordelia, you know, from *Buffy The Vampire Slayer*? I think something, I say it, people look at me like they want to rip the tongue right out of my head. Sorry.'

I started shovelling food into my grand canyon of a mouth, then swallowed. I didn't see the need for chewing. I wanted to get away as quickly as possible.

Part of the reason I'd run away from London was so I could stop spreading my foot in mouth disease. I could reinvent myself. Be quiet, demure, sophisticated and – most importantly – not get involved.

I'd even sat on the train and formulated my own Commandments. (No offence whatsoever to God was meant. I knew I couldn't come up with a set of Commandments to rival His, but I needed something to work towards.) They went something like this:

1. Thou shalt sort out thy cardiovascular system
2. Thou shalt NOT get involved in other people's lives
3. Even if they're really, really nice thou shalt remember Commandment 2

4. Thou shalt think before thy speaks
5. Thou shalt think again before thy speaks
6. Thou shalt watch less *Angel*
7. Thou shalt remember that Angel is a 250-year-old vampire who dated Buffy The Vampire Slayer, not the man you're going to be with for ever and ever.

Simple. No? Easy. No? And I've broken two of them within, oooh, four hours. A personal best.

When my throat was definitely taking no more lodgers, I put down the fork and swallowed hard to get rid of the food lump so I could speak.

'Anyway, I'd better get going, I've got to meet another lecturer and find out what I'll be doing for them.' *In an hour and a half.*

I put my hands on either side of my tray, stood. 'I'll see you both around?' I knew I sounded desperate, but I couldn't help it, I thought I'd managed to get myself some friends then. Nothing major, just a couple of people to sit with in the canteen, extend my social circle in college to two.

'Yeah, course,' Mel said.

'When you're assigned an office, I'll come over and we can have a coffee, if you want,' Claudine said.

'Great, I'll see you soon.'

Yeah, yeah, I'll be lucky if I see either of you again.

37

SPRING TERM

(and it was 'term', dammit. No one is going to make me call it a semester)

CHAPTER 4

DRESS REHEARSAL

'I really don't know why you've asked me to come here,' Jess said, from the comfort of my bed. She was supposedly helping me to choose what to wear for my first lecture tomorrow morning, but in reality, she was under the covers watching *Coronation Street* while I paced the length of my room – of which there was quite a lot – and fretted about my first day as lecturer proper.

Me. Ceri D'Altroy, a lecturer.

The very thought made my stomach turn and twist like a wind chime in a strong breeze.

This had all been fantastic in theory. Y'know, like the heart's desire thing, I wanted to do it when it was an idea I'd scrawled down on a piece of paper under the heading 'goals'.

I'd always quite liked the idea of being an academic. That was why I'd applied for a PhD all those years ago. I wanted to carry on learning while helping with the teaching process. I liked lecturing, enjoyed the power it gave me. You stand up there, in front of people, you tell them what you know, they interject with their theories and together you helped to build a new theory, a new understanding.

41

I'd been seduced by that idea; of having that power all the time. Even though over the years, Jess had told me that students had changed. 'They don't have a thirst for learning like they did when you were a student,' she said. 'They're more interested in what they need to know for the exams than in expanding their minds.' I suppose that was part of why I wanted to do this as well. I wanted to see if I could help turn back the tide. Stop students being simply fixated on the exams. When I was a student, we – rather sadly some might say – used to look forward to certain lectures when we could debate stuff. Like in Jess's lectures, the philosophy of psychology. There was so much to think and talk about we'd often overrun. Or we'd stop at the end, go get coffees, come back and debate some more. I wanted that with my students. I wanted them to be so into my lectures they didn't mind if they overran.

Of course, with this lecturing lark, it didn't hurt that I'd get to talk, too. I loved talking. Not speaking, *per se*. I loved to think out loud at someone, to formulate theories and ideas and self-invectives through communicating with other people. I loved listening and having that spark of understanding or that flame of indignation lit in my head. So, on top of continuing to research what had, over the years, become my specialist subject, this was my idea of a dream job.

I just had no idea what to wear.

'I asked you here because I needed a second

opinion on what to wear tomorrow. I can't very well ask Jake or Ed, I've only lived with them for three days, they'll think I'm mad. So, you'll do.' Jess had planned to spend the evening with her husband and daughters, and had got quite far into that plan, which meant when she'd turned up at my place she'd been shrouded in her mac and Wellington boots. Underneath them she was wearing the grey fleece pyjamas I'd bought her last Christmas – they matched mine. She'd got straight into my bed and put on *Emmerdale*.

Jess's eyebrow arched up and her head creaked round to face me. 'Oh will I now. D'Altroy?'

'Yes.' Her expressive eyebrows didn't scare me. Much.

'What I meant was, I don't know why you asked me over for this. We all know what you're going to wear.'

I stopped pacing. 'Do we?'

Jess flung back the covers in a move born of frustration, got out of bed and marched across to the large oak wardrobe, threw open the wardrobe doors. 'OK, let's see what's in here, shall we.' She reached into the wardrobe's depths, pulled out an item of clothing on a hanger. 'What's this?' she said, raising the hanger so I could see it.

'My white long-sleeved top.'

Jess flung it onto the floor – the bed was too far away for her to hit it. She reached into the wardrobe again. 'And what's this?'

'My red long-sleeved top.'

43

'Hm-hm.'

That went on to the floor too.

'And this?'

'My white v-neck top,' I said, testily.

'But what has it got?'

'Long sleeves.'

'Right.' On to the floor.

'And what about this?'

'My grey top.'

'Does it by any chance have long sleeves?' Jess said, sarcastically. 'Oh, look, yes it does, now there's a surprise.'

She reached into the wardrobe again, pulled out another top. 'Tell me Ceri,' Jess said, turning to me, 'do you see a theme developing?'

'Maybe,' I said, petulantly.

'Far be it for me to criticise, but you'd think a person starting a new life would start off with a new wardrobe too.'

'Oh yeah, says Mrs "I've Been Wearing The Same Clothes Since I Was Twenty". What was that, fifteen, twenty years ago?'

Jess, surprisingly, laughed. Surprisingly because usually she'd throw something at me. 'Ah, but you see, I haven't spent however many years working on fashion magazines. You'd think some of it would've rubbed off.'

'Whatever,' I said, flopping my arms around. 'I still need help deciding.'

'I understand, no, really I do. Should I wear the round-neck long-sleeved top or the v-neck

44

long-sleeved top? Those decisions will keep a girl up all night.'

'Do you want some chocolate cheesecake or not?' I replied.

'Ceri, it doesn't matter what you wear,' Jess said. Ever the mum, she started picking up the tops she'd dropped on the floor. 'I mean, when I was lecturing you, did you ever notice what I was wearing?'

I thought about it. I didn't remember now what she used to wear. And I can't remember at any point thinking. *Wow, she should not be wearing* that. 'Suppose not.'

'My rule of thumb for dressing for lectures has been,' she went back to my bed and got in, taking custody of the remote controls again, 'to wear what makes you comfortable. Cos people will notice if you're fiddling with your waistband or bra strap.'

'But do you think they'll have a problem with the fact none of my tops ever cover the waistband of my trousers and that there's always this strip of midriff showing?'

'No, sweetie, I don't think they'll be sat there going, "Who cares what Piaget said, look at that midriff on her".'

I went to my wardrobe, opened the door, took out my favourite long-sleeved top, the white one with a slightly plunging v-neck. 'I think I'll wear this one with my dark blue jeans,' I said, decisively.

'Good, you look lovely in it,' Jess replied, without looking away from *Corrie*.

'Trainers or shoes?'

'Shoes.'

'Why?'

'Because you're going to wear your trainers anyway.'

'Funny.'

Jess deigned to tear her attention away from *Corrie* and rested it on me. 'I'll tell you what you should wear, though.'

'What?' I glanced anxiously at the open wardrobe.

'Your bloody glasses, you vain madam. You won't be very authoritative if you're squinting at everyone.'

'We do not talk about them,' I hissed. 'They do not exist and we do not talk about them. Ever.'

'OK, Mrs Magoo.'

'Grrr . . .'

Jess was right about one thing, I didn't really need help in deciding what to wear, I'd hauled her over here from Horsforth because I needed company. Someone to fret at. I didn't know Jake and Ed well enough to unravel in front of them. And it didn't work down the phone, so that ruled out most of my London friends. The only person it could be was Jess. She knew that, which was why she came, I guess. She was my surrogate boyfriend in such situations. It had to be said, I wasn't usually the fret out loud type. I was the gnaw on my fingers, stare into space, sometimes scrawl out a list type.

But then, I'd never taken such a huge leap of faith before.

Whenever I'd started a new job before, it'd

always had an element of sheer terror because I'd always moved upwards on the career ladder: first from junior sub-editor to sub-editor, then to senior sub-editor, then to chief sub-editor and then, finally, to contributing features editor. My career jumps had always been into a position I wasn't sure I could handle. Naturally. I'd lie awake panicking about being sacked; being 'found out'. In comparison to this, what I'd felt then was a mere smidgen of terror. A small quantity of fear that could be beaten into submission by ordering a desk tidy and sending my first email. With this lecturing lark, a desk tidy wasn't going to cut it.

What did I think I was doing?

This was just one idea on a page. I'd written down what I wanted to do on a piece of paper, as per instruction in one of my self-help/follow your dreams/Oprah books. *Write down all your dreams. If you could do anything, what would it be? Go on, write it down. Even if it's ridiculous, write it down. No one else will ever see it, so what's the harm if you put it down on a piece of paper?*

What's the harm? I'll tell you the harm. Once it's in blue and white, once it's written down, it seems possible. Not quite so ridiculous. Not quite so airy-fairy. And, once something seems even remotely possible, it starts to grow. Like a baby growing inside you, your idea – your dream – grows, takes from you, feeds off you, gathering strength, slowly but surely becoming part of you until it's ready to be born. To become something

47

tangible in its own right. Then, without realising it, nothing else seems as exciting or important or worthy. Everything you do comes back to your dream. Comes back to whether your current life is helping to feed, nurture and strengthen your dream. Next thing you know, you're pacing the floor of your bedroom fretting about giving your first lecture. Me, lecturing. For real. Full-time. Well, seventy-five per cent of the time, but full-time in the sense of what my title was and what I was paid to do.

'If you don't stop wringing your hands you'll have no skin left on them.' Jess commented.

I glanced down, my hands were twisting and twisting themselves together as I paced the floor. I hadn't even noticed.

I went over, climbed into bed with Jess and pretended to watch *Corrie*.

'We'd better not move about too much,' Jess said. 'Ed and Jake will think we're having some kind of love tryst.'

'I should be so lucky,' I said. It'd been a while since I'd had sex.

'You would, to get me.'

'Ha-ha, ha-ha, ha-ha.'

'You would be lucky to get me. Haven't you heard how hard it was for Fred to convince me to go out with him?'

'Yeah. He said "hello", you were his.'

'You're a cheeky cow, D'Altroy,' Jess laughed.

I slid out of bed again. I couldn't settle. My insides

were in flight, my mind was in flight, my body needed to be in constant motion too. I started to pace the floor of my bedroom again. I was lucky, this bedroom seemed to have been constructed for fretful pacing.

'I feel like I've made the biggest mistake of my life,' I admitted suddenly.

'Bigger than moving in with Whashisface Tosspot?' (We never spoke the name of the man I lived with for a year, because that would be asking for him to get in touch. That would be like standing in front of a mirror and saying 'Candyman' three times when you're the star of a film called *Candyman*. In other words, that was asking for the unholy to blight your life again. Or, in even fewer words: that was looking for trouble.)

'Yes, even bigger than that catastrophe.'

I met Whashisface Tosspot when I was doing my journalism masters in London. We were together for two years and I spent most of the time wondering why I was with him. I moved in with him at the end of college, when we'd both been looking for somewhere to live and he suggested we get a place together. I'm still convinced he used some kind of Jedi Mind Trick on me because I'd stood there, looking at him, thinking, '*You what?! Move in with you? We are so not on the same page, are we?*' but 'All right then' came out of my mouth.

Jess had laughed when I told her he'd asked me to move in with him. When I told her I'd said yes, she'd hung up on me. She'd previously spent the better part of a month coaching me into dumping him, and that night was the night I was supposed to do the deed. The night I was supposed to rid my life – and therefore Jess's life – of him for ever. Instead, I came away, having agreed to live with him. Having, basically, further ensconced him in our lives.

'At least when I realised he was Prince Of The Undead I got out . . .' I said to Jess.

'Eventually,' Jess cut in. 'Very, *very* eventually.'

'Yes, all right, eventually. But the point is, at the time I didn't know it was a mistake. Not really. I kind of thought I was doing the right thing. At least I convinced myself I was doing the right thing. With this . . .' My voice trailed away as terror took over again.

'With this, you're feeling lost. And that's only natural. But look at what your life was like before. Remember how unhappy you were? Almost everyone you met or talked to wanted you to sort their lives out; all those dramas you were involved with. I couldn't believe half of them and as you know, I watch all the soaps. You couldn't untangle yourself from all those lives. But you can start again here, can't you?'

Jess was right on that score. I had managed to embroil myself in the most ridiculous dramas when I was down in London. None of them were mine, though. Not one of them. When most people heard I was leaving, they'd gone into shock. Not

50

because they'd miss me but . . . well, put it this way, when I went to resign, my boss had paled, she'd lost all her natural colouring and her whole face had become a study in horror. In fact, she'd reminded me of that hideous picture, *The Scream*, but with more hair. She'd stared at me from across her desk, her thin but muscular face contracting and convulsing as she struggled to speak. 'I thought we were friends,' she'd finally managed in a shocked whisper.

'I just can't do this job any more,' I'd replied, neatly avoiding the 'friends' issue. 'I'm sorry. It's nothing personal.'

'Couldn't you have come to me before? Talked to me? I thought we were friends.'

Just because I know that your husband has to call you 'Mummy' before he can have sex, and just because I know you had a fling with your husband's sister, doesn't actually *mean we're friends. It simply means I know too much about you. You and the rest of this office. In fact, the rest of this city*, I thought darkly. And that was how it was. Somehow, some way, I'd become the person everyone came to tell their secrets to. People would often sidle up to my desk, say, 'Ceri, can I have a word?' in a desperate manner and my heart would skip a beat. Initially, I'd thought something big and bad had happened. When I realised this was rarely the case, my heart would still skip a beat because it might well be the one time when something hideous was wrong. I'd get up from my seat, follow them to the smoking area outside the building with my heart racing in my chest. 'What's up?' I'd say.

They'd launch into some tirade that they'd been too chicken to direct at the cause of their rage. I'd listen, nod, go, 'Ah, right,' in the required places, then when they finished I'd follow them back to the office, knowing that *they* felt better for having got that off their chest but being none the wiser as to what it was all about. I was Sounding Board/Vent Your Spleen At/Share Your Secrets With Woman and I'd been looking to shed that persona when I started following my heart's desire. I didn't want to do that any more. I had to get my own life. In fact, I had to get a life. Hence the Commandments. All right, so I'd broken a couple of them with Claudine and Mel, but that could be rectified, all I had to do was not get involved.

'I suppose,' I mumbled, in response to Jess's comment cum question about how I could start again up here.

'Ceri, you're a natural control freak so it's equally natural that doing something you've not really done before is going to unsettle you. Or freak you out.'

I started making the eeey-orr sound of a woman hyperventilating.

'But, but,' Jess added quickly, 'so many people spend their lives wishing and wondering, "What would it be like to live my dream?" You've done it. You're doing it. That takes a particular type of courage. You wouldn't believe how many people wish they had your type of strength. Or could get out of their rut and take that chance.

'But the thing about you most people would love to have is your ability to appreciate chocolate as much as me. Speaking of which, didn't you lure me over here with the promise of chocolate cheesecake?'

I stopped in my floor-pacing tracks. *Oops*. 'Now there's a funny thing about that. You'll laugh. You'll really laugh . . . Jess, put down that remote control . . .'

'You will be all right, you know,' Jess said later. She was back in her Wellingtons and mac, Fred was waiting outside in the car with the engine running. 'There's only one thing you really need to remember tomorrow and every day after that.'

'And what's that?'

'The students don't know that you don't know everything so, if they ask you a question you can't answer, just bullshit. That's how I got through my first year of teaching.'

She hugged me and left.

CHAPTER 5

LIFE ORGASM

Elephants stampeded across my stomach as I walked around before the lecture started, leaving four-page handouts on the desks. To say I was nervous was like saying Madonna is a bit of a pop star. Things hadn't got better in the time that had elapsed between Jess leaving last night and this morning. If anything, I'd got worse. I'd started to have wild nightmare-like fantasies and vivid visions about what would go wrong. Which was one of the reasons I was putting handouts on the desks before the lecture.

Most lecturers dispense handouts as the lecture progresses, but I'd already seen the potential pitfalls. Literally.

Scenario One: I pick up the pile of handouts, ready to give it to one student for them to pass on, I trip, I fall and find myself lying face down in a pool of paper.

Scenario Two: I ask the students to come up and get them, there's a stampede, someone knocks over my drink – necessary so my tongue doesn't Velcro itself to the roof of my mouth – and all my overhead projections are ruined.

Scenario Three – Anyway, there were quite a few scenarios. I'd actually forgotten how vivid my imagination was. I'd begun to think it'd been blunted over time, taken up as it was with visualising Cupid sorting it out so me and Angel could end up together. But no, when I was in need of truly nightmarish scenarios, there was a rich vein of horror just waiting to be let.

I was putting out handouts in a room that was situated at the top of a building right in the middle of the All Souls campus. This block was an octagonal with a paved over quad at its centre where students lurked and lunched. The room I was to teach in wasn't huge, not as huge as I'd expect after yesterday's foray into the land of the giants. Light streamed in from the arched-top windows, leaving pools of light around the room. The ceiling was quite low, surprising considering the windows. The floor was still parquet, scuffed slightly, obviously well-trodden ground with bits more scuffed than others.

The forty or so chairs with little desks attached to one side were set out in a kind of arc. Behind me hung a white board which I had to bring my own non-permanent markers for. Above and behind the chairs was a wall to wall two-way mirror because this room doubled as a psychology lab and next door was an observation room. Thankfully, there was a heavyweight blue curtain that could be drawn across the mirror so I wouldn't have to worry about looking at myself for two hours or there being someone else observing me lecture for two hours.

I sat on the edge of my desk. Just stopped. For a second, stopped. Took time to breathe. To breathe and think about what I was doing. What was to come.

And it happened. Total peace descended upon me. At the very core of my soul, a celestial being touched me and I felt peace. I was peace. Pure peace. Suddenly I was flooded with power and joy and happiness. All I'd yearned for when I'd accepted this job. I was complete. Whole. This was it. I was there, on the brink of it. On the brink of a life orgasm. I'd only ever felt this sense of pureness when I'd orgasmed. Right in the middle of an orgasm, you are nothing but pure emotion. Nothing else exists except that one moment of sheer, unadulterated bliss; when your body and mind give themselves up to immaculate pleasure. That's what I'd been chasing when I gave up my life in London. For that moment, sat on the desk, I felt it. How life was meant to be. How life could be if I carried on with this.

The first student arrived five minutes before the lecture was due to start. Tall, malnourished thin, long greasy hair, wearing a baggy jumper. He was the type of guy you'd expect to come in last to the lecture, but no, he came wandering in, nodded a hello at me then sat himself at the back of the class.

Next came a girl who was very money. Chatting

on a chrome phone, dark brown hair cut with very expensive scissors, the kind of clothes I used to see all the time on the pages of the pricier magazines I worked for. She smiled at me, but wasn't going to finish her conversation until the lecture started. A chunky lad came next, Scouse, again with long hair, surrounded by a gaggle of good-looking women, all of them laughing at something he'd obviously just said. He grinned at me as he walked over to the far corner of the room, sat himself under the large window, and the women sat at other seats around the room.

More of them poured through the open gash of the door: a blonde with a tight perm; an older woman with short blonde hair and petite body; an older man who had 'pervert' scrawled across his scraggly beard: another older man who had 'narrowminded Thatcher lover' written in his eyes; a woman with black plaits right down to her bum; a man who put me in mind of a Wham-era George Michael, more and more until the room was full with about forty students.

I put on a charming, welcoming smile for them all. Hoping I looked confident, a natural, as if I'd been doing this for millennia.

OH SHITE! my brain screeched.

I'd lectured before, but that had been on the understanding I wouldn't see those people again. I'd be like hundreds of guest lecturers they'd encounter in their lives: transitional, flibbertigibbety. Nothing more than the sum of notes on the page, a voice on a tape recorder, a name in a handbook. It was like a one-night stand. You tried to enjoy it while you were there, but you could be someone else, flamboyant, tarty, even dominant because you'd never see them again. It didn't matter how you behaved because it was only ever going to be for a few hours. Whereas I'd be expected to bond with this lot. I had to leave my phone number, answer their calls, reveal more and more of who I was. Form some kind of lasting relationship with them over the coming year.

I was about to be found out as the fraud I was. I didn't know jack about anything and I'd sure as anything couldn't impart it, ensure it entered other people's minds and stayed there long enough for them to write about it in essays and exams. I was going to be publicly ridiculed. Laughed and pointed at in the street. Tarred and feathered, branded a liar and cheat then sent packing through the streets of Leeds with my rucksack on my back.

OK D'Altroy, back away from that panic. Calm down. If you don't calm down you'll start getting sweat patches all over your lovely white top and then it'll be see-through. They'll all be able to see your bra . . .

OH MY GOD, WHAT THE HELL HAVE I DONE!

I should be sat in London, reading about make-up, I thought. This thought was swiftly followed by *Run away! Very fast. Just leave everything where it is and leg it.*

I smiled at each and every one of them, waiting

58

until almost all the seats were occupied. Most of them talked with each other until a natural hush, then a silence fell upon the room.

Ms Money flipped shut her phone.

OH MY GOOD GOD.

All right, smile. Smile, goddamn you. Now open your mouth, say: 'Hi.'

Expectant faces gazed upon me as though I was about to impart the meaning of life, the universe and everything. That I was going to explain it wasn't, in fact, forty-two, but ninety-eight – and I had proof. Or maybe they thought I was going to give them next week's lottery numbers. Whatever it was, each face was so expectant my voice dried up as I croaked, 'I'm Ceri. Ceri D'Altroy. It's written on th—'

The door slammed open, and 'I'm sooooo sorry,' a voice cried out from nowhere, as a woman hurried in. 'I'm so sorry I'm late. The bus didn't turn up. I ran all the way here from the bus stop.'

She rushed off to her seat across the room, no one blinked, she obviously did this all the time. I, meanwhile, having leapt in shock, leant with one hand on the desk, the other hand clutching my chest, and breathed like *I'd* been running.

The class weren't sure whether to laugh or be scared.

I laughed. Couldn't help myself when I'd tried so hard to get the lecturer look right and it all fell apart when someone made me jump. The room erupted into uneasy laughter with me, until we all relaxed into normal laughter.

OK, this is better. I can work with laughter. Didn't they always say you should start a presentation or speech with a joke? And you don't get much funnier than old lecturer lady having a coronary cos someone comes late. 'All right,' I said, feeling my body relax a fraction, 'as I was saying, I'm Ceri. Ceri D'Altroy. I'm taking over Eva's teaching for the rest of the year. I'll be teaching you the history of psychology as well as taking tutorials and doing all the other things that Eva did and I don't know about yet.

'On the sheets in front of you, I've written out a brief rundown of the modules as I see it. Before we get into a more detailed discussion about what you should have done as told to me by Gwen and what you've *actually* done, I wanted to get something clear.'

I took a deep breath. 'I'm here to help you learn. If you don't want to do the reading or prepare stuff for tutorials, that's fine with me. I'm not your parent or God, I can't make you do it. But, what you do or don't do will be reflected in your marks. And, to be very honest, I've got my degrees so feel free to piss about, make excuses, not do your work. I'm not open to bribes so it'll only hurt you in the end. I really hope, though, that you get into the learning stuff and if not enjoy it then at least understand the History of Psychology.'

This all sounded very cool and very laid-back,

60

I'd fancied myself as a cross between Robin Williams in *Dead Poets' Society* and Miss Jean Brodie in her prime. Experienced, but 'down with the people'; friendly, but worthy of respect. Which was clearly why I delivered my speech with sweat trickling down my back, making the white v-neck top cling to me.

Thankfully, I'd stopped short of writing it down before prattling it off – *prat* probably being the operative part of that word – because I'd be triply sad if I had to read my cool and laid-back attitude to the class. An audience of faces gazed back at me. It was still to be seen if my speech had worked, but for now, no one looked as though they were about to leave. Which, when it came down to it, was the important thing.

CHAPTER 6

ED'S WORLD

'Someone called for you,' Ed, my new flat-mate, said, with only his head stuck around my bedroom door. His long blond hair hung like grease-sodden chips around his thin face, his eyes watched me like I was an alien species.

I'd been living here a week and was still becoming acclimatised to the houseshare experience, so spent a lot of time in my bedroom, reading, working on seminar stuff or watching TV. I didn't want to get in their way, what with being new girl in the house and all.

Ed and Jake, my two flatmates, seemed nice. From what I remember of being a flatmate, though, a week wasn't enough to tell. Most flat-mates were fine, friendly and fun – until you borrowed a splash of their milk and suddenly you'd been bashed over the head and buried before you could say 'carpet that doesn't show blood-stains'.

I hadn't done the housesharing thing since I left Leeds, six years earlier. I'd lived with Whashisface Tosspot for a year when I was in London, but that was different, I felt at home there. It was 'our

62

place'. When I bought my own place and our relationship finally ended, I'd had over two years of being able to walk around naked, if I so wished, and as it turned out, I did so wish, quite often. I was no weirdo naturalist/naturist/flasher, it was simply easier to know I could roll out of bed and answer a call of nature or put on the kettle without scrabbling about for a dressing gown. Especially since I lived on the first floor and most of my windows were obscured by trees. That'd all changed the day I went to fill the kettle wearing only a pair of black knickers and a casual glance to my left, out of the six-foot sash window, had shocked me twice over.

Shock one: The creepy man who lived downstairs had cut down all the trees that obscured the view of my windows.

Shock two: A queue of people at the bus stop below were staring open-mouthed at my floppy tits and black tanga briefs.

I'd developed a closer relationship with my dressing gown after that.

Flashing the neighbourhood not withstanding, I enjoyed living alone. I could leave the bathroom door open to hear the stereo or TV when I was in the shower; I could talk to myself out loud all the time, and I didn't have to rely on other people to pass on my messages.

At the time of Ed's appearance with my message, I was curled up in bed, watching an episode of *Angel* on video.' (This, of course, meant drawing the curtains, putting on my side lights, changing into my pyjamas, surrounding myself with junk food and beer. Watching *Angel* was like taking part in a ritual. Ed was privileged, I was usually out to callers when it started.)

'Oh? Who?' I said to Ed, having pressed the mute button on the TV remote.

'A bloke. Dan? Um . . . Derek? Drew? Yeah, Drew. Said he'd call you back later or you should call him back when you'd stopped, er,' colour rose in Ed's cheeks, 'stopped, er, creaming yourself over, er, Angel.'

'The git!' I replied. Was too outraged to be embarrassed by my outing by my so-called mate. Ed was obviously going to find out about the man in my life at some point, he wasn't meant to be told that said man only existed in the nineteen-inch world of my telly so soon into our living relationship.

'When did he call?' I asked Ed.

Ed coloured some more, his eyes shifted about. 'Um, this afternoon. Meant to, uh, write you a note but couldn't find a pen. Then I forgot. Sorry.'

'Don't worry about it. Come in,' I shifted up to make room on the bed for him to sit, 'if you want.'

Ed pushed open the door, came in, perched himself on the very edge of the bed, only a fraction of an inch of his butt was on the bed. Ed was doing a PhD in English at The Met and he was into heavy metal. His clothes suited his hair and his heavy metal reputation: dirty blue jeans, black

T-shirt with a lurid, heavy metal band picture on the front. Over the top he wore a red and black lumberjack shirt. But, under the dirt and grease, under the clothes, he was the cutest boy. Young and untouched by life. It showed in his clear green eyes, his smooth skin and the contours of his face. He just needed a wash and blow-dry all over.

Ed glanced at my TV screen, smiled when he saw what I was watching. 'Is he your boyfriend? This Drew bloke,' Ed asked, refocusing on me.

'No,' I replied. 'Just an old mate. That's a mate I've known for a long time, not a mate who's old.'

I was rewarded with one of Ed's blank stares. They were a natural miracle: his clear green eyes would glaze over, his face would become flat as he stared at you. Maybe he was computing something behind that look or maybe he was wondering if he should make a run for it. 'Do you have a boyfriend?' he asked, coming out of his stare.

'No, I'm currently between relationships and boyfriends. What about you? Are you seeing someone?'

He nodded grimly. 'No.'

I inhaled deeply.

Ed was on the verge of confessing something deeply personal to me. He was going to do to me what people had done to me on buses, trains and in cafes and pubs for years: invite me into their world. Drag me into their life; their innermost secrets.

On one level, it was flattering, I was trustworthy

enough to know people's secrets. But on almost every other level it was bizarre. Perfect strangers giving me flashes of their hearts. Telling me things they didn't even tell their best mates. It was also exhausting because I couldn't just listen, walk away. I had to listen, then I had to give my opinion, advise, *get involved*. Hence my Commandments. Hence walking around without making eye contact. It was easier all round to appear miserable and moody than to start getting involved.

At this point in the night, though, I was too tired to fight it. I had to go with it. Take one giant leap into Edness. And besides, he'd earned the use of my ear, by bringing my bags upstairs on the day I'd moved in. I'd just not get involved. Listen. No involvement. I could do that.

'Complicated is it?' I prompted.

'No. Not really. It's quite uncomplicated. I love her, she doesn't know I'm alive.'

Your typical stalker scenario, then.

'She's doing a drama MA at The Met too. Her name's Robyn. You might've seen her. She's been on telly and stuff, she's so beautiful.'

Definitely your typical stalker scenario, then.

'But it's more than that. She's so funny. I've spoken to her, I've spoken to her loads. She's almost a friend. She's really nice, and clever, and interesting a—'

'You really don't have to justify your feeling for her to me. You like her, that's all that matters,' I interjected before he ran out of adjectives. For an

English student his vocabulary was distinctly third rate.

Ed's whole persona relaxed. 'Most people I tell think she's just wank material cos she's so beautiful.'

'I believe you like her. But, can I just say, even if she was just wank material, that's OK too. Some of my best relationships have been based solely on physical attraction. That's how these things happen sometimes. Not that your thing with, er,' *shite, what was her name, what was her name,* 'Robyn! is like that.'

Ed, who now he'd unburdened his soul obviously felt more at ease with me and in my room, rested back on his elbows, turned his head upwards and stared wistfully at the ceiling. 'She's perfect.'

I wanted to say that no one is perfect; to label someone as perfect was to set yourself up for disappointment when the one fatal flaw in their character that proves them to be imperfect makes an appearance. One look at Ed's face was enough to tell me he didn't want to hear that. Most people didn't want to hear it. They'd much rather get their expectations up, then have them dashed.

'She reminds me of this line from a song, "I feel so lucky loving her, tell me what else is magic for?".'

He was quoting Robert Palmer. Ed, heavy metal Ed, was quoting Robert Palmer. I'd underestimated his feelings for this woman. No one reached for Robert Palmer lyrics unless they were more than knee-deep in the mire of love.

Without warning, my heart started to race. Really pound, hammering and hammering against my rib cage. The sound filled my ears and made me quiver slightly. This was what Ed was feeling for this Robyn one. The emotions he felt ran deep, that was obvious. Robert Palmer had been the first clue to how he was feeling. How he looked now, the expression on his face, was the next clue.

Beyond his limited vocabulary flowed unfathomable seas of emotion. She made him smile, inside and out. He wanted to make her laugh, he often thought of something and wanted to call her to tell her about it. Sometimes he'd lie on his bed, replaying their conversations, enjoying the fact that he'd spent time with her, not knowing that hours had passed while he lay there. She made his heart beat faster by just entering the room.

And his lust. She wasn't just wank material but . . .

Every cell in my body pulsated with his passion. I was suddenly, inexplicably turned on. I hadn't felt like this in a long time. Not even when I'd last had sex, it wasn't like this. Every part of me burnt with lust. A cold shower wasn't going to cure this. How Ed got through the day with all this pumping through him I didn't know. Watching *Angel* now would be a bad idea – I'd probably end up dry-humping the TV screen.

If anything, Ed was understating his feelings.

Maybe he just didn't have the right words to explain how much he felt. Well, with me he didn't need to. Sitting next to him told me how he felt.

'So, she doesn't know you're alive, what are you going to do about it?' I asked.

Ed froze for a few seconds, then his head creaked around to face me. 'Do?!' He'd screwed up his face. '*Do?!*'

'Are you going to ask her out?'

'Don't think so,' he scoffed.

'Why not?'

'Erm, possibly because she goes out with actors and businessmen, she even went out with a duke once. Those are the kind of men she goes out with – famous, important men, not people like me.'

My legs ached from sitting cross-legged. I prised my lower limbs apart, stood up a little shakily because they weren't used to being contorted like that and shook them out to get the blood circulating again. 'How do you know she doesn't go out with people like you if you've never asked her out?' I asked Ed.

'I just do,' he said with the conviction of a man who knew someone was totally out of his league.

'What if she doesn't go out with people *like* you but actually goes out *with* you.'

'She wouldn't.'

Seeing as I was in love with someone who happened to be a 250-year-old vampire that lived only in my telly, I didn't think of anyone as out of my league, so didn't see why Ed, when he knew this person, should think like that. I mean, if I knew I was going to end up with said vampire, then why shouldn't he at least ask this woman out?

'There's this expression us old folk use,' I said, staring at Ed. 'It goes something like, "Faint heart never won fair lady". Be a coward about this and you'll be dreaming about you and her until you read about her wedding in *Hello*. Besides, the worst that can happen is she'll say no.'

'No, the worst that can happen is that she laughs in my face, tells me to piss off then emails all her friends and they laugh at me too. Or she could publish my picture on the Internet with a transcript of our conversation, so the whole world will laugh at me,' Ed replied.

'Or she could say yes and turn out to be a total cow, which'll mean all this time you've loved her from afar has been wasted on some silly bint. That's the worst that can happen.'

'No, the laughing thing is definitely the worst.'

He had a point. I took my seat back in the bed, covered myself with the duvet again. 'I know how you feel.'

Ed smirked. I'm sure he thought I had no idea what love of the unrequited sort was all about. He'd be surprised. My unreturned affections hadn't been exclusively aimed at fictional TV characters.

'No, really I do,' I reassured Ed. 'I spent over nine years in love with someone and, it's a long, loooonnnnggg story, but the short of it is, I'm between relationships. And, sometimes, I mentally kick myself when I talk to him. Or he leaves messages with my new flatmate.'

'Ohhhh . . . Drew! He's Drew?'

'Yes. He's Drew.'

Drew and I had been in the same psychology classes and I'd had a major thing about him since we were assigned to work together on a project in first year. We'd become friends after that assignment, but despite us being very close friends, I'd never really known how he felt about me. On the one hand, we'd spend hours on the phone often talking about sex (some of our conversations were so pornographic they bordered on phone sex), we'd sit too close, hug for too long, stare too much. He'd often turn up at the house I shared with three other people with a six-pack of beer and a video and we'd cuddle up in my bedroom and watch it. On the other hand, nothing happened. *Ever*. Not during college, not after college. I sometimes got the feeling that he was thinking about kissing me, thinking about taking our relationship to the next level, particularly when we were lying on my bed watching something he'd taped, but it was all just think with him. He never *did* anything. I did consider kissing him, of course, but I was never sure how it'd be received. You see, if there was one thing I'd learnt about men, it was that if they liked you enough, nothing, except possibly an act of God – and even then it was a close-run thing – would stop them making a move. So, why did Drew never just lean down and cover my lips with his, even when his arms were holding me close to his chest? Because he didn't like me enough, was the short answer.

Still, even though I knew this, even though I had this short answer, I was confident that would change over time. He went out with other people, I'd see other people but none of those relationships ever lasted. Because the two of us were going to end up together, weren't we? When we were single, we'd flirt till it hurt, all preparation for us getting together, I thought.

Three years ago, he met his girlfriend, Tara. Met her, then rang me up in a tizzy saying, 'Ceri, it's happened, I've met her. I've met the woman I want to spend the rest of my life with. I've met *The One.*'

I'd always listened with interest when he'd met other women. It was the kind of interest that came from knowing it'd never last because, well, they weren't me. He and I were meant to be. It was written in the stars, in the Domesday Book, practically anywhere you looked it said 'Drew & Ceri 4 ever'. This time had been different. I could hear it in his voice. The excitement and joy and shock that he'd met his ideal woman. He was in love. After two hours, he was in love. She was, indeed, The One. And she wasn't me. Or like me in any way. (Whashisface Tosspot asked me to move in with him about six hours after I got that call from

Drew. By all rights, I should've taken to my bed with a bottle of wine and a box of tissues, instead, I'd gone to meet Whashisface Tosspot. Maybe I'd suddenly realised that now my long-term plan for happiness was heading off into the sunset with someone else and I needed a back-up plan, a sunset companion of my own, Whashisface Tosspot became it. It could've been that, but personally, I favour the Jedi Mind Trick/Work Of The Devil explanation.)

I'll never forget the sudden horror that rushed through me when I heard Drew's words. It'd hit me, right then, that we weren't eventually going to end up together. That maybe, if I'd told him earlier how I felt, things would've turned out different. I didn't want that for Ed. Or for anyone. 'What if' was no way to live your life. 'Always regret the things you did do, never the things you didn't,' someone once said. They weren't wrong.

'I'll tell you Ed, nine years of unrequited love that results in nothing more than friendship hurts, quite a lot. Hate to see you waste your twenties like I did, mate. Ask her out and if she says no, at least you'll know. You can find someone else to lust, I mean, love.'

Ed was silent for a very long time, he pursed his lips slightly and his eyes clouded over, he was thinking very hard by the face on him. My eyes strayed back to the TV screen and to the gorgeous but silent David Boreanaz. I jumped guiltily when Ed rejoined me in the land of the speaking.

'You really think I should ask her out?'

'I do,' I replied. 'I would. But only because I know now that the one thing more painful than rejection is looking at yourself day after day and wondering "What if". There's this line in *Strictly Ballroom* that I remind myself of whenever I start to chicken out of stuff. It goes, "A life lived in fear is a life halflived". And, let's be honest, who wants to live half a life when you can have a whole life? That's like eating half a chocolate bar when you're hungry enough for a whole one and you've got a whole one in your hand.'

'All right, all right, all right,' Ed mumbled, nodding slowly.

'Anyway Ed, I've got to watch *Angel* now, but feel free to stay.'

Ed smiled at me wryly. 'Is that OK?'

'Course. But no talking.'

'Are you sure you don't want to enjoy it, you know, alone.' Ed waggled his eyebrows suggestively.

I grabbed a pillow and thwacked him with it. 'Listen you cheeky *get*, you ask out actress woman then you can take the mick out of me and how I run my love life, all right?'

Ed grinned, accepted my proffered can of beer and lay back on my bed.

Bless you, but you still need a wash and blow-dry.

What if?

I asked myself that a lot. A lot. I still, for example, thought: What if I'd taken English lit A-level instead

74

of politics A-level? Would I be the politically-minded journalist I'd become before I ran away to Leeds? Or would I be someone else? Would I have become interested in Psychology or have done an English degree? And what if I'd done an English degree, would I have met Jess? What if I'd never met Jess . . .

Thinking 'What if' always made me homesick. And after talking to Ed, I started feeling homesick. Not for London, I had nothing to be homesick about in London. My parents, my sister, my brothers, their various families, a few friends were there. I'd left them behind, but since I didn't live with any of them, I didn't miss them. In fact, I'd probably start to see them more now I didn't live within an hour's journey of them. Two hundred miles apart was probably exactly what I needed to inspire me to see my family more often. No, I was starting to feel homesick for my time in college. To see all the people I'd gone to college with. Pastsick, really.

After Ed gave up on *Angel* and went off to bed (or to play heavy metal quietly), I got my photo albums out and lay on my bed looking through them. Pictures of my room in halls, pictures of the living room in my last student house, three streets over from where I was now. In that pic, I'm stood by the stone fireplace, wearing my floor-length blue velvet, long-sleeved ball dress. Specially bought – at a bargainous £10 in Oasis – for my graduation ball.

I flicked on a few pages and there was a picture of me and Drew at the graduation ball, a few hours later. Him in his smart black tuxedo, black bow tie, his razor-cut blond hair and cheekbones making him look rather effete. I was *so* in love with him when that picture was taken. At least I thought I was in love with him. That fierce, all consuming love hadn't changed until, what, three years ago. Like I said to Ed, I spent most of my twenties in love with a man who didn't even know I was alive. We had our heads close together, in the picture, my jet black bob almost touching what was left of his blond hair, our faces glistening with sweat because we'd spent half the night dancing and we were both flashing 100 watt smiles at the camera. Drew's arm was slung casually around my shoulders. I knew exactly what I would've been feeling – quivery and giggly, thinking, 'Oh, GOD! Drew's touching me in front of a camera! It's a sign! He does love me really. Tonight could be the night.' I stroked my fingers across the plastic covering the photo, as I got another pang of past-sickness. Awww, young Drew, young Ceri. So bloody stupid. We didn't even get less stupid the older we got. Well, I didn't.

After the initial shock of Drew meeting 'The One', which resulted in me moving in with Whashisface Tosspot, I'd gone into denial. I'd hung up the phone, sat staring into space for ages until I reached a very important decision: *I'm not going to think about it. At all.* Drew, my love, my long-term plan for happiness had met his dream woman, so the best course of action was to enter denial, quietly and calmly, without any fuss, and not think about it.

Since I'd decided not to think about it, I could think about nothing else. It was always there at the back of my mind. Kicking away, dancing up and down, waving a red flag, demanding attention. When I woke up in the morning, when I got ready for work, when I sat at work, when I came home from work. When I made dinner, when I ate it, when I watched telly, when I was having sex. I thought about it. My stomach churned; dipping and rising, spinning and twisting. I found it hard to eat without feeling sick afterwards. I'd be sat at my desk, editing copy and find my right leg perched on the ball of my foot, bouncing nervously up and down. And all because I'd decided *not* to think about it.

Three months later, exhausted by the effort and nausea involved in not thinking about it, I decided to think about it. I decided to let myself off the hook, stop being such a brave little martyr and go into the pain. Go into it, embrace it, accept it. I was, at least, allowed to cry about it. I picked a weekend when Whashisface Tosspot went away to his parents' (of course, they had a huge house in the country but he was always pleading poverty). As he drove off very late Friday night, I got myself all the tools for grieving I'd previously denied myself – a couple of bottles of wine, a multipack of tissues and some appropriate CDs – and took to my bed.

Except, my mind, twisted as it was, refused to collapse. Refused to let me cry and wallow and give in to how much pain Drew's news had caused me.

As I lay under my duvet, *Can't Live If Living Is Without You* playing on loop in the background, there was no emotional retching. No physical heart-break. No tears. No open-mouthed ugly cry. Not even when I squeezed really hard. All that came to me were all the negative things about him. About this Drew, this man who I thought I was going to spend the rest of my life with.

My brain kept dredging up examples of his caddishness any time 'but I love him' thought of rearing its pathetic head. How he'd cuddle up with me, but never made a proper move on me. How he'd go out with other people and flaunt it in my face (how many times had I heard how great his latest woman was, how sexy, how good in bed? Too many, that's how many). How he'd disappear from my life if he met someone else and only call me to ask for advice when they were going through a hard time. How he'd give me the cold shoulder for days if I snogged someone and would refuse to listen to anything about them, at all.' (When I'd admitted I'd been seeing Whashisface Tosspot for three months, Drew had blanked me for a whole month. Didn't return my calls, didn't text or email me, ended calls after a minute if I caught him in. *Nada*, for a whole month.)

It wasn't just that, though. I started remembering how most of his girlfriends hated me, would be blatantly rude to me, probably because he told them that I had a thing about him. How he didn't come to visit me when I was in hospital for a week with pneumonia – even though the hospital was only a twenty-minute bus ride away. How he'd once forgotten my birthday. Me, his best mate, he'd forgotten my birthday. How he'd got all our mates together for a do one Christmas after we'd all left college – and neglected to invite me. On and on my mind went. By the end of the weekend, I actually hated Drew. Every time I thought of him, I mentally growled. He was an emotional tease. He'd get me all whipped up, let me believe that some way along the line we'd be together. It wasn't all his fault, though, I'd been led on by all those movies and books which propagated waiting it out. Which told you that if you just hung in there long enough, he'll realise that you're the one for him and give up going out with supermodel-types who'll smash up his car windscreen because he didn't call. (Yes. one of his girlfriends did that once and I'd gone with him to get it fixed.) No. he'll discover he wants to be with the woman he comes running to emotionally and physically when he's single.

Suddenly, I realised he'd been a bastard to me but because I thought I loved him, I hadn't wanted to see it. And this falling for 'The One' was the final act of treachery as far as I was concerned. It was all right for him to go meet his perfect woman, all right for him to fall in love, all right, even, for him to realise he wanted to spend the rest of his life with her. But why the bloody hell was I the first person he called up about it? Because he had no respect for me or the feelings he'd nurtured in me, was the short answer. (I was good at short answers, but this was the first time I'd actually paid attention to one.)

Drew. my beloved, was a bloody bastard who wasn't worthy of my love or attention.

By four o'clock Saturday afternoon I'd thrown back my duvet, leapt out of bed and called up a couple of friends to meet me in Soho for a late lunch. Three of us had sat in a café on Old Compton Street, London, drinking wine and eating cake. It'd mutated to going to a pub, going to a club, then staying at a friend's house in Fulham. We'd then gone for a pub lunch and got some more drinks in. By the time I got home, Whashisface Tosspot was back – unimpressed by how legless I was at six o'clock on a Sunday evening – and I'd re-entered my place called denial.

Except, this time, when I decided NOT TO THINK ABOUT IT. I really didn't. I wasn't nauseous and jumpy. I'd crossed the desert, the wide, barren landscape that was my feelings for Drew. I'd made it through the hardest times, the mirages of plentiful water supplies that were his jealousy at me seeing other people; I'd made it over the sand dunes of hurt that left me feeling worthless when he met someone else; and I'd survived those months of craving for the merest drop of affection to wet my lips on when he blanked me. Now, thanks to a weekend of negative thinking, of being surrounded by nothing except the cacti of his bad behaviour, I could see the other side of that desert and I was almost there.

Two months later, I finally reached the other side of the desert when someone called and asked if I'd spoken to Drew recently and I realised I hadn't needed to shove him to the back of my mind because he hadn't even entered my mind.

When you're so infatuated with someone, like I was with Drew, it's very difficult to see them for what they really are. But once I'd made that desert crossing. Drew stopped being the man who could do no wrong. He also stopped being the man who would one day wake up and find he loved me, because it was not going to happen. Once I could see him clearly, he became a good friend. A proper friend with no undercurrent of 'What if?' He became a friend because, well, I can forgive my friends most things, but I couldn't forgive the man I was supposed to love for not even liking me enough to make a pass at me. How embarrassing was that? He could cuddle me, he could flirt with me, he could talk sex with me, but he couldn't even close his eyes, think of Leeds, and kiss me full on the mouth.

Part of me clung to the notion that Drew was the one who got away, that I wouldn't feel this for anyone else – three years on, I could see that I really didn't want to. Because that wasn't love. Love is a two-way street, except with me and Drew it had been totally one way. If he'd loved me, even a little, he wouldn't have emotionally teased me.

I flicked through more pages in the photo album. We all looked so young.

I stopped over a picture of me that Drew had taken a few days after our final exam. I was lying on the grass in Hyde Park with sunglasses on, a huge smile on my face and sticking two fingers up at him. I looked quite good then, even if I say so myself. I was happy. I'd just finished my finals. I had a few weeks to go until the results. The world was my lobster. A group of us had gone to the park to play a game of rounders and I'd taken a break, lay on the grass not caring about getting grass marks on my short red dress (with white cycling shorts under it for decency).

As a shadow fell over me, I opened my eyes and found Drew stood over me, his camera poised. Just as he hit the button, I'd stuck my fingers up at him.

I didn't look that different in that photo, actually, not if you looked at the photos of me then. But when you looked at the photo then looked at me . . . I was older. Not particularly wrinkly (wrinkles weren't a worry of mine), just older: I suppose I'd done a lot and it showed on my face. I'd run a department on a women's magazine. I'd found out that love had to be two-way for it to mean anything. I'd discovered that I'd much rather stay in with a video than go out 'on the pull'. And then, of course, I lived with a man I'd torn out of every photo he'd managed to infiltrate. This was against everything I ever believed in, I loved to take photos, to take snapshots of every time of my life. To have it there to look back on if I ever got pastsick. With Whashisface Tosspot, I just couldn't bear to be reminded of the biggest mistake of my life. It was bad enough that I'd slept with him for two years, did I really want to look at him too? No, was the short answer to that, too.

I slammed shut the photo album. Didn't I just say to Ed that 'What if? was no way to live a life? Erm . . . maybe I didn't say it, but I'd meant to. And, constantly dipping into my photo album was no way to live a life in Leeds, either. *Yer have to look forwards* I reminded myself.

And I will, right after I've watched a couple more episodes of Angel . . .

CHAPTER 7

BLURTING

Before I'd touched down in Leeds this time around. I'd decided to doff my cap to health and fitness. Devote some of my time and effort to what probably should come naturally. Not go crazy, not become a gym bore, not even attempt to lose weight or start chasing that mythical dream of 'firming up'. I simply fancied the idea of being able to walk up more than two flights of stairs without making the asthmatic donkey sound of someone who'd had a thirty-a-day habit since she was sixteen. It was downright embarrassing that Jess could do the stairs thing without a hint of a donkey about her when she had been a thirty-a-day person since she was *fourteen*.

The gym on the college campus, a stand-alone annexe, was adequate for my purposes – a line of treadmills greeted you as you entered, flanked on the left by a large handful of exercise bikes. On the right was the weights area, plus rowing machines; further on and then down a short flight of stairs was a swimming pool and a circuit training gym.

I'd come here, the first day at college, straight

from my final meeting with the last lecturer, Sally. (Sally had been lovely. The meeting with her had been left till last because she was the woman I'd be sharing an office with. Out of all the other three lecturers I'd met, she was the only one who seemed to be able to speak in short sentences.) That night I had my body introduced to the equipment and the ways of the gym. That should be reintroduced, welcomed back into the fold of the gym.

This wasn't information I liked spread around, it was a shameful secret I'd buried and hidden from – but I'd joined a gym once before.

I was in college then too. Young, impetuous, easily brain-washed. If that wasn't bad enough, I joined then, dot, dot, dot, *went on a regular basis*. To add insult to potential injury, I went every other day, in fact. On alternate days, I did aerobics.

It'd been a membership of necessity, though. Everyone I knew had gone travelling for the summer, or returned to their home towns, or had left college. They all had a life. I did not. And, that summer, I became depressingly thinner and healthy. Depressingly, because I'd always have lodged somewhere in my memory the image of what I'd look like if I took care of my body, exercised, drank less and slept more. And, much as I'd love to be bright-eyed, clear-skinned and a size ten all the time, I'd much rather have a life, see my mates, drink alcohol, eat what I want and watch telly. It was a fair trade off, as far as I was concerned.

Now, however, I was lost all over again. Whilst Drew worked as a management consultant in Leeds, he lived in York. So on those days when he left work on time, he liked to drive straight home to spend time with his girlfriend. Also, when I finally saw Drew for the emotional tease he really was, I stopped calling him as much. Didn't need to ring him up to say 'hi' or to just listen to his voice. Didn't need to ring him to get a laugh. He was simply a good friend who I didn't speak to that often.

My only real anchor in this city was Jess. And she liked to see her daughters and husband quite often, too. With only a handful of acquaintances in Leeds, and the knowledge that it'd be a while to get some – particularly if the Mel/Claudine/ lunch/mouth-foot thing was any indicator – I was forced to take refuge, once again, in the high-energy embrace of the gym.

This time, though, I was treadmilling or cycling, just to sort out my lungs. To make my cardiovascular system work properly. Nothing more. My hands, my body were going nowhere near any weights or complicated machinery. I knew my mind, all it'd take would be one well-timed movement in front of a mirror and I'd be launched back into trying to get that final year of college body again.

Just in case my body decided it was going to stay any longer than necessary in the gym, I wore the most ridiculous outfit: royal blue, daisy-covered cycling shorts and a baggy sweat top with 'Michigan State' emblazoned across it. My black socks were rolled down to just above my ankle bones and my trainers had seen better days. To stop my hair frizzing, I'd scraped my black bob under a scarf. Gorgeous was not the word for me. Truly.

I stood with my feet on either side of the treadmill's moving part as I keyed in **30 mins** to the treadmill.

I paused, stared at the LCD. A bit too ambitious for my first time here in eight years.

I pressed CLEAR, then keyed in **10 mins**. *Wimp. You're a big girl's blouse.*

All right. **20 mins** it is. *I can do twenty minutes. No problemo.*

I focused on the TV screen in front of me. *The Simpsons* was on. Without sound, though. In the background, around the gym, the constant beat of something lively and funky pulsed. It was designed to get you moving in time to it. To get you motivated and moving. The genesis of perpetual motion. I opted to walk quickly, but not in time to the music. If I wasn't careful, I'd train myself to head to the gym every time I heard that beat. I'd become a Pavlov-type animal, not salivating every time I heard footsteps because I thought food was coming, but wanting to run everywhere, simply because I caught a snatch of something high-paced in a passing car. And th—

'Hi, Ceri?' A voice cut into my thoughts.

Without breaking stride, I turned to the person who'd spoken.

AAAGGGH! Claudine. Damn.

I might've known she'd frequent these parts. Very few people got those elongated, willowy looks with clear, glowy skin if you didn't habitually visit the gym. Of course, the first night I make it here since receiving my training programme, she appears. And on the treadmill next to me. I'd spent the last few days keeping an eye out for her and Mel, then running away. Very fast. I still physically cringed at how I managed to fit the whole of my foot very neatly into my mouth. I hadn't wanted to do that again. And now look.

'Hi,' I said brightly. Too brightly. That sounded fake. Like I'd been avoiding her and now was over-compensating. Which, of course, I was.

'Are you all right?' She stood with her legs wide open, each foot resting on the platform beside the moving part of her treadmill. She'd paused in keying in information into the treadmill display. 'You looked pretty fierce just then. Is something bothering you?'

'No.' I jumped like I was doing a jumping jack, so I could get off the moving treadmill and stand with my feet on either side of it. My heart sprinted in my chest, my whole body heaved in my attempt to get more oxygen. 'I'm fine.' *Breathless, but fine.*

Claudine's face became a picture of concern as she said: 'You looked like you had something on your mind, that's all. You can tell me if you want.'

'I, erm, I was actually thinking about Pavlov's dogs, brainwashing and music and if it's possible to brainwash people in the same way that Pavlov did with the dogs, but using music.'

Claudine's concern mutated to fear. With every moment her impression of me was lowering.

'*Really?*' she asked.

I nodded, aware that I sounded like a complete loon. 'Unfortunately, yes. I don't have big subjects like boyfriends to occupy my mind.'

'Right.' Claudine pulled the big red button on her treadmill display to get it working, hopped on then started walking. 'You'd better not cool down too much, unless you're about to stop.'

I hopped back onto the treadmill, started to walk again.

Beautiful as she was, Claudine was clearly proof of my gymlife relativity theory. She had trendy, up-to-date label gear that was obviously used. After about two seconds of warming up, which I was still doing, i.e. walking briskly, she started to jog. Slowly, at first, each step carefully considered, expertly dealt onto the machine. She'd obviously done this before, several times, regularly. Ergo, no life. The worst part, as she increased her pace, her slender arms pumping away, her long, svelte legs working without wobbling, was that there was no moisture in sight. Me? After five minutes of my brisk walking, my body was a tidal wave of sweat. Every ounce (I still hadn't got around to metric-sizing my thoughts) of moisture in me was taking a day-trip to my outer epidermis. Claudine didn't even have the decency to 'glow', she simply increased her stride, running. Now that was a concept, running. On a running machine.

My feet moved quicker. Didn't want to be outdone. There was my pride at stake. My lungs, clearly left out of the pride rousing lecture, complained almost straight away. They burnt their displeasure into my chest. *Piss off!* my brain replied. *No one outdoes us.*

I monitored Claudine from the corner of my eye – each time she upped pace, I upped pace. I matched her stride for stride, step for step. Soon, we were running equally. Both of us heading for the imaginary finish line neck and neck. While she had eventually started to glow, rivers of perspiration washed down my back, making my top stick to me, oceans of the stuff cascaded down my face.

'What are you doing after your workout?' Claudine asked, over the din of the treadmills. She spoke in her normal tone of voice, she could even breathe, the bitch.

'Whuh-huhow?' I replied.

'Yeah. I'll only be doing an hour today. I was wondering if you fancied going for a drink afterwards?'

I tried to speak, my lungs refused (they'd gone on strike since that 'piss off' thing from my brain). I nodded, instead.

'How long are you working out?' she asked.

I gave up, slowed down. I'd never win against

her in this race. I glanced down at the LCD display. Held up three fingers. 'Three minutes.'

'You're not doing anything else?' she asked.

I shook my head.

'You really should do weights as well . . .'

Suddenly, things got nasty. Claudine's mouth started spewing filth about more exercising. Workout, weights, swimming, muscle tone, endurance . . .

Why don't you just call me a whore and be done with it?

The beer was divine on my tongue, in my mouth, sliding down my throat. I gulped at it the second the pint glass, cloaked in condensation, touched my bottom lip. Claudine did virtually the same thing with her glass of wine.

'See, isn't that better?' I almost said. I'd talked her out of that 'workout' nonsense and had flat out refused to sit with her if she ordered a soft drink.

'Bliss in a glass,' I gasped, finally giving my drink a reprieve.

'You're not wrong,' Claudine said.

We both sighed deeply at the pleasure that could be found in the form of alcohol, then sat in silence as we contemplated how easily pacified we were. She left the air between us silent for a few seconds more before she asked: 'Were you really thinking about Pavlov in the gym earlier?'

'Um . . . yeah.'

'I see,' she said, eyeing me suspiciously. She

sipped more of her drink. 'I suppose being a psychologist those things come to you all the time. Kind of like an occupational hazard?'

There was that . . . there was also the fact it was a mad, scary world inside my head. I once spent the better part of a night thinking through the intricacies and possibilities of being battered to death with a teaspoon. I'd seen a news story about being battered to death by a hammer, the teaspoon thought process followed from there. Naturally.

'I teach contemporary and cultural studies,' Claudine said.

'Oh. How long have you taught that then?' I asked.

'Since I finished at The Met. My tutor said I should think about doing a PhD because I'd done so well over the three years. So I signed up for a PhD at All Souls and eventually, when they realised they couldn't get rid of me, they gave me a job. I've done it properly for two years now.'

'Do you enjoy it?'

'Yes and no, like most jobs I'd imagine. There are good times, there are bad times.'

'I know what you mean. That's why I left my job and London in the end. I found that the bad times were getting longer and longer and the good times were so few and far between that they'd virtually disappeared.'

'What made you decide to do it then?'

'No one thing. It all built up I guess. Then

someone said something and I knew, kind of, what I had to do.'

'God, they must be pretty wonderful. Who was it and what did they say?'

Claudine thought I was odd anyway, and I wasn't trying to impress her, but she, like most people, wouldn't understand the whole 'Oprah told me to do it' thing. And did I really want to still be repeating that line when I was very nearly thirty? 'Oh, just a person,' I supplied. 'It's been fun though, being able to start again.' Fun and scary.

'And it's a nice place to do it at. Small, intimate. It's like a family college. I like lecturing there.'

'It seems nice,' I agreed.

Claudine sipped her drink. 'The thing with me and Mel is complicated. It's not a simple case of us being friends and you being wrong about us. It's . . . it's so complex.'

I wasn't shocked by this non sequitur in conversation – at all. If people who are about to invite me into their lives didn't do odd little things like Ed had done a few nights earlier, they just blurted at me. Stopped mid-conversation and blurted.

It'd taken time to understand what was really going on with these confessions and heartfelt blurts. When blokes would spontaneously confess that they were single and looking to settle down/meet the right woman/fall in love, I'd used to think they were secretly coming on to me. I'd excitedly tell my friends about it and would sometimes go as far as asking them out. I'd only cottoned on after several blokes ran away at the very idea of dating me, and several more spent the 'date' unloading their hearts and minds and problems on to me, instead of flirting that I understood. I had booked an honest-to-goodness night out with the possibility of a song at the end of it; they wanted a confidante, someone who wasn't backward at coming forward with advice. Or, failing that, the phone number of that gorgeous woman they'd been after for ages.

I wasn't stupid, just a dreamer. I still hadn't completely accepted that Cupid, Venus, Eros or whoever governed the laws of love had a grievance against me. I lived in constant hope that a bloke would want to go out with me for me being me. Not a free therapist.

With women, I soon discovered their deeply personal blurts weren't on a quid pro quo level; it wasn't a precursor to a long and/or meaningful friendship. They didn't want to know about my stories, my worries, they wouldn't be there during my upsets or in my times of need; what they wanted was a non-friend to listen. Someone who couldn't judge like a friend might. They latched onto Ceri, the listener, the someone who wouldn't expect the favour returned in kind.

Sometimes it pissed me off, usually when I'd had a four-in-the-morning panic and knew that if Jess wasn't around the next day to listen, I'd be carrying the weight of that panic around for days and weeks, because when it came down to it, more than half the people in my phone book didn't want to know my problems.

But that disgruntlement was only sometimes. Most of the time I just put up with it. What else was I going to do, tell them I'm not interested?

'What do you mean?' I asked Claudine, my latest blurtee.

'We . . . well, we're very close,' Claudine said.

'I see,' I replied.

Claudine cast her dark, smouldery eyes over me – assessing if I could handle the truth. Like you could tell by the cut of my jib how sturdy my mind was. Weak chin, weak mind.

'Can you keep a secret?' Claudine asked.

If I couldn't I'd hardly say no, would I? I'd most likely not realise I couldn't keep a secret. As it happened, I could keep a secret. I could keep several million secrets. My head was like the Fort Knox of secrets, except, of course, no one tried to break into my head to steal the twenty-four carat stuff stored in there. Not yet, anyway. 'I can,' I said.

Claudine swigged some French courage. 'The thing is . . .' more courage down her neck, 'last year, that is, a few months ago, around Christmas . . .' big gulp, 'Mel and I, well, we . . .'

Made love? Wore each other's underwear to work? Spent the limit on your credit cards on ice-cream?

'Kissed.'

Right. *And that's bad is it?* 'Was it the first time it'd happened?'

95

'It was a bit more than kissing.'
My mistake, shan't interrupt again.
'Quite a lot more, actually.'
I sipped my drink.
'We were practically naked.'
I sipped more drink.
'And in his bed.'
Sip.
'And we were totally naked.'
Some kiss, I thought as I watched her from over the rim of my glass.

Claudine looked me in the eye as she delivered her next earth-stopping revelation. 'We didn't have sex, though. I didn't want to do that to my boyfriend and Mel didn't want to do that to his, er, wife.'

'Mel's married?' I asked. *I seem to remember him saying 'I'm not seeing anyone special.'*

Claudine twirled the stem of her wine glass between her forefinger and thumb; with the other hand she pulled wisps of her cropped hair around her face. 'They split up not long after, you know.'

You didn't have sex? 'Ah. Right.'

'Like I said, it's complicated.'

'I guess so. How about I get the next round in and you think of the least complicated way to tell me about it.'

'Get me a large wine,' Claudine called after me. 'I'll leave the car at college and get a cab home.'

The bar of the Fox & Hound, down by Horsforth train station resounded with dark broodiness.

Most of it came from its dark wood interior, the lead pattening of the windows. We were sat in the larger of the two alcoves that looked out to the bar. We'd rested our exercised carcasses on highly upholstered booths beside the empty fireplace.

I stood on the foot rail and leant forwards over the bar, waiting for the barman to notice me. While I waited, I checked out the only other person at the bar. He was leant across the bar too, waiting to be noticed, but his height excused him from needing the chrome foot rail. His body, leant across the bar as it was, turned him into a sleek line, like smooth easy brush strokes on a page. If I blurred my eyes he'd be colours and smudges against the dark canvas of the bar. More aesthetically pleasing than if I did it to other people in this bar. I stopped watching him before he caught me and I found myself in one of those eye contact situations. I concentrated, instead, on getting the barman's attention. The barman was busily working through a large round. I'd probably get two rounds in at once, that would save me interrupting Claudine's story by doing anything as wanton and thoughtless as needing more alcohol.

The hairs on the back of my neck tingled suddenly as though someone had stroked ice-cold fingers across the base of my skull. My head snapped round and my eyes connected with the man who looked like brush strokes on a page. Unusually for me, my eyes didn't immediately rip themselves away, they were startled still. Startled by the way he was blatantly staring a hole into my head. He had his head slightly to one side, studying me as though I was something he'd just discovered under his microscope.

Worse, he didn't even stop, now I was facing him. He continued to stare away like it was the most natural thing in the world to watch a woman who'd caught you watching her. I offered a very small, very nervous smile; he didn't. He carried on staring for a few more seconds, then looked away, leaving an air of faint disapproval as he did so.

What the hell was that all about? I thought as my whole body burned in indignation at being so closely scrutinised. He'd probably even studied the huge flea bite that was developing on my neck.

I didn't dwell on it for too long though. I had to listen to Claudine's tale . . .

'After that night, you know, the night we got naked and physical, everything about our lives changed. Mel . . .' She paused, drank deep from her drink, then swished what was left around the bottom of the large wine glass. 'Mel says he loves me. And that he's in love with me.' She sighed, glanced at me, was probably surprised to find my face interested but impassive. I was, in the main, unshockable. Not even *Jerry Springer* had thrown me – it may have disgusted me, but not shocked. I'd heard it all before – literally.

'I don't know what to do. It's been, what, four

months since it happened, but I don't know what to do. I keep thinking about it, but it's not any clearer.'

I knew what I had to ask now. It was in my script. I could do this listening, confessor thing from any level of consciousness. There was a set way to coax these stories out of people, not that by this point they needed much coaxing. They just needed me to follow my script to get them to tell me everything. And the question next on my list wasn't: 'How do you feel about him?' It was . . .

'What's your boyfriend like?'

'Kevin? Oh. Um. He's one of the best blokes you'd ever want to meet. He's great. Really great.' Claudine twirled her glass between her fingers again. Then sighed. Then sighed even deeper. 'But he's not Mel.'

'I see,' I said.

Time for a little assessment of the situation. OK. Kevin isn't Mel. Mel says he's in love with her. Mel's no longer with his wife. He isn't seeing anyone special. A fair summation of what she'd told me, no? The question on my lips now was, of course: 'So why don't you leave?' Not that I'd ask her outright.

'I don't leave because it's not that simple.' I didn't need to ask. 'You don't just walk out on a life. Not when we've been together for four years. I mean, most women struggle for some kind of commitment from their boyfriends. I didn't. It was Kevin's idea for us to move in together after two years. We bought our house, we've built a life together from scratch, we've been happy together for ages. You don't just walk out on that.'

'I see,' I said. *You wouldn't be the first, you wouldn't be the last*, I thought.

The world is chock-a-block with people – male and female – who've walked out on a marriage, family, kids, friends, jobs on a whim. On a look. Let alone a near-shag and a confession of love both offered and felt. Not that I was advocating leaving (I'd never advocate anything I haven't done myself and even then, just cos it worked for me, doesn't mean it'd work for anyone else), it simply seemed . . . it came across that Claudine was, to all intents and purposes, waiting for something.

'It's not like Mel's putting pressure on me. I get the impression he'd wait for as long as it takes.'

'What about you? How long are you prepared to wait?'

'Wait?' Claudine replied. 'Wait for what?'

'Sorry, my mistake,' I said, started gulping down my drink at the rate of knots. *That was a question I should've thought, not said.*

'No, no, tell me. Say what you meant.'

'I'm probably wrong, so don't take what I'm about to say as anything other than my opinion.' I sighed, silently. *I am a big-mouthed old slag.* 'When you were talking just then, I got the impression that you were waiting for the answer to present itself. We all do that when we're in the middle of something big, but it's as though you've pressed pause on the whole matter and are kind of waiting for someone else to press play and sort it out. Unless Mel's going to make it up with his wife, or Kevin finishes with you out of the blue, that's not going to happen. The remote control is firmly in your grip. But, like I said, that's just my opinion. My last relationship that lasted longer than three weeks was two years ago. I know very little about very little.'

Claudine swirled her wine a bit slower and stared into her glass, as though hypnotising herself.

I often did this to people after a blurt session. I often made them think about something so deeply they checked out of the conversation and became sad. Upset that there was something they could be doing but weren't. An option that was staring them in the face that they couldn't see. It was all right for me, I could come out with these theories, because it wasn't my life. I could see what to do clearly if it wasn't my life. Couldn't everyone? One step removed you had twenty-twenty vision.

However, the result of my clear-sightedness sat opposite me, swirling pale wine around her smeared glass, looking so forlorn, she probably qualified to have her picture beside the entry for 'forlorn' in *The Oxford English Picture Dictionary*.

If there was one thing I shouldn't do, it was offer my opinion. I was getting better, though. Better at not saying everything I thought, even if others had started it by telling me far too much, way too soon. There was a time when I would've said all that stuff about people leaving on a whimsy to Claudine, thereby totally alienating her. Whilst now, there was only about seventy-five per cent alienation going on – if you factored in the lunch thing.

'What would you do?' she asked me.

'Me?' I replied.

Claudine nodded vigorously. 'In my situation, what would you do to "press play"?'

'To be totally honest, Claudine, I don't know. I don't have all the facts, because I wasn't there. I don't know how Mel acted afterwards, how he's acted since. I don't know if Kevin's noticed a change in you, if you've been off with him or trying too hard. Like I said, I've not got all the facts so I don't know what I'd do.'

I'd actually forgotten what a mind terrorist I was. I came wandering in, lobbing confusion grenades left, right and centre and then when I was asked how to disarm them, I shrugged and said, 'dunno mate'. I should be locked up.

'Thanks Ceri,' Claudine said as I stumbled out of the taxi an hour or so later. 'Thanks for listening, you were a great help.'

'Any time,' I slurred.

She grabbed my cuff before I reeled away from the open door and fell into the house. 'Don't tell anyone what I told you,' she said, frantically searching my face for understanding.

102

'About what?' I replied.

'Me and Mel,' she said.

'I know. I was being funny.'

'Oh. Ha ha. That wasn't very funny.'

'No, I guess not. Bye.' I shut the car door before she took that the wrong way too.

CHAPTER 8

COPYING

Apparently, photocopying was an ordeal round these parts.

Either you spent hours camped out in the photocopying room situated in the furthest, darkest corner of the social sciences department, waiting your turn to watch lights flash back and forth, back and forth, back and forth, back and forth; battling with toner and collating and getting the book to lie flat enough to get a good copy. Or, you took it to the reprographics department and had them do it. Because that's what they were there for. They worried about getting good copies and stapling and other stuff like that. Our department just paid for it.

The whole reprographics department was situated just opposite the library, had swing doors and a photocopied, laminated sign outside that said: REPROGRAPHICS in block capitals. The whole demeanour of the place said, 'Don't come hither. And if you do, expect to be insulted'. Sally had warned me about them. Said to not go there if I was sensitive. But I wasn't sensitive. I could handle most things, I was a South

East Londoner. You didn't survive 'Darn Sarf' if you were sensitive.

I headed down there the day after I'd been out with Claudine and did not feel well. Every step reminded me I did not feel well. In fact, how I was still standing was a mystery. How I'd got out of bed in time and got to the bus stop and managed to stay upright long enough for the 731 to arrive I'll never know. At one point last night it'd looked like I wasn't going to get to bed . . .

I'd opened the door after Claudine's cab pulled away, trying to be quiet and normal just in case the boys were asleep. Still going for the quietness, I moved to shut the door, but it sprang out of my hand and slammed.

'Shhhh!' I hissed to it, bashing my finger against my lips. 'Shhhhhh!'

'You all right there, Ceri?' a voice asked.

I leapt around to look at him. Jake. *Uh-oh. Landlord. Act normal. Don't want him to evict you.* 'Fine,' I said, trying to stand up straight. Never mind I smelt like a beer mat and swayed like a blade of grass in a gale.

'Do you want a cup of tea or something?' he asked.

I shook my head violently. 'No. Thank you. No. No thank you.'

I seem to remember him looking confused. 'OK,' Jake replied. 'Did you have a good time?'

'I went to the gym,' I said. My arms started making running movements. 'I ran on the treadmill.'

'It's midnight. Must've been a long run.'

I nodded enthusiastically. 'Twenty minutes.'

Jake frowned. 'Right.'

I pointed to the stairs. 'I'm going to bed now.'

'OK. Night.'

'Night.'

'Oh, Jake, Jake,' I called urgently, even though he hadn't moved at all.

'Yes?'

'Thank you. I really like living here.'

'I'm glad.'

'No, no, really. It's a nice room and it's so cheap and you and Ed seem like nice blokes and I don't even think you'll smack me over the head and drag me out over the carpet that doesn't show up blood stains cos I used some of your milk. Not that I have. I don't really drink milk, but I don't think either of you would. Thank you. Good night.'

I started up the stairs, then realised how mad I must've sounded. So, on the top step of the first flight of stairs, I turned around and went tearing down them, practically ran into the kitchen where Jake was filling the kettle.

'I'm not really mad,' I said, loudly.

Jake jumped so much he almost dropped the kettle. 'Sorry?' he asked.

'I'm not mad. When I first looked around you asked me if I was a weirdo and I'm not. I'm in love with Buffy The Vampire Slayer's ex-boyfriend Angel, and I'm addicted to *Star Trek* but I'm not a weirdo.'

'OK, I'll take your word for it.'

'Good night.'

I went happily skipping off to bed after that.

And woke up red-eyed, shaky and with a thirst that could not be quenched by water alone. I'd stopped off in the canteen on the way in this morning to get water and had nearly passed out at the food smells. The week-old oil that had been used to fry that morning's hash browns, clung to the air. Even the cereal smelt enough to make me want to hurl. And, on top of that, I had three sets of tutorials to do *and* see Jake later.

First things first: photocopying for the next morning's lecture.

The wire-mesh windows of the reprographics swing doors were obscured by paper so you couldn't see in as you reached out and pushed open the right door. The room was brightly-lit, a waist-height wood counter separated the world from the department. High shelves seemed to go on and on as you approached, stacked with piles of photocopying, reams of paper, lots and lots of different colours. It was like walking into a library of paper.

'Hi, I'd like these photocopied forty times for tomorrow,' I said to the woman behind the counter. I even managed a smile with my dry, furry mouth.

The woman looked up slowly from the book she was making notes in and gave me a partially-hidden sneer that suggested that I hadn't actually asked for photocopying. I had, in fact, informed her that her biological mother and biological father were close blood relatives.

Time crawled on as she looked me up and down from behind her large, plastic-framed Deirdre Barlow glasses. Once she'd appraised me, she opened her mouth, which had been so clenched it was almost caving in on itself, and sneered, 'Photocopying has to be brought in at least fifteen days in advance.'

'Fifteen days?' I said.

'Fifteen days.'

Do you see this face? It is suffering. It does not need to be told it has to wait fifteen days for something it needs tomorrow.

Sally had warned me. '*Show no weakness,*' she'd said. '*They do not understand weakness. They do not respect niceness. They chew up nice people until they are mulch, then they spit you out and stamp on you.*' I knew all this, but I still said, 'Can't I get it done sooner?' in a pathetic, 'be nice to me' voice.

She sighed with her whole body.

'I do not have time to explain everything to you. You should know all this if you're a lecturer.'

'How? By subscribing to the college's psychic newsletter? Or by simply putting my head against the reprographics sign outside and letting it seep in by osmosis,' I replied.

'You *are* a lecturer, aren't you?'

'Yes, but I'm also a new lecturer so I don't have a handle on everything yet.'

'That's not my problem, is it. *Dear.*' Her superiority had clambered up to a new level now she knew I was in a weak position. I was a novice. 'Fifteen days.'

'But I don't know what I'll need that far in advance,' I replied. 'Sometimes I only find books and articles that are necessary a couple of days in advance.'

'That's not my problem either, is it,' the woman behind the counter replied, picking up a stack of forms and tapping them on the counter to straighten them while wiggling her head in an officious manner. 'Maybe you should plan your lectures more carefully.'

Even in my state, even as hungover and unwell as I was I couldn't abide that kind of rudeness. (Particularly not from someone I could soooo take in a fight.) 'Excuse me?' I replied.

'I was under the impression that lecturers were meant to work to a set timetable. You know, *plan things.*' As she spoke she waggled her upper body in that selfsame officious manner. 'Be prepared.'

I picked up my stack of books and articles. 'Tell you what, you don't tell me how to lecture and I won't tell you how to press the little button on the photocopier machine.'

'You cannot speak to me like that,' she said. 'I will report you to your head of department.'

'Right. Well, you do that. Don't forget to read the college's psychic newsletter to find out my name, and when you've reported me to the head of department, why don't you report me to God too because He's the only person I'm really scared of.'

Had I been able to, I would've slammed the swing door behind me. But I kicked it, leaving it fump, fump, fumping open and shut behind me.

WHORE! I said in my head. *Whore-faced old bag. Who does she think she is? No one talks to me like that and gets away with it. Stupid old mare.*

I'd stamped my way to the Senior Common Room before reason pierced my anger: I'd been insulted by some officious mare in a department. And she couldn't do that if I wasn't part of the grand scheme of things.

Hey, I'm a proper lecturer now.

I slid my key into the front door and almost collapsed with happiness as the door swung open. I never thought I'd be so happy to see the inside of a place in my life. I never thought I could sleep with my eyes open, either, but I could. I'd just done it.

The nonsense I'd heard about developmental psychology this morning had almost put me to sleep for real. But I'd propped my eyes open with sheer willpower and had nodded and asked questions when people read out their work.

The worst part was, to sit there, listening to students spewing what was essentially something they'd put together on the bus . . . it made me think of all the times I'd done that and thought

I'd got away with it. It hadn't occurred to me that lecturers would see through it. That they'd be sat there thinking: *Are you kidding me? Do you really want me to believe that what you were talking there was a week's worth of extracurricular reading?*

I went staggering into the living room, dropped my papers and books onto the sofa and flopped down beside them, dropped my head onto the cushion. I could stay like this for ever. And ever. And ever.

'Hi Ceri,' a male voice said. I hadn't been here long enough to work out who it was. I turned my head a little to look at him. Ed.

'Hi Ed,' I replied.

Ed threw himself down onto the other sofa, picked up the remote control and turned on the television. 'Suffering?' he asked.

'Yeah. I've had to deal with photocopying psychos. And this lecturing lark's a lot harder than it seems,' I mumbled.

'So it's nothing to do with being laroped last night?'

'Jake told you?' I said.

'Jake told me. He said you wouldn't stop talking.'

'Oh, Godddd. Did he sound scared when he told you?'

'Well, he was quite pleased that you took the time to reassure him that you weren't a weirdo. And that you didn't think either of us would whack you over the head if you borrowed our milk. Not that you drink milk.'

'Ohhhhhhhh.'

'He thought it was quite funny, actually.'

'Yeah, they all think it's funny until they ask you to move out,' I said into the cushion.

'Hi Ceri,' Jake said.

I sat bolt upright. Dragged my hands through my hair to make it lie flat. 'Jake, about last night . . .' I began.

'Forget it,' Jake said, brushing away my apology before I'd even started it. He sat beside Ed, wrestled the remote control off him and flicked the TV over.

Ed wrestled it back, flicked it back to the other side.

Jake nudged Ed, held him back with his elbow, got back the control and turned over the TV. 'We're having sausage casserole for tea,' Jake said, he'd got Ed in a head lock and was holding the remote out of reach.

'Yeah, and I made Angel Delight for dessert,' Ed choked.

'You do eat meat, don't you?' Jake said.

'I do,' I said, watching the fight progress.

'Cool. But don't have any Angel Delight, Ed's a really bad cook even when it's just whisking powder into milk.'

Ed managed to grab a pillow from the sofa and started to bash Jake with it. I lay face down on the sofa again. I had moved into the right place. I could feel it in my soul.

CHAPTER 9

THE BOSS

Time moves quickly, time moves slowly.

The longer I stayed in Leeds, the more I understood Einstein's theory of relativity. Not the entire theorem, more the relative part. How things seemed.

Time sped by at weekends, time almost stopped when I was giving a lecture, from the looks on some of the students' faces and the way they stared forlornly at their watches, they felt the same. And, for some reason, every day seemed to be the day before Wednesday, or Wednesday. Wednesday was half-day at most universities and colleges so the students could pursue physical activities and play sports. Most uni competitions and matches were held on Wednesday afternoons. This meant I could pursue my favourite activities – cooking, eating, watching television without infringing upon official work or study time.

The relativity of Wednesday to every other day of the week should, then, have been joyous. It was not.

The usual drill for Wednesday pre-lunch, post-morning, was for Gwen, my boss and the head of the psychology department, to come in after giving a cognitive psychology lecture and flop down next to me, offer me a cigarette (I'd always refuse, emphasising how much tobacco smoke bothered me with a reply of 'I don't smoke') and proceed to chain-smoke her way through the entire two-hour lecture. That is, recounting it between long drags of her high-tar fags.

'I don't know why I bother, I really don't,' she said, searching her handbag for something. Cigarettes I presumed. This was my third Wednesday. She'd assumed the flop beside me position and was now searching for her props before the drama that was lecturing unfolded. I braced myself for a face and body full of the brown stuff people had to use paint stripper to get off pub walls. 'Do you know what they've done now?'

I'd been in Gwen's office a few times since I started, and discovered it was like walking in to an Ashtray Temple. Ashtrays littered the desk, her bookshelves, there were a couple on the window sill. Each was different in size and colour but her office was clearly a holy place for the things. Drawn here to worship at the fingers of the great, white smoker. Each and every ashtray had some kind of cigarette debris in it, as though she stubbed out her cigarette in whichever ashtray she happened to be passing at the time. Most disturbingly, every cigarette was fully-smoked.

I'd sat opposite her at her desk and studied the

114

cigarettes the first time I'd been in her office. First, I'd looked at the ones in the ashtray by her computer, then at the ones in the ashtrays I could see. Every cigarette was smoked, right to the edge of the filter. No fag escaped her ownership unsmoked or half-smoked. Or even three-quarters smoked. That showed a particular type of dedication. She didn't simply want a boost of nicotine, she wanted every last drop, every last microgram. Gwen was one step away from injecting nicotine.

'Do you know what they've done now?' she repeated, her hand still digging around the bag.

Rather conversely to all laws of physics and biology, Gwen spoke with the girliest voice. The kind of voice I used to affect when I wanted to get around someone by pretending to be pathetic and unable to think due to a lack of brain cells. She spoke with an educated squeak that became posher and squeakier the more riled she got. Her voice suited her clothes though: Laura Ashley-style skirts or dresses, pink or powder blue blouses. And, most bizarrely, always, *always* thick black tights. We'd had a rash of hot, sunny days recently, but still Gwen's sixty deniers stuck to her legs, and stuck out of her black open-toe sandals. She wore those whether it was sunny or cold or rainy, too.

Gwen found her cigarettes and pulled them out of her big, flowery cloth bag. She flipped the top of the packet open. 'I really don't know why I bother,' she repeated.

'Why, what's happened?' I said, catching on that, unlike previous Wednesdays, I had to work for the information this time. She lit her cigarette with her solid gold lighter, a present from her husband – I'd seen the inscription – and inhaled almost all of the cigarette in one suck. It was bad. It was very bad. I didn't yet understand just how bad it was, though.

'Not one of them had done the reading. Not one,' she squeaked, a notch or two higher than normal. She was very agitated. 'And then one of them had the audacity to . . .' huge draw, 'to say she didn't know what I was talking about. She didn't know what I was talking about. Can you believe it?'

My heart sank, my throat tightened and I swallowed hard. Unfortunately, yes, I could believe it. In fact, I could've prevented it.

My second lecture with the first group I'd taught as a proper lecturer, I'd relaxed into the role far more. I wasn't reading straight from the script in front of me. I could ad lib, drop in little quips. I was working up to big detours and anecdotes. That second lecture, they'd relaxed with me, too. We'd only been in the room for a few minutes when the woman with the tight, blondish perm raised her hand slightly.

'Er, yeah?' I asked. 'Oh, do you mind saying your name before you speak? I still haven't learnt your names.'

'Um, I'm Roberta. Can I ask you something?'

'Yeah, course.'

'Do you think Gwen's mad?'

'Sorry?' I replied.

Mr Wham-era George Michael raised his hand. 'I'm Joel, I think what Roberta's trying to say is, we don't understand what she's on about half the time. And none of us are learning anything.'

'No, Joel,' Roberta said, 'I was asking if Ceri thought Gwen was mad. There is a difference, even if you're too polite to notice.'

'Right,' I said. *Oh bollocks,* I thought.

After that, the flood gates were bust open as a tidal wave of disgruntlement crashed down onto the room. Gwen was boring. Gwen was confusing. 'She scares the b'jasus out of me with the way she teaches,' one of them said.

I'd listened to the first wave of discontentment, then said: 'She speaks very highly of you, too.'

Another tidal wave of disgruntlement crashed down on us then: most of them skipped her lectures, they said. The ones who did go to her lectures were far too scared to point out how little they were learning. Or to even reply to her questions. They all lived in mortal fear of her asking them a question. They simply weren't learning anything, but were too worried about being given a failing grade to say owt to her.

I wasn't stupid. Stunned, but not stupid. The general gist of what they were saying was, 'Could you say something to her for us?, i.e., could you get her to stop being Gwen and be a little human when it comes to her teaching style?

I tried to impress upon them that they were responsible for what they learnt, no one could put it in their heads. But they were having none of it. They merely dragged out more examples of how bad a lecturer Gwen was and how it was practically my duty, as the new, young, trendy lecturer who'd started off by being nice to them, to say something to her. That'll learn me to try to be cool.

With the burden on my head, I'd meant to say something to Gwen. Really I had. I simply never found the right moment, the right time, the righ – OK, OK, I was scared. She was the head of department. My Boss. She could revoke my position with the stroke of a pen. How was I supposed to tell her, she who had years of teaching experience, compared to my fifty hours' experience, to stop it. Besides, I'd be trapped in her smoke-filled office while I tried to explain their position to her. I had meant to at least broach the subject. I'd just kept putting it off and putting it off until, well, now. Woman thy name is coward.

I looked at Gwen as she finished off her cigarette. 'I, er,' I began, not sure what I was going to say before I opened my mouth. But then, I was rarely sure what I was going to say before I opened my mouth, and it hadn't stopped me before.

Again, I was saved by Mel. He blew into the Senior Common Room, a mass of papers and folders. Papers slipping, eyes searching the room, he always moved as though someone was chasing him. 'He could cause a riot in an empty house,' that was a phrase my mum used and it was so apt for Mel. He approached the low coffee table Gwen and I were sat in front of and I had my feet on, paused – giving me a silent one-second warning to move my feet, before they were avalanched by his lecturing materials and essays. I pulled my feet away just before he dropped his load. He then reached into his back pocket and pulled out a picture postcard.

'Guess who I got a postcard from?' he stated to the room. It'd filled up a little, but not much. Not enough for him to be making such a big-voiced announcement, anyway.

'Who?' Gwen replied for the room. Her demon year group forgotten.

'Eva.'

The name sparked a couple of 'awwws' and some interest around the room. A couple of people – mugs in hands – wandered over, others looked up from what they were doing to listen.

'Listen,' Mel said, cleared his throat.

Dear Everyone – and Mel. Greetings from Barcelona. Am having the time of my life. Even better than I could have hoped for when I left. It's warm here and I'm walking

119

around in a lot less than I would in Britain. There's so much to tell but not much space. Have met a couple of nice people and we'll be working our way across to Spain's Atlantic coast and then on to Tangiers. I can tell I'm going to be a travel bore when I get back. Miss you all but don't miss College. At all.

Love and Peace, Eva.

PS Mel, you waster, you'd better pass this on.

'Cheeky cow,' Mel muttered.

A few pleased sighs went around the room. Eva was the woman who'd kindly vacated her position about three days before I wrote to the college.

'Wish I was travelling,' Gwen mumbled, a petulant tone in her voice.

'Have you been travelling before?' I asked, grateful that we didn't need to talk about the demon year group any more.

Gwen lit another cigarette with her lighter, breathed it to life, shook her head. 'No. My husband and I didn't ever get around to it.' She snapped her head around to me. 'We meant to. We simply got tied up in our careers. It's just, the first ten years were devoted to getting ourselves established in our careers, and then it was too late. But we did mean to.'

I'd avoided asking Gwen much about her family because:

a) I hadn't forgotten she abandoned me at lunch on the first day

b) I wasn't allowed to by The Commandments

c) I didn't want to get into any conversation that would end up with me having to accept an invitation to dinner. (If I'd only narrowly escaped becoming a Jehovah's Witness, how much more would I be able to turn down an invitation to dinner? It wasn't in my nature to say no to people when they asked me nicely.)

There were inherent dangers in any Gwen-related dinner invitation: if the chintz her house would surely be decorated in didn't burn the retinas off my cornea, then the smoke would get me. And if her husband smoked half as much as she did, I'd end the night in an oxygen tent. Of course, there was also the small talk factor. ST had never been my forte. It was pretty unnecessary when most people came out with deeply personal stories from the off. But I didn't want that with my boss.

You needed a little mystery with the people you worked for. I remember when I'd been a secretary during the summer holidays from uni. I got to know far too much about my bosses. One boss in particular when I temped in a media agency used to take me out for drinks to whinge on about her relationship. She often told me things my fragile mind didn't ever want to hear. I suppose the bedrock of my unshockability came from that

121

summer, with her. I'd lie for her when her partner called, I arranged her life, I even cleared out her office when she moved floors. And the stuff I unearthed in there unsettled me. Let's say, I'd never seen things like vibrators or crotchless knickers up close until I worked for her. I came to her a non-virgin innocent. I left knowing too much about sex – like how having a threesome with your partner's best friend could really mess you up emotionally.

Basically, there was no mystique between us and that's necessary in a boss-employee relationship. How could you take seriously someone shouting at you for being late when you knew she'd once cried in the street because Shelley's had sold out of white stilettos?

I did not want to cross that line with Gwen. Having said that, guilt gestated in my conscience. I wanted to go back in time and warn her about the coming student revolution. That they were not going down the *coup d'état* route – they wanted blood and beheadings. I couldn't go back though, despite all *Star Trek* had led me to believe, so I had to be nice to her in the present. 'What does your husband do?' I asked, risking the dinner invite.

'Do? He doesn't do anything. Whatever do you mean?'

'You said about your careers . . . I just wondered . . .' *Freako*, I thought.

'Career? He's a banker. One of the top executives in the City.'

122

'Right. Sounds interesting.' I.e. boring as tooth plaque. Although, I shouldn't malign tooth plaque – under a microscope it was probably more interesting than her husband's job.

'Vernon seems to suit it.'

'But you'd rather be travelling?'

'No, no, of course not. It's just a pipe dream that we, well, I think about. Sometimes. Only sometimes. How can you not when you hear postcards like that? Of course I wouldn't rather be travelling. I love my life. I love my life.'

Chill baby, you don't have to convince me of owt. I don't care if you travel or stay in Leeds. 'I see,' I replied, absently. I'd tuned out, fuzzed my brain to Gwen, focused instead across the room on Mel and Claudine.

Claudine and Mel sat alone at the table at the left end of the SCR, while he described something on the front of the postcard to her. He'd obviously been to Barcelona, his right index finger traced something along the postcard, every two microseconds his eyes would go up to her face, keen to ensnare her in his tale. She, while clearly interested, kept her dark eyes focused on the postcard, nodding to show she was following him but studiously avoiding eye contact.

There was something going on there. Yes, she told me that last week, after the gym, but there was something more going on between them. It wasn't purely body language that gave the game away. Not with them, not with other people.

123

It was the way people looked at each other in unguarded moments. The way they didn't look at each other in guarded moments. I'd become a bit of an unintentional expert in nonverbal communication over the years. I'd studied people on the sly, listened to their tales and watched them afterwards. Despite what people pretended, despite what people said to my face, they couldn't stop those tell-tale signs showing through.

With Mel and Claudine it wasn't as simple as the picture she painted for me the other night. I'm sure they had 'got physical', but *how* physical was still up for debate. Not that Claudine was a liar, she wanted to believe what she told me, which was why she'd been able to look me in the eye as she said it; you can lie if you want to believe the lie enough. Maybe more had happened, maybe less had happened. The point was: something had happened. And they were both struggling to deal with the consequences of it. Claudine, from the way she was behaving and talking the other night, was clearly racked with guilt over whatever it was. (I'd personally not worked out how anyone could cheat. It was far too much guilt to live with on a day-to-day basis. To look in the mirror day after day, knowing what you'd done . . . that was too much like hard work.) And, like I said to her, she was waiting for the answer to her dilemma to fall into her lap so she could decide what to do.

Then there was Mel. Sitting beside Claudine. Nice guy Mel who'd cheated on his wife with his best friend. Those weren't the actions of a nice guy. But, as I'd found over the years, nothing was as simple as we all hoped it would be. You could rarely point your finger at the average person in the street and say, 'All bad.' 'Completely evil.' It was only the people who'd gone out of their way to cause destruction and death and hurt and pain and ignorance who could be classified in such terms. Most people, your average Joanne Public, your next-door neighbour, your lecturer in the common room, had levels of behaviour, levels of badness, reasons for doing the things they did. Even if they did destroy other people's lives. Mel was one of those people.

Take the way he was with Claudine now. How he was looking at her, how he was talking to her, he cared about her deeply. If he and his wife only split up a few months ago, *after* his indiscretion with Claudine, then that would mean he couldn't be feeling rebound love for Claudine. He'd most likely loved her for years. If he'd loved her for years, then why wait until he got married to make a move on her? And *then* finish with his wife and tell Claudine how he felt. Something more was going on. It was more complicated than love. Love was great. Love was everything as far as a lot of people were concerned, but with Claudine and Mel, it was more complicated than love. They had depth of friendship; years seeing other people; a present that meant working together. For them, love was only a small element of it, a tiny piece of the Mel and Claudine jigsaw. If love was the be all and end all in their case, they'd be together, wouldn't they?

Mel and Claudine. Claudine and Mel. I really needed to hear his side of the story to get the fuller picture of their jigsaw. However, it was nothing to do with me. At all. It was j—

'Well, would you?' Gwen asked, impatiently.

I turned to her, smiled. I trawled my memory for what she'd been saying while I'd been observing Mel and Claude. I'd heard it, but not enough. And Gwen's face, lined and freckly and obscured by cigarette smoke as it was, hung on a precipice of either pleasure or upset. The guilt that had been gestating earlier was almost ready to come out, kicking and screaming the truth, the whole truth and nothing but the truth. I was very close to either telling her I'd known about the students hating her, or I'd invite her to dinner myself.

'Why not,' I replied, careful to keep my tone ambiguous so she wouldn't know I'd completely tuned out.

Gwen's face broke into an unexpected grin. I'd never seen her grin before, it suited her. She should smile more often. She should probably relax more often, too. 'Fabulous. I'll let you know,' she squeaked. 'It'll be within the next month or so. I'll have to check with Vernon, but I'm sure he'd love having you over for dinner.'

CHAPTER 10

TEA CIRCLES

Mel was the new Levi's type. The kind of lad who always had the latest style of Levi's, two minutes after it hit the shops. I bet he had the latest DVD machine, the toppest-of-the-range stereo. I'd heard, though, he'd supplemented his wages by giving private A-level sociology lessons.

Currently on Mel's wear list, as he stood at my front door, was the distressed blue denim with the twisted seams. Jeans and jacket. He'd teamed them with a black polo neck. He didn't look like a dork, though. I'd always been theoretically against putting same-coloured denim together, it looked like you were trying to wear a casual suit. But what did I know? I lived in combats, jeans and long-sleeved tops.

I smiled a welcome at Mel, he grinned at me. Maybe he didn't look like a dork because he stood erect, showing off all of his six foot frame. Or, possibly because of the chaotic way his brown hair curled on his head. Or maybe it was his light hazel eyes. Whatever it was, Melvin looked at ease in his gear. He always did. When he had his large

128

blue rucksack slung casually over his shoulder and he wandered the corridors of the college, he seemed more student than lecturer, which was probably why so many of the students looked genuinely pleased to see him, why he often stopped for a quick chat and why he got invited to lots of student parties. He was Mr Popular, not only at our college, but also at The Met.

His popularity at The Met was how I'd found out so much about him. I'd mentioned to Ed and Jake a nice young sociology lecturer who'd helped me on my first day. When I said he was called Mel, they told me they knew him from playing footie at The Met. When I'd said we'd sat at lunch together, they'd sat me down and imparted every morsel of info about him they knew. There'd been more than a hint of the 'you get in there, girl' as they told me about him. 'He's single now, you know,' Jake and Ed had said at various points. *If only you knew*, I thought back at them.

Mel had never shown up at Ed and Jake's before then – over a week after I'd been for a drink with Claudine.

'Come in,' I said, stepping aside to let him into the warm hallway. The mid-March air still had a winter's bite about it and I'd begged and begged Jake to let me have the heating on. He'd relented but he and Ed took to walking about in shorts. Ed, though, still wore his red and black lumberjack shirt. I was pretty sure he'd die wearing that shirt.

'I forgot you lived here,' Mel said, taking off his jacket and loosening his scarf.

Lie. Total lie. I mean, if he'd truly forgotten, then why no surprise when I opened the door? In the hundred watt lighting of the hallway, I could see the different shades of pink that made up Mel's blush. He knew I knew he was lying so he avoided eye contact as he handed over his jacket, then took it back to stuff his scarf in the side pocket. The blue scarf spilled out like the jacket's guts were falling out. I draped it over the hook.

'Who is it?' Ed called from the depths of the living room. We'd all settled down to watch the second instalment of *It*. (When I'd said that if I watched the film I'd end up sleeping on the floor of one of their rooms, because I didn't 'do' horror films, they'd both laughed like broken drains. 'You think I'm joking,' I said. 'Wait till you wake up and find me kipping on your floor with a teaspoon for protection.')

'Mel,' I called back.

'All right mate,' Jake called.

'All right,' Mel replied, sticking his head around the living room door. 'Room for a little one?'

'Depends if you've brought any stuff,' Ed replied, putting his forefinger and thumb close together and moving them towards his thin lips.

'Nuh, huh, no drugs, we agreed,' I said, returning to my space on the sofa furthest from the widescreen telly.

'Yeah, Ed,' Jake added, 'Ceri's old, remember.'

130

Wouldn't mind if the cheeky *get* wasn't only a couple of years younger than me. And Mel was my age.

'Oh yeah,' Ed said.

'Whatever, just wait till I've gone to bed.'

'With your slippers and cocoa,' Mel chimed in.

'Watch it, you, I get a vote in if you're allowed to stay or not, you know.'

'While you're up, Cezza, put kettle on,' Ed said.

My bum had almost touched the seat, as well. I sighed and hoisted myself up.

'Mel can help, to earn his keep,' Jake decreed.

Funny he should say that. I got the impression Mel was going to help me anyway.

Being a Southern Softie, I'd bought a water filter – to the amusement and constant abuse of the lads. I filled the filter from the tap while Mel helped by leaning against the worktop closest to the back door and staring into the mid-distance. The water dribbled and dripped through the filter, I found clean cups, dropped three ordinary tea bags into the three white cups, dropped a strawberry, Southern Softie bag into the fourth black mug. Mel's latest contribution was to stand still in the kitchen.

'Claudine's nice, isn't she?' Mel eventually said. Very eventually. So eventually I'd thought he'd never get it off his chest. That he'd leave with his soul still burdened with whatever it was he felt so compelled to travel here to see me about. That wasn't arrogance, his lie about forgetting I lived here proved that. And, I didn't want to prompt him to tell me what he wanted to tell me. I could prompt him to reveal the wrong thing.

'Yeah, she seems nice.' I wasn't sure how much Claudine had told Mel about our impromptu night in the pub, or if she'd even mentioned that night to him. So it was best to use my new-found power of keeping shtum.

'Oh, she's lovely. I've known her, what, ten years now. We met at The Met.'

'Ah, right.'

'We were in the same halls of residence.'

'Right.'

Silence. More silence. *Come on Mel, spit it out, it might be a bus. And, to be honest, I'm getting spooked stood here in silence near the sink. You know, where water comes from and where the scary clown from the film comes up and grabs people.*

'It was funny you saying that the other day,' he said.

'About?' I stopped myself adding: 'I'm that funny, I need constant reminding of my witticisms.'

'About me and Clau and how long we'd been together.'

I grimaced. Even though I now knew what I knew, I still physically cringed every time I thought about how I'd done that on my first day here. 'Yeah, sorry about that.'

'It's all right,' Mel shrugged. 'It was just funny that's all.'

'Funny how?'

Mel shrugged again. 'Because you obviously guessed how I feel about her. Even though we really are just mates now.'

'And you weren't before?'

'I know I probably shouldn't tell you this, but Claudine is the love of my life, she always has been. I was, er, married for four years.' Mel watched the sink while he talked. He cleared his throat. 'My marriage fell apart over Christmas. The happy season was not happy for me, I can tell you. It turned into the worst few days of my life. But,' Mel had the grace to look ashamed, 'even before I tied the knot I was gone on Clau. I fancied her from the first year. I mean, you've seen her. She's gorgeous. And, well, last year, just before Christmas we got very drunk and . . . made love.' Mel paused, obviously waiting for judgement or shock from me.

'I see,' I said. Probably not the time to mention Claudine remembers it differently.

'It was the first – and only – time it happened. Clau was so ashamed she'd cheated on, Ke— her boyfriend and what we'd done to my wife that she wanted to pretend we'd stopped at the last minute. She and my wife used to get on really well, they were mates actually. They often went out together on their own cos they got on so well. We'd actually planned to spend Boxing Day together, the four of us. My wife and I weren't getting on anyway, but what happened with Claudine turned out to be our death knell. Clau still feels ashamed about it. I try to be normal but she can't seem to forget it.'

'It's hard to be normal if you think you've ruined someone's life. Especially if yours is still intact,' I replied. This was actually a cleverly-disguised question. I was trying to get him to reveal more about the state of his marriage before he and Claudine got physical.

'I don't know why she'd think that. She of all people knew that my marriage was far from perfect. I'm sure Fran, that's my wife, told her about it – Clau spent more time with her than I did at one point. We talked, me and my wife, but it always seemed to be about bills or what was for dinner. That's how I got to know Jake and Ed so well – I started spending almost every night out, joined a footie team. Then I spent time here with them. As it got to Christmas time, I spent all my time with Clau . . . I'm not saying the means justify the end, but for me it was always going to be that end. Me and my wife splitting up.'

'So it could've been anyone, not just Claudine?' I asked.

Mel's face narrowed into a fierce frown. 'What are you saying? I adore Claudine.'

'So you said,' I replied.

His eyes narrowed to slits, his face twisted.

Mel was the angry type. Great time to find *that* out. The Angry Type scared me. They were the type neighbours said of, months later, as bodies were unearthed from their back garden, 'I always thought they had killer eyes.' I had no intention of going that way. I opened a cupboard, the nearest one to me, and started moving things around, seeking biscuits and sugar, even though both things stood in clearly labelled jars on the worktop. I couldn't face his look of anger and betrayal and not fear for my life.

'Why did you marry your wife?' I asked, my head still in the depths of the cupboard.

'Because she was beautiful. And nice. And funny. And clever and lovely.'

'Did you love her?' I might as well get buried for a cow as a mouse. (The saying went something like that.)

Mel slammed down his cup with such force, I expected a loud smashing sound to follow it. His tea was surely slopped all over the worktop. I couldn't see, I still had my head in the cupboard.

'*What?!*' he snarled.

'You said you were gone on Claudine,' I said, moving the pepper onto the marmalade. 'You adored her when you got married. So, did you love your wife at all?'

'Course,' Mel said quickly. 'Of course I did. It wasn't just a simple case of I loved Clau and didn't love Fran.'

'Right, I see. Did you like Fran?'

Silence was Mel's reply. Not angry silence. Not even silence lightly flavoured with indignation. Just plain ol' silence. It was safe to out myself now. I withdrew my head from the cupboard. Mel was staring down into his cup of tea, making patterns on the worktop with the spilt tea. Jake would love that, Mel staining his real wood worktop with his thought-filled tea circles.

'Yeah I liked her,' he mumbled. 'Course I liked her.'

'Oh, so she was a mate, too? I mean, did she match up to all your other friends?' In other words, was she as good a friend as Claudine?

Mel's tongue started to explore his mouth, seeking renegade bits of food to dislodge and chew on. I stared at him rather openly as I waited for his answer. *Come on, tell me, did your wife match up to Claudine in the friendship stakes?*

'Erm, the lads will be gagging for these by now,' Mel said. He threaded his fingers through two cups with one hand and picked up his cup with the other hand. 'You know how much they love their tea.'

The poor cow never had a chance, did she Mel? I picked up my cup, the strawberry scent filling my senses. *She thought she was marrying someone who she was going to spend the rest of her life with; you, well you wanted something completely different. She stood a snowball's chance in hell. Poor, poor woman.*

During the second part of *It*, Mel cast me long, thought-filled looks, redrawing those tea circles with his eyes over the space I occupied in the room. He was rethinking his marriage; his 'friendship' with Claudine. The lads probably thought he was running through the *Kama Sutra* in his head with me.

Ed started to skin up the second the credits rolled on the film. I dragged myself from the sofa, and headed for bed. *Can I hold off going to the loo or brushing my teeth until morning?* I wondered as I shuffled out of the room. *No way am I going near any kind of water when that clown could appear out of the plug hole. In the morning, the lads will hear sounds of my demise if the clown does appear.*

'See ya,' I called. *Only goody two shoes brush their teeth twice a day anyway. And remember how you once held off going to the loo for six hours when you were in Egypt? If I go to bed straight away, I'll wake up in the night and not remember the clown until after I've used th—*

'Oh, Ceri, hang on.' Mel handed the joint to Jake and skipped out of the room after me. I stopped on the second step, my eyes hurt from telly-watching without my glasses, I blinked a couple of times to ease their discomfort and strain.

'Yup?' I asked Mel.

I could feel, rather than see, the lads leaning out of their seats to catch a snatch of our conversation.

'You won't tell anyone what we talked about, will you?' Mel asked in a lowered tone.

'Course not,' I replied in the same low tone.

Mel smiled at me, placed a hand on my hand. I could feel the lads' eyes widen. I took my hand away before they gave him a pack of condoms and directions to my bedroom.

'Thanks for listening,' he said.

'My pleasure,' I said. 'Good night boys.'

'Night Cezza,' they called back.

And good luck with all that thinking and rethinking you've got to do, Melvin, I know it won't be easy.

CHAPTER 11

ONLY THE LONELY

Who thought that seeing this little bit of dirt track road, made up of pebbles and mud and huge great holes, would make me so happy. That I'd feel my heart leap with joy as I turned off St Michael's Lane into the road I now called home. I'd been deeply depressed for the past five hours or so. Actually, for most of the weekend.

I was returning from a weekend in London.

London, my home. Ha!

I'd decided to go back, visit my parents, visit my brothers and my sister, get some more of my belongings and remind myself that London was a trillion times more hip than Leeds. That while I was settling in Up Norf, my heart was buried deep in the south. Ha, ha, ha. (That was a humourless, bitter laugh.)

Bloody Oprah and bloody heart's desire.

It'd felt like I was entering a strange land when I got off the train at London's King's Cross. Even in a month things seemed to have changed. By the time I got to South East London, where my flat was, I felt as though I was on the moon.

Ridiculous really, since I'd grown up in London. Twenty-four of my twenty-nine years on this planet had been spent in London. But, I didn't feel like I knew anything. Everything seemed smaller, dirtier, stranger. Alien. I felt like ET walking into my flat (he wouldn't have spent so much time bealing on about going home if he'd been confronted with what I had when I'd stepped over my own threshold). The woman who'd taken over my flat for the year had made her mark on the place. Not with the decor, she hadn't painted or lain new carpet or owt, which would've been nice cos I hadn't really done that in the two years I'd lived there, either. But she'd taken down the huge framed photo of Angel/David Boreanaz that previously hung over my fireplace. My videos had been stacked up in boxes, in their place were books. *Her* books. Rows and rows of the tomes and 'intellectual' novels people put on display but few people actually read.

My books, of which there were over six hundred, had mostly been boxed up too. They had those 'intellectual' tomes amongst them, and I had actually read them. And I'd read all my Judge Dredd graphic novels too. I was widely read like that. Her tomes all looked untouched by human hands. My cushions and stuff had been moved to the spare room, which was now an office again. An office-cum-second bedroom. The metal-framed futon was now put up as a sofa instead of put down as a bed. My clothes were all folded and hidden away in suitcases under the futon. My beloved Batman bust was back in its box.

She and her boyfriend had moved into my bedroom, of course. I'd valiantly ignored thinking about the two people having sex in my bed thing, just made a mental note to buy a new bed the *second* I moved back to London. I'd felt like I'd sold my flat years ago and was visiting to see what they'd done with the place. It was my place still. Except it wasn't. My name was on the mortgage papers and on the lease, it was my furniture but that was it. The shell was mine, the soul of the place now seemed to be hers.

I thought it'd always be my place. Home is where the heart is, *n'est-ce pas?* I hadn't been prepared for the shock and ill feeling I'd got when I went around. I could've made those adjustments, I could've had those brown suede cushions and cream cotton cushions on that cream throw in the living room. I could've put up those blinds. I could've had rugs, dammit. It hurt so much I had to spend the night with my parents. I'd have been cheating on my own taste if I'd slept there. Just to compound the upset, none of my London friends had been around for the night, owing to having husbands, wives and children to think about, so I'd spent the night in with my parents. Saturday night with my folks. Much as I love them, fun as they are, Saturday night sipping cherryade in front of the news was akin to hell.

As the woman who'd possessed my flat made

me tea (fancy that, someone making me tea in my own flat, treating me like a guest), I'd had another wave of wondering if I was doing the right thing. Yes, I was enjoying it in Leeds. But maybe my heart's desire could be found at home in London. Originally, when I started doing the 'follow my heart's desire' thing, I'd thought of Leeds because it seemed the perfect escape route from all that nonsense I got myself embroiled in in London. I could walk away from living other people's lives. Well, look-see, I was doing the same thing in Leeds wasn't I? It was just now condensed into a smaller area and had been done in a smaller amount of time. While in London it'd taken me years to get truly embroiled in everyone's life, I'd done it in under three weeks Up Norf. Mel, Ed, Claudine, a couple of the students.

On top of my feeling like a failure because I had managed to get involved in Leeds, I was going back to London and feeling displaced, lost in the nowhere land between living in someone else's home Up Norf and not having a definite home in London. I'd made South East London my home when I finally returned to London from Leeds six years ago and I never thought I'd feel this loneliness. It was so illogical. Why did I feel like this? I could get my flat back whenever I wanted, I had loads of contacts in London I could freelance for, I could go back if I wanted. I could be a home-owner and journalist again just like that. It wasn't as though I'd *sold* everything to come to be a lodger and an employee far down on the career ladder. Just loaned it out. I felt so lost though. I'd often felt like this when I was younger – displaced and homeless – emotionally. Not really sure of where I fitted in the world.

Maybe I should just accept I'm not good with people. I may listen to them and advise them, but like I said, there were very few people who'd be there if I had a four-in-the-morning panic and wanted someone to talk to. Jess was only there when her family life would allow and I didn't even think Drew would be there should I need him. I was in constant wonder at how many people kept in touch with friends from school and college and beyond. I had friends from college, but I always felt on the outside looking in. That I wasn't one of the first people they thought of when it came to births, marriages and reunions.

I trundled up Stanmore Vale, sighing inwardly. That was the truly ironic thing about my life, really. I could connect with people quickly. People dragged me into the deepest enclaves of their lives in the blink of an eye, but I had hardly anyone I could do that with. I gave – my time, my ear, my advice – but rarely received. Ceri D'Altroy, she who was open to callers twenty-four/seven, couldn't get the time of day from most people.

Already on my list of advisees were Claudine and Mel and Ed. Although Ed was slightly different. He'd just opened up to me the once and had gone about his business, completely ignoring

143

what I'd said. Claudine and Mel were, I could tell, long-termers. They'd keep coming back and coming back, neither of them noticing that when they were getting their advice and listening ear, while they unburdened their souls, I was dying to talk about myself. Talk about why I had very, very few close friendships. And why I couldn't keep a relationship going for toffee.

My relationship history read like a horror story. During college, I had a few boyfriends, but nothing serious. I met The Love Of My Life during the third year of college – which sent Drew into such a jealous rage he'd picked a fight with me, told me to f-off and walked out, only to reappear properly when The Love Of My Life left me for someone else. I never craved anything serious after that, partly because I was still holding out for Drew, partly because relationships or my lack of them weren't the be all and end all. Telly, junk food, reading – far more important than bemoaning the lack of a man in my life. Then I moved back to London and did my masters, where I met Whashisface Tosspot. I saw him for a year, then we moved in together. I then spent *that* year trying to escape whatever Jedi Mind Trick/Work Of The Devil he had me under. He was nothing like a boyfriend. We had sex, we sometimes went out, I didn't go out with anyone else, but still, he was nothing like a boyfriend. I had no burning passion for him. Mainly because, when I'd origi- nally snogged him I'd been trying to make him

144

feel better. And it'd rather spectacularly back-fired . . .

I knew N——Whashisface Tosspot, from college, he was in the next halls to me, he had friends in my halls and I'd spoken to him a few times. He seemed nice enough, not overly friendly, not overly unfriendly. Just nice enough. About two months into the course, I'd gone to a party with a group of people from my halls and he'd happened to be there. I'd been contemplating the wisdom of leaving my coat in one of the bedrooms; wondering what the likelihood was of it being used by someone to have sex on when he'd come over to talk to me. During the conversation he'd asked if I was seeing anyone and I'd said no. Out of politeness, rather than genuine interest, I'd asked him if he was seeing anyone (those were the kind of questions that led to people pouring their hearts out to me).

'Umm . . .' he'd said, then looked very uncom-fortable. 'My last relationship was cut brutally short, six months ago.'

'Right,' I said, and sipped on the home-made punch in my hands. It contained vodka and cran-berry I was pretty sure, but there were a few other things I couldn't quite place.

'Yeah,' he'd continued, 'my lady and I were going to get married and she left me. Smashed my heart into smithereens. Now she's cohabiting with someone else. I was completely blindsided by that. As I said, my heart was smashed into smithereens.'

145

I'd had a strong suspicion that the conversation was going to become a blurt session when he'd asked if I was seeing anyone, but now we were heading up that path, I was determined to take us down another route. It was Friday night, I was at a party. For once, this man who had hunted me out to blurt at me was not going to get a listening ear. I just couldn't be bothered. It was Friday night, for God's sake!

I decided to avert the blurt session with a bit of levity. 'I've forgotten what kissing's like,' I joked.

'I'll be more than happy to help you out in that matter,' he replied.

I jumped inside. Actually, physically jumped, then my body froze. That'd never happened before. No one who'd been on the verge of blurting at me had taken a flip comment like that the wrong way. Then again, none of them said 'smashed into smithereens' either.

My head moved slowly as I turned to look him over properly. I'd seen him before, of course, but I hadn't been offered the opportunity to kiss him when I'd contemplated him before, so I hadn't *looked* looked. He wasn't bad. He had receding dirty blond hair, a largish slightly hooked nose, small eyes. In his favour, he didn't have a mono-brow. He wasn't bad, but he wasn't exactly overly endowed with attractiveness, either. Nothing about him said, 'snog me'. I'd snogged men before who weren't even vaguely good-looking, but had something about them that drew me to them.

'No, you're all right,' I replied. I really hadn't drunk enough to snog someone whose best feature was not having a monobrow. 'I'm being silly. I, er, need to go to the loo. See ya.'

Later, much later, back in halls, when the group of people I'd gone to the party with had broken out the tequila and hash, I went to make coffee. It was going to be an all night session and I wasn't drunk enough for more tequila nor sober enough to go to bed. Whashisface Tosspot came to help with the coffee making. Even though I was only making one cup for myself.

'I didn't mean to offend you earlier,' he said as he fussed around the sink and I stood beside the kettle waiting for it to boil. 'I simply find you enchantingly interesting. And attractive.'

Who talks like that? I asked myself. 'It's OK, I wasn't offended,' I replied and willed the kettle to boil faster. He fancied me, I suddenly realised. He'd more or less told me I was a bit of all right, in that odd language of his; he'd taken my comment earlier the wrong way and had been overly eager to kiss me and now, he was looking at me. I could just tell he was looking at me, acting shy and nervous – as you did around someone you fancied. I could feel something from him and at first glance it seemed to be attraction. Except, on closer inspection, it wasn't really a genuine type of attraction. The fact of the matter was, he only *thought* he fancied me. Like people start to fancy their therapists or their priests, he thought

147

he fancied me because I'd listened to his story, all two seconds of it. He could probably sense that I'd listen to his story again, should he feel the need to open up some more. And this having someone there to listen, in his mind, translated into fancying me.

It's so obvious what his problem is, I thought, as I watched steam funnel up out of the white jug kettle. He needed someone to make him feel attractive. He'd been hurt when his (ahem!) lady left. He was probably cautious around women. Unsure of his feelings and how they'd be received. What he wanted, what he needed, was to win. Just once. To get an ego boost that would send him off into the world feeling like a man. Feeling that he could pull. What he needed was a mercy snog. A small act of charity that would get him back on the dating horse.

Besides, if I didn't snog him, there was every danger he'd start talking again – and completely ruin my night.

Instead of pouring hot water on the coffee granules, I crossed the kitchen, put my arms around his neck and kissed him before I could think twice about it. He was a bit taken aback but soon his lips were kissing me back. He wasn't that bad at it, either. We stood snogging in the kitchen for ages but when he murmured, 'Let's go to your room' things came to an abrupt halt.

Kissing was as far as my charitable acts were going to go. Besides, I'd grossly underestimated the vital roles of Messrs Vodka and Cranberry in this merciful act and as I was sobering up, I was feeling far less charitable.

'No, I don't want to rush things,' I replied, not wanting to undo all the good work by telling him I didn't even fancy him.

As it turned out, he didn't want to rush things, either: he started coming to see me every day. He wanted us to 'date'. A lot of the time I'd open the door and wonder how to tell him that I really wasn't interested. That I'd wanted him to get up enough confidence to find himself a girlfriend, not think he was dating me. Because, with Whashisface Tosspot, dating involved two things:

1. Coming to my room and pouring his heart out about the long-term relationship that went wrong

2. Watching telly in my room.

I was more than partial to a bit of telly, as the world had probably guessed, but watching it with him was an ordeal. He had something negative to say about everything I watched: *EastEnders* (dull); *Corrie* (people with funny accents); *Brookside* (people with funnier accents); *Sliders* (odd non-sense); *Star Trek* . . . well, he realised the second he opened his mouth that it could end violently. He'd survived slagging off *Sliders*, slagging off *Star Trek* was giving me mitigating circumstances at the resulting murder trial. However, because of his negativity about my viewing habits, I'd invariably be sat watching television, my body tense, waiting

149

for some comment he thought was highly original and highly incisive.

The more I saw of him, the more he riled me. Particularly his story of woe, which, on the scale of one to ten (ten being worthy of a made-for-Channel 4 drama) was a minus five. To him, being dumped by a woman he'd thought about maybe one day asking to marry him was the end of the world; to most blokes it was a lucky escape. He felt his heart, broken and damaged as it was, needed to be poured out at every given opportunity.

I listened because I listened to almost everyone and he had no one else to listen to him, but not even I, listener extraordinaire, could listen to him murder the British language for more than thirty minutes at a go. After half an hour I'd lean across and kiss him just to stop him talking. He'd willingly kiss me back . . .

Our relationship developed from there. I started getting used to him and his language loosened up. He found other things to talk about, so I stopped getting riled by him. Also, there was no one else on the horizon, so we started to see each other – in a very casual way. In other words: no one was allowed to know about us.

To be honest, I don't think either of us really went beyond liking each other. Actually, neither of us went beyond tolerating/liking each other. We had nothing in common, we weren't always gagging to have sex, even in the first few weeks, and I got more laughs off the evening news. We were a passion-free zone.

Despite all this, he wouldn't let go. He wouldn't accept there was nothing between us and let me go. He seemed to have a sixth sense for me deciding to do the decent thing and end things. I say this because whenever I found the right time and the right words, he'd treat me to breakfast in bed, would book a weekend away in a nice hotel, or tell me how much he liked (*liked*) me, to remind me he wasn't all bad. When he knew I'd made up my mind to move on, though, and that croissants and orange juice weren't going to cut it, he'd dust off his *pièce de résistance* – reminding me how much he'd been hurt in the past and how grateful he was that I was helping him get over that. (My instinct to help always won out over common sense.)

At every other time he treated me with the kind of contempt most people wouldn't put up with from someone they hated. When it came to telling people about us, he developed a mental block that stopped him actually saying the words. People thought we were friends – particularly his family (he'd never tell his family that we were together because that would mean he'd gotten over his heartbreak and he would never admit that). When we looked for flats together, we had to get a two-bedroom flat and have our own bedrooms so everyone would know we *weren't* living together. Sex was rationed out so we only did it on Friday or Saturday nights, i.e. the nights when he didn't have to get up for work. If I tried to initiate it any other day of the week, he'd always reject me, reminding me that we weren't actually seeing each other so probably not a good idea to have sex.

I did get the last laugh on that score, though: when I started to extract myself from him I went cold turkey with sex and turned down his seduction attempts. In response they became more elaborate and fervent, even started coming on 'school nights'. After a couple of months of 'er, no, I don't think so', he realised he'd have to seek his sexual favours elsewhere and so took to pleasuring himself. Unlike most other blokes, though, he pleasured himself while stood over the loo so he wouldn't have to clean up the mess afterwards. (And thus, his full name was born. Jess had always called him 'Whashisface' because to use his name would mean she'd accepted him as part of my life – and she'd never do that. When I walked into the bathroom and caught him *in flagrante dewanko*, the moniker 'Tosspot' was added.)

'He sucks the life out of you,' Jess constantly said. 'I'll never understand why someone as vibrant as you is with someone as turgid as him.' She was right, of course, but I couldn't seem to snap out of it.

I often looked back on that time and wondered why I put up with it. And then I'd have my answer:

152

Jedi Mind Trick or some kind of power endowed him by the devil.

Theoretically, after I'd extracted myself from him, the quality of blokes should've increased. To get any lower, they would've had to start digging because Whashisface Tosspot really was rock bottom. So, the only way should've been up. Up, to lads who wanted sex on week nights, who didn't tuck their jumpers into their trousers and who could watch telly in silence for a bit. Except, it didn't work like that. The blokes I met were after a free therapist or were psychopaths. It was one or the other, nothing in between. In fact, by the time I met the last bloke I was seeing, I was convinced that I had NORMAL BLOKES NEED NOT TRY stamped across my forehead.

Maybe I should just accept I'm not good at human relationships, full stop. I was crap at getting close friends, I was crap at not getting embroiled in other people's dramas and I was crap with love.

I pushed my key into the door of 17 Stanmore Vale feeling very lonely and sorry for myself. I could talk myself into a bout of self-pity faster than anyone I knew. *Woe is me*, I'd probably be sobbing as I fell dramatically onto my bed, the back of my hand covering my forehead. *Woe is me without any friends*.

I pushed open the door, hoisted my rucksack onto my shoulder and pulled my holdall through the door. As if by magic, Jake and Ed appeared.

'Hello!' they both screamed. 'Hello!'

I jumped at the loudness of their hello, then took a step back, eyed them even more suspiciously. 'Hi?' I offered cautiously.

'Did you have a nice time?' Jake asked. They were both grinning maniacally.

'It was fine,' I said, remembering everything I'd felt like a kick in the guts. But that wasn't for them to know. I even managed to sound happy.

Jake and Ed's faces fell slightly, but then, in unison, they both grinned again. Now they were freaking me out. Should I close the door and run away? Should I try to make it upstairs before they attempt to sacrifice me to whatever god they'd taken to worshipping over the weekend?

'Let me take your bags,' Ed said, coming towards me.

'Yeah, and I'll make you a herbal tea. I filtered some water earlier. And I went to town yesterday and bought some chocolate cheesecake.'

'I got the Jaffa Cakes,' Ed said.

'Yeah, well I got the caramel digestives,' Jake replied.

'And I got the green olives and chorizo slices.'

'But who remembered the focaccia?'

They were going to fatten me up before the sacrifice. I stepped even further back, ready to run for it.

'Come in and sit down,' Jake said.

Ed wrestled my rucksack and holdall out of my grip.

154

Jake came to me, and led me into the living room. I sat cautiously on the sofa nearest the window. I could make it out of the window if it came down to it. One foot on the window sill, short jump down into the paved-over front garden and I'd be away down the road before either of them could even blink.

Ed raced upstairs with my stuff, Jake legged it to the kitchen and returned with a tray of biscuits, a cup of strawberry tea and a bowl of big, juicy green olives. One of the many things on my favourite foods list.

Jake and Ed sat on the other sofa, looked eagerly at me.

'All right, what have you done?' I said.

'Done?' they asked.

'What's going on, why are you being so nice? What have you done?'

They looked at each other, looked at me. 'Nowt.'

'Have you rented out my room and are now trying to soften me up before you break the news?'

'No.'

'Have you accidentally burnt my belongings?'

'No.'

'Oh no, you haven't broken one of my *Angel* tapes, have you?'

'Noooo,' they chorused.

'Didn't you say we'd die horribly slow deaths if we touched them?' Ed added.

'Yeah, well, you'd be surprised how ineffective that threat is nowadays,' I mumbled.

'We haven't been near them, we swear,' Jake said, hand on heart.

'Then what is it?'

Jake and Ed looked at each other. 'You tell her,' Ed said.

'No, you,' Jake said.

They carried on like that until Jake finally gave in and said, 'The thing is, Ceri, we really missed you.'

'Yeah,' Ed added. 'We didn't realise how much a part of our family you were until you went away.'

'And then Ed started saying that if you had a good time when you were in London you'd probably want to move back there.'

'You were the one who said she'd probably realise what a strain it was living with two lads and would decide not to work her notice and go straight back to London, Jake.'

I didn't know if I should laugh or cry. But tears crept into my eyes.

'And it were you who were almost crying at the idea that we'd end up going back to stained teaspoons and toothpaste smudges on the taps, Edward.'

'You actually started crying.'

'Liar!'

'Is that why you bought all that food?' I asked.

They nodded in unison. 'And we got you some wine.'

'And beer.'

'Yeah, and beer.'

I started laughing, causing a tear to break free and crawl down my face. I wiped it away with the back of my thumb. 'I'm not going anywhere.'

'Sure?' Jake said.

'Really?' Ed said.

'Positive. Ceri D'Altroy is in this house for the duration.'

Both lads grinned like I'd promised to get them subscriptions to the porn channels of their choice. I had to laugh. Just when I was feeling so low I could take to my bed with an armful of *Angels* and a bottle of wine for a week, Ed and Jake had made me feel loved. Wanted. That's what I needed when I got my bouts of loneliness dressed up as depression.

How I got sometimes wasn't, I knew, depression. Not hopelessness when I couldn't get out of bed. More, teariness at being alone. Emptiness at not having a someone who had it in their job description that they had to be there for me. Pain at never quite getting it right on the relationship level. I could make friends, acquire confidences at the drop of a hat, tell other people how to fix their relationships, but when it came to intimacy with men, things fell apart. Having to accept my life would probably be a love-free zone for ever.

These were the thoughts that dogged my night times, made my heart heavy and achy. That, I suppose, had been part of what I'd been feeling as I traipsed from London to Leeds.

There, in the midst of it, were Jake and Ed. Two

157

lads who actually wanted me around. Who'd panicked at the thought I wouldn't be around.

'Thanks for all the effort boys,' I said, getting up. 'I missed you too.'

'Group hug!' Jake screeched, then they both charged at me, leaving us all in a laughing bundle on the soft-pile living room carpet.

CHAPTER 12

PARTY PEOPLE

'Oh come on, Cezza, there'll be men there,' Jake said.

'There's men on my telly,' I replied, stuffing garlic mash potato in my mouth.

Ed and Jake were off to a party being held by some of their Met buddies and, seeing as this was my first weekend back after my visit to London, they weren't going to leave me alone. They'd put me on a kind of suicide watch since that Sunday, where one of them had to know where I was every hour of the day. I was constantly called or emailed at college. I had them knocking on my door to offer me tea or food if I sat upstairs. I had two shadows who wanted nothing but my happiness – that phrase 'be careful what you wish for' kept replaying itself in my head when I started griping that no one would miss me if I wasn't around.

They weren't going out this Saturday night without me – and Jake seriously thought blokes at a party would be enough to prise me out of my pyjamas and away from my bowl of comfort food. The choices were: garlic mash, pyjamas and a blockbuster movie on TV or traipsing through the streets, going to a party where I only knew two people and having to move from my sofa to get ready. There was no contest. I was going nowhere.

'Yeah, but these men will talk to you,' Jake persisted.

'The men on my telly talk to me. And, sometimes, I even talk back.'

'But you might get a snog off one of them,' Ed chimed in.

What do I say to that? 'I'll get a snog off one of the men on my telly?' *And* not sound like a freak?

'All right. But if I don't get a snog, you lot are in for such a hard time.'

They laughed.

'Obviously, neither of you realise how hard I can make things for two boys like you.'

They both grinned as I put down the bowl of garlic mash, threw back my duvet and stomped to the stairs.

'Wear your leather pants,' Jake called.

'How do you know I've got leather trousers?' I called back.

'You just look the type.'

'Yeah, and wear your sparkly gold top, too.' Ed added. Fashion advice from Mr 'Live In My Lumberjack Shirt', himself.

I got showered, dressed, brushed my teeth and put on make-up in record time. The lads, very wisely, wolf-whistled when I descended the stairs.

I was indeed wearing my leather trousers and my sparkly gold top.

With most proper student houses you had to enter through the back door because the front door usually led into someone's bedroom. It was a way to make a four-bedroom house into a five-bedroom house. This student house, where the party was being held, was no exception.

Ed and Jake went to find their mates – aka the people with the drugs – as soon as we walked in through the back door. They left me in the living room with the rest of the partiers. 'It'll increase your chances of a snog,' they reasoned, 'not having two men around.'

'Yeah, cos I'd even look twice at either of you,' I replied. 'No offence.'

I leant back against the wall of the living room, ignoring the way my jacket stuck to the wall.

This was a proper student house. The single red light bulb did nothing to mask the horrors that had been regurgitated on the carpet. The furniture had been pushed back to the far end of the room and showed signs of overuse. Generation after generation of student had skinned up on the arms of that browny sofa and non-matching armchair. God alone knew what those stains between the threadbare bits were, but I had my suspicions.

I leant against the wall and let my mind wander back in time. Back about twenty years, actually.

I couldn't help thinking that the eighties may well have been the decade that fashion forgot – actually, that fashion taunted – but at least they knew how to put together a choon in those days. Every other song you got in the eighties you wanted to dance to or sing along to – even if you were wearing a puff ball skirt, a batwing top, bright blue eyeshadow and your perm had been back-combed and hairsprayed to stand at a ninety-degree angle. And anyway, all the people you were dancing to were just as badly dressed as you, they too found joy in frilly white shirts and lip gloss.

Harking back to another era instantly doubles your age, I thought, and started gulping beer. And being stood at a party while doing the harking tripled my age . . . but it was true. Music was music in those days: Duran Duran, Spandau Ballet, Madonna, Luther Vandross, Haircut 100, Barry White, Howard Jones, Phil Collins all so much better than the trendy nonsense served up nowadays.

Please, put a bit of Howard Jones on. Seriously. Anything but this 21st century nonsense.

Erm, Ceri, how old are you? I asked myself sternly.

Time was when I'd be elbowing my way to the centre of the room so I could be seen by everyone as I danced. I had that much faith in my body-moving abilities. Time was, though, when I wouldn't have turned up to a student party in leather trousers and heeled boots. In my student days, any person turning up to a party in leather trews would've been lynched for being the capitalist, cute-ickle-animal-hurting bastard they were. Nowadays I was more likely to get stock tips on which type of animal you got the best hide out of.

Not that I dwelt entirely in the past, but when I was a student, I had things to worry about beyond where my next joint was coming from, mainly because I didn't do drugs. (I was completely of the 'do what you want within reason' mentality but drugs were not for me. Alcohol did strange things to me; adding drugs to that equation would be asking for my parents to identify my overdosed body.) Even in sixth form I was politically-minded. I stood on the picket lines with the ambulance men; I organised a convoy of coaches to go to Brighton to march in protest against student loans. In school I boycotted any company that had holdings in South Africa.

In college, I lobbied Parliament; I joined the Students' Union and actually tried to get students involved in political stuff. It goes without saying that I actually got down on my knees and thanked God the day Thatcher resigned. I cast my eye around the room, I'd be lucky if most of this lot knew who was Prime Minister at the moment.

Right Ceri, lighten up. It's a party. I cast my eye about the room again, this time less critically. This time, looking for boys.

Ohhh, he was all right. Him with the shaved head, beautiful brown skin, huge eyes, flat nose, pouty lips. Hmmmm, very all right. Now, fix him with a look that says you're interested. No, *interested*, not desperate, lighten up on the eyebrows, smile a little more, hey, he's smiling back . . .

I peeled myself off the wall, smiled a little more, fixed him with my dark, mysterious eyes . . .

The lad smiled back. He nodded, 'come here'. I finished unsticking myself from the wall and a young slip of a girl skipped over to him, flung her arms around his neck and started snogging his face off.

He looked about fifteen anyway.

I guzzled beer, looked even further around the room. And this time, I caught someone's eye. He was definitely looking at me, his eyes were practically drilling into me. I'd recognise that stare anywhere – he was the man from the pub a couple of weeks ago. Across the smoke and flashing lights and music, he was leant back against the wall, can of beer in one hand, glaring at me. I knew it was me because I glanced around me, there was no one else even remotely close enough to be on the receiving end of that glare. Maybe I knew him. I peered through the smoke and moving bodies to get a closer look. But no, he didn't look familiar. I was pretty sure I didn't know him. Maybe he was a writer I'd commissioned in London who was unhappy with the final edit of his feature, so he now scowled at me in revenge.

Like the time in the pub, he made no attempt to hide his glare now that I'd spotted him: if I was caught giving evils to someone – even someone I hated – I'd at least have the good grace to look away, go back to glaring in a minute or two. This man clearly had no grace. He glared and stared and evilled like I had my back to him.

Well, two can glare at that game. I shifted slightly, blanked my face so my mouth was a flat line, my eyes flat, then returned his stare. Mine wasn't so vicious, I'd save the viciousness for later. I simply stared at him like he stared at me. Pretending the music and dancing people and haze weren't ther—

'Fancy seeing you here!'

I jumped slightly as Mel stepped between me and Staring Man. 'How you doing?' he shouted above the music.

'Fine. How you doing?' I shouted back.

Mel shrugged untidily. 'Do you want a drink?'

I raised my can. 'Got one, thanks.'

'Oh,' Mel replied. He swigged from his can of beer. He was, of course, wearing a Levi's combo, but this time he had on a white T-shirt instead of a jumper. 'Are you all right, then?' he asked. This had all the hallmarks of becoming a small talk conversation. He was embarrassed because he'd shown me a side to him very few people saw. And, while part of him yearned to get back to that intimacy, the rest of him was horrified about it. Why would any sane person tell a virtual stranger all those things, especially one who they saw in and out of work? Why indeed. I often asked myself this when someone had dragged me into their life.

'Yeah, I'm fine, Mel. How are you?'

Mel shrugged again.

'How come you're here?' I asked. 'I came with Jake and Ed.'

'What?'

'I came with Jake and Ed,' I said loudly. 'Who do you know?'

'One of my students from All Souls. She lives with The Met lot. And I know quite a few of The Met lot anyway. But my student asked me to come here.'

'Right.'

'Do you want to dance?' Mel asked, indicating to the now packed dance space in the cleared out living room.

'Honestly?' I replied.

'It's shite music, isn't it?' Mel laughed.

I nodded.

'Give me a bit of Wham any day. I only come to these parties cos it beats sitting home alone.'

There spaketh a lonely man. Mel was used to company. His marriage had just broken up. It was, I suppose, understandable that he needed someone. The noise and the distraction. The only way to stop the constant noise in your head. To stop thinking about what you did to ruin your life. Going out was so much easier than living with the pain. Than thinking the thoughts and feeling the feelings.

'I know what you mean,' I replied. The music mutated into another 'song' bastardised from a good tune, dubbed into oblivion.

'I've been doing a lot of thinking,' he said, 'since I came to your place.'

I nodded. I *thought you might.*

'It's . . . I've been doing a lot of thinking.'

'Thinking's not all it's cracked up to be, is it?' I replied.

'No. No it's not. I, er, almost called my wife.' *Oh?!* 'Oh?'

'But I didn't know what I was going to say so I didn't.'

'You could try what I do: open my mouth, say whatever words find themselves in my mouth at the time. It's almost as good as having a plan.'

'If I did that, I'd probably tell her about . . . you know . . . and she'd be devastated.'

And she isn't now? 'Why did you split up? I mean, if she doesn't know about,' I waved my hand about expressively, 'why are you apart?'

Mel looked about him, checking the coast was clear before he shouted more of his love life story above the music.

'COME DANCE!' a student screeched in our faces. Young, dark-haired, not as pretty or sophisticated as Claudine.

'No,' Mel laughed. Almost like an ageing uncle telling his young niece he didn't want to dance at her older sister's wedding. (Well she wasn't going to be talking to me, was she?)

'Oh, come on!' she persisted, she grabbed his hands, pouting. 'Don't be an old git!' Did she give me a sideways glance, when she said 'old git'?

Cheeky cow. I should get out there, show her what dancing's all about. Or just slap her.

Mel gave me a 'should I? Well I'm going to anyway' look. I dutifully took his beer and his carrier bag of cans from him.

The young lady dragged Mel out into the middle of the living room, elbowing aside anyone who had the audacity to get in her way. She had her man and she was going to make sure everyone knew it. She soon wrapped herself around Mel, arms around his neck, body welded to his. She was angling and positioning herself for a kiss, her head kept looking up at him from a side angle, just perfect for him to lean down and place his lips over hers. She was the student who'd invited him to the party, I'd guess. And she'd taken it as a personal come-on that he'd shown up. If I was her, I would – I'd once taken it as a declaration of love that Drew gave me 10p because I didn't have enough to buy an ice-cream; a man coming to a party that I'd invited him to would've meant he was proposing marriage and offering painless childbirth. It wouldn't occur to her – or me if I was in her position – that he'd come out to escape the silence in what would've been his marital home.

Mel openly wasn't interested. His body moved in time with the music, but his attention moved everywhere, settling nowhere. And it went nowhere near the woman who was attempting to become his second skin.

In a microsecond of silence between tunes, the atmosphere charged up, someone stuck the whole room into a plug socket and flicked the switch. I felt the electricity of the moment bolt through every cell in my body. Mel froze mid-dance, as though someone had just pressed the pause remote at him. But it was just his body that froze, his face mutated itself into the very picture of horror and terror, his eyes fixed to the door that led from the back door. I looked to the door. Claudine. She was ex-Met. He was ex-Met. The party was Met. It'd stand to reason she'd be here.

Now, from Claudine's standpoint, this didn't look good. I could clearly see how this might come across: Mel, who'd been confessing love and all sorts to her, who'd been saying 'leave your boyfriend' without actually saying it, was dancing rather closely with a good-looking young student. Those last two adjectives ('good-looking' and 'young') and one noun (student) when applied to someone Mel was dancing with weren't going to help matters, either. From Claudine's point of view, these weren't the actions of a man who's madly in love with you. Or even in love with you.

Claudine wrenched a smile across her face and came into the room, followed by her friends. Not lecturers at All Souls, but most of them were her age, well-dressed and very sophisticated. (That was how I wanted to look, all the time. Well-dressed and sophisticated, even if I wore a bin liner. And, whilst one of them looked like she was wearing a bin liner, she still looked sophisticated. I bet her farts smelt of flowers, too.)

Mel extracted himself from the student and, smiling, went to Claudine. The student followed him, stood beside him as Mel and Claudine talked. It was quite comical really. The student slung her arm around his waist every other second and Mel kept shrugging the arm off, while talking to Claudine. No matter how much he removed the arm, the following second, it tried again to re-establish itself on Mel's body. She didn't even seem to mind the fact he was completely blanking her. Mel and Claudine talked for a bit, then Claudine gave the most bothered 'I'm unbothered' shrug and stalked across the living room with her friends. They were soon surrounded by the men. Real men. People who were nearer my age than the rest of the students' ages. *Where the hell had they come from?* I thought as I watched them salivate over Claudine and her friends. *I've been here since, like, for ever and I didn't notice one single eligible man and now they've all come out of the woodwork. That's fair, isn't it?*

Mel, followed by his student, came back to me, snatched his carrier bag from me. He raked his hand through his hair a few times, all the while glaring at Claudine. 'I'm going home,' he said. 'Do you want to come with me?'

Clearly, the best offer I was going to get all night.

CHAPTER 13

CHEAT

Mel made angry tea.

That's not tea that was called angry, he made tea angrily, huffing and puffing as he slammed cups onto the breakfast bar, then slam-dunked tea bags into them. Having said that, if *Like Water For Chocolate* was to be believed, all his anger and frustration would come through in the drink and I'd soon be choking on his fury by simply taking a sip of the tea. As it was, I was too scared to tell him I didn't drink proper tea unless it was an emergency.

He lived about three streets away from the party and it'd been an angry pound from there to his house. Part of me had been scared. Not that Mel was a scary man, *per se*, it'd been his nefarious mood upon leaving the party. Of course, the other night I had thought he was kill-and-bury-you-under-a-patio material. But, even in the dark of the party I could see he needed a friend. *And, yes, all right, all right, brain, I'm not meant to be doing this sort of thing any more, but you try walking away from someone who's suicidal.*

Mel wasn't overtly suicidal. Mel wasn't booze

171

and overdose, or take a shotgun to his chin suicidal. He was down a bottle of whisky and go pick a fight with a really large individual suicidal. He would get the living daylights beaten out of himself, to hurt physically so he wouldn't hurt emotionally. So he wouldn't have to feel what he was feeling. That's what happens in his situation: first, the only way to douse your feelings is to drink. Then you drink, and drink more. Then, the booze stops helping and the going out being surrounded by other people while totally bladdered stops helping, so the next stop is physical pain. Punching the walls, or going out to pick a fight with an obliging thug so you could get your head kicked in. I'd felt Mel's desperation, his eagerness to be hurt at the party, started to feel desperate too, so, naturally, I went with him.

'My wife is an interior designer and decorator,' Mel explained as I oohhed and awwed over his American-style fridge, his huge sixties leather chairs, the cream carpets, white walls, padded breakfast stools, fake fur rugs, light wood and chrome fittings. This is how my flat was meant to look. How it was always going to look – until I actually moved and discovered how expensive and time-consuming decorating was.

'Ah, right.'

'That's how we met,' he said, plonked a cup of tea on the glass-topped side table in the living room and threw himself into one of the leather sixties chairs. He slumped in the chair, his head hanging, his feet not quite reaching the ground, swinging his legs back and forth. Mel reminded me of my five-year-old nephew and how he sat when he felt unjustly blamed for something.

'I'd just bought this place. It was a student house the landlord had got bored of running so I got it dirt cheap. I even had money left over to get some decorators in. I found her number in the book and booked an appointment. I went to her office and . . .' Mel stared down into his tea, suddenly less angry, more lost. 'And she was the most beautiful woman I'd ever seen.'

He paused. 'We flirted outrageously during that meeting and, of course, I asked her out. She didn't date clients, but she made an exception with me. About six months later, she moved in here. She started her own business in that time and our house became a bit of a show home for what she could do. Philippe Starck chairs, Bang & Olufsen speakers, Habitat rugs, chrome, light wood, Smeg fridges, etc., etc. . . . Her office was upstairs and my office was upstairs too. The rest of the house had to be kept immaculate cos of clients coming round. My room – my office – it's a tip. Always has been. Always will be.'

I sat on the sofa playing with my mug of angry tea.

'We got married about a year later. We didn't even need a wedding list cos we had everything most newlyweds ask for.'

'Did you feel that you missed out on starting a new home with someone?' I asked.

Mel's face registered surprise; looked at me as though realising for the first time I was still there. Shrugged. 'Maybe. Who knows?'

'You still haven't told me the reason you split up, if she doesn't know about you and Claudine.'

Mel perfected the stance then, looked so much like my nephew I wanted to bundle him up, saying, 'It's all right, I know you didn't mean to do it.' He sighed. Then smiled, bitterly.

'The thing with Claudine happened just before Christmas, the weekend that Fran went home to see her parents in Sheffield. Basically, we'd decided this was going to be the first Christmas that we spent together at home, alone, no parents, no siblings, no friends. She's dead close to her family, so she went home a week before to have an early Christmas with them. That was the same weekend we had our staff party at college. Clau and I shared a taxi back, one thing led to another . . .

Fran got back on the Tuesday night. I'd spent all that time trying to work out how I felt. I mean I wouldn't have done that with Clau if I truly loved Fran, would I?

When she got back, she walked through the front door and I wanted to tell her what had happened. I'd never done something like that before. I mean, I'd never cheated before, that wasn't me. I didn't do things like that. I just wanted to get it off my chest, out in the open. But I kept thinking, how's she going to take it that I'd done that with someone she thought was her friend? The worst thing was, she felt bad cos I'd been alone all that time – it was the longest we'd been apart. And she kept trying to apologise. She'd even bought me an early Christmas present to make up for it. A games console, imagine how that felt. That first night I left it. And the second night. But the third night . . .

She was sat where you are, I was sat here, I just looked over, stared at her for ages. She was all curled up reading a Jane Austen book and I said: 'I don't love you any more.' I still can't believe I said it like that.

She just carried on reading.

'Did you hear me?' I said, 'I don't love you any more.'

She looked up from her book, her face was set like stone. 'I heard you,' she said. 'I was just wondering what you expected me to say.'

'I don't know. I just thought you should know.'

'Do you mean you don't fancy me, or you don't love me?' she asked.

I shrugged.

'Don't you dare shrug at me, Melvin Rivers. Don't you dare sit there, tell me to fuck off and then shrug at me.'

I stared at my feet for ages, then I said, 'I still fancy you. I'd still have sex with you, but I don't love you.'

'So it's not my body, it's me.'

'I suppose,' I said.

'Is there someone else?' she asked.

What do I say to that? Maybe it was someone else, maybe it wasn't. I just knew I wouldn't have been with Clau if I loved or respected Fran.

'No. Not really.'

'WHAT DO YOU MEAN "NOT REALLY"?' she screamed at me. She even threw the book at me, luckily it missed, cos it was a hardback.

'I mean, I have an idea of the person I love in my head and it's not you.'

'YOU WAITED UNTIL WE'VE BEEN MARRIED FOR FOUR YEARS TO DECIDE I'M NOT THE PERSON YOU LOVE IN YOUR HEAD?'

'NO! YES! I DON'T KNOW. I ONLY KNOW I DON'T LOVE YOU ANY MORE. I CAN'T HELP IT.'

I thought she was going to throw something else at me, but she fell apart. I'll never forget how she sat there sobbing, how it felt to hear her cry and sob. I wanted to go to her but I couldn't move.

'So what are you saying?' she asked. Tears were pouring down her face at this point.

'I don't want to be with you any more.' Yes, I actually said that.

She went upstairs and I sat here for ages because I couldn't move. I think I was in shock, more than anything. I'd never been such a bastard in my life. I mean, there I was, breaking her heart, ruining her life and I was so cold. So cold. I was just . . . cold. Eventually, I went up to her and she was lying on the bed. She kept saying between tears, 'Why? Why? What did I do wrong?'

You're probably thinking I couldn't get much worse, but I could, I did. I started comforting her, cuddling her, then kissing her and then . . . then . . . I ended up making love to her. All the time I was resenting her, wishing she was Clau. Fran just cried the whole way through and then afterwards she said, 'What did I do wrong?'

We talked for ages, and all I could say was, 'You're just not what I want.' Anyway, when I fell asleep a few hours later, she got up, packed a bag and left. It was three days before Christmas. I went out on the day before Christmas Eve to the pub, I couldn't stand the silence in the house. That was the one thing I hadn't really been prepared for. The silence. It was awful. When I came back she'd cleared out her stuff. All her office, her clothes, make-up, books, CDs. I figured she must've had help. All she left was a cheque for the bills and half the mortgage for a month, her keys and a phone number where to direct all her business enquiries. I haven't seen or spoken to her since.

Christmas was hell. I couldn't work out how to tell my family, or anyone else. How do you tell the world you've failed at a marriage to the most wonderful woman on earth? How could I tell everyone that for the past year or so we'd hardly spoken? Or that the longest conversation we'd had in twelve months was the night she left me. Clau rang but I couldn't speak to her of all people. I spent the whole of New Year's Eve and New Year's Day on dope, beer and whisky. I thought I was going to die on 2nd January. Part of me wanted to die on 2nd January.

If I could go back in time, I wouldn't have been so cold. I would've been . . . Oh I don't know, I can't go back in time, I'm officially separated from my wife and I haven't spoken to her cos I haven't got a clue what to say to her. Neither of us has started divorce proceedings and I'm sure she'd call me if she had anything to say to me. So, the official reason we've split up is that I'm a total bastard and she was blind-sided by that, just before Christmas . . .

Had I, Ceri D'Altroy, been a person without a predisposition to saying what I thought, I would've

178

said, 'You're not a total bastard.' As things lay, I was, and he sounded like a total bastard. Not a fraction of a bastard, or a bit of a bastard, a *total* bastard. However, it did take two to wreck a marriage. In Mel and Fran's case, even though I'd only heard one side of the story, it did indeed seem that they'd both neglected their marriage. And, of course, there was Mel's 'thingy' with Claudine.

'Don't worry, you don't have to say I'm not a bastard, I know I was. I still get pole-axed when I think about what I did.'

'I wasn't going to say you weren't one.'

Thankfully, he laughed instead of fitting me up for a patio foundation. 'So anyway, Clau hates me. She thinks I was perving over that student.'

'Did she say that?'

'No, she didn't have to. All she said was, "You look like you're having a good time, don't let me interrupt you" and then she and her four harridans of witchville went prancing off.'

'She doesn't hate you.'

'She's just jealous, right? Cos that will make all the difference.'

'Look, Mel, we all bandy about the word "hate" as if it's as whimsical as air, but it's a very strong emotion. I can't see her feeling that in an instant and then it staying with her till she dies.'

'You reckon,' Mel replied.

Touchy-feely reasoning wasn't going to work. I changed tactics. 'You do know that student fancies you, don't you?' I said.

179

Mel sighed. 'Oh she's just an ego boost.' He registered my raised eyebrows. 'Yes, I know, I'm a bastard. But my wife's left me and the woman I love is with somebody else, I need an ego boost.'

'Ever thought of a career writing country and western lyrics?' I said before I could stop myself.

Mel laughed.

'You knew what you were doing when you let her drape herself all over you. You should be grateful she wasn't trying harder to kiss you when Claudine walked in.'

'Suppose.'

That feeling, my curse, brewed itself in my heart. The need to make things better. And the more those big hazel eyes simpered at me, the stronger the feeling got. I clamped my teeth together, trying to stop myself from saying something, anything to make him feel better, to make this situation all right. The last time I did that, I'd ended up with Whashisface Tosspot. But, even as I wrestled with myself, I knew I was fighting a losing battle. I might as well have tried to stop watching television for a year or two.

'Claudine doesn't hate you. She's just jealous and,' *Lord forgive me for what I'm about to do, but he needs it, you can see by the look on his face he needs it,* 'being jealous is a good sign. She was probably taken aback at the strength of her reaction to,' *God, I promise I'll make it to church sometime soon if you don't let this blow up in my face,* 'seeing you with another woman. Even if she is a student.'

180

He threw himself forwards in his seat. 'You really think so?'

I nodded, unable as I was to say 'yes' to the nonsense I'd put out there. It was probably true, but also not as uncomplicated, what with Claudine still being with her fella and all.

'You think I should tell her the student meant nothing?'

'No, Mel, I think you should make sure the student knows it meant nothing. That there was no "it" in the first place, before it gets blown out of proportion and it gets back to the college that you're knocking off a student. Ignore the Claudine thing. It'll be all right. You've been mates for years, it'll blow over.' *And anyway, have you forgotten she's with someone else?*

Mel slid out of the seat, slid onto the floor, still managing to keep his tea upright. 'I did love my wife, you know,' he said. 'I didn't stop as quickly as I made out to her. I was so busy making her leave, I guess I never really thought about how much I was hurting her. I thought about getting rid of her, stopping myself being unfaithful to her, but I never thought about how much I was hurting her. Can you believe that?'

Er, yes I could, actually.

CHAPTER 14

LOST

Jake wasn't wrong about how far it was from here to up there, aka, my bedroom. The relevance of *Star Trek*'s space time continuum wasn't lost on me at moments like this. I'd got the space, but did I have the time (or energy) to get up there? (It regularly occurred to me that the reason I was still single had something to do with my ability to drop *Star Trek* into normal conversations.)

Mel had ordered me a taxi at three, it'd arrived at four-thirty. Saturday night-morning was clubbing till all hours night, so taxi firms, naturally, concentrated on getting them home first. People like me who wanted to go a couple of miles down the road had to wait till the large fares were dealt with.

I'd gone to say to the taxi driver that I should charge him a waiting fee in the same way he'd charge me one if I kept him waiting for an hour and a half but, uncharacteristically, my mouth didn't work. Possibly tiredness. Or, possibly, because he was a big white geezer with a shaved head, a gold tooth and a grunt for 'hello'.

After I'd paid him plus tip (I was a veritable coward in the face of such scariness) I found myself at the bottom of the stairs looking up at them, realising how never-ending they were. In fact, they reminded me of that scene in *Poltergeist* where the corridor seemed to lengthen each time the mother tried to run down it. By the time I hit the second set of stairs I'd be climbing a stairway to heaven. Or thereabouts.

Luckily, I hadn't taken my duvet upstairs from earlier. *Jake and Ed won't mind if I kip down on the sofa, just this once, will they?* I asked Narcissus, who was still silently checking out his reflection over the fireplace. Unsurprisingly, he didn't answer.

I peeled off my leather trousers – never as good an idea at four forty-five in the morning as they were at ten last night – and sighed as air hit my legs and flesh gave way to gravity. I was never so grateful as that moment when the trousers were pulled away and my flesh could return to its natural place on my body. I yanked the gold top off, but left on my bra and knickers. If I kicked off the covers by accident I didn't want Jake or Ed to come wandering in to find me sprawled naked on the sofa. And, in my universe, it'd be the weekend their parents decide to visit.

Birds had started to chirp and cheep and generally create a 'we're awake, why aren't you' row outside, and the sun was obviously going to be putting in an appearance quite soon.

I wrapped the duvet around me like a cocoon

so my skin wouldn't become stuck to the leather of the sofa, snuggled down, lay on my side facing away from the window. There was a time when the reason I was coming home at this hour was because I'd been out having sex. When I'd got into a taxi at four-thirty in the morning with dull throbs left by another person tingling across my skin. I'd need to have a shower before slipping between the sheets, wondering how long I should wait before I called them.

I most certainly wouldn't have spent the night in the company of a good-looking man and not even considered jumping his bones. Cos even on the many (MANY) occasions when I discovered a bloke wanted me for my ear not my body, there was a time limit. Chucking out time at the pub, usually. Possibly midnight if he was very, very lucky. No bloke had exceeded the two in the morning mark before. Not if sex wasn't ever going to be on the agenda.

But Mel, with his suicidal tendencies, had made me stay. It hadn't even occurred to me to leave. In fact, if he hadn't started to fall asleep at three o'clock and hadn't been completely spark out at four-fifteen I would've spent the night with him. Listening. *Only listening.*

I'd got worse. Moving up here had made me worse, not better. I hadn't 'started over'. The Commandments were so underused I'd forgotten how they went – much like the real Commandments.

I hadn't started over at all. I'd become so

184

embroiled in people's lives it didn't even enter my mind that I had a life. In fact, did I have a life? What was I feeling before the party? I can't even remember. I can't actually remember what I was feeling or thinking about before Mel. I pulled a cushion over my head. I'd lost myself in other people's lives.

Click, went the front door, as someone closed it quietly. I peeked out from under my cushion as a form slunk past the living room and went towards the kitchen. That looked like Jake.

Except it didn't. It looked like a depressed version of Jake, his head hung low, his body moving listlessly. He could be coming down after a major drugs binge or, I took a moment, yup, no mistaking it. The air in his wake sparkled with sex. And it *certainly* wasn't from me.

I threw back the covers, got up, picked up my duvet and wrapped it around myself in the manner of a movie starlet after she's had sex and is off to the kitchen. (Those beanpole actresses made it look so easy, wrapping heavy bedding around yourself AND walking. It wasn't. At all.)

Jake sat on a stool by the breakfast bar, staring out the back window even though the blinds were closed. He hadn't turned on the light and the kitchen was in semi-darkness.

'Where've you been, you dirty stop-out?' I whispered. Whispering seemed to fit the mood.

'Getting screwed in every way possible,' Jake replied.

EASTER HOLIDAYS

CHAPTER 15

JUST GOOD FRIENDS

First day of the Easter holidays. First day of my first official holiday as a lecturer. *God knows what I'm going to do with it.*

Saturday was officially the first day of my holidays, but after the whole Mel/Jake thing on Friday night/Saturday morning, the whole of Saturday spent in front of the TV with Jake and Ed, recovering, and most of Sunday spent in front of the telly with Jake and Ed, I hadn't really felt like I was on holiday.

I snuck down under the covers. And besides, this was the first weekday in ages that I got to sleep in. Weekday after weekday of lying in would follow. Kids' TV and eating chocolate. There was no bad here, at all.

I rolled over and listened to the silence in the house. It was pure silence. Jake and Ed had both gone home to see their parents last night. Both had been concerned that I might be scared being on my own in the house. 'Not me,' I'd said bravely. The scary clown from *It* hadn't entered my mind until Jake had hit the M1. He'd left last. He'd dropped Ed down at Leeds station in town,

Ed had a very long journey down to Cornwall so wouldn't reach there until sometime today.

Jake had then come back and had something to eat before getting himself ready for the drive back to Scotland. Involuntarily, my body sighed as I thought of Jake . . .

After I'd gone into the kitchen, Jake had filled me in on the details of his love life.

Jake was a good-looking lad, nice personality, had the capacity to be a bastard but only if really pushed. I did often wonder if he was too sensitive. Cared too much about other people, took them at their word even though he didn't trust anyone. He thought too much about others. (That was probably the pot calling the kettle black but I had no choice in it. I had the wants of others thrust upon me, Jake was just too considerate.) If he saw something he thought someone would like, he'd most likely buy it for them. They'd be surprised, pleased, but rarely did he get it back in kind. As in, very, very, very few people did the same for him. Few people thought that much beyond their own world. The way Jake was so giving was odd considering he was an only child, some might say. However, it's likely that was part of Jake's motivation – he wanted to give too much to be loved too much. He probably thought he had to buy presents for his friends to make them play with him. As an adult, he thought he had to be extra nice all the time to make his friends love him.

Jake did realise that the buying of presents and niceness was a fragile basis for a friendship. That he could never be sure if they liked him for him or his niceness. If he showed them his nasty side would they still be there for him? A couple of times I'd been tempted to sit Jake down and tell him to scrub that 'trample all over me' sign off his forehead. I mean, take the whole 'you don't need a reference to move into my lovely home' episode with me. I could've been anyone from that chick in *Single White Female* to Michael Keaton in *Pacific Heights*; I could have been on the run from a mental hospital. But Jake took me at my word when I said I was normal. Jake was too nice. Which was why he'd been screwed over in his love life.

Basically, the story went like this: Jake had known this guy, now renamed The Git, for years. They'd been good mates, had a laugh, but The Git had a long-term boyfriend. A year or so ago, they'd got drunk together, one thing led to another and Jake and The Git ended up in bed. Jake, not having any confidence in his attractiveness knew that The Git wouldn't leave his fella, so they just got on with being mates. But, they were constantly flirting and one day, when they were both sober, they'd ended up in bed again. It'd happened regularly after that; every month or so, Jake and The Git shagged.

That night, at the party, Jake had gone to find The Git, not to find drugs, they'd gone home to The Git's place, had sex, ended up having a long chat.

Jake had basically gone vocal with his feelings, told this guy how he felt. Not a great big, I love you, more a 'I've felt a lot for you for several years and I'd like to know how you feel. Cos we can't be sleeping together every month and let it carry on like this indefinitely. I just want to know if there's some hope for us, you know, somewhere down the track. I'm not expecting you to leave your fella, I just want to know how you feel.'

And The Git had told him to f-off, but in a lot more words. It'd sounded so cruel, so unnecessary, I felt like I'd been slapped. *And I wasn't there.*

'Go on, say it,' Jake said tiredly when he finished his hideous tale.

I'd made tea and we'd gone outside onto the patio to watch the sun come up. I was sat in my underwear, hidden and warmed by the duvet; Jake was curled up in his chair with my long black coat draped over him.

'Say what?' I asked.

'What everyone else says: "You should just forget about him now. Put him right out of your mind and move on." Go on, say it, you might as well, everyone else has.'

'In case you hadn't noticed, I'm not like everyone else,' I said, a little offended that Jake would think that of me. 'And anyway Jake, I'd never say that. Not to you, not to anyone.'

'Really? Why not?' Jake asked, eyeing me suspiciously.

'People only say "move on, get over him"

because it's a nicer way of saying, "I'm sick to death of hearing about this, just shut up will you."'

Jake double-took. Clearly a 'thought into head, out of mouth' moment. But it was true, I simply should've dressed it up a bit nicer. 'It's true. I'm sorry to put it like that, but it's true. People get to the point where they're so frustrated at listening to a tale, they shut off from it. And how do they stop you from wittering on about it? Tell you to move on. I'd never say that to you.'

'Why not?'

'Because if you knew how to move on, you'd have done it already.' I pulled my knees up onto the chair so I could double-up the duvet. Watching the sun say hello was very nice but also very cold on a late March morning. 'I know it's not a simple case of forgetting him. If it were that simple, half the books and films and songs out there wouldn't have been written. Actually, half the books, films and songs out there shouldn't have been written . . . but that's beside the point. In the grand scheme of things, getting over someone isn't easy. And you shouldn't harass yourself or let anyone else harass you about it. If you want to hurt over this guy, go right ahead. They're your emotions. It's your life.'

'What do you think I should do?' he asked.

'That's the whole point, isn't it Jake? It doesn't matter what I think, or what anyone else thinks. What matters is you do what comes from the heart.'

'I did, and look where it got me. I told him how

I felt in a light way, nothing heavy, not making any demands and he told me to fuck off. I just don't think I deserved to be treated like that. I mean if like he said, he knew all those years how I felt, then why sleep with me? You know he said he slept with me out of friendship. Like I couldn't have handled a rejection. Rejection's bad, but this is worse. I mean, why wait until now to tell me to get lost?'

'Because, sweetheart, it was a lot easier to ignore it. And, of course, it didn't do his ego any harm.' Ouch. Another head to mouth moment that got away from me.

Through the pale blue light of sunrise, Jake stared at me, surprise smeared all over his face.

'Yeah, well, it's true.' I looked down at the pattern embroidered on my duvet. 'All that noble, "I slept with you out of friendship" stuff is nonsense. Once is pity. Twice is being too nice. Once a month is enjoying it. The attention and the sex. Mate, if I had someone as good-looking, lively and good-hearted as you following me round, I'd be flattered. I wouldn't want to get rid of you, I'd be sending out mixed signals left, right and centre. I'd probably end up sleeping with you. It's human nature.'

'Maybe,' Jake said quietly.

'I'll let you in on a little secret that I've gleaned from all my years as a listener of tales and as a rejected woman. You can flatter almost anyone into bed. There's only a small, small,' I raised my finger

194

and thumb and showed Jake how small, 'minuscule number of people who are immune to flattery and they're the ones who don't like sex very much. Because the way to anyone's libido is through their ego. I mean, think of the people you've slept with solely because they were extra nice to you or made you feel special or kept on about how great you were. Everyone has their ego trigger and almost everyone can be flattered into bed once you find it. If you hang around this guy long enough, you'll get him into bed again for sure. Even though you've had this chat and he's said all this stuff.'

'You think?' Jake said a bit too keenly. Considering how badly he'd been treated not an hour ago.

'Yup. He's done it once, he'll do it again. It's just a question of how long you're going to put your life on hold till it happens again.'

Jake stared off into the distance, he seemed happier. Which wasn't the point. It so wasn't the point. He shouldn't have been fixated on the fact he could shag The Git again if he wanted to.

'Ask yourself Jake, is just another shag good enough for you? Because, mate, now that he's treated you like that and finds out he can still get away with it, a shag and ill-treatment is all you're likely to get.'

I lay back in bed, listening again to the silence. To my breathing. My life force going in and out. I looked down at my chest, moving up and down.

I held my breath, then let it out. I could've gone home too. Returned to London for a few days or the complete break. But London was my *béte noire* now. Somewhere I'd rather not go to unless it was to see specific people. Because it wasn't my home. My bank statement with all my mortgage payments and loan payments and insurance payments may say that London was my home, but in my heart, home was where my body was. Not where my accent was from.

I jumped when the phone rang. The house was that silent, that still. I rolled over in bed and picked it up. 'Hello.'

'Right, D'Altroy, get out of bed and get your arse round here.'

'How do you know I'm in bed?'

'You're always in bed.'

'True. And why, exactly should I extract myself from it at only midday on a Monday when I've got *Oprah* starting in an hour and a half?'

'Fred's gone away with his football mates; the girls are off in Spain, so we're going drinking, and you're staying over afterwards,' Jess said.

'What now?'

'The very second you get here.'

'But . . .'

'But what?'

'But nothing, I suppose.'

'OK, get a bus round here and we'll start in the Grey Horse, work our way down Town Street.'

'Are you sure you want to do this?' I asked.

'What do you mean?'

'You're not as young as y—'

'Brrrrrrr,' the dialling tone replied.

We'd been sat in the Hog's Head, the fourth pub down Town Street, for less than an hour when the barman came over with a clear drink in a clear glass on a silver tray.

'Excuse me love, sorry to interrupt, but someone asked for this drink to be sent over to you,' he said. He was blushing profusely.

'Ahh, it's from you, isn't it?' Jess laughed.

'No, love. It's him over there, by the fruit machine.' Jess and I went to look. 'Don't look,' the barman hissed. 'He asked me not to tell you who it's from straight away.'

'Did someone really send her a drink?' Jess asked, looking at me and on the point of laughter. Cheeky mare. Obviously didn't realise that my beauty inspired such acts from men.

'No, love, it's for you.'

CHAPTER 16

PULLING

We're in a pub in Horsforth, not a bar in bloody LA,' Jess said, looking around the bar. A tall, tanned man grinned at her and raised his glass to her.

'You've pulled,' I hissed at Jess. He wore a shiny suit, the kind that no man looked good in – not even my beloved Angel would look good in that.

'He probably meant it for you.' Jess slid the drink over to me.

'You wish,' I replied. 'Oh God, he's coming over.'

'Hide!' Jess shrieked quietly. For a women of her age, she moved with lightning speed, but she wasn't quick enough for me. I grabbed her arm, held her in the booth. 'You're going nowhere, lady,' I whispered, then: 'Smile for the nice gentleman.'

'How you ladies doing?' the man said in the fakest American accent I'd ever heard. His eyes sparkled in Jess's direction.

Neither of us spoke. Shock, I think. It's not every day you're confronted with a man who sends over drinks, wears light-reactive suits and talks with a fake accent. 'Fine,' I finally said. I was, after all, far more used to this than Jess.

I kicked Jess. 'Ow!' she said. 'Ow, I'm fine.'

'Do you mind if I join you?' he asked Jess.

Jess's head swung round to look at me. *Rescue me* was written in her eyes.

Not on your life, I said back. I'm sure there was something I needed to get her back for. 'If you'll excuse me, I'll just be off to the *bathroom*,' I managed with a straight face, slid out of the booth and went prancing off to the toilets.

I took my time returning from the loo. Jess, who I was sure never fully appreciated what it was like to be constantly approached by weirdos, needed time. To learn. As I reached them, her eyes swung up to look at me.

'I was just telling our guest here that we're off to meet our husbands for dinner, aren't we?' she beseeched. She was two seconds away from throwing herself on her knees at my feet and begging me to get her out of there.

'Yeah,' I replied, trying to keep a straight face. 'I just noticed in the *john*, that we'd be late, if we didn't leave now.'

Jess grabbed her bag.

'We could finish our drinks though, if you want,' I said.

'No, no, you know how my other half gets when we're late.' Jess shot out of the booth.

'At least let me have your phone number?' the man begged.

I felt a little sorry for him then. He wasn't just some weirdo, although he was a weirdo – nobody persisted with that fake accent unless they were a little strange – he genuinely liked Jess. I could sense that. He thought she was beautiful, he liked the way she laughed and had watched her for a while before sending over the drink. *That* was why he'd sent over the drink. He liked the way she pushed me away when she really laughed. The way her hair flowed down her back, the way her eyes were intense when she was listening.

'Oi,' Jess said, shaking me, 'come back to earth, we're leaving.'

'Sorry?' I said, struggling to focus on her.

'You checked out of reality then. We're going to be late.'

'Yeah, right,' I said. For a second, I hadn't been myself. Now that was weird, that was an out of body experience. The way I expected drugs to feel. How I felt then was the reason I didn't take drugs – I always wanted to be in control of who I was.

'Have I seen you around The Met?' The guy was very good-looking. Shaved head, brown skin, very dark eyes framed by long black eyelashes. And he was, of course, talking to Jessica Breakfield. A woman who was clearly old enough to be his mother. Not that I was bitter or jealous or anything.

'Maybe,' Jess replied, cautiously.

The guy took this as a green light and sat opposite her at our table. 'You're in the psychology department, aren't you?' he said keenly.

'Have you been stalking me?' Jess asked.

'No, I've just seen you around college and always wanted to come talk to you but never had the courage and here you are in my local.'

'You want to talk to me about psychology? I only do that Monday to Friday between nine and six.'

'Not particularly. I just want to talk to you.'

I was whistling silently, checking my nails, running my tongue around my teeth because it made no difference if I was there or not.

'Can I get you a drink?' the guy asked.

'Erm, Ceri, do you want a drink?' Jess asked.

The guy looked at me, surprised. He really hadn't noticed I was there, all he saw was Jess. 'I'll have a double vodka and coke,' I said. If you're going to ignore me, you're going to pay for the pleasure.

'I'll have the same,' Jess said.

'Two double vodka and cokes,' he said and toddled off.

I turned to say something to Jess and found another man had appeared. He was crouching down beside her, grinning, talking to her. *God, it's going to be one of those nights.*

I glanced around the pub, drinking in the atmosphere. I liked the Black Bull. It had an old worldliness about it. Twee with its flowery curtains and matching flowery seats and flowery carpets. All worn with constant use. The bar, which was down the steps from where we were sat, was a big square overcrowded with its drinks and hanging glasses and peanut packets. At this time of a Monday evening, the pub was quite empty. A few people stood in groups, others stood alone.

Unexpectedly I was confronted by a pair of eyes. Eyes that were staring straight into mine.

I tore my eyes away, but too late. Too late. The damage was already done, the eye contact already made. And, from the corner of my eye I saw he was coming my way. Maybe if I just kept my eyes down and looked like I didn't want company he'd just walk on by. Y'know out through the wall and window behind me.

'Hi,' a voice said beside me.

I looked up from my drink and found myself looking into deep, dark eyes.

'Hi,' I replied.

'Do you mind if I join you?'

A lot of words telling him to go away came out of the great big mouth in my head, but they didn't come out of my mouth in reality. I glanced over at Jess, with her four men chatting away to her. 'If you want,' I said.

'You looked so lonely sat here on your own.'

'Me and the Lone Ranger, we've got a lot in common. Except I can't ride horses. And, of course, I don't do the mask thing.'

He laughed. 'I know a lot about loneliness,' he said.

'Why, are you the real Lone Ranger?' I asked facetiously.

'In a way, I suppose.' His tone was so serious I

wondered for a moment if he was the Lone Ranger reincarnated. If the original one was dead, not that I knew. 'I was just stood over there, watching you and thought, She looks like a woman who knows a thing or two about loneliness.'

This was true.

'It hurts, doesn't it? Being alone and lonely and not really knowing when it's going to end.'

'I suppose.'

'I did find a way out of it, though, in the end.'

'Really? How?'

'I turned to God.'

So this is it, is it? Jess gets three, no, four good-looking men clambering over each other to get her attention while I get some kind of soldier of God, who goes out to pubs to recruit his victims.

'I found a group of people who showed me the true way forward. They became my family. My salvation. The ones who I turned to in my hour of need.'

And, I'm sure they don't ask you to give them lots of money, try to distance you from your family and brainwash you into doing whatever they decide The Bible *says you should do.*

'Do you believe in God?' he asked.

'I was brought up a Catholic.' Y'see, at this point, most people would be lying or saying get lost. Not me. Heaven forbid that of me.

'And do you still go to church?'

Lie. Just lie. 'Not as often as I should.'

'Maybe you should give our group a try. We meet

once a week down in Headingley. Maybe I can give you the address?'

'Yeah, why not,' I said.

He pulled a card out of his jacket pocket, started writing on the back.

'My name's Brad. Can I look forward to seeing you there?'

'Maybe,' I said. 'Possibly.'

He grinned. Far too wide for someone who'd only secured a possible maybe out of me. Maybe because he'd got that far in his spiel. I'll bet few people gave him that long. Certainly not in a pub.

'Anyway, Brad, it's been nice talking to you, but I think I should rescue my friend over there.'

Brad and I both looked over at Jess, who currently had four men around her. Each talking, trying to get her attention.

'She might not need that much rescuing,' Brad replied as Jess and her admirers laughed, quite heartily. 'Why don't we talk some more about loneliness.'

'Yeah, sure, why not?'

'It were you,' Jess said, gesticulating at me with her half-smoked cigarette gripped between her forefinger and middle finger. 'It were. That's the only explanation for it. I was fine until you got here. No, actually, I wasn't fine, I was perfectly happy. And, suddenly, we go out for a few drinks and I'm being chatted up left, right and centre.'

'But—' I began.

'No.'

'But—'

'NO!' She punctuated this with her cigarette.

Jess had spent the rest of the night fending off the advances of the four men; I sat sipping my drinks supplied by her admirers, talking to Brad The God Botherer about loneliness. Jess got to have her ego flattered by young good-looking men desperate for her to choose them; I got to hear all about his salvation. From being a lonely boy to a lonely man who thought he was homosexual but was saved from all that by the group.

Then, to add insult to injury, ten hours later, Jess had reassessed the situation and decided it was all my fault. *MY* fault. *MY* fault that I had to drag her out of the pub after last orders and pour her into a taxi while she was wailing, 'Let's go to their party. I'm sure it'll be fun.' And *MY* fault I'd also had to hold her hair while she threw up in the gutter outside her house. How, exactly, it was my fault I wasn't sure. I hadn't sent the men to come talk to her. I hadn't forced alcohol down her neck. I'd been the one trying to go home at nine o'clock, only to be told no by a certain Dr Breakfield.

'How—' I began.

'No,' Jess said firmly, her finger silencing me. 'It were you. I'm old and happily married. I don't need you dragging me out and letting me drink too much, making men fancy me. You are a bad influence, Ceri D'Altroy.'

Jess drew long on her cigarette, expertly flicked ash into the ashtray. 'You know, Ceri, you're my best friend and all that, I love you and all that, but God, I'm not going out drinking with you again.'

'Fine by me, Dr Breakfield,' I said, lying back on the floor. 'But just remember, it was your idea to go out in the first place. And there's another two weeks left of the Easter holidays.'

SUMMER TERM

CHAPTER 17

COLLISION

I always leave it too long.

Always. Right to the point where I have to run the last bit while trying to cross my legs and think of deserts and dried earth and other things desiccated. In this spirit, I hit the door of the staff loos on the top floor with the speed and force of the London to Leeds Intercity Express at full speed, thereby causing somebody who was trying to leave the toilets to reel back. Luckily, she wasn't knocked over, but her bag flew out of her hands, its contents exploding over the white tiled floor. We both stopped, startled still, for a second.

'Ohhhh, I'm sooooo sorry,' I said, coming alive and going to her. She was the colour of new-fallen snow, her body trembling as she held onto the basin nearest the door. Her grip on the basin anchored her as she said, still shaken: 'It's all right.'

Clearly it wasn't. I'd never seen someone the colour of new-fallen snow. So white, so pale she was almost luminescent. 'I'm so, so sorry,' I repeated. 'Are you OK?'

'I'm fine.'

My need to pee wasn't gone, simply postponed. It pressed on my bladder, wanting to be let out. 'Here, let me help,' I said.

I bobbed down, gathering her belongings: battered diary, three blue pens, one red pen, black leather purse, four 2p coins, bulging make-up bag, No7 mascara, toothbrush, black mobile, Clear Blue pregnancy test. The usual stuff you found in a woman's handbag. Apart from the pregnancy test, obviously. Or maybe it was just me. Maybe I was behind the times and every sexually-active woman carried pregnancy tests as well as condoms.

As I retrieved each item, I placed it on the side of the basin. She hadn't moved, she still stood with both her hands behind her as she clung to the basin for dear life. 'Um, is there anything else I can do? Can I get you a drink of water or something?' I asked. The word 'water' instantly shrank my bladder and doubled its contents. I tried not to do a 'gotta pee' jig as I stood beside her, but I probably swayed a little.

'I'm fine. Really.' She turned to face me. 'I'm fine. You go.'

'Sure?' I replied, not too keenly I hoped the second the word was out of my mouth.

She bent stiffly and picked up her bag. 'Absolutely. I'm fine.'

'OK.'

I ran to the nearest stall, almost ripped off my

jeans. I probably even let out a sigh as I relieved myself.

When I finally left the stall she was still there. She'd put most of her belongings back in her bag, but was staring at the pregnancy test as though it'd threatened to kick her head in if she so much as moved. *Now what do I do? Ask her if she's OK again and embroil myself in someone's drama? Or walk away, leave her to it? Not in my nature, obviously*. But, I was already in the Mel and Claudine drama. It'd been more than two weeks since I listened to Mel's tale after the party. And then there was Jake's drama. (He was walking around putting a brave face on things. He'd even declared to Ed and me, 'The Git is dead to me. We do not mention him in this house, we do not think about him in this house. He is gone from my life.' I don't know if Ed was convinced. Because I was. Not.)

Could I take any more? *Should* I take any more? *Walk away*, one part of me said. *Just dry your hands and back away from that upset woman*. Another part of me argued: *Can't just leave her here. She needs a friendly shoulder, someone who cares*. Sickness speared my stomach unexpectedly, almost kicking the lunch out of me. The sickness pangs of someone who was so scared, lonely and damaged they could hardly breathe, gripped me. I reached out to the sink for support. This was the sickness of someone who was just about keeping things

211

together. Every part of them was on the verge of cracking.

I'd only come in here to wee, I wasn't meant to be feeling any of this.

As it was, fate took matters out of my hands because the mystery woman suddenly burst into tears. Silent sobs, with plump tears that rained down onto the pregnancy test box, her face crumpled in pain, her whole body quivered. She held onto the basin with both hands, her blonde hair swinging back and forth as she cried and cried and cried her heart out.

Without a second thought, I went to her, put my arms around her and gently pulled her into a close hug.

'I don't know what I'm going to do,' she sobbed.

Trudy stopped crying after a couple of minutes. Her nose still ran and she trembled in a way that meant she was just about controlling the tears. She'd managed to tell me her name as I steered her into a cubicle.

She took the wad of loo roll I offered her.

'I'm a bit upset,' she offered in return for the loo roll. She dabbed at her wet eyes. 'Just a bit upset.'

I was 'just a bit upset' when an *Angel* episode finished. *This ain't 'a bit' upset, baby*. I didn't say that, obviously. I leant back against the wall of the disabled cubicle, watched her sit hunched over on the loo.

'Do you want to talk about it?' I said. 'I mean, you can if you want. I'm a good listener. I've actually got an honorary degree in listening from the International University Of Auralogy.'

She said nothing.

That was meant to make her at least smile.

'You don't have to if you don't want to, of course. We can stand and sit here in silence for as long as you want. I haven't got any more lectures today.'

Trudy ran a hand through her bobbed hair. 'There's nothing to talk about. I'm getting what I deserve.' Then she ran her sleeve under her snotted nose, forgetting the loo roll in her hand.

'What's that then?'

Her eyes flashed with venom at something. 'You reap as you sow, isn't that what they teach you in school? You reap as you sow. You get what you deserve.'

I ransacked my memory but I couldn't find the exact point in time when that phrase entered my repertoire. Or when I started using it, but I doubt it came from school. 'I went to a convent school, but I don't remember hearing that from there. I do know the phrase.' *It's entered my mind a few times with the types of things I hear.*

'Well it's what I'm living now.' Trudy paused, balled the tissue up in her fist a bit tighter. She looked me up and down as though I was wearing a nun's habit and I was about to start lecturing her on the Good Book. 'I suppose you disapprove

213

of me, you being a Catholic and me having this,' she raised the pregnancy kit packet, 'but no wedding ring on show.'

'I'm not exactly a virgin . . . um, I'm in no way a virgin and I'm not married either, so let she who is without sin and all that.'

Trudy's face turned. She suddenly became a vicious, poison-spitting demon. Her blue eyes narrowed to slits and her features became so contorted, they looked like they could actually reach out and punch me. 'Do you sleep around? Do you sometimes wake up beside someone and not know his or her name? Do you hate yourself after every single time but can't stop yourself doing it anyway? Do you have to use one of these,' she lifted the box again, this time like a trophy, 'and not know who the father might be?'

That would be no – to every single question. 'Um . . .'

'Didn't think so! So you can drop the "I'm down with your pain, sister" bit because you have no clue how I feel.'

Not exactly true. I had some clue how she felt. And I was only trying to help. I meant no harm. I was offering her an ear in a time of need. There was also, of course, that saying, something about hell and its lovely path constructed with good intentions.

'In fact, why the fuck am I in here with you? Who the fuck are you? Just piss off, will you! PISS OFF!!'

I stood my ground. Not because I knew she didn't mean it; not because I wanted to reason with her. I was too shocked by her change in mood to do much else. Not the humour, so much as the suddenness of it; the severity. She'd gone from upset to brutal in 0.21 seconds. Naturally, I'd been told to 'get lost' before. But never so forcefully – not by someone who didn't know me a lot better, anyway.

'DIDN'T YOU HEAR ME?' Trudy bawled. 'PISS OFF!'

I attempted a smile, to show her there were no hard feelings. There really were no hard feelings, on my part anyway. I was only doing what came naturally, and it wasn't me who was crying in the work loos. All right, that's not true. There were some hard feelings. Outrage pumped in my chest as I fumbled to slide back the lock and exited.

Outside, a woman with wet hands stood staring at the disabled loo. She double took as I came scurrying out, then she jumped as Trudy slammed and locked the loo door behind me.

I stood, frozen in time, immobilised by embarrassment. No one was meant to hear me being ordered to leave a cubicle. Ever. In the probability of life, the grand scheme of things, no one should hear you being ordered to leave anywhere, let alone a staff loo cubicle. The woman stared at me. I stared at the woman.

In a moment that Dali would've been proud of, I reached out, pulled a couple of blue tissues from the wall dispenser and handed them to her. Still staring me straight in the eye, she accepted the towels, said thank you and proceeded to dry her hands.

I wandered away, my work here was done.

CHAPTER 18

DON'T LISTEN

The thing with Trudy bothered me for days. No matter how hard I tried to forget it, it niggled at me. Not just in my quiet moments when I had nothing else to occupy my mind, even in my manic moments, like running for the bus; trying to find the right green olives in the supermarket; teaching. Even when I was sat in the library, reading journals, concentrating really hard, I was besieged by her.

It'd been a week, as well. A week when I should have been able to get her out of my head. And this wasn't a week to be trifled with. Seven short days in the future I had a meeting with my research supervisor. The professor who would assess how well I was doing, if my non-lecturing work was up to scratch, or if I was on a wild goose chase. And, ultimately, if I'd have to go back to London to pick up my life where I left off.

All the same, Trudy invaded my thoughts. It wasn't simply the 'piss off' thing that replayed itself and replayed itself in my mind – that naturally smarted my pride – but, two Twix, one

Crunchie and a packet of Doritos later, I was calm enough to see the funny side of it.

What kept drawing me back to Trudy, what made her a persistent ghost in my mind was the way she'd cried. How in an instant she'd fallen to pieces in the arms of a stranger. What she'd said about herself upset me too. What she did. How hard it must be for her to know what she was doing wasn't making her happy, but to keep doing it. To keep on keeping on, even when it was making her so unhappy she hated herself. She might've thrown it in my face, but I really was down with her pain. It hurt me as well. I'd experienced what she'd experienced as she wiped snot off her face with her sleeve; as she gripped the basin. I'd literally been tangled up in her aura of misery as sure as if I'd been her. Trudy was alone. And terrified. I'd felt that through her and it'd almost knocked me off my feet.

That was nothing new.

Feeling through others, others feeling through me was nothing new. My version of that thing called empathy went beyond simple understanding. It was the actual feeling. The actual emotion. Like the time with Ed when I understood how he felt about Robyn. Like the night when I felt Mel was suicidal. Like the moment I understood how that dodgy man in the bar felt about Jess. And now this thing with Trudy. I understood how these people really felt because I felt it too. Their emotions jerked through me just as they jerked through them. Their emotions crushed or consumed or energised me as sure as they did to them. I felt others in a cloying cloud that seemed to descend then transport me to the midst of their souls, the very core of their hearts.

Before, these experiences were periodic, the occasional sensation. Like getting into a lift and suddenly being over-powered by morning sickness. Someone in there was pregnant and there was no chance whatsoever it was me. This person was keeping it a secret because she didn't know what to do yet, and how I knew it, I didn't know. I simply felt it.

Another time, I was sat on the tube, reading, when the page was splashed with a fat teardrop. I reached up, touched my cheek, I was crying. A flood of sadness followed. I hadn't been sad two seconds earlier, the book wasn't sad but I was overwhelmed by unhappiness. I wiped the tears before anyone saw, but the sadness and teariness only left me when the man next to me got up and left. Just like that, one minute my emotions were swimming in a sea of despair, the next, when the man next to me got off the tube train, I was fine.

Yet another time, I'd been stood in a bank queue and I couldn't stop myself laughing. Waves of joy kept coming and coming until I found myself covering my mouth to stop the giggles. Soon I was laughing so much I had to leave. Outside, I had no clue as to what had been so funny.

But those things only happened when I was tired. When my mind was relaxed and weary and finding it difficult to keep a grip on reality. It was like a seventh sense. Not quite being psychic. Just having a super-enhanced perception. Extra Extra Sensory Perception for feelings, I guess.

Except that was stupid, wasn't it? What I felt was probably based on understanding people. And if there was one thing I had a lot of, it was understanding. Understanding how they got themselves into certain situations and how they felt about them afterwards. How people just kept going over and over, trying to sort things out but couldn't because they couldn't get any perspective on them.

Like with Trudy. She was crying because she was scared and alone. And she had to do that test alone.

She's probably done it now, I reasoned. *She's done it now, got the result, decided what she's going to do. And she's done it without me holding her hand or sharing her pain. Just like a few million other people around the globe manage to do every second of the day.*

I sighed, sat back in the library chair, rubbed my eyes before I put on my glasses. I'd been in the library most of the day and my eyes were exhausted. The best cure: the blue-framed glasses I'd had a tantrum about being prescribed. (The woman in the opticians had stared at me in disbelief as I turned down every frame in the shop because, 'I look like my dad in them'. I proceeded to try to talk her into finding that I didn't need them after all. You know, couldn't the diagnosis have been wrong? Anyone would've thought that I needed to have them welded to my face, not that I needed them to see things more than ten feet away. That was why we never mentioned them, not even if I was wearing them.)

I closed my eyes. Trudy. Her face, her crying face, appeared behind my eyes. That was how my mind worked. I didn't focus on her snarling, 'Who the hell are you, PISS OFF' face, the heartbreaking one plagued me.

She bugged me, harassed me, upset me because I couldn't, with a word or deed, make it all all right for her. If anything, I'd made things worse: Trudy wouldn't have said all those things about herself if I hadn't hugged her. Now she was walking around, knowing that someone else in the world knew how she felt about herself. Usually, too, saying things out loud made it all the more real, all the more horrific. I'd prompted her to go vocal with her traumas.

A chill crawled across my skin, tingling my scalp, someone was watching me. My eyes flew open. Across the wide, light wood table on which were spread the spoils of my hours in the library, stood a lanky man. His close-cropped blond hair made his ears stick out, he wore baggy charcoal suit trousers, a white shirt with the top button open. He looked familiar. But then, most people looked familiar to me especially when there were so many faces in the college. This man, though, grinned at me as if he knew me, his green eyes excited as he yanked out a chair and deposited himself on it.

'I've done it, Ceri,' he said.

I physically jumped out of my seat at his voice. 'Jesus Christ, Ed! I didn't recognise you.' I *still* didn't recognise him.

'Huh?' Ed replied.

I waved vaguely at his head, the white shirt.

'Oh,' Ed ran a hand over his head, 'that.' He brushed off my shock with a blase wave.

'That?! Ed, you're a different man. You're a man.'

'Shhhhh,' a couple of people replied. This was a proper library, even though it was in a college. People actually came here to work and they expected silence with it. When I was a student, the library was an extension of the common room. Here, these merchants of no fun wanted to study.

I leant forwards too. 'Done what exactly?' I whispered just as loudly.

'I took your advice.'

My blood froze, my bowels turned to water, my hands grabbed the table for support. Ed had just uttered four words I *NEVER* wanted to hear.

I may dish out advice, I may think of myself as a cross between Oprah, a therapist, and Gynan from *Star Trek: Next Generation* but, Jeez, I never wanted anyone to *take* my advice. To listen to me, yes, but not to hear me so well they do what I say. For all the 'faint heart', 'life half lived', 'life's too long' speeches I gave, I never wanted people to screw up their lives by following them. They'd only partly worked for me, and *I* believed them. I'd hashed together my theories and insights from a lifetime's telly-watching and a couple of months of self-help book reading. How could anyone do what I said from just being told about it? By me, too. Who was I in the grand scheme of things?

'Which advice was that then?' I asked cautiously, knowing it wasn't that he start ironing his clothes inside out to stop them getting a sheen to them.

'Faint heart never won fair lady. I asked her out. I. Me. Ed. I. Asked. Robyn. Out. Me. I asked her out!'

'You never!'

'I did.'

'Shhhhh!' From around the library.

Moving like a woman possessed, I grabbed papers and pens, my glasses case, books that were mine, picked up my bag. 'Come on.'

We stood outside the library in the long, wide corridor with light wood parquet floors and beige walls. It was late afternoon, most students were either heading for late lectures, heading for home or were heading for the canteen. Everyone had somewhere to head to, except me and Ed. Ed, technically, shouldn't be here anyway, what with his educational institute being way down in town.

Not caring about the mess I made, I dropped the bundle in my arms and leant against the notice-board outside the library. Ed leant facing me.

'So . . . so,' I prompted, with a frantic 'come on' gesture.

'I went up to her when she was in the union. That's our union, the union at The Met.'

Yes Ed, I get the idea.

'She was with all her mates. She's so popular . . .'

Usually I'd go sit on my own cos I don't like going up to her when there's loads of people but this time, I went over, asked if she wanted a drink, dead cool like. She was a bit taken aback. But she smiled at me with her beautiful lips, her eyes still looked surprised, like, but she said, 'I'll have a vodka and tonic.' I mean, I'm never that forward, not in front of her mates. I always wait until we're alone to talk to her. I'm just too shy and she's just so beautiful.

My palms were all sweaty and my heart was beating dead fast as I spoke to her, Ceri. You would've been so proud of me, I kept thinking, 'A life lived in fear'. I bought the drink, took it back and then asked if I could have a quiet word with her.

'Sure,' she said. I think she was impressed with my change in image. She kept looking at me as though she was seeing me for the first time and she couldn't stop herself smiling.

We went to the other side of the bar and I looked her in the eye. Right in the eye.

And I said: 'I was wondering if I could take you out to dinner next week, Robyn.'

Just like that. No stuttering, no ums, no ahhs. I just asked her.

And she said: 'Sure, why not. When?'

I said: 'Wednesday?' Cos you know, Wednesday's the night most people have free isn't it? I wouldn't presume she'd be free Friday or Saturday.

And she said: 'Give me a call over the weekend and I'll come round to yours first. My flatmates will give us a hard time if we meet at my place.' Then she asked the barman for a pen and look . . .

Ed raised his hand. Across the back of his right hand, in curly-girly writing was a phone number.

'Bloody. Hell.' I couldn't think of anything else to say. I was stunned he'd done it. Even more stunned that she'd said yes.

'I know!' Ed replied.

I looked at him again: eyes sparkly, face flushed and excited.

'*Bloody hell!*' I repeated.

'I KNOW!' Ed grabbed me into a bear hug. 'And it's all thanks to you.' He rocked me as he squeezed the life's breath out of me. 'Thank you, thank you, thank you.'

Ed's happiness was infectious. The Mount Fuji of grins spread across my face as he smothered me with his joy.

From the corner of my eye I spotted a cloud. A dark storm cloud on the horizon of happiness Ed and I were hugging on. I shifted slightly in Ed's arms to face it head on.

It was him. The man from the pub a few weeks ago; from the party the other week.

Staring Man. Standing there – glaring at me.

'Who's he?' I asked Mel.

It was late in the day. I'd got into a routine of doing research during the day and prepping (oh yes, I was a proper lecturer now, I even used lecturer terms) in the early evenings. That way, students wouldn't catch me in the library because they were either in lectures, the pub or their beds during the day; and they wouldn't wantonly drop by my office in the evenings because they generally thought I was away home. I'd sent Ed off earlier with promises to listen to the entire retelling of the 'I. Asked. Robyn. Out. Me. Ed' tale again when I got home.

I dropped by the Senior Common Room to have some time away from essays and my computer and found that I wasn't alone in how I planned my working day: there were quite a few other lecturers in there too. About fifteen of us, dotted around the SCR, either eating dinner or prepping or marking, or doing what Mel and I were doing, sat side by side taking a break.

When I asked my question of Mel, Staring Man had walked into the SCR. His body, which had looked like an artistic stroke on a page, moved very easily, elegantly almost, as he'd crossed the expanse. He went to make himself a cup of something in the kitchenette area.

'That's Bosley,' Mel replied.

'Bosley?' I asked. 'What kind of a name is Bosley?'

'Bosley, as in *Charlie's Angels*,' Mel said, speaking slowly, as though I was thick for not immediately getting it.

'Right,' I said. 'Course . . . Why do you call him that?'

'It's not just me, everyone calls him that. The thing about Bosley is, he's got an army of women friends and that's all they are friends. He's always surrounded by good-looking women, whenever we bump into him he's got some gorgeous woman at his side and nothing ever happens between them. You know, like Bosley in *Charlie's Angels*, sexy women, no sex. And our Bosley is always rescuing these gorgeous women from some drama or another.'

'Really?' I asked, trying not to sound too interested.

'Yep. A couple of weeks ago, me, Bosley, Craig, and another guy got together at my place to play cards. Bosley arrived last. He'd literally walked in and sat down when his mobile rang. One of his friends was stuck in Sheffield, she was pissed and had lost her coach ticket home. She was crying and saying she didn't have enough cash to buy another one. So, Bosley gets up, goes and drives over to get her. He went all the way over to Sheffield and back, just cos she's his friend.'

'And he wasn't trying to get into her knickers?' I asked, as casually as possible.

Mel leapt forwards in his seat, twisted to look at me. His eyes were alight with the suspicion of my question having a double meaning. It did, but not how Mel thought. I wanted to find out what sort of man he was. If he was driving miles out of true friendship or if he was doing it because he ultimately wanted to get a shag out of it. Either way you looked at it, it was a nice thing to do, but the motivation behind it would have a bearing on why he was glaring at me. Was he stalker material or just someone who had an unfortunate stare that I got in the way of? Obviously, trying to get into her knickers was stalker potential; not trying to get into her knickers was unfortunate stare.

Mel, who had no idea what went on in my head, thought I was asking because . . . it was obvious from the grin on his face what he thought.

'No,' Mel said, 'he wasn't trying to get into her knickers.' His eyes twinkled even more. 'Why? Are you interested?'

'No,' I said. *Not in the way you mean.*

Mel's grin spread, infecting more of his face. 'You are! Ceri loves Bosley. Ceri loves Bosley!' he started chanting under his breath.

'Shhh,' I whispered and pulled him back down beside me. 'Stop it. I do not. I just spotted him at that party the other week and was wondering what he was doing here if he's not a Met boy.'

'He lectures in the Media department – that should interest you, seeing as you used to be a journalist. And he was at that party because he shares a place with a couple of Met people,' Mel said, still grinning, 'just like you. And, he's from London, just like you. You two have got so much in common. You're meant to be together.'

'Don't start, Mel,' I said.

'I could put a good word in for you if you like,' Mel said, behind his grin.

'Stop it. I'm not even remotely interested.'

'Now, are you sure? He's a mate. I'll just mention you were asking about him. It's no trouble.'

'Don't you dare,' I hissed, then pinched Mel's leg. He yelped, loudly. A few people in the room looked up at us. 'You are such a big girl's blouse,' I whispered. 'I didn't even pinch you that hard and you're practically screaming the place down.' Staring Man, who was leaning against the kitchenette counter, was doing what he did best: staring. He glowered at us from over his coffee cup. I shifted uneasily in my seat and looked away.

From the corner of my eye I spotted Mel waving at Staring Man. I looked up in time to catch SM's reaction: he nodded a slight hello back, then looked away. Looked away in a manner that suggested he was studiously avoiding looking at us again.

'I think Bosley fancies you,' Mel whispered, leaning in close to my ear. 'He looks well jealous. I've never seen him look that pissed off, ever.'

'Yes, he does look jealous,' I agreed. 'And you've

229

just told me that he's always surrounded by gorgeous women but nothing goes on.' I turned to look at Mel. 'Ever thought that he might fancy *you*?'

CHAPTER 19

SEX, *PLEASE*

I sat on the edge of the bath, smoothing handfuls of conditioner into my hair.

I loved conditioning my hair. Knowing that with every stroke I was making it shiny and soft. I got a real sense of joy from squidging it into my hair and running my fingers down from the roots to the tips, feeling my hair soften under hand.

The simple things in life pleased me. I'd discovered this the longer I lived this life in Leeds. Seeing Jess once, maybe twice a week; and not so much as a sniff of male action. Well, not if you didn't count Ed and Jake. Both of whom I didn't count. Since that weekend back in London thing, the three of us had become very close. It was like having two more brothers, except now one of my brothers was white, with shorn blond hair, and hailed from Cornwall; and my other brother was white too, with rusty hair, an eyebrow piercing and a faint Scottish accent. Was it any wonder I found true happiness in conditioner? And *Angel.*

I slowly pulled a comb through my hair, thinking about what had happened in my life since I'd touched down in Leeds. In ten weeks.

Ed and his date, which was, what – Sunday, Monday – in four days.

Claudine and Mel. Mel and Claudine. She wanted to pretend nothing had happened between them. Mel kept saying he was in love with her, conveniently ignoring his wreck of a marriage. And between them nothing was being sorted.

Gwen. I'd become her new best mate. The dinner invite hadn't materialised, but she'd started sitting next me on days that weren't Wednesdays – she even came to my shared office to find me and sat around until I made her coffee. Then I had to make conversation. She talked to me like we had anything in common. She was younger than Jess, but she was most definitely madder than Jess. Always it was with the demon year group. She could never forget them. Or ignore them. When I tried to change the subject, it worked for a few minutes. She was like a crying child you tried to distract with a toy – it'd work for a while, but their attention would come back to why they were crying in the first place. With Gwen it always came back to that first year group. I'd started to keep score of how often she mentioned them in a neutral conversation. Her personal best was twenty-five in one Wednesday.

For my sanity and because I could see how much it bothered her, I went to the demon year group, as a group and in tutorials, and suggested they attempt mediation, to explain to her what was wrong. 'Don't just sit there and say, "I don't gerrit".

232

Explain what your problems are in a practical way that she can sort out.' My idea had fallen on deaf ears and consequently they fell on my ears via Gwen.

Trudy. The mystery crying woman. I wondered if she existed. I hadn't seen her. Not in the SCR, not in the canteen, not even in the corridors. The whole thing was so surreal. Possibly a reminder from on high that I shouldn't be involving myself in other people's lives?

I tossed the comb into the bath, which was lined with islands of shampoo foam, and went back to running my hands through my hair, feeling the conditioner squidge and slip through my fingers.

Saturday night and I was sat here alone, rethinking my life. Ed was out with his mates, Jake was out with other mates. I suspected he was sneaking off to see The Git, but hadn't said owt. This was a sad state of affairs. I was young, vibrant and nearly thirty and I was getting my pleasure from conditioner and the prospect of watching David Boreanaz be a 250-year-old vampire. And, let's not forget, said vampire couldn't have sex because one moment of true happiness would result in him losing his soul and turning bad again.

Speaking of which, when *was* the last time I'd had sex? Or even a snog. Or even the hint of a snog. Two months ago? Nope, I've been here two months and I've certainly not had sex here. Two months before that? Nope, that was Christmas and no action there. Six months. Hadn't had sex or the sniff of sex in six months. Time really does fly when you're not getting laid.

The weird thing was, for someone who loved it as much as me, I hadn't really noticed. Not till I got here and ninety-five per cent of the people I encountered seemed to be motivated by sex. They all seemed to be at it or trying to be at it or had been at it but were pretending they hadn't been at it.

They all served to remind me I wasn't at it. And, for the foreseeable future, I wouldn't be at it. I hadn't even spotted a man I fancied. And that was rare. I could talk myself into liking the most unfanciable of men. Whashisface Tosspot, who I lived with for a year, being the prime example. Not only was he the individual put on earth to make me believe in God, by proving the devil did exist, he wasn't even good-looking as a compensator. All he had was . . . nope, nothing, can't think of one thing that he had going for him. Actually, no, he got married nine months after I moved out. That proved that he wouldn't bother me again. Ah, see, there *is* good in everyone.

Part of the not finding anyone else to even fancy, I suppose, was because my last 'relationship' with Mr Perfect Penis (PP) had petered out to an open ending, before Christmas. (He'd earned himself that moniker because it was the most perfect specimen of male manhood I'd ever seen. Not that I'd seen that many in my life, it was just huge and belonged to someone who knew how to use it.

Despite its size he hadn't used it like a battering ram.)

I'd met Mr PP through work friends and I'd been instantly drawn to him. He was so overtly sexual, but didn't realise it. His dark hair speckled with grey, his dark eyes, his mouth, his body, were all rather unremarkable – on anyone else. On him, that combination turned my head. Unusually for me, I decided there and then that I was going to have him, that night. I spent the whole night talking to him and generally trying to wow him with my sparkling personality. I hadn't bothered with make-up that day, not even lippie, so had to resort to Plan B: my sparkling personality.

We'd laughed and joked all evening, then I'd invited myself round to his house for coffee. Even then he didn't get it. Didn't realise I fancied him. He'd been the perfect gentleman and made me coffee, got me biscuits and offered to order me a taxi home if I was tired. 'So you don't fancy me then?' I'd eventually said when I realised I was going to get sent home without so much as a lascivious look.

'Well, yeah,' he said, shyly. 'But, I didn't think you'd be,' he looked down at his coffee, 'well, I didn't like to assume . . .'

'And there was me thinking I was being so obvious.' My eyes held his dark eyes. 'Any more obvious and I would've been wearing my knickers on my head.'

We both burst out laughing, until the laughter slowly petered out. Our eyes met over his coffee cup and we leapt on each other. The cup became a casualty of passion.

During the night as we cuddled up and laughed in bed, we laughed like we'd been taking drugs, except we hadn't. Odd things were he-lare-re-us! Like how he'd once got locked out wearing only a towel and it'd taken him ages to wake up his flatmate. Not at all funny unless you were there, but we'd laughed and laughed about it for ages. Going through lots of different 'what if' scenarios, like 'what if' his flatmate had taken a sleeping pill and hadn't woken up for ages? 'What if' he'd had to walk down to the end of the road to the phone box and reverse the charges? Like I said, he-lare-re-us. I'd been snuggled into his chest and his arms were around me when he'd said suddenly, 'I want you to know I don't usually do this kind of thing. Don't usually meet someone and then go straight to bed with them.'

'Er, me either,' I replied. I had no problem with going straight to bed with someone. In general, people spent far too much time judging others on trivial things like how soon they slept together. All that mattered was that I was OK with it. At that point of my life, though, I didn't just leap in to bed with just anyone, more out of a lack of opportunity than anything else.

We'd walked to work the next day, both shell-shocked that we'd had amazing sex – six, *six* times

236

in one night – when we'd met five hours earlier. You don't usually expect quality and quantity when you hardly knew someone, but we'd lucked out.

Mr PP and I saw each other a couple of times a week for a couple of months, but he had a lot of emotional baggage and I'd decided not to help him carry it. Whashisface Tosspot had helped me see the folly of trying to help a man with his luggage. He was never grateful afterwards – he just found someone else to share his luggage-free life with. Under Mr PP's workload, his connection to his ex and my new-found ability to not put my life on hold while I waited for him to sort himself out, it'd ended with neither of us ringing or emailing each other.

Before, I would've put it in the lap of fate. *If it's meant to be, it'll be*, I'd think and say, while checking phone, mobile, email several times a minute. With Mr PP, I'd decided that I gave it my best shot, I offered him the best minutes of my shagging life – and if he was too busy or caught up with his ex to get in touch, then there was nothing I could do. That was the thing about giving my best – I could walk away, conscience clear, memory clear. No way I could rework things, rewish things, cling to something that was well past its shag by date. I only wish I'd learnt that sooner. It could've saved me a ton of heartache and tissues and humiliating phone calls when I was pissed and lonely.

★   ★   ★

Through the stillness of the house, I heard my mobile ringing in my bedroom and dashed for it. I picked up the phone gingerly between my forefinger and thumb, not wanting to get conditioner on the plastic cover, pressed a button to answer it.

'Hi, Ceri, it's Claudine.'

I'd given her my mobile number in case she wanted to go out sometime. Which she didn't because she'd been avoiding me since the last time we went out. She had most likely woken up the morning after we went out and been horrified by what she'd spontaneously told me.

'Hi,' I husked back. I was still a bit out of breath from the epic dash up the stairs from the bathroom. So much for my gym membership.

'What you doing tonight?' she asked. She had an edge to her voice. Not upset. Not angry. Hard to put my finger on the exact emotion, but distressed was nearest.

'Erm, washing my hair.' I replied. She was going to think I was the most exciting woman on earth. Pavlov, hair-washing on a Saturday night. If only she knew I'd been planning on updating the work I'd done on my research study later.

'Oh.' Claudine replied. 'So you won't be, erm, wanting some company then?'

'Is everything all right?' I replied.

'Of course. Course. I was just, erm, ringing on the off-chance that you were . . . no. No, it's not all right. It's all wrong,' her voice wavered, teetering

238

by the tips of her vocal cords before falling into an abyss of tears.

Ah. Not really in the position to be receiving visitors. Especially not ones so gorgeous they gave me – secure and comfortable with my looks and body as I was – bouts of self-doubt. Just walking beside tall, willowy, elegant Claudine made me want to walk on tiptoes to extend my five foot four frame.

Bad Ceri, bad, bad, bad. Can't believe you're thinking twice about letting her come around because you've got slicked down hair and no contraptions holding you up and in. Especially when you can make yourself presentable before she gets here. And besides, she's not coming to look at you, just talk to you. Stop being so bloody vain.

'Do you want to come over? I can't go out cos I've got wet hair and stuff, but come here. I've got some nibbles and the boys are out.'

'Are you sure?' she asked cautiously.

'Course.'

'OK. Thank you. I'll be there soon.'

'Erm, how soon?' I was doing mental maths on how long it'd take her to arrive and how much time I'd have to put on a bra and change out of my tatty Judge Dredd T-shirt and Mr PP's paint-splattered jogging bottoms.

'Um, about two seconds. I'm outside.'

Few people who I haven't had sex with have seen me braless. Jess has cos I've spent so many nights

239

at her house over the years. Jake and Ed have but only during my bedroom to bathroom stumble if they're up. Claudine had just become the latest person to see me *sans* mammarial support. Not that she showed any signs of noticing or caring. In fact, she didn't seem to notice how unlike me I looked. Unless, of course. I always looked dishevelled and underdressed and everyone expected it.

I'd braced myself for her to come stumbling in, tears in eyes, body quivering, ready to collapse into sobs. Instead, she'd arrived with four bottles of wine in her arms. 'I didn't know which colour of wine you liked so I bought two of each,' she explained, leaning forwards to offer me the bottles. I took two, led the way into the kitchen. Claudine stood by the worktop near the back door and from her voluminous coat pockets she produced eight cans of beer. 'I thought you might prefer beer, so I bought that too.'

While I busied myself with glasses and a packet of tortillas and dips I'd been saving for later. Claudine returned to the living room, to do what she was doing now. Pacing. She stalked backwards and forwards in front of the fireplace with its fake coal fire nestling in its black belly: her reflection catching in the *Metamorphosis of Nareissus* every time she passed him. She was intent on walking a groove into Ed's cream fake fur rug. Occasionally she'd stop, sit herself in the sofa under the window, cram a handful of tortilla chips into her mouth, gulp down red wine, then clench her fists as she ground her teeth.

I said nothing. Not one word during all this. I wanted her to start her way. Even saying something as innocuous as 'What have you been up to' could tip her into a dialogue about her weekend instead of her getting to the point.

'Kevin and I had a row,' she explained after I'd drunk a can of beer, very slowly. She held up her hands, like she was showing me the size of a fish she'd caught. 'A huge,' she widened the gap between her hands, '*huge*, row.'

She picked up her wine glass, knocked back its contents, pushed her hand into her black hair, causing the top to stand on end. 'About Mel.'

'Oh' my face said. My mouth didn't ask any of the questions that were fighting to get out, most prominent being: 'Did he guess about you and Mel?'

Claudine sighed. Then sighed again, threw herself back into the sofa. 'It's all such a mess,' she rubbed the make-up off her eyes as she seesawed across them with her fingertips. 'And it's all my fault. I just want two men at once, and I . . . Kevin said some horrible things. He was right though.'

'What happened?' I asked.

She sagged in her seat. 'Earlier, Mel rang, asked if I wanted to come for a drink up in town. Kevin and I were only watching telly and I thought, why not. I asked Kevin if he wanted to come and he lost it. I mean, he totally and utterly flipped out.

He grabbed the phone off me, told Mel we weren't going anywhere – except with a lot of swear words – and hung up.'

Shit. I filled her glass of wine to the top, she needed it. 'Oh God,' Claudine began again . . .

He started ranting on that Mel was always around. That we couldn't get through one day without Mel's name being mentioned or him calling up.

'Our weekends are fucking precious, Claudine, we don't spend any time together during the week and now HE's imposing on the only time we get together.'

'He's my best friend,' I replied.

'I'm your boyfriend. You see more of him than you do of me.'

'No I don't,' I said.

'You spend morning, noon and night with him, Monday to Friday. And tonight, the one fucking night we get to be alone together, you want to go out with him. ALWAYS HIM.'

So I said, 'He's my best friend.' Lame, I know, but I couldn't think of owt else to say.

'Why do you have to have a man as a best friend?' Kevin asked. 'Are you fucking him?'

I must've gone pale cos my whole body went cold. But I screamed back: 'You bastard.'

'You are, aren't you?' That's why he's

always around, why you light up when he's around. You're fucking him.'

'I am not!'

'Well, you never let me near you nowadays.'

'That's not true.'

'When was the last time we made love, Claudine?'

'A few days ago, I don't know, I don't keep score,' I said innocently.

'Try three months. And even then I could tell you weren't into it.'

I nearly fell over, Ceri. I mean, I didn't know it was three months. Three months? That's impossible, we couldn't not have had sex in three months. 'THAT'S A LIE!' I said.

'Is it? All I know is, you're not getting your kicks at home, so you must be getting them somewhere. And my money's on your precious Mel.'

'What are you saying?'

'I'm saying you and Mel are at it every chance you get.' He started pointing at me. We were both on our feet at this point. 'And the pair of you are laughing at me behind my back.'

'You bastard!'

'Whore!'

I slapped him. He pushed me. And I fell back onto the sofa. He looked so mad, so crazed at that point but also really hurt, then he stormed off upstairs.

I just sat there shaking. After a few minutes I grabbed my coat and keys and left. He heard me shut the door I guess cos he opened the bedroom window, leant out and started screaming: 'GO ON, GO OFF TO YOUR FRIEND. GIVE HIM ONE FOR ME!' all the way down the street until I turned the corner.

And I ended up here.

'Why didn't you go round to Mel's?' I asked.

'Kevin would love that,' she replied. 'Me going round to Mel's now.'

'You're not so angry you'd go round to Mel's and shag him to spite Kevin?'

'*No!*' Claudine seemed aghast at the idea. I examined her face, her widened eyes, her turned down mouth. She *was* aghast at the idea. 'Of course not.'

'Never even crossed your mind, huh?'

Claudine's forehead folded up like finely-corrugated iron as she frowned, then shook her head. 'No.'

'I would,' I stated, after a few draws on my beer can. 'I'd have brought a bumper pack of condoms and would've tied him to the bed and rogered him senseless. If I was as angry as you were when you first arrived, Mel would be getting the shag of his life right about now, but that's just me.'

'I wouldn't do that,' Claudine stated simply.

No, unfortunately, you wouldn't. 'Might as well get hung for a cow as a mouse,' I said.

'Eh?' Claudine said. That look of 'you're a nutter' was back.

'I mean, if you're accused of something, why not do it to make it worthwhile getting accused.'

'It was only an argument with Kevin.'

I nodded. 'But I thought you said Kevin was nothing compared to Mel? This was your chance; what you've been waiting for. If not to leave, then to start an affair. It was what you needed to press play.'

Claudine was back to downing wine. 'I only slept with Mel that one time because I was very drunk and the thing between us had reached fever pitch.'

Should I mention that she'd told me, while looking me in the eye, that she'd *almost* slept with him? No. No one likes a reminder of their lies and half-truths. 'Like I said, Claudine, I know very little about very little.'

She didn't hear me. She ploughed on: 'It was Christmas, we were all in a festive mood, Mel and I got a taxi home together like we'd done a hundred times before. We sat so close in the taxi, his leg pressed against mine. As we turned into his road he kissed me on the cheek. Then we looked at each other and we kind of leapt at each other, started kissing properly. Kevin was away, I didn't want to go home to an empty house . . .'

'Is he a good shag?' I asked. 'I always get the impression that Mel would be quite adept at it.'

Claudine smiled like the cat who got the cream – several times. 'He was . . .' big salacious pause, 'what was that word you used? Adept? He was *adept.*'

I grinned back, while my heart sank like a tank in quick-sand. Claudine's answer to that red herring of a question presented me with many, many problems. I didn't give two figs what Mel was like in bed, it wasn't as though I'd ever find out, was it? I just . . . let's put it this way: say I was in her situation and I'd had the biggest row ever with my boyfriend. If my boyfriend called me a whore, accused me of shagging around, I would've stormed around to the cause of the row's house, with booze and condoms, got myself good and drunk, attempted to shag said man, realised I couldn't do it, burst into tears and passed out, with the strong likelihood of choking on my own vomit. Failing that, I would've at least gone round to a good friend's house and repeated the scenario, minus the condoms and hopefully without the attempted shag bit.

I certainly wouldn't be sat in the house of some bird I'd met a few times. And if this person I didn't know very well had asked about the love of my life's sexual prowess I would've thought and said, 'Mind your own business, you nosy mare.' I certainly wouldn't *tell* her. I'd automatically think she fancied him. I didn't know her well enough not to assume that. Which led me to deduce one thing . . . From the depths of the corridor, the theme of *I Dream Of Jeannie* started. Claudine's mobile.

'That'll be Kevin. Ringing to check I'm all right.'

Kevin? Yeah, right! It's Mel. He's rung back cos he rang you at home and Kev's given him a mouthful then hung up on him, so he's ringing to check you're OK. Kevin won't be calling. He thinks you're mid-coitus with Mel.

Claudine stumbled blindly around my living room, searching for her coat and mobile like a heat-seeking missile looking for an iceberg. She finally found it, in the corridor where I'd hung it. 'It's Mel,' she said, after checking the mobile's screen.

'Is it?'

Claudine nodded, drunk and miserable. 'Shall I answer it?'

How the hell should I know? 'Do you want to talk to him?'

'I want to talk to Kevin,' she wailed.

That's the Kevin who isn't a patch on Mel, right? That Kevin?

The mobile stopped playing *I Dream Of Jeannie*.

Claudine stumbled drunkenly back to the sofa. She was, it had to be acknowledged, a lot drunker than me. And I was on the verge of closing my eyes and sleeping where I was. Why had I let her drag me into this piss-up session? I was so easily influenced. Offer me alcohol and I rarely said no. This wasn't my trauma but I was drinking like it was.

I Dream Of Jeannie started again. Mel, again.

Claudine snatched up the phone, looked at the

screen, visibly sagged. 'Mel.' She spat his name out as though it was phlegm.

'He probably won't stop calling until he knows you're OK,' I offered, kindly. This was nice speak for: PLEASE STOP THAT PLINKING MUSIC HACKSAWING INTO MY BRAIN. NOW!

She answered the phone and spoke at length to Mel. It sounded like:

'Fnugh.' (Fine.)

'Hml, know.' (I know, I know how you feel.)

'Dwnan know.' (Don't know.)

'Fnugh. Fnugh.' (Yes, I'm fine, stop asking.)

The only thing I really understood was: 'Ceri' which probably meant she was telling him she was with me.

From the way she pursed her lips like a sulking school girl unfairly separated from her favourite toy, it was clear she wanted Kevin to be on the other end of the phone.

I poured Claudine into a taxi right after that phone call because she was on the verge of tears. I knew, even if she didn't, she'd get a lot further in making up with Kevin if he saw her shed a few tears. She didn't look like a habitual crier and Kevin, after their row, would probably appreciate it. There was no point her crying on my shoulder, I was already on her side.

I collected glasses and bottles and cans by the light of the television. I threw away what was left of the dips, then got down on my hands and knees to rid the carpet of tortilla bits and dip drizzles.

Jake was fanatical about certain things such as food bits on his cream carpet, but the bathroom could go uncleaned for months and he wouldn't care. (Not that it did go uncleaned for months, *I* couldn't stand it.)

Wearing my hair-washing clothes, I got into bed, switched on the TV, turned down the sound and lay in the flickering light, thinking. Not just about Claudine and Mel. More the wider implications of Mel and Claudine.

The fact your life can change in the blink of an eye; the misunderstanding of a phrase; the kissing of someone you shouldn't. The pain of wanting something you simply can't have.

Wanting something so much that you make yourself and everyone around you miserable because you can't have it. It was madness, but we all did it. There was this film I saw once that encapsulated that madness quite neatly. It was a shite film, but I remember one of the main characters saying something like, 'Why do people love those who are not in love with them? Is that not madness? Does a man go to the airport to pick up his brother when he has no brother?' It *was* madness, but we all still did it. Even when I could see the hopelessness, when I knew there was no chance whatsoever of getting what I wanted, I craved things, made myself sick over things. Even when I knew, no matter what I did, I couldn't have that thing (Drew Tucker, case in point). Mel and Claudine were doing it now. Deep down they both knew what they wanted, it was simply easier to ignore it. Pretend it wasn't happening, wasn't staring them right in the face. Part of that was self-flagellation. Punishing themselves for what they did that one night. Fair enough, they did a bad, bad thing. Feeling guilty was part of the cheating package. What I wanted to know was, why was I being dragged in to share in the punishment? I mean, I hadn't had sex in six months.

CHAPTER 20

THE MORNING AFTER(ISH)

'Have you seen Claudine? Is she all right?' Mel, complete with chaos, had flung himself into the seat opposite me in the canteen. I'd only nipped down there for a break from library duties. I was not having a good day. Gwen's demon group had been excruciatingly fractious, most of them hadn't done the set reading, the rest didn't understand the reading and thought, for some reason, I would understand it better than they did. Admittedly, I was being paid to understand it better than they did, but I was only human. I had a life – of sorts. I hadn't meant to get ridiculously drunk on Saturday and spend Sunday recovering and then staying up later, reading and planning.

It'd hit me as I had to re-read something for the sixtieth time, while drying and tonging my hair, that I wasn't as young as I used to be. The days when I could pull an all-nighter and still function the next day were gone. I'd wanted to tell the group that. Instead, I stood in front of them, trawling my brain for any dregs of my psychology degree that would help me get on with this so I could get to the library and read up some more for my meeting with my research supervisor tomorrow. Eventually, we'd all admitted defeat, I sent them off to do the reading and come back next time with valid questions instead of their favoured refrain of 'I don't gerrit'. I'd scuttled off to the library for some eleventh-hour reading. Trying to work out what the supervisor may ask me about. What she'd think was wishy-washy in the stuff I'd sent to her.

I'd staved off hunger pangs until two-thirty so anyone who was likely to want to communicate with me would be off doing something better. Ha.

'I last saw her at about three Sunday morning, and she was fine then. Drunk, but fine.'

'She's not in today. I'm really worried about her.'

'Have you spoken to her?' I replied.

'No. Her mobile was switched off all of yesterday. I called the house once and HE said he'd kick my head in if I showed my face around there. I'm really worried. I think he might hurt her.'

'How do you mean, hurt her?'

'You know, get physical.'

And you didn't think to go round there, try to rescue her? What a man.

I mentally slapped myself for thinking such a nasty thought. I was tired and wound up, my life could unravel tomorrow. The supervisor could put an end to my heart's desire. But that didn't give me an excuse to be nasty. Even if it was just mentally nasty.

'Has he ever hit her before?' I asked.

'No.'

'And has she ever said she's scared of him?'

'No, but he sounded so angry.'

'I'd be angry if I was him. And if the person I saw as the root of all my problems kept calling, I'd probably threaten violence too. Just threaten it, mind.'

Mel's silence said, *'I'm not convinced.'*

'They've got a lot to sort out,' I added.

'It's just not like her to miss a lecture. Something must have happened.'

'Must it?' I snapped.

'Yeah!' Mel said desperately. 'You don't know her like I do. This just isn't like her.'

I didn't growl, I didn't sigh. I counted to five, threw down my fork. 'Why can't it be something good that happened? You know, they took themselves off somewhere where they could be alone without the phone constantly ringing and people dropping around so they can talk.'

Mel shook his head. 'No. No, I don't think so.'

I sighed. Couldn't help myself. I didn't have the time or energy for this. 'Two things I've learnt about these things, Mel, if something bad had happened, you'd have heard about it by now – bad news always travels faster than good news. And,' I softened my voice, made an effort to sound sympathetic, 'because you're part of the problem, you probably can't be part of the solution right now.'

Mel's big hazel eyes watered up. I knew that look well. It plucked on my heart strings. 'You're right of course.'

Usually. Usually those eyes played my heart strings like a harp. Today they aggravated every nerve in my body. I tutted. 'No, I'm not. You said it yourself, you know Claudine and Kevin better than I ever will, so only you know what the problem is.' Mel's face brightened a little.

'Look, Mel, I'm sorry, but I have to go. I've got a really important meeting in the morning and I haven't done even half of what I'm supposed to do.' I got up, taking my half wolfed down food with me. 'I'm sure it'll be OK. Bye.'

I almost got to the library. Almost. All right, I got outside the canteen, my heart strings playing such a loud instrumental of 'Endless Love' that I couldn't hear anything else. Not the people leaving the canteen, not the students in corridors, not anything. I stopped, took a deep breath, turned around and went back to Mel. He'd looked so dejected, so genuinely worried . . . I'd obviously learnt nothing from the whole Trudy episode. And it wasn't like this meeting tomorrow was my first proper assessment or anything. My future in Leeds didn't rest upon the outcome of this meeting tomorrow, did it?

'All right,' I said, sitting back on the orange plastic chair.

Mel glanced up, his face brightening as he saw me. Rarely are people so pleased to see me.

'This is what we're going to do,' I said. 'I'll call Claudine and make up something about her leaving something at my place on Saturday if Kevin answers. And then, if there's no answer, we can go around, check it's all OK.' *Although if it isn't, I don't know what we'll do.*

'Really?' Mel said. 'You'll do that?'

I hate myself sometimes. I am weak. I allow myself to be swayed to the will of others too easily. Saturday night, case in point. This moment, another case in point. 'Really. But first, tell me what you're so worried about.'

And he did.

'You're too nice for your own good, you,' Jess said to me later.

'So you wouldn't have gone back?' I replied.

'Oh yes, course I would, but if I'd told you that story, you'd have said, "You're too nice for your own good, you", so I'm saying it back to you. It's what friends are for.'

'I suppose.'

'But it was all right in the end? With Claudine?'

'Oh, yeah, it was fine. They'd gone away, like I said, to sort things out.'

'I bet Mel was pleased.'

'I wouldn't say pleased. More like, relieved, plus . . .'

'Plus?'

'Plus a whole rainbow of emotions I wasn't sure one person could feel in about three seconds, but, anyway, love, I'm going to try to get some reading done before this meeting tomorrow.'

'Try to do some reading?'

'Yes.'

'Ceri, do or do not, there is no try.'

'Yeah, all right, Yoda. I'd better go.'

'All right, good luck. Call me tomorrow to let me know how it went, bye.'

'Bye.'

CHAPTER 21

ADVERTISING

I'd practically stripped my left thumb of its top layer of nail by the time Craig arrived in my corner of the Senior Common Room.

Craig, who was researching his PhD and teaching in the sociology department, gave me the impression that he'd been waylaid on the road to something bigger and better. I also suspected he'd be studying for his PhD for nigh on for ever for that same reason. He was a man with far too many things on his mind. He'd be talking to you one minute, his dark brown eyes watching intently behind his thin framed glasses, then he'd 'sit back'. Not physically, mentally. Mentally, he'd take a back seat to the conversation, his mind calculating something of extreme importance.

'There you are, Ceri,' he said, dropping his regulation paper pile on the table where I sat. 'I've been halfway round the college looking for you.'

'And you didn't think to look in here?'

He thought about it for a second, shook his head. 'No.'

'I've been here since,' I looked to the large white

clock on the wall above the far door, 'eight-thirty. My office partner had tutorials from 8a.m.'

'Oh,' Craig said.

'You didn't try my office either, did you?' I said.

Craig's brown eyes stared at me as he shook his head.

If I wasn't so nervous about my assessment, I would've laughed. As it was, I was so nervous I'd worn a skirt. I'd even flirted with the idea of wearing a blouse, I'd gone as far as taking it out of the wardrobe but I didn't actually put it on. I stuck to my favourite long-sleeved red top that was slightly bobbly, but fit me perfectly.

When Craig had come bursting in, I'd been contemplating another herbal tea. The last six hadn't calmed me down. Maybe lucky number seven would do it. I wasn't used to these kind of nerves. It felt like my first day on the job all over again. Only worse. With this, there was no blagging, she'd had a chance to read what I'd done so far. I had a whole lot of reading stored in my brain cells. But still, I felt I should be doing something more. Something. Anything. I was of the busy generation. I couldn't do one thing at a time. I was often writing and watching television; reading and listening to the radio. It also felt unnatural to be prepared and finished in time; I was usually working right up to the wire. Some of my best work had been done two hours before a deadline.

'Anyway Craig, what was so important you looked practically nowhere for me?' I asked.

'Oh, oh your research supervisor called. She's got food-poisoning, she can't make your appointment.'

'What?' My chest loosened, my stomach tightened. 'WHAT?' I slapped my hands onto my cheeks. 'Why didn't she call me?'

'She called you at home, your flatmate said you'd left; she tried your mobile, it was off; so she called here and I told the secretary that I'd find you.'

I flopped forwards on to the table, all my muscles unclenching. 'I've been terrified the whole weekend for nothing. Nothing.' I could've enjoyed getting drunk on Saturday night. Not been so brusque with Mel yesterday.

'At least you've done the work,' Craig offered.

I met his philosophical gaze with one as hard as flint. 'Don't get all positive on me Craig, I'm not in the right frame of mind. My nerves are shot. I've been dreaming about this meeting. It's so important.' I got up, went to the white jug kettle on the kitchenette sideboard, flicked it on. I raised a cup to Craig, he shook his head.

'It's like getting all dressed up but with nowhere to go.' I folded my arms, leant back against the counter top, lightly butting my bum against it. I pointed at my dark denim skirt. 'Literally.'

Craig checked his watch, sat down. He obviously had time to spend with me. 'What's your research about anyway? I know you said before that you're not doing a PhD, you're just doing research but I never got around to asking what it's about.'

He hadn't 'sat back' yet – this was a good sign, I still had someone to talk to. To unload on. And after the way I'd worked myself up into a frenzy, there was rather a lot that wanted to be unloaded. Poor Jake and Ed had been tiptoeing around me all Monday night – even offering me herbal tea and cheesecake had been tantamount to offering me an 'outside' (i.e., calling Angel a big girl's blouse, and asking me to step outside for a fight to the death). Neither of them, rather cleverly, said, 'You've got nothing to worry about.' I would've battered them if they did.

Craig was actively listening right then. He probably realised, though, I'd be unloading whether he was listening or taking a jaunt through his mind.

I poured hot water onto the tea bag. The scent of peppermint wafted up in the steam leaving the cup. 'I'm writing a paper on subliminal advertising,' I explained. It was, of course, more than that. More than just a case of 'subliminal advertising'. It was more to do with perception and communication and the way our conscious and subconscious minds worked independently and dependently. How we found out things without being directly told; how we told people things without actually saying them. On the most basic level, it was about how we perceived things without realising we'd perceived them.

Take for instance the case of someone calling you a few minutes after you've thought about them. You think, that's strange, I must be psychic. However, it might not be psychic ability at all. It could actually be that at an earlier date you'd said you hardly went out on Wednesdays. Maybe you'd mentioned that telly was much better on a Wednesday night, or that you preferred going out on a Thursday rather than a Wednesday night. So, that person you're talking to unintentionally, subliminally, has it in their head that Wednesday is the best day to call you. You, without realising it, always think of that person on a Wednesday because you've started on some level to associate them with you not going out on that night of the week. Also, subliminally, you've told them that the best day to call you is a Wednesday. So, when they call, it's not cos you're psychic or have super-enhanced women's intuition, you have subliminally communicated when to call you.

And that was my study. On subliminal perception, on the ways people subliminally advertise things.

This information had a strange effect on Craig. A light bulb seemed to go off in him and he physically sat forwards in the chair. 'Yeah, course. It's quite obvious if you think about it.'

I frowned, put down the kettle, stirred the tea. 'What do you mean it's obvious?'

'Well, that's what you do, isn't it? You subliminally advertise sex.'

The spoon slipped from my fingers. Huh? How had he come to that conclusion? Wasn't I the one who hadn't had sex in over six months, and who had accepted the most exciting my life was going to get was through trying a new hair conditioner? And had Craig actually looked at me? Apart from today, which was a glitch in the otherwise normal wardrobe, I had an asexual way of dressing. I wore combats and jeans. Long-sleeved tops. All right, so I wore big hoop earrings and I occasionally slicked on lipstick, but I in no way advertised sex, subliminally or otherwise. Pamela Anderson had nothing on me breast-wise, but there were hoards of men who would swear on the continued longevity of their penises that the last thing that came to mind when they looked at me was sex.

'I don't,' I stated with a frown.

'You do,' Craig replied. 'You make me want to have sex every time I see you.'

The spoon, which I'd picked up, slipped from my fingers onto the side again. 'What?'

'You make me want to have sex every time I see you.'

I stared at him. 'It's true,' Craig shrugged.

'Craig, have you seen me? I'm hardly *Baywatch* material. Apart from these babies,' I said, pointing at my chest, 'I'd probably be turned down for *Readers' Wives*.'

Craig shrugged again. 'I don't know what it is about you. You don't show flesh, except for that little bit of curved abdomen where your tops never quite reach the top of your trousers. And your bum's not exactly pert, but it's juicy and round. And your breasts, always encased in jersey tops, but . . . I don't know, I really don't. Maybe it's the way your hair's so black and the way it touches the nape of your neck, or the way you smile and show all your teeth . . . to be honest, Ceri, I don't know what it is, but I can guarantee that after I've seen you, I'll have sex with my ex-girlfriend. Most of the time I can hardly bring myself to talk to her, but I've been with her almost every day since you started. We even have a laugh together.'

'Bollocks.'

'It's true. I don't know why, but it's true. I mean, before, I hated her. Really hated her. I'd go out of my way to avoid her or anywhere she might be, but I swear to God, since you started working here, I can't keep away from her.'

I picked up the teaspoon, ran it under the tap. I dipped it back into the cup of brown liquid, an oily film had formed and when I withdrew it, clumps of the film stayed on the spoon.

Without thinking, I poured milk into my tea. Stirred. I put the cup to the lips, the strong scent of peppermint stopped me drinking. I looked into the cup, it looked horrible, it would've tasted worse.

'Anyway Ceri, got to go, but good luck with the research.'

'Mmm?' I replied, looking up. Craig was halfway out the door with his papers in his arms.

'See ya,' he called.

'Oh, yeah, see ya.'

'Well, it's obvious, isn't it?' Drew said to me on the phone. 'He fancies you.'

'No he doesn't,' I said. Drew now knew the conversation with Craig word for word and I'd waited with baited breath for his opinion. He came next in the list of people to consult when I had a dilemma. Jess, with her several trillion degrees came first, she was the smartest person I knew.

Drew, who went under the moniker of 'my other best friend' only seemed to be contactable via phone nowadays even though we worked in the same city – in fact, I saw him more when I lived in London.

'Only a man who fancies you notices all that about you,' Drew added.

I sighed. 'Will you stop. He doesn't fancy me. It was only when I told him about my research that he brought it up. I mean, I'd told him I was single before, he never leapt on that. It was only the subliminal bit that got him to say that. He was obviously speaking as he thought, not flirting.'

'Oh.'

'Anyway, it'd be a pretty bad way to flirt with me, wouldn't it, saying he was still knocking off his ex-girlfriend?'

'True.'

'And he's not the first person to say it to me. Someone else said the same thing but not in the

264

same way. And *they* certainly didn't fancy me.' That's what had freaked me out about what Craig said, it reminded me of Jess saying that I made men fancy her. I made people do things and that couldn't be right. I had to get a third opinion. Hence the calling of Drew at his management consultancy conference, which I'd never do unless it was a real emergency. Which this was, in a way. 'Do you want to have sex after you see me?'

Drew thought about it for a few seconds. 'No. Can't say I do. Sex doesn't even enter my mind.'

Big foamy waves of relief washed over me. I wasn't a freak. I didn't send people scurrying off to satisfy their lusts elsewhere. Then I was completely affronted. The Git. After flirting with me for all those years, after cuddling up to me and having pornographic conversations with me, sex didn't even *enter* his mind. He really was an affection tease, wasn't he? Or, horror of horrors, had I always been so sexually uninteresting to him that he could flirt with me by rote? That thought made me shudder.

'Tell you something, though, I did always pull with you around,' Drew's voice said thoughtfully.

'What?'

'Yeah, thinking about it now, whenever we went clubbing, I'd always pull. Always. It was weird. It never happened when I went out without you.'

'WHAT?!'

'It's true, you were like my lucky charm. I couldn't get a girl to look twice at me when I went clubbing without you, but with you, I was like the most popular man on earth.'

'So how did you pull Tara then?'

'That was a fluke. And she didn't go for me for my looks, it was my personality that attracted her.'

'I didn't realise just how bad her taste was.'

'Funny. Anyway, are you sure this guy wasn't coming on to you?' Drew asked.

'No. I mean, yes, I'm sure he wasn't coming on to me. At least I think he wasn't.'

'So you admit the possibility?'

I thought about it. It was a possibility that Craig was coming on to me. So slim a possibility it didn't even qualify as a poss. 'It is possible. Less possible than, say, me marrying Angel, but a possibility.'

'You're a freak, you know that?' Drew replied.

'And that's why you love me, right?' I said.

I could hear him smile down the phone. 'Absolutely.'

'But what does it mean?' I said, flopping back into the office chair.

'Don't know,' Drew replied, the line rustled as he switched his mobile from one ear to the other. 'Maybe you just appeared in one of his dreams – of the moist variety.'

I sighed. 'It didn't sound like that.'

'Or maybe it's an X-file. Y'know, one of those mysteries we'll never work out, like how you, an almost thirty-year-old woman, could still believe you're going to marry Angel.'

'You know, sod you Drew, time will prove me

266

right on that. And when it does, you're going to be a bridesmaid – and wear a dress.'

Drew laughed.

'Oh, you laugh, but you will.'

Drew laughed some more. 'Anyway gorgeous, gotta get back to it. Talk to you soon?'

'Yeah, talk to you soon.'

'And don't worry about what that bloke said. He probably just has a very poor flirting style. You know, trying to get you into bed by being clever. He wouldn't be the first, that's for sure.'

'Yeah, you're probably right,' I said. A voice at the back of my head said, *He's not right, you know he's not right.*

CHAPTER 22

GOOD ENOUGH

The day of Ed's Big Date dawned and I was nervous.

Actually I was shitting myself, for want of a better expression. This was Ed. This was his one big chance to impress the gorgeous Robyn. And I'd been the one who'd pushed him into doing the deed.

Oh God, what if this all turned nasty? What if she was a nightmare and she made his date hell? Who would he blame? Who would he have every right to blame? Me, of course. *Then* what would I do? Find him another woman to lust after? Yeah, right. Most people needed love in their life. And if not love, then someone or something to lust after. Robyn was Ed's *raison d'être*. The reason he got out of bed most mornings. The reason he'd hacked off his hair and retired his lumberjack shirt. And I'd practically held a gun to his head and forced him to ask her out. I wouldn't be surprised if he turned that very same gun on me and blew my brains out.

He'd have every right. I would, if he took away my *raison d'être*. My purpose, the one thing that kept me believing in love and happy endings. There were times, during those barren weeks, months and years where all you had to keep you going was seeing that one person, that perfect computer, those exquisite shoes – that one thing that made the rest of the bad times that plagued your existence worthwhile.

Case in point: my obsession with *Angel*.

I was enough of a psychologist to know that it'd gotten out of hand, that I'd started to believe he and I were meant to be together for ever because I hadn't seen a man or a computer or a pair of shoes that gave me the same kick. Nothing got my undivided attention like him. Nothing made my heart beat faster, or my stomach tingle or my face smile like he did. Consistently.

But, finding out that your perfect shoes would, over time, amputate your little toes; that the computer would give you incurable RSI; or that person you loved was actually sent to this earth to make you suffer a lifetime's worth of indignity (or, after one shag would lose their soul, then hunt down and kill all your friends, oh, wait, no that's Angel) was information you could live without. And you usually only found out the downside of your dream when you got the thing you wanted, in other words: be careful what you wish for, it may come true. In Ed's case, going on a date with Robyn.

I went to work on that Wednesday morning as usual, but I left after my last lecture. Didn't hang around in the library or work in my office or go anywhere near the Senior Common Room to get my weekly dose of Gwen. I came straight home and spent the entire bus journey offering up a prayer that Robyn would like the posh restaurant he'd planned to take her to. That she'd laugh at his jokes. She'd appreciated the sacrifice he'd made with his hair. That she wouldn't lurch with disgust if he tried to kiss her. That she would see past anything that could possibly put her off and realise what a genuinely decent guy Ed was. He and Jake had gone out of their way to make me the third wheel on their Stanmore Vale tricycle. They didn't have to, they just did because the pair of them were good people. *Please God, let her realise that.*

Ed was in his room when I got home. I didn't disturb him, didn't want to add to any anxiety he might have with anxieties of my own. I pottered around the kitchen, attempting to cook but getting distracted by thoughts of Ed coming home after his date a broken man with nothing left to live for. Every self-help book I'd read and started to read had mentioned something about visualisation – visualising the result you wanted from a situation, seeing it in your head helped it to come true. Would it work for other people? Who cared? I settled myself on the sofa nearest the window.

OK. Ed and Robyn. Had to visualise something great. The perfect date.

I didn't know what she looked like, Ed's description – 'an angel on earth' – hadn't been particularly helpful, so in my mind's eye she became Halle Berry, a gorgeous woman, no mistaking.

Right, visualise Robyn/Halle and Ed sitting in Teppanyaki, that Japanese restaurant in town, he tells her a joke. And she . . . she tuts and carries on eating. No. No. She . . . tuts and carries on eating. OK, change scenario.

Ed says he'll see her home. She smiles, agrees, says most blokes just put her on the bus. They get to her front door, which bears a remarkable resemblance to our front door. Once there, Ed says he had a great time, can he see her again? She smiles and says yes. Ed asks if he can kiss her, she replies: 'Euck, no!'

Noooo, that was going so well.

I opened my eyes. *Ah, sod it. If she upsets him, I'll just do away with her and visualise my way through the perfect murder.*

I answered the door to Robyn at seven-thirty.

And double-took at her. Halle Berry had nothing on her. She was so stunning, *I* had faint stirrings in my loins. Her hair was plaited to waist length (when I had plaited extensions, they never looked that perfect) and framed her slender face with its wide nose. She had dark brown eyes, full lips and styled eyebrows. And her skin, flawless. It could've been make-up, but I was sure it was natural beauty. And probably not drinking, not smoking and doing the gym thing. Her and Ed would make a great couple: her, all slender limbs and poise; him,

271

tall and, when he stood up straight, he looked quite manly. At least she'd made an effort, I thought with relief. Having said that, she didn't seem the kind of woman who'd leave the house without making an effort. She certainly wouldn't do a Ceri D'Altroy and leave the house to get a newspaper and bottle of water with her uncombed hair squashed under a scarf, wearing crumpled clothes, an uncleansed face and unbrushed teeth.

'Come in,' I said, stepping aside to let her in.

She stepped in, headed straight for the living room, like she'd been invited to do so. She certainly knew how to own a place by doing something as innocuous as walking in to it. Probably something she learnt in acting class. She was an artist, *darlink*.

'Would you like a drink or something while you're waiting?' I asked, with a smile. 'Ed shouldn't be too long.' I was on my best behaviour, didn't want to do anything to ruin Ed's chances.

'No,' she said. 'I'd rather we got going.'

'Oh, Ed won't be much longer.'

She moved her face as if to say. *He'd better not be*, then sat on the left-hand sofa, instantly brightening it up.

'Music?' I said, moving to the stereo.

'Do you have any acid jazz?'

What, that music that makes me think of bad and lengthy elevator music? 'Er, no. I'm sure I can find a radio station that plays it though.'

'Don't bother.'

272

Right. 'What about telly? *Corrie*'s started.' I had one hand ready to hit the 'on' button.

'I don't watch *Coronation Street*. I went for an audition once and I didn't get it. It upsets me to watch it.'

H'OK. I withdrew my finger. I stood by the television, with this incredible urge to twiddle my fingers and hum out of tune. Minutes passed. More minutes passed. I knew Ed would've heard the doorbell. Even he wouldn't be stupid enough to keep her waiting. Not if he wanted the date to start off well.

Robyn's dark eyes flickered over me, giving me the distinct impression it was my fault Ed wasn't in front of her.

'I'll just go see what's keeping him,' I said to her.

She hinted at a thin smile of gratitude with her lipsticked lips, then decided not to bother.

Ohhhh, does she not like me. She's not the first woman not to like me. I doubted she'd be the last. Just like I didn't particularly like girly girls; girly girls didn't particularly like ungirly girls. Which was cool. As long as we both stuck to our respective areas of expertise – her: hair, make-up, boys: me, science fiction, psychology and using my brain.

I pegged it up the stairs, turned the corner, sped to Ed's door and tapped on it.

'Ed?' I whispered loudly through the door. The living room door was still open, I didn't want her to hear.

No answer.

I tapped again.

'*Ed!* Ed, Ed, what you doing? She's getting really wound up down there.'

Nothing in reply. I knew he was in there, I could hear him walking around. Pacing, whispering.

'Ed. What are you doing in there?'

Nothing. Pacing, whispering. I tapped the door again, louder. 'Ed, open this bloody door,' I hissed. 'What are you doing?'

The door unlocked, his head appeared in the fraction he opened it. 'I'm stuffed, Ceri.'

His blue shirt collar stood on end on one side, horizontal on the other side. His tie was tied over it, his face flushed, his eyes wide and desperate.

'What do you mean, stuffed?'

He was breathing hard, a possessed man who still had the devil at his heels.

'She's going to leave if you're not careful,' I said.

His terrified eyes searched mine. 'I'm stuffed, Ceri, I'm stuffed.'

'Stop saying that! You're not. Tell me what you mean.'

Ed jerked the door open. 'I mean, this.' He pointed to his lap. I followed his pointing finger.

Outlined in his trousers, loose as they were, was a long, thick shape. The material of his loose trousers was taut around it emphasising it. You couldn't miss it. I tore my eyes away, thinking, *Who'd have guessed that skinny Ed was so big?*

He grabbed my wrist, pulled me into the room,

shut the door behind him. 'I can't get rid of it,' he said.

'What?'

'I can't get rid of,' he pointed southward again, '*IT!*'

He paced the length of his room. 'I've tried everything I know. I've tried playing with it, orgasms, ignoring it, cold showers, flicking the top of it . . . nothing works. I can't get rid of it.'

'Not even flicking the top of it?'

He shook his head.

'How hard did you flick?'

'Hard! Fucking hard! It hurt. It bruised, but it wouldn't die. I can't go on a date like this. She'll think I'm a sleaze. And I can't even change cos these are the biggest trousers I've got apart from my jogging bottoms.'

He was indeed, stuffed.

'And, and, I swear, it's got bigger. It was never, well, you know.'

'Eh?' I said, trying hard not to stare at it.

'I'm not saying I was small or owt, but it was never that big.'

From my side of the room, I raised my hand, held it up in that area so Ed's lower half would be hidden and I wouldn't be tempted to gawp at it.

'How long have you been like this?'

'All day. I was pleased at first, I kind of hoped I'd be up to the challenge. I mean, I'm nothing. I'm not as good-looking or funny or famous as her other fellas. I don't know, I just . . .'

'Hoped, prayed, wished you could be better in one way,' I cut in. 'Just one way, you want to outshine the competition. You can't change your looks, you can't change your bank balance and it'll take her a while to get to know your true personality. But in one way, just one way you want to stand out. Be superior, be worthy.

'This is, this was, your one chance with someone you've wanted, yearned for, for months. This person is number one. You never thought this day would come and now it has come, you're terrified that you won't live up to the challenge. That now your dream's come true, it's all going to go wrong because of you. Not cos she's a cow, but because of you. You not being good enough.'

I suppose you could say I had some vague idea of how Ed felt. That deep yearning, that not good enough feeling, that wondering 'when will it be my turn to get the big prize?' Self-help book, smelf-help book, when you never got the boy – or girl – you didn't feel good about yourself. Your positivity was eroded, you seized on every little sniff of romance as THE NEXT BIG THING.

'That's all very well, but what the hell am I going to do?' Ed wailed.

I shifted my hand a fraction, peeked at what should have been his very big pride. The first – and last – time I saw a male member nearly as big had been attached to Mr Perfect Penis and I'd initially been disturbed by its size. When I got to know it, it'd been all right. But I'd been overcome with lust for him from the instant I saw him. It remained to be seen if Robyn even liked Ed; if he went out on a date like that, she'd think he was disgusting. She'd leave before he even got to the restaurant, let alone offered to pay for dinner.

'There's only one thing you can do, mate,' I said.

CHAPTER 23

THE LOVE CV

'You told him to what?' Jess said, when I told her the sketchiest details of Ed's predicament.

We were back in the Black Bull. So much for her not drinking with me again. Although, technically, she wasn't drinking with me again in that respect. We were about to go shopping in Morrison's, Horsforth, so we'd done our usual and gone for a fortifying drink down the road beforehand. We used to go shopping every Wednesday night when I lived up in Cookridge years ago. After *Star Trek: Next Generation*, she'd drive round, pick me up, we'd shop then go back to our lives. We'd slipped back into that routine, but this time on Tuesday, after *Star Trek: Voyager*.

'Well, it was either that or cancel the date. And, short of maiming himself and being rushed to casualty – which I'm not sure would've convinced her anyway – he couldn't cancel. Not if he wanted another date with her. It'd taken the poor lad months to work up the courage to ask her out in the first place. Which, I suspect, was why he was in that state.'

'But still . . .'

'What would you have got him to do, Dr Breakfield?'

Jess shrugged. 'Cover it up.'

'I kid you not, it was huge. Not being funny, right, but I've only ever seen one penis that large and, to be honest, it wasn't as big as Ed's was and I was a little scared of that one. Every other part of Ed's trousers were baggy on him, but it was like a huge pole, straining there. I can't get the image of it out of my mind. And I don't want to think like that about Ed. Not ever. Anyway, if I'd told him to cover it up, he'd have had to hide behind a large *AA Road Map* for the rest of his life.'

'Did your plan work?'

I shrugged. 'I don't know.' I sipped from my pint of beer Jess had bought me. 'But I haven't seen him since that night. Neither has Jake.'

Jess stopped. She'd leant forwards to scrunch out her cigarette in the ashtray but stopped and looked at me. 'You're joking! Tell me you're joking.'

I shook my head. 'Jake said that he got a message on his mobile from Ed and it was just hysterical laughter.'

'NO!'

'Oh yes. And that's not all. When Jake called him back, Ed just mumbled "bliss" and hung up.'

Jess put out her cigarette and shook her head incredulously. She turned to me, shook her head some more. 'Let me get this straight. You advise someone to tell a woman he's got the hots for her so desperately that he's perma-erect and it *works*? She actually buys it?'

I pushed the ashtray closer to her. 'There was more to it than that,' I replied. 'I told him to tell her the truth. To explain how much he liked her, why he liked her, because it was more than her looks. The guy genuinely adores her. So he told her. Not the "I adore you" bit. More the *reasons* he likes her, for example, he remembers exactly what she was wearing when they first met, he listens when she speaks, he gets excited every time she even looks at him. He often wants to tell her something because he knows she'll appreciate it. So he told her. And he also told her how inadequate he feels compared to her other boyfriends. How he was terrified that he'd screw up on this date and he'd not get another chance. And how his perceived inadequacies had worked like Viagra. I'm assuming it worked.

'With an ego the size of hers, I'd have been more surprised if it hadn't worked.'

Jess nodded slowly, her face deep in thought. She leant forwards and took a cigarette from the packet that lay between us, her arm slung across her stomach.

'Don't take this the wrong way, Ceri, but it occurs to me that you live everyone else's life with the volume turned right up, but your own life is pretty barren.'

'Barren?' I said.

'Don't get that pet lip with me, Ceresis D'Altroy.' Now she was using my full name. What was she going to do next, slash my throat with a broken bottle? 'I said not to take it the wrong way.'

'What way is there to take it?'

'What I mean is, you can do almost anything with someone else's love life but yours, well, you think you're going to end up with Angel.'

'I can't help it if all the men I meet turn out to be freaks.'

'What about Vincent? He sounded nice enough.'

'Yes, and he could only have sex if *Inspector Morse* was playing in the background. He couldn't even get it up if it wasn't on.'

Jess's face double-took into true disgust.

'I don't tell you everything, you see. I do try to protect you from the horrors of my love life.'

'What about, erm, what was his name, Luke?'

'Forgot to mention his girlfriend was eight months pregnant.'

'Adam?'

'His ex-wife cheated on him so all women, particularly his girlfriends, are devil's spawn. Of course, then there was the time some guy smiled at me and he almost beat him up.'

'Paul? I met Paul, he was lovely.'

'Yes, when I saw him, he was lovely. But he kept disappearing for weeks after we'd seen each other. When I called it a day, he started sending me pornographic emails telling me how much he wanted to F star star K me.'

'What about the, erm, television producer?'

'Was getting married and I was his last fling. I found out when I opened the local paper and there he was with his bride.'

'The graphic designer?' Jess's voice was waning.

'Some bloke pushed him in the street, so he went out the next day with a knife in his jacket in the hope he'd see the bloke again and stab him.'

'The other graphic designer?'

Jess braced herself to hear about this one.

'Erm, let's see, his best male friend turned up one night, to join us in bed. And he was really "upset" when I said no, got dressed and left.'

'The guy working on his novel?'

'He stopped calling me after three dates. You can go through the whole list of men and at the end of it, you'll find they all have one thing in common: they are all freaks. I don't do it on purpose. I don't go out looking for them. But they seem to have this ability to track me down. Hunt me out of the crowd, as it were, like I'm a wounded animal.'

'Doesn't that worry you?'

'Yeah! These are the thoughts that keep me awake at night. I'm convinced I'm going to spend the rest of my life alone or dating freaks. I don't know what it is, but I can pick a nutter at thirty paces. And I'm scared I'm going to keep doing that for the rest of my life. The closest I've got to a relationship was with N— Whashisface Tosspot, and look how that turned out.' (It turned out with me sneaking around for months buying a flat without telling him so he couldn't stop me with his line in emotional blackmail (aka Jedi Mind Trick/Work Of The Devil). He was a man about it, though: when I told him I was moving and started packing, he didn't say anything. At all. Or try to stop me. It had nothing to do with my brothers being with me, I'm sure.)

'What about that thing with you and Drew?' Jessica asked, looking in her cigarette packet and finding it empty. She tossed it back on the table.

'Drew has a girlfriend, remember?'

'Yes, I remember. But he was always so keen on you, why weren't you interested?'

I almost choked on my beer. 'Me, not interested? I think you'll find it was the other way around.'

'No,' Jess said, thoughtfully, 'the way he used to look at you . . . I remember in lectures I'd always catch him staring at you. Even when you'd both finished college, I remember at parties he'd be all over you. Or would look so jealous if he saw you talking to another man. It was . . . I reckon you were his reserve option.'

'His what?' I said, eyeing my best friend. I didn't like the way this conversation was going. Actually, I didn't like this conversation at all. I didn't need to be reminded that my love life was, as she said, 'barren'.

'I think he thought of you as the woman he'd end up with if something better didn't come along.'

My head creaked round to face Jess full on. 'Excuse me! Who are you? Because I'm sure my best friend isn't allowed to say such things to me.'

'God, Ceresis, you're being really touchy today.'

She was doing it again – calling me by my bloody full name.

'Touchy?' I stated. 'You've just said that I wasn't important enough for Drew to fall in love with unless he had no other options. And you've just called me Ceresis twice. Why wouldn't I be touchy?'

'No sweetie—'

'Don't you "sweetie" me, Dr Jessica Breakfield,' I cut in.

'So you'd prefer Ceresis?' she replied.

I gritted my teeth and bared them at her.

'OK, *sweetie*, what I'm saying is, there's something about you. Makes men think that they can be . . . I don't know. Whashisface Tosspot did it, he sucked the vitality out of you so he could get a personality. By the time you and he ended, he was a different person. He didn't speak in that ridiculous way and he actually had conversational skills. He'd even stopped tucking his jumpers into his jeans, if what you told me was true. As a result, he ended up getting married less than a year after you got away from him. Drew used you as some kind of surrogate girlfriend, always coming back to you when things were going wrong, his safety net for not getting disheartened when another one

284

of his relationships went pear-shaped. He kept coming back to you until he met his current girl-friend . . . there's something about you.'

A chill went through me and what Drew said to me the other day came to mind. '*You were like my lucky charm. I couldn't get a girl to look twice at me when I went clubbing without you, but with you, I was like the most popular man on earth,*' his voice said in my head.

'Loads of women get treated badly by men,' I said to Jess, trying to dislodge that thought from my head. This was all going down the 'you make me do things' route. A particular route I wasn't keen to venture down right now. Or ever again, for that matter.

Jess nodded. 'True. But you're different. Have you ever been in love, Ceri?'

I didn't have to think about that question. Not at all. Have I ever been in lust – absolutely (Mr PP, prime example); have I ever been in deep like – yup (man I usually called 'Love Of My Life', who left me for someone else); have I ever been in stupidity – damn right (Whashisface Tosspot, take a bow). But love? It was odd when I thought about it. When I really thought about it. I was, the coming summer, about to start the fourth decade of my life and yet, I hadn't experienced romantic love. I hadn't said it to someone and meant 'I love you and I'm in love with you'. Well, no one who wasn't Angel, Arnold Schwarzenegger, etc. I'd never looked at someone in front of me and thought, 'I love you. I can't live without you' and knew he felt the same way.

I'd been through the whole spectrum of emotions in my life, anger, lust, hate, rage, joy, happiness, indifference, anticipation, but I'd constantly skipped over the segment where romantic love lay. Jess was right, my heart was barren. It'd never been toiled over and planted and weeded and watered by someone else. It'd never been loved, like other people's hearts had been loved. If I told people that I'd never been out with anyone, they'd immediately bring up the man I lived with. Not knowing, not understanding that I'd *shared* a flat with him. I had my own bedroom. That everyone around us, particularly his family and his friends, thought I was his flat-mate – and the woman he sometimes shagged – and because of that, I was never invited to weddings or christenings or family parties. And people who thought I'd lived with someone never knew that the one time he ever said 'I love you', he'd immediately taken it back by adding, 'You do realise I mean I love you as I love all my other friends, don't you?' If I told people I hadn't been out with anyone, they didn't realise I meant, I hadn't ever been with anyone long enough for the L word to come up.

So, no, I didn't need to think about whether I'd been in love before.

'Not with anyone who's loved me back,' I replied to Jess. 'None of my relationships last long enough for me to fall in love and have them fall in love with me.'

'That's really shit, Ceri,' Jess said. Her voice sounded how I often felt when it came to the subject of my love life, defeated. Others may whine about their troubles with men, but I'll bet every one of them had some good relationship years to show for it. They'd experienced that mythical state known as 'In Love'. I had . . . Whashisface Tosspot. And if there was ever a man you didn't need on your love CV, it was him. For him to be the best you can do, well I wouldn't employ me as a partner if he was the best reference I had.

'I know,' I said to Jess, agreeing with her my love life was indeed shit.

'But at least we've got chocolate and beer,' she said, her voice rallying suddenly Trying to drag us out of the bog that was my love life.

'True,' I agreed.

'So, let's get going to Morrison's and not leave until we get some of that.'

'God, Jess, you're going to be fifty,' I said, wondrously.

It was one of those moments where I said what was on my mind. I'd looked over Jess, tall, slender, waves and waves of auburn hair and hardly a wrinkle in sight – despite those propagated theories on smoking and skin. She looked about thirty-two, thirty-three at the most, not closer to fifty. Fifty. My best mate was going to be fifty when I hadn't even cleared my thirties. Which was why I said it.

Jess froze as she put mushrooms in a plastic bag. 'Thanks a lot Ceri,' she said incredulously.

'I didn't mean it like that,' I said.

'Oh, and how *did* you mean it?'

'That you don't look that old.'

Jess's eyes widened.

'No, no, no, no, that came out wrong, too.'

'Hmmm,' Jess replied, twisting her face to show how unimpressed she was.

'It was a compliment,' I floundered. 'Honest.'

'Hmmm,' Jess replied.

'I suppose I'll go get the peppers,' I said, waving around the plastic bag in my hand. I turned on my heels and headed towards the capsicum section of Morrison's.

'You're going be fifty too one day,' Jess said as I walked away.

'I know,' I said. 'I wasn't saying you would and I wouldn't.'

'If you're lucky,' she hissed.

Jess, who was generally laid-back about most things was probably cross with me now. I really hadn't meant it like that. Even though she'd not an hour ago told me my life was barren, reminded me I'd never been in love and called me Ceresis (*twice*), I hadn't meant to upset her. To curry favour, I wandered past the peppers and round to the next aisle, I'd get her a frozen pizza, then jazz it up with vegetables and make fresh garlic bread.

Then she'd forgive me. The route to Jess's forgiveness centre was, like mine, through her stomach.

I turned the corner, to the next aisle. And there he was About to lean in to grab a frozen pizza. My heart skipped a beat.

Staring Man.

Instinctively I jumped back out of sight. My heart galloping in my chest. I pegged it back to the produce aisle.

'Jess, Jess,' I hissed loudly.

'What?' she replied, still in a strop.

I beckoned rapidly to her. 'Quick, quick, come here.'

She glowered at me for a second.

'*QUICK!*' I hurried.

She came wandering over. I grabbed her arm, dragged her to the corner. I stuck my head around the corner; she did the same.

'There he is,' I said.

'Who?' she asked, even though he was the only one down that aisle.

I pointed. 'Him!'

'Who is he?'

I shrugged. 'I don't know, but he hates me.'

'Why?'

'I don't know.'

'You must have done something.'

'I haven't! I've never even spoken to the man, but every time I see him at college or in the street or in the pub, he just stares at me.'

'Really?'

'Yeah.'

'And you've never spoken to him?'

'Nope. I just turn around and there he is,' I opened my eyes wide, 'glaring at me. I don't know why.'

As if he had a radar for people staring at him, SM looked up.

Jess and I both jumped back, clinging to each other. We got ridiculously silly and ran back to the trolley, both of us shaking and giggling.

'But why is he always staring at me?' I asked, when we were sure that he hadn't clocked us and stopped giggling.

'Hmmm,' Jess said, thoughtfully. 'I don't know. You're this striking woman with this presence wherever she goes, and two of the biggest, natural breasts known to man, I haven't got a clue why he stares at you.'

'Even when you're being nice you're a sarcastic cow.'

'Something to do with being nearly fifty, I think.'

'I didn't mean it like that.'

'Yeah, yeah.'

'Can we get back to the matter in hand? Staring Man. It's really disturbing.'

'I've told you before, disturbing things happen when you're around.'

'But why does he stare at me? Those big eyes staring at me from this blank face. It gives me the willies.'

'Ceri, sweetheart, I'm sure that's all he wants to give you.'

My eyes almost leapt out of my head. 'JESSICA BREAKFIELD! I can't believe you just said that.'

Jess shrugged. 'It's true. Him, man. You, woman. He wants to, what's that phrase you youngsters use? Oh yes, roger you senseless.'

My eyes widened and my mouth fell open. 'Filthy mind.' I took over the trolley-pushing duties. 'Filthy mind.'

I pushed the trolley down the aisle, towards the long line of narrow checkouts. 'Filthy, filthy mind.'

Jess lit a cigarette against the strong breeze in the car park, then stood smoking it by Fred's car, while I pushed the trolley back and went to retrieve my pound coin. I was still reeling from her filthiness. My best friend wasn't meant to say things like that. That was one of the advantages of having a best mate who was older than you, they didn't say such things. Having thought that, Jess and I were of a similar mind, and I did have a tendency to let my imagination run free when it came to sex.

Especially, when it came to Angel . . . I stood patiently behind someone as they struggled to retrieve their pound coin from the trolley contraption while I contemplated Angel. I often wondered what it'd be like if *he* gave me the willies. Well, I knew, from the detail and the vividness of my imagination what it'd be like. Fantastic. One of those nights you'd never forget. Even when you were eighty-nine you'd drag it up from your memory and hold it up to scrutiny. And every time, you'd get those chills and tingles down below. Oh yes, one night with Angel would be like one night in heaven. A bad pun, but so tru—

'This thing's broken,' the man in front of me said. My knees involuntarily weakened at his voice. It was deep and warm, like sinking into a hot bath after a hard day; like snuggling down in front of a real fire when it's snowing outside. His voice made all my body tingle with pleasure. (I really was rather sexually frustrated, wasn't I? I was getting excited over a voice!)

I looked up at the source of the voice. He looked back at me. We both started at who we were looking at. Staring Man.

I ripped my eyes away, my face and body suddenly aflame. This was the closest we'd ever been. And after what Jess had said about him wanting to give me the willies, my body started to burn with embarrassment. My knees had gone weak when I heard his voice. Him, the man who obviously disliked me. Waves of red-hot mortification crashed down on me all over again.

'This thing's broken,' he repeated. His voice still had the same effect on my knees, even though I knew it was him.

'Oh,' was all I could think to say as I looked back at him. I suppose I'd never thought he had a voice. He seemed to glare at me more than anything else, so I knew he had eyes and a face. But not a voice. I'd also now worked out that he had a thing about Mel. It was abundantly clear. He'd been giving me evils because he fancied Mel. He'd seen me leave the party with Mel, so was pissed off about it. Then, he'd seen me hugging Ed, jumped to the conclusion that I was doing the dirty on his Mel. I'd be the same if, say, I thought Fred was doing the dirty on Jess. Then in the SCR, he'd seen me acting all normal with Mel and probably thought I was some two-faced slut who was going to break his precious Mel's heart.

'I suppose we should go find someone to report it to,' he said.

'But that would mean queuing and talking to someone who will invariably decide that my need for my pound back gives them licence to patronise me,' I observed, even though I was still rather overcome by this ill-meeting. All we needed was a spot of moonlight and I'd be well within my rights to start quoting Shakespeare.

'True,' he replied.

'Do you have a hairpin or a nail file? I've got a mean trick to get pound coins out of these contraptions, no probs. It's a South Londoner thing.'

'Really?' His eyes doubled in awe. He was impressed.

'No,' I replied. I'd not have said it if I thought he'd be *that* impressed. 'I just say things like that,' I explained. 'I can't help myself.'

'Oh, right. Kind of like Lieutenant Barclay?'

My heart stopped. 'You reference *Star Trek*,'

I breathed. My heart started beating again, but I was suddenly breathless with admiration and awe. It was always a genuine shock and moment of true kinship when I met someone who wasn't me or Jess, who could drop *Star Trek* into a normal conversation. If he didn't hate me and fancy Mel, I'd be seeing him in soft focus, hearing romantic harp music and melting in his arms, right about now.

'You know my references to *Star Trek*.' He sounded equally surprised and impressed. We let a moment of silence pass between us as we formed a bond of mutual admiration.

'Are you *DS9* or *Voyager*?' he asked.

'I'm *Next Gen*. But *Voyager*'s second.'

Anyone listening to us would think we were talking in code, unless they watched *Star Trek*. *Star Trek: Next Generation* (my favourite); *Star Trek: Voyager* (my second favourite); *Star Trek: Deep Space Nine* (I'd grown to love it over time); and then of course there was the original series, but not necessarily the best.

SM raised his eyebrows. 'I'm a bit torn. *Voyager*'s good, but then, so's *Next Gen*. I think, though, I prefer *DS9*.'

'Most men do cos a lot of it was war games and politics. I had a bit of a *DS9* marathon once and really got into it. I can't help liking old Avery Brooks either.'

'What, Mr Hawk himself?' SM teased. 'You like all that wearing shades at night stuff?'

'You did *not* watch *Spenser: For Hire*,' I said, aghast. *God, maybe I dismissed those harp players and the soft-focus visuals too quickly.*

'I did too!' SM replied, not one hint of embarrassment. 'I've even got a few episodes on tape.'

'Me too!' I replied. 'But despite Hawk being in *DS9* I, er, can't give up my love for a spot of Will Riker and Jean-Luc. And Worf.'

SM's face broke into a huge grin, softening his chiselled features. He was really quite attractive – but that was probably a lot to do with us having such a big thing in common. Television. 'I like a bit of Worf myself, but I was glad he and Deanna didn't get together in the end. I can't abide Deanna Troi.'

'Me either!' I laughed.

'Have you seen *Enterprise* yet?'

I shook my head. 'Nope.'

'Me neither,' SM replied.

'Can't say I'm that keen on the idea, but I'm sure it'll insinuate itself into my affections like all the others did.'

'True,' he said.

We let another moment of *Star Trek*-induced admiration pass in silence.

'So, how long have you known Mel?' I asked, groping for the only other subject we had in common, hoping to bond there, too.

SM looked down at the trolley he had his hand on, started fiddling with the lump of metal that held on tight to his pound coin. *I'm right, he does*

295

have a thing about Mel. And this is my chance to show him Mel and I are just mates. That I'm not trying to muscle in on his territory.

'Not long. Well, since I started at All Souls, about two years ago. He's a good bloke is our Mel.'

Our Mel. 'Yeah, I really like him, h—'

'Oi, D'Altroy, what are you doing?' Jess's voice cut in. I jumped slightly, then turned around. She was leaning out of the driver's window of her car, looking rather impatient. By standing there, trying to ingratiate myself with what was, essentially, The Enemy, I was lengthening the time between cigarettes for her.

'Hey,' SM said, 'how about I give you a pound and you give me a pound then it'll seem as though we've got our pounds back from the trolleys.'

'Good plan,' I said. I rummaged into my jeans pocket and handed over a pound coin.

'Got change for a fiver?' he said, holding out a five pound note.

I looked at him, unimpressed.

'Only joking,' he said, with a smile, then took a pound coin out of his jeans pocket and gave it to me.

'See you around,' I said, then scuttled around the metallic blue Mondeo and got in.

'Yeah,' he said. Staring Man started off across the car park towards, I presumed, his car.

'So,' Jess said as she pulled out the car park onto the road, 'hates you, does he?'

'Thanks to you, missus, he still does. I was just

about to tell him that Mel and I were just friends, so he knew I wasn't trying to get off with his man, and you came along tooting your horn and shouting your mouth off.'

'I did not toot my horn. Besides, I think the only horn going on around here came from him – and it wasn't for Mel.'

'JESSICA BREAKFIELD!' I screamed. 'WHAT HAS GOT INTO YOU?'

'Nothing for a while, actually.'

'OH MY GOD!' I screeched, then clamped my hands over my ears, 'DON'T YOU DARE SAY ANOTHER WORD UNTIL WE GET TO MY HOUSE.'

CHAPTER 24

BRUISER

'What the blinking hell happened to you?' Craig said as I wandered into the Senior Common Room.

Being Craig, he said this so loudly, most people in the SCR looked up, double-took at me.

After taking a deep breath, I replied: 'I walked into a door.'

How did that sound? Exactly. Had someone said that to me, I would've looked the same way as Craig and most of the people in the common room who were openly paying attention were looking at me then: *Yeah, right. Who were you fighting with, why were you fighting and do they look worse or better than you?*

Some of the faces around the room went back to conversations they were having, the notes they were reading, the coffee they were drinking. Some of the faces carried on openly staring at me. I didn't blame them, I'd got it on the bus into work, I'd got it in the street, I'd got it wandering through the corridors, I'd got it in my lecture first thing this morning. Anyone would think people hadn't seen a woman with a huge, great bruise on her face before.

298

Craig frowned very hard at me and my reply.

'I did,' I said. I carried my paper pile and my body, then slumped into the seat I always sat in. The tan leatherette seat would soon have a groove in the shape of my butt, I sat there so often. I noticed people who were sat there when I came in, moved. I probably unintentionally glowered at them for being anywhere near my seat. I liked that seat. It gave you a good view of most of the room, the dining/kitchenette area and both doors.

Gwen was sat next to my favourite seat, but I didn't care. If it was a toss up between the seat and her, or any other seat and not her, I'd take my seat. It was a fair pay-off.

Craig, the man I supposedly subliminally incited to have sex, followed me from his area of the SCR, sat himself down on the table opposite me.

'What happened, babe?' he asked. First time he'd ever called me babe. I recognised his softened tone, his brotherly expression. They were subliminally saying, 'Tell me who it was and I'll go get them for you.'

I did look a fright, though. Even I had to admit it. I'd worn my glasses – the cursed glasses – to take the edge off the vicious bruise that currently resided on my left cheek. I'd been surprised by its severity – and I'd been there when I'd been bashed in the face. What with my skin being such a dark brown, I thought it wouldn't be so bad. But this bruise was darker than my skin, tinged with black and purple and yellow. I'd baulked at myself in the mirror. Spent a lot of time trying to find angles to stand from that didn't make it look so bad. I did indeed look as though I'd been on the wrong end of a prize-fighter's rage.

Gwen was staring at me too with maternal concern. Nice though it was that they all cared, their concern was misplaced. I'd got double the amount of affection and care and attention from Jake. Again, trying to coax out of me what really happened.

'Do you really want to know what happened?' I asked Craig, tiredly.

Craig nodded.

'And do you promise you'll believe me, no matter how obscure the story?'

Craig nodded again. His whole face was frowning with concern.

'I walked into a door. Or, rather, a door swung into me. I was coming out of a sweet shop down in Headingley and someone coming in at high speed smacked me in the face with the door. It was all rather embarrassing cos I stumbled back-wards, reached out to steady myself and pulled down a free-standing rack of greetings cards with me. I don't know if you can imagine it, me, lying on the floor, under a rack of cards, writhing in agony on a Saturday lunch time, but it is truly my idea of hell. And then, to add insult to injury, liter-ally, I woke up Sunday with a mind-splitting headache and this huge bruise on my face.'

'Really?' Craig said.

'Yes, Craig.'

'Sure?'

'Positive, Craig.'

Craig still eyed me suspiciously.

I sighed. 'Thank you for your concern though, it's really touching.'

'OK, but if you need to talk . . .'

'I'll come find you. Thanks.'

With one last suspicious look, Craig got to his feet and went back to his life. I'd be telling this story for ages. I wondered who'd be the first to bring up the fact that where there's blame, there's a claim. I knew exactly who I'd be suing.

I was going to get stuff photocopied. In reprographics.

Since that encounter with Deirdre Barlow Glasses woman I'd done what other people did and camped out in the photocopying room and did it myself. Anything to avoid a row. Today, I didn't have the energy or time. I needed far more doing than normal and to be honest, why should I stand there breathing in fumes and getting Repetitive Strain Injury from pushing buttons when she and the rest of her 'gang' were paid to do it?

This time, I'd got Sally to get me the forms in advance and I'd filled them all in. All I had to do was take down my load, explain what needed to be done and to put them on 'Urgent', which meant I could get them done in forty-eight hours.

301

'Emergency', which would cost the department more, would be done in twenty-four hours. Deirdre Barlow Glasses hadn't explained that to me, had she?

Standing outside, I read REPROGRAPHICS (they'd changed the colour of the sign from orange to yellow because that was the kind of krazy with a 'k' type of people they were), took a deep breath and pushed open the swing doors. I even managed to put a smile on my face. Try not to annoy the people who can screw you over, was one of my many mottos. *Great.* The woman on duty behind the counter was, of course, Deirdre Barlow Glasses.

'Hi,' I said. 'Could I get these done on urgent?' I had my sweetest voice at work as I showed her my bundles, each with clearly marked instructions on Post-Its.

Her face remained like stone. Without moving any other part of her body, her arm reached out and retrieved a stack of forms from their envelopes on the wall beside her and slid them across at me.

'I've already filled in the forms,' I said, still smiling. I dumped the books on the counter, plucked off the forms and handed them to her.

She looked at them as though I was offering her a turd.

'They're the wrong forms for an urgent request. You'll have to fill these in. And make sure you've got the right budget code.'

Deep breath. Stay calm. She can screw you over.
'OK,' I said, took the forms. 'Can I borrow your pen?'

'We don't lend out pens. We have this problem with getting them back. Or not, as is usually the case.'

'Good thing I always carry one, then, isn't it?' I replied and pulled one from my pocket. 'Wouldn't want me walking off with your million-dollar pen.' That bit I said in my head.

I heard the swing doors open behind me and moved to one side to let the person coming in take their chances with the photocopying bitch from hell.

'Hi,' the male voice said. 'I've come for my stuff.'

My knees weakened at the voice.

'Ticket?' the woman demanded.

'Here we go,' he replied. 'I brought it in three days ago.' My knees did that melting thing again. I glanced up to see who it belonged to.

The man glanced sideways at me. Again, we both started at who we were looking at. Staring Man. I should've known by the effect he had on my knees.

I ripped my eyes away, my face and body suddenly aflame. I put the pen back to the sheet, but my hand was shaking. I couldn't even write properly because I knew, KNEW he was staring at me now. I could feel his eyes on the side of my face. I lowered my head even more, twisted my neck slightly so all he could see was the back of my head. I could still feel it though: I could feel his gaze, steady and unwavering, burning holes into the back of my black hair.

'We haven't finished your photocopying,' Deirdre Barlow Glasses said. 'You'll have to come back.'

'What?' Staring Man said.

'You'll have to come back later.'

'Don't talk to me in that tone of voice,' he said. 'I'm not the one in the wrong here. I asked for urgent repro and I've not got it. Would you like to accompany me to my lecture and explain to my students why I haven't got the material ready?'

Go Staring Man, go Staring Man.

She said nothing. Maybe she'd shaken her head.

'No, thought not. So don't give me attitude, lady. Just so you know, I'm not paying full price for this job and I'm going to be reporting you to my head of department.'

'While you're at it why don't you report me to God too?'

My head shot up. Cheeky cow. Not only was she rude to me, she actually had the audacity to nick my sarky retorts. Deirdre Barlow Glasses had gone, disappeared into the depth of the repro world and Staring Man was glaring at me. Actually, he was glaring at the part of my face which currently housed a massive bruise. I thought we'd sorted out all that stuff between us the week before last, but no. I hadn't got around to telling him that I wasn't interested in Mel. And, as it turned out, ten days was a long time between Staring Man and me.

'Er, look, I was, erm, hoping to run into you,' Staring Man began, then winced, looked down and started blushing furiously. 'I mean, I was hoping to see you.'

'Oh,' I replied. My heart was going ten to the dozen. Things had gone distinctly downhill between us since those halcyon days of the supermarket car park – because that person who'd been coming into the newsagent's at high speed and who'd helped the door connect with my face had, in fact, been Staring Man.

When I'd opened my eyes, dazed and confused as I was, I'd looked up and through the hail of greeting cards, there he was, doing what he did best, staring at me. Although, to be fair. shock and horror were carved into his features.

I'd let him and a couple of other people help me up but I'd legged it before anyone could say anything, including 'sorry'. Like I'd said to Craig, moments like that were my idea of hell. It'd been so busy in there, I couldn't bear to stay. I'd just pushed my way through the crowd of voyeurs and walked away as quickly as possible, clutching my face. I'd had to lie down for most of the afternoon when I got home because I felt so dizzy and sick every time I moved.

'I'm really sorry about, erm, your face,' Staring Man said. 'Is it painful?'

I shook my head. 'Not really. I mean, not any more.'

'I'm really sorry,' he repeated. 'You left far too quickly on Saturday for me to apologise properly.'

'It wasn't your fault, I wasn't looking where I was going.'

'Aww, you can't be blaming the victim. I was worried that you might have had concussion or something. Is there anything I can do?'

'Breathe?' I said, then cringed. *How the hell did that get out of my mouth? How did it get into my head in the first place? I can understand 'battered to death with a teaspoon', I can understand 'carpet that doesn't show up blood stains', but, 'breathe'?*

'Sorry?' he asked.

'Umm, you asked if there was anything you could do and, well, it's obvious that you can breathe.' *So, just as obviously I had to say it.*

Surprisingly, SM laughed. He had a laugh that matched his voice. Rich, deep. More tingles of pleasure flickered through my body. 'Another Lieutenant Barclay moment,' he said as though he understood. 'But, I must say, you're right there, I can breathe. What I meant was is there anything I can do—'

Deirdre Barlow Glasses chose that moment to reappear. 'If you come back in half an hour, we'll have your stuff for you,' she told SM. It didn't seem to bother her that she'd just interrupted our conversation.

SM turned his glare on her. 'I'd say thank you,

306

but I've nowt to thank you for, have I?' he said. 'See you around,' he said to me, then left. He'd obviously been put back into a bad mood by Deirdre Barlow Glasses. I watched the swing doors flump together behind him.

'Hi,' I said to the woman behind the counter. 'Filled in the right forms this time.'

Had she not:

a) nicked my sarky retort
b) interrupted my attempts to re-bond with SM
c) been a miserable old whore

I would have offered her a sympathetic smile – I knew what it was like to be on the receiving end of a Staring Man glare.

'Forty-eight hours,' she said. 'And don't forget your slip, you won't be able to get your photocopying without it. We will charge your department, though.'

'Thanks,' I replied. 'You have a nice day now.' *If you know how.*

'Ceri, hi,' a voice called from down the corridor as I was heading towards my office later that afternoon.

I stopped, looked around. I should have known by the squeak. Gwen. She came bounding towards me.

'I wanted to talk to you about the other day,' she said.

'Why? What did I do?' I asked, trying not to act shifty. Deirdre Barlow Glasses had reported me. The cow. She was probably in church now, reporting me to God, too.

'Nothing, nothing,' Gwen squeaked.

'So why do you want to talk to me?' I asked, eyeing her suspiciously.

'Maybe it's best we have a word in private,' Gwen said.

The cow. The miserable old cow had *reported me.* I was so going to be chucking a lighted flame in there at some point. All that paper and chemicals would go up in an instant. 'Are you sure I haven't done something wrong?'

Gwen rested a reassuring hand on my forearm. 'Of course not.'

Now she was plain scaring me.

'How about we go to my office. I think it's empty,' I said to Gwen.

'Perfect,' Gwen replied.

Gwen sat on the green tweed, armchair-type thing beside my office door, then patted the seat beside her. She'd piled her hair up into a bun today, she had on her usual flowery uniform, but her face was all maternal concern and sympathy again.

Something bad has happened, I realised as I sank into the seat beside her. *She hasn't even got a cigarette out.*

'Ceri, I know I am your line manager but I think we've made a connection. We've become friends, haven't we?'

Have we? I thought. She wasn't like my other boss who thought we were friends because she told me too much about herself. But we still weren't friends. Not by a long stretch of the imagination. But, I nodded.

'Good,' she smiled, 'I'm glad you feel we're close. Which is why I wanted to talk to you about your face.'

'My what?' I said.

'The bruise on your face.'

I raised my hand to my cheek. It'd gone down quite a lot in the past three days, and it'd stopped hurting so I'd forgotten about it, I didn't go in for looking in mirrors that much.

'What about it?'

Gwen looked down at her hands. 'I know it's very hard to admit what has really happened, especially to people you don't know very well, but I want you to feel you can come and talk to me. About anything.'

I don't get you, I thought.

'I mean, when one of my friends was being physically abused by her husband, it was virtually impossible for her to talk about. She had bruises all over and an excuse to match each one. I don't want you to feel you have to suffer in silence like that. I understand. I mean, last year, I was attacked.'

My eyes widened in horror.

'In the street. It was hideous and very, very frightening. They only took my mobile phone, but I had bruises and scratch marks all over my face. I found it very, very difficult to talk about it. So, you see, I understand what you're going through. You can talk to me. Any time.'

'Gwen, thank you. But I really was smacked in the face by a door.'

She bunched up her lips in an 'are you sure?' fashion. Jake was still on that kick as well (Ed would've been too had he not spent ninety-nine per cent of his time Missing In Action with Robyn). The only person who believed me was Jess, who knew I was prone to daydreaming and that accidents generally followed. My daydreaming was the reason why I'd never learnt to drive.

'Thank you, though, for your concern. It's good to know I can turn to you if I need to. But in this instance I don't need to. I should've been paying attention to where I was going. But thank you. I'm touched you care.'

Gwen left, having made me promise to talk to her if I needed to. I had considered for a fleeting moment telling her what was on my mind. It was a moment so fleeting it was gone before it entered my head. After she was gone, I moved to my side of the desk, collapsed onto it, rested my forehead on the cool work surface.

God, this obsession with Angel had to stop. It'd gotten so bad I was actually seeing him everywhere. And I mean. every where. It was he who gave me the stupid bruise in the first place. Couldn't very well tell Jake, Ed, Craig or Gwen that, could I?

I'd thought I spotted him, David Boreanaz/Angel on the front of a magazine and double-took as I reached for the newsagent's door. Next thing I knew there was a blinding pain in my face and I was groping for support as I went flying backwards. Then, I was lying on the floor and it was raining greetings cards.

Just earlier, with Staring Man, I'd actually thought he looked like Angel. Except Staring Man had the most amazing eyes and I'd never seen David Boreanaz's eyes in real life. SM's eyes were a bronze colour. Shame he used them to glare at me. Shame, actually, he fancied Mel. But, at least now we'd made some sort of contact (pun not intended but very painfully true). And now he felt guilty about the door-face thing, it would hopefully be the end to those glares.

If SM didn't fancy Mel, though, he could have been my Angel replacement. The one I lusted after until Angel/David Boreanaz came up to me in the street, asked me for directions, looked deep into my dark eyes and realised there was no other woman on the earth for hi—

Oh my God, I need therapy. I thumped my head on the table. I need to get a grip. And then keep that grip on reality. I was never going to have sex again if I carried on like this. And that *would* kill me.

CHAPTER 25

CONFESSIONS

'I'm going to tell Kevin everything.'

Claudine was stood in my shared office doorway and she said this like she was asking if I fancied sneaking into her office for a crafty joint. There was a hint of the naughty, but total casualness about it. My pen hovered over the marking of a below par essay while I looked at her.

'I'm going to tell him about me and Mel. That I slept with him and that we've snogged twice since. But it's all over.'

Are you mad?! He'll kill you, bury you and build a patio over the spot before the 'we snogged twice' bit is out of your mouth. 'That's, er . . .' I hazarded, didn't know what to say except 'stupid' so stopped.

'Do you want to come in?' I asked instead.

Claudine stepped into my office, shutting the door behind her. She sat on one of the armchair-type things by the door, placed her bag and pile of papers on the armchair-type seat next to the ceiling-high bookshelves.

'I'm definitely going to tell him,' Claudine said, in a 'don't try to talk me out of it' fashion. She clasped her hands in her lap, and leant forwards over her knees. I was surprised anew that Claudine didn't smoke; she was the type of woman I always expected to smoke. I watched her from my position across the desk; her agitated manner made me want to smoke.

'I decided last night,' she paused, 'and this morning, but that's not important. The important thing is, I'm going to tell him.'

Claudine's tone had the conviction of someone who, if they talked long enough, would convince you they were doing the right thing. They knew they'd never convince themselves, so they didn't even try.

'I didn't realise it was over between you and Kevin,' I said neutrally.

Her eyes doubled in size. 'It's not. Why would you say it was?'

'Because you're going to confess to him. I just assumed . . . I suppose I shouldn't assume.'

'Assume what?' Claudine said quickly.

'Well, if you're willing to do something that's going to end your relationship, I assumed you'd reached the end of the road.'

Claudine gave me a wider-eyed demented look. 'What I have reached is the end of my tether. I can't deal with it any more. I can't go home, look at Kevin, talk to Kevin, sleep beside Kevin . . . all the time, carrying this secret with me. It's driving me insane. And every time we have sex, I'm so wary that I'll say "Mel", I can't relax. It's doing my head in. I can't bear it any longer.'

I nodded, as though in understanding but the last thing I was feeling was understanding. 'What are you going to do when Kevin breaks down and starts sobbing his heart out?' I asked.

'He won't cry,' Claudine said, aghast.

'What will he do?'

Claudine shrugged. 'I don't know. He'll get angry I suppose.'

'You suppose? You mean, you're going to cause him all that pain and you haven't thought about how he'll react?' *What, are you some kind of sadist?*

'He'll be angry, of course, but when he calms down . . .'

'Calms down? Claudine, he's not going to calm down. He'll probably not forgive you. Ever. *EVER.*

'The calming down and talking things through are for films and story books; the anger and shouting and smashing things and never wanting to see you again, that's reality. That's what you've got to accept will probably happen if you confess all.'

Claudine stared at me with her mouth and eyes agog. I'd never been stern with her before. I wasn't being stern now. Not really. I just wasn't condoning her decision, as she'd expected me to. Claudine's eyes watered up.

My tone had been a bit sharp, though. I shouldn't have gone from nice Ceri to cross Ceri in one go. It was bound to jar her. However, she was talking nonsense. I sighed internally, looked down at my desktop to get myself calm and make

314

my voice nicer, less harsh. 'Claudine, tell Kevin if you want, but don't forget he has a heart too. Don't break his just to make yours lighter.'

'But our relationship is based on a lie,' she wailed. Next would come the wringing of the hands. Swiftly followed by gnashing of teeth and rending of clothes.

'No it's not,' I reasoned. 'Your relationship is based on all the things that brought you two together all those years ago. Your relationship is based on all the things you've done and worked towards together in the past however many years. Your relationship isn't based on a drunken shag that happened six months ago. It may very well influence and affect your relationship, but it's not the basis of it. If it *were* based on that shag . . . well, I don't know.'

'What about Mel?'

Rat-a-tat-tat. The office door opened before I had a chance to say 'come in'. Mel stuck his head around the door. 'Hi Ceri. I w—'

His face lit up and clouded over at once when he saw who was in the office with me. Claudine's face did exactly the same thing.

World War Three was about to kick off in my office.

'I'll come back later when you're not so busy,' Mel said, focused on Claudine.

'Are you following me?' Claudine snarled at my visitor. 'On top of everything, are you following me too?'

'You're off your head, you,' Mel said.

'Look who's talking,' Claudine said.

'What the hell is your problem?'

'Everything to do with you.'

The volume of their voices was rising. I got up, went to the door, to shut it.

'Listen babe, it was you who stuck your tongue down my throat last time.'

'Yeah, and it was you who stuck his dick in m—'

Whoah! Not for sensitive ears. I shut the door on my way out. I paced the corridor for a while. Then I checked the clock at the far end of the wide corridor. Eight o'clock. The canteen was shut. I had nowhere to go, except, possibly the bar. Much as I enjoyed the odd drink or eleven, I couldn't face going in there alone; sitting alone. If it were a proper pub I wouldn't feel so worried, I'd have something to read too, but in college, students would see me all alone – I'd be one step away from being the lecturer with a tweed jacket and pipe, emanating pathetic aloneness.

I turned, started my slow walk back up the corridor. Maybe I *should* go to the bar. Get myself a pack of cigarettes. With Mel and Claudine, I was tempted to take up a life-threatening habit.

In fact, between those two, what Craig and Jess said, Ed disappearing to be with Robyn, Gwen, Jake wearing the aura of a man wronged, and Staring Man, I was quite tempted to take up heroin. Have an out of body experience that would remove me from this world I'd moved in

316

to. London was crazy, Leeds was certifiably insane.

Time ticked on, I wore a groove into the corridor carpet, voices rose and fell from my office. But there were no smashing sounds or blood-curdling screams of anguish and death. I couldn't even go home because my bag, coat, iBook and the essays I needed to finish marking tonight were still in my office.

An hour later, I jumped back as the door was wrenched open and Claudine came stalking out, throwing: 'If you fucking come near me again I'll kill you,' over her shoulder. She completely blanked me as she marched down the corridor, heading for the stairs to the next floor and her office.

Mel's head popped around the door. 'SLUT!' he screamed after her.

Thankfully, no one else was around at that hour, so only I jumped at its suddenness and severity.

Claudine did the smoothest 180-degree turn I'd ever seen, came stalking back up the hallway, growing about a foot with each step. By the time she reached us, she was twenty foot tall.

Her face had narrowed into a knot of anger. So scary and hideous did she look at that moment that I leapt out of her path and flattened myself against the wall as she stormed past. I don't know if Mel saw it coming, but I felt it, heard it, winced at it when her fist connected with his face.

She didn't even stop, she spun on her heels in

another smooth 180-degree turn and stalked away again.

'That's going to be a right shiner,' I said to Mel, who was holding his cold beer bottle against his cheek.

He took the bottle away and nearly pulled a sarcastic smile, hindered by the pain in his face. 'Thanks, Ceri, you're a great help. I always like it when people point out the bloody obvious.'

I tried not to laugh. 'How long have you known Claudine, again?'

'Nearly eleven years.'

'And even though you know her so well, you didn't think calling her a slut would end up with her smacking you one?'

'I wasn't thinking, that's the point. I wanted to hurt her; get the last word in.'

'Well you did that. "Ow!" wasn't it?'

Mel glowered at me. I probably shouldn't be taking the piss. I'd no doubt added to Claudine's foul mood by vetoing her plans to unburden her conscience.

'Why were you two rowing anyway? You were, are, mates,' I said, feeling a tad responsible. What I'd said had been in Kevin and Claudine's best interests. And Mel's. He would've been in for a sound beating if Claudine had blabbed. (Never understood what was sound about a beating. Surely it should be unsound? That was the whole point.)

Mel returned his bottle to his face, right after he rolled his eyes. 'Who knows. I don't.'

'So you spent an hour in my office listening to Claudine shouting, and said nothing?'

'Yes.'

I planted my tongue in my cheek and raised an eyebrow at him.

'Well, a little. No. She shouted, I shouted, we both shouted.'

'Why?'

'Ever since that weekend, you know the lost weekend, she's been off with me and, I suppose, I've been off with her.'

Don't ask why, don't ask why. Don't get any more involved. Not your problem. NOT YOUR PROB-LEM. 'Why?'

'You know Ceri, I'm really pissed off. I mean, it's all right for her, she's got someone, she can just bugger off for the weekend and be happy with him and I'm alone.' Mel slammed his bottle onto the table. 'It's not fair. I care so much for her and I know she loves me. You don't make love to someone like she did if you don't love them. (At that moment I couldn't believe Mel was thirty. You don't make love to someone like she did if you don't love them, indeed. Where did he get that sort of idea from? Reading too many love stories, and watching too many Hollywood movies, I'll bet. I was more than a little partial to them, myself. But even I didn't believe what he'd just said.) So why is she still with him? Why?'

319

'I don't know,' I sighed. *Except I do know, and you, buddy, don't want to hear it.*

Mel sighed slightly, looked away across the bar. I looked him over again. The man who Jake and Ed used to try to set me up with. He was good-looking. Fresh-faced but experienced. Long lashes around hazel eyes, sexily-curly hair, distinguished but friendly features.

Mel caught me checking him out and his eyes held mine. Lust shivered through me. Things were bad – I was starting to have impure thoughts about Mel.

'You're actually quite vaguely attractive, aren't you?' Mel said.

Talk about your damning with faint praise. 'Thanks Mel, that's probably one of the most insulting things anyone's ever said to me.'

'I didn't mean owt by it, I only just noticed. You're all right looking. And I had this sudden urge to kiss you. I was thinking about Claudine and I get that urge every time I think about her.'

I leapt on that like a woman who hadn't eaten in days offered a slice of hot buttered toast. It reminded me of what Craig had said about me subliminally advertising sex and inciting him to have sex with his ex-girlfriend. 'Really? You think about Claudine and you want to kiss any woman around? So it's not just me?'

Mel thought about my question, even though I wasn't sure he understood it.

'It has been happening a lot lately, I think about

Claudine, I get the urge to kiss someone. But I can't say it happened before you arrived on the scene.' Mel sipped his beer, returned it to his face. 'In fact, I can categorically say, a lot of things have changed since you got here. Things between me and Clau were fine until that day you asked us if we were going out together. Our friendship deteriorated right after that.'

Oh.

Mel saw my face fall. 'It's all right. To be honest, I feel better now it's come to a head – smack in the face notwithstanding. Maybe now she'll realise what this is doing to us and leave that idiot.' Mel talked on, explaining why he was glad I'd ruined his life.

CHAPTER 26

KNOCK OUT

'Ceri, we've been waiting for you,' Jake said, practically greeting me on the front door step.

'We? Who? Why?' Suddenly I had visions of an intervention, where all your friends and family wait for you – usually in your living room – to tell you in no uncertain terms that your addiction is destroying you and they love you too much to stand by and watch you do that.

Obviously Jess had blabbed that I watched too much telly. Well, too much *Angel*. I'd slipped from being a recreational user to a full-blown, gotta have it everyday, twice-a-day addict.

'Ed and Robyn are here.' Jake looked rattled. His face was pale, his features were set to permanent frown and even his hair looked shaken. Why? Had he walked in on them at it and been permanently scarred by how truly disgusting sex could be?

I couldn't take any more drama though. Whatever it was, I couldn't handle it. It'd been less than two hours since Mel and Claudine's blow-up, I was still fragile. It'd jolted me to my very core, especially to know that Mel – and probably Claudine – thought I was the cause of that. I incited Craig to sex; I motivated Claudine to violence and I made men fancy Jess. I didn't want any more drama unless it was on the television.

'What's the matter?' I whispered anxiously.

Jake simply gave me a hard stare, then led the way into the living room.

Ed beamed at me as I approached, although how he managed to get more smile behind that grin was a mystery. Robyn, she of the girly, haughty, 'I didn't get a role in *Coronation Street* but I'm not bitter' visage was beaming too. I wasn't sure she knew how to smile.

'Hi,' I said, clocking how close they sat, their fingers entwined.

'Hi, Ceri,' they both said. They'd become Stepford Couple. In the space of, what, three-and-a-bit weeks. This wasn't what I'd been expecting when I'd seen Jake's face. I'd expected Robyn to be holding a gun to Ed's head or something.

'We've been waiting for you,' Ed said.

'So Jake said,' I replied.

'Before you say anything else, babe, I just want to say thank you to Ceri.' This was, rather scarily, from Robyn.

'For?' I replied.

She gave Ed a loving look, the kind of sweet look that diabetics would need an insulin over-dose to get under control. 'For making Ed ask me out.'

'I didn't make him do anything,' I snapped. I didn't need this bullshit on top of everything else.

'Yes you did,' Ed said. 'You were the only person who gave me any advice worth listening to. Twice.'

'He's perfect. Thank you.' Robyn again.

'Hmmm,' I mumbled. Would anyone understand if I started upending furniture and screaming, 'IT'S NOTHING TO DO WITH ME! YOU ALL FUCK UP YOUR LIVES ON YOUR OWN! STOP BLAMING ME FOR EVERYTHING!' I glanced at their faces, no they probably wouldn't understand at all.

'Anyway, what we wanted to tell the two of you is, we're moving in together,' Ed said.

My heart double-flipped. Oh. My. God. It'd been under four weeks. I tried to keep an impassive face, but now I could see why Jake was so shaken.

'When?' I managed from my shocked mouth. I really did think I was unshockable.

'As soon as possible. Robyn would ideally move in here cos it's bigger than the place she shares, but if Jake says no, we'll move in to her place.'

'Oh.'

'And, this bit we haven't told anyone, not even Jake, but, I'm going to give up college, get a job and next year we're going to get married.'

'Give up college?' Jake managed.

I did not speak. I was lying spread-eagle on the carpet, KO'd by the news.

*   *   *

'This is all your fault,' Jake said to me in the kitchen.

Ed and Robyn had skipped off upstairs to their little love nest and Jake had asked me into the kitchen for a quick chat. He might as well have ripped off his shirt and offered me an outside for the friendliness he'd put into the request for a talk in the kitchen.

He'd practically dragged me to beside the back door, shoved me roughly against the sink worktop, and then stood over me like he was going to resurrect the bruise that had just started to fade on my face with his fist. Jake was really quite big and scary when it came down to it.

'How? How is this my fault?' I said.

'You made him ask out that gold-digging hussy. And now look.'

'Gold-digging?'

'Ed's minted.'

'What?'

'He's a millionaire's son. She's no doubt found that out and now he's going to give up college.'

'Millionaire's son? Don't talk soft. If he's minted, why does he live here?'

'He doesn't have to. Ed could buy this whole street of houses if he wanted. But he doesn't want, he just wants a normal life. And he's not going to get that if he gives up college.'

I ran my hand through my hair. What the hell is going on? Ed, a millionaire's son. Ed and Robyn moving in together. Claudine punching Mel. Had the world gone mad?

'Ed's life was going fine until you encouraged him to ask her out,' Jake said.

'He wanted to,' I said lamely. 'I couldn't have made him if he didn't want to. I mean, I didn't hold a gun to his head.'

'Ed looks up to you. You've got this, presence . . . he said that after that first day you moved in here. When he talks to you, he feels like anything's possible, even if it's the most stupid thing on earth. I've been telling him to either ask that, that,' Jake lowered his voice, '*woman* (I never knew anyone could get that much venom into a two-syllable word) out or forget her. All his friends have been telling him that for ages. One word from you, and he's cut his hair, wearing smart clothes and asking her out.'

'I didn't tell him to cut his hair,' I said, lamely.

'Whatever. Just sort it out.'

'What?'

'Sort it out. Stop him from doing this.'

'How?'

'I don't know. Just sort it out. Stop him. It's your fault he's about to chuck his life away, so it's down to you to sort it out.'

I just looked at Jake.

He jabbed his finger viciously at me. 'I mean it. Sort it out Ceri. If Ed ruins his life because of this. I'll never forgive you. And I doubt Ed will either.'

Jake went slamming out of the house and there was me thinking he'd be devastated if I left. 'I was the only one who didn't tell you to get over The Git,' I almost called after him. 'I listened, I let you own your feelings.'

His trail of bad vibes still hadn't dispersed when Ed came trotting down the stairs minutes later. And I hadn't moved from my semi-cowering stance by the back door. Three shocks in less than three hours was more than I could take.

'Has Jake gone out?' Ed asked, heading for the kettle.

I nodded. Ed bounced as he walked, a jolly little spring to his step. He was happy. Any idiot could look at him, listen to him and know that. Ed was in the happiness zone. It might not last, but was that any reason for me to do as I was told, nay, ordered and tell him he was moving too fast.

'We're going to get a takeaway, want some?' Ed asked as he plugged the kettle back in. 'Pizza. I can tell Robyn wants a Chinese but she said to get pizza cos you and Jake might want some. And if we get garlic bread and stuff it'll make a right old feast.'

What are you doing Ed? And is it anything to do with me? Have you too become a victim of whatever it is I'm supposed to do to people? Or is it a coincidence?

'So, do you?'

'Um, um, no. I'm not that hungry.'

'Oh come on, you know you want it,' Ed coaxed. 'What's that expression you use, I'm sure you could choke some down.'

'Go on then, you've twisted my arm. I never could say no to a good feeding.'

Ed grinned. Went to leave, stopped, came back. Kissed my cheek. I put my hand to my cheek, his kiss had been as light as a feather. 'I wouldn't be feeling like this if it wasn't for you, thank you.' Then he bounded out of the room.

CHAPTER 27

THE QUESTION

I have no life.
It's official. I have no life, I am merely living vicariously through other people.

Take, for example, Mel and Claudine's drama. They were actively avoiding each other. Even in the Senior Common Room, when one entered, the other one left. They'd got an official face on it, of course. A 'hi' face that told the world that they're both so busy they haven't got time for each other. While everyone we worked with believed that, I knew the real story.

I, for example, happened to know that they'd once been more than friends. And I also knew that the lamppost Mel walked into that caused his bruise happened to be five foot eight, with black hair and a surprisingly strong right-hook for her slender frame. She was also very angry at the time. (I noticed no one sat him down and asked him if he was being abused. They all believed his heinous lie without a second thought.)

The most unsettling thing about the Mel and Claudine story was, though, I didn't just know their story. I *was* their story, I was part of their

329

drama and I experienced their emotions. What they felt, I felt. It was my seventh sense magnified.

I was Mel, in love with someone who wouldn't leave her partner for me. Clinging to the hope that one day she'd wake up and see sense. I was Claudine, convinced that I could be in love with two men at once and almost breaking my heart to try to reconcile that. I was both people, knowing how I felt, suspecting how the other felt, not really knowing what I should do.

But the seventh sense didn't end there. Not by a long shot.

I was also Ed. Rushing into something because she really was The One. I had no fear, no doubt, no indecision. All I knew was, when I left her place to return to mine, I felt as though I'd left my arm behind and needed to go back and collect it. And, within seconds of shutting my front door, she was calling me, begging me to come back because there was an Ed-shaped hole in her life. I'd never known anything so easy, passionate, comforting, so right.

I was Gwen. Suddenly dissatisfied with everything. It wasn't just the demon year group any more. Every year group wound me up. Every lecture rankled me. I smoked more and more, trying to push down this feeling of powerlessness; this knowledge that I'd chosen this path and I was going to be doing this hideous thing called lecturing for the rest of my days.

I was Jake, scowling now about what Ed was doing with his life. Scared that he was doing the wrong thing. Worried my best mate was about to do something monumentally stupid, something he couldn't go back on. And under it, really scowling about the twat who was meant to be my friend but used me for sex then treated me like dirt when I told him how I felt. I was also jealous. How come Ed got it right and I got it so wrong? Robyn was a stuck-up tart, The Git was meant to be my friend, but Ed was happy, I'd been used.

I was Craig, in desperate need of a reality check on my feelings about the ex I can't stop sleeping with. She winds me up, she's a bit of a psycho, but nowadays she's the one person I want to spend all my time with. I can't possibly love her, could I?

And then, of course, there were the students. Constantly trailing to the door of my shared office, pouring their hearts out. Not that I was their tutor. Just, it seemed, available. *Did I have such an eventful life as a student?* I'd often wonder as another student poured out a plot more complicated than anything I saw on *Sunset Beach*. There was something very disconcerting and disturbing about standing in front of a group of people and knowing who'd shagged who, who'd screwed over who, who really hated who. The students spent so much time pouring their hearts out in my office that whenever there was a knock on the door these days Sally picked up her papers and cup and left because she knew the people wouldn't be visiting her.

My brain, my heart, my time were crammed with people's passions, loves, hopes, hates, sorrows, emotions. I had to keep track, remember who had told me what, who hadn't told me what. What was told only after swearing me to secrecy, what I was supposed to pass on, but discreetly.

I wasn't simply listening to problems and stories and lives, I was living them. At least, that's how it felt. I felt it all. Not empathy. Actual feelings. The actual emotions. I ached when they ached; I vacillated when they vacillated; I loved when they loved. I'd had this before, only not as consistently like now.

Before, like with Ed, like with Trudy, like with Mel, like with the man who fancied Jess, it was periodic, the occasional sensation. Now, it'd got worse. Intensified, concentrated. Never-ending. When someone cried, I genuinely experienced those ripples of distress and teetered on the brink of tears myself. If someone told me of their joy, I felt my heart leap and do an excited jig. Like. I suppose, some men get sympathetic labour pains, I got sympathetic life experiences.

I felt all their joys, all their fears, all their upsets, as though I was doing the living myself.

And it was sucking the real life out of me. Even the unmitigated highs and joys of other people's happiness didn't make up for it. It wasn't my happiness. I may as well have described my perfect birthday present, down to the Bagpuss wrapping paper, then watch someone else unwrap it without so much as a glance at the paper, then smile, say it's lovely, then put it aside and never pick it up again. You were happy they had it, but you, sure as eggs is eggs and chocolate is chocolate, wanted it yourself. It was *meant* for you. *Built* for you. You deserved it, just as much as the person who had it. You'd appreciate it more, too.

All this emotion by proxy meant I hardly knew what I felt any more. *If* I felt any more. What did I have to feel about? Everyone else had the life, not me. I experienced the emotion, but I didn't get closure. Didn't get the end result when others got their problems sorted or they went back to the thing that made them ecstatic. I ran the race, but never finished and got my medal. I was constantly jumping from one race to another, running every race just as hard, but never finishing. The roads to hell, perhaps?

And it showed no sign of abating. I literally had no life. My only time alone were those moments I fell asleep and those moments when I woke up. In between, my mind was in constant motion. My mind was sampling everyone's life, snatching titbits here and there until it was a constant soundtrack to my waking hours. Snatches and excerpts of other people's experiences playing on loop in my head.

One night, at the end of May, I found myself outside Jess's house. She was marking very important final year experimental reports, but let me in anyway.

I lay with my head on the kitchen table, crumbs from the sandwich she'd eaten earlier grinding into my right cheek.

'Jess, you've got to help me,' I said, staring forlornly at the side of the tea cup she'd placed in front of me.

'I don't know why everyone comes to tell me everything – good, bad or indifferent – or why I can't say no, but I really think I'm going mad. What is it about me? Why me?'

Three days later, she had the answer.

CHAPTER 28

THE ANSWER

'I think I've worked it out,' Jessica said, stretching out on her sofa. 'Finally.'

I sat on the floor, the soles of my feet touching, my knees splayed out.

'I'm all ears,' I said.

'Actually,' Jessica said, 'you're all heart.'

'Hey! All right, I might not be the kindest person on earth all the time, but I do try. So less of the sarcasm.'

Jessica drew on her cigarette, exhaled, waved the cigarette smoke away from my direction. 'No, no, I really mean it. Literally, you're all heart. Basically, we can talk philosophically, or we can talk biologically, or we can talk physics, but the end result is the same.'

'What the blinking flip are you on about?' I replied.

Jessica smiled. 'Remember how Craig said you advertised sex? He was right. 'Remember how I said you made men fancy me? I was right. And, remember how poor Ed got himself into that state before his date and he said he thought he'd got "bigger", well he probably didn't realise that you had something to do with it, too. And you know how everyone has been blaming you for all the changes in their lives? They're right too. Basically, Ceri, you're Cupid.'

CHAPTER 29

STUPID, CUPID

'Pay attention, this is complicated.

'In chemistry and biology, there's the law of osmosis. I don't know if you remember it from school, but basically, say there are two substances that are separated by a semi-permeable membrane, you know, like a barrier that has tiny, tiny holes in it. If the molecules of the two substances are small enough, and there's a very concentrated amount of the substance on one side and a slightly less concentrated amount of the substance on the other side, the side with less will attempt to move into the concentrated area through the holes in the barrier. You understand? Less will move into more.'

I nodded, not knowing where this was leading.

'It's the same with you, Ceri, but in reverse. You have so much love and affection and sexuality locked up inside yourself, it's started to leak out. In the form of pheromones. As we both know from all that work you did on subliminal perception, there's evidence to suggest that love and sexual attraction are governed by those tiny hormones called pheromones. With you, and the abundance

337

I suspect there is of love and sexuality inside of you, it's leaving the concentrated area that is you and dispersing into the outside world which has less. It's osmosis in reverse. More is moving into less. You see, you've never really used that love and sexuality and affection inside you. so it's being secreted out of your body as pheromones. Out where it's needed.

'Think about it, people think that negative emotions if internalised for too long can cause illness, well with you it's love, a positive emotion. So love's not going to cause illness, so it's going outside to where it's needed. And because you've never really used all that love and affection and sexuality, it's been building up in your body and your body needs to let it out. The only way it knows how to release that pressure is to leak it through your pores. And, as you know, skin is a semi-permeable barrier.

'Everyone knows that women's periods synchronise themselves once they live together for a time and the reason they do that is because of pheromones. What I didn't know until I read your original degree thesis on subliminal perception was that when women live long-term with men, it's been found that their periods become more regular – again as a result of pheromones.

'Now, the main reason I think that what's happening to you is mostly down to pheromones is Ed. Remember his predicament with his penis? I'll wager you were extremely nervous for him, very worried that he wouldn't be good enough for that date. You were probably sending out so many conflicting pheromones and vibes that his body subliminally picked up on it and he ended up in that state. Physically, his body wanted to be good enough and that was the only way it knew how to do it.'

Jess paused. 'Are you following me so far?'

'Yeah, sure, why not,' I replied flatly.

She lit herself another cigarette, slowly breathed life into it.

'All right, now, let's link all this to what we know about Cupid philosophically. The Romans, who had Cupid as their god of love, needed a way to explain the often irrational ways that people behaved once they fell in love, the seemingly bolt-from-the-blue, narcotic state people experienced love as – hence they drew Cupid as having a bow and arrow. To get that "wham" thing across. Your love, affection and sexuality – released as pheromones – are hitting people like a bolt from the blue. That's what Craig meant about you subliminally advertising sex. Your pheromones are, subliminally, like your bow and arrow, they encourage people to have sex.'

Jess paused. Smoked in silence.

'Sticking with philosophy, I have to say, the way you behave is like the original philosophical incarnation of Cupid. The thing is, Cupid, the original Cupid, was a life messer-upper. He may well have been the god of love, but he's only seen as all-good

339

since the Christianisation of the Roman and Greek religions. The Christians couldn't leave the god of love as a naughty entity who went around making people do things they wouldn't normally do – so they fixed the stories and myths so that people falling in love with the wrong people were just cute little mistakes. Not huge great problems.

'But the original incarnation of Cupid was quite disruptive. That's what's so true about you saying that you keep messing up people's lives—'

'No, *I* didn't say that, it was everyone else who said that,' I cut in.

'OK,' Jess conceded, 'everyone else says that you mess up their lives, that since you've arrived things have gone wrong. Or, at least, have been disrupted. Disruptive, that's what you are. You can't help it. You turn up somewhere and lives are transformed. Wherever you go, people are experiencing that bolt from the blue, they are facing up to things, admitting their feelings, following their heart's desire. And, it must be said, you do have this knack of making people open their hearts. You've always been like that.

'Take me, for example. I keep in touch with my ex-students, but you're the only one who has changed my life and made me a friend, influenced me. Made men fancy me. And that's why, I reckon, you have very few lasting friendships. It's as though once you've disrupted someone's life long enough for them to make the necessary changes you move on. You don't even realise you're doing it. You're like the Littlest Hobo, but with people's hearts and minds.

'I reckon it's only come to a head now because you're following your heart's desire. And, I suppose, you're releasing lots of happiness hormones out there. Showing everyone what's possible when you do what your heart really wants you to do. But following your heart's desire isn't easy. In fact, it's hell, the most disruptive thing you can do to your life. The reason why people keep coming to you, keep blaming you is because you're modern-day Cupid. And you leave The Cupid Effect wherever you go.'

I let Jess's words settle like dust around us. Let them soak into the atmosphere until the air was saturated with the nonsense she'd just come up with.

'You're insane,' I said. 'I thought I was mad, but you want locking up.'

Jess just smiled, lit herself another cigarette. 'Sweetheart, your track record alone proves you're Cupid. Look at the men in your life, I couldn't believe half the things you told me the other week. And I'm sure there've been more of them. Ones that you've kept from me, but, after all that, with not even one decent relationship, without ever having experienced real love, you still believe in love. You're still *capable* of love. You must be Cupid. Because only Cupid would take all that nonsense and still be the loving, caring soul you are. Most people give up over less, but not you.

And you still have room in your life for everyone else's dilemmas and problems.

'Apart from everything I've just told you, probably the most damning thing of all is your name.'

I said nothing, waited for her to explain.

'When you shorten your name to Ceri, you're actually shortening it to a name that comes from the Welsh word meaning "love". I don't know where your parents got it from but your full name, Ceresis, comes from a very obscure and ancient Latin phrase which literally translated means "Heart's Desire". You're actually called Heart's Desire. How more modern a Cupid do you get than that?'

I turned from her to look outside at the trees, the sky, the world. Everything beyond the window was normal, the same, all right. Everything had changed and flipped and upended in here. I turned back to Jess.

'D'you really believe that?' I asked.

'Absolutely,' she said.

I nodded in reply. Nodded because I couldn't speak.

Then burst into tears.

CHAPTER 30

RELUCTANCY

'I don't want to be Cupid,' I gulped between sobs. 'I just want to be me. Ceri. Ceresis, at a push. Not "heart's desire" or disruptive. I just want a normal life.'

Jess rubbed my back, hugged me and let me sob while variations on the 'I don't want to be Cupid' theme spilt from my mouth. Eventually, she left me crying my heart out, went to the kitchen and came back bearing tea mugs. I'd heard her rummaging around the kitchen drawers, probably looking for chocolate or anything with chocolate in it. Like that would help. My reality had been smashed to pieces and she was giving me tea and looking for something with forty per cent cocoa solids in it.

Jess handed me a blue mug with a big smiley sun on the side. Tea. Real tea, very, very strong and very milky. If I drank real tea, I drank it so strong it could tarmac roads. I suppose this was a real emergency. I was still shaking from my epic cry and Jess held onto the cup a fraction longer so I wouldn't drop it.

'It's only a theory, love,' Jess said, freeing another

white stick from its packet. 'It's not the gospel. What do I know about biology and chemistry and physics and philosophy?' She put a flame to the cigarette, breathed life into it. 'All right, I know about philosophy because I teach the philosophy of psychology, and I know a bit about biology and pheromones, but what do I know about the rest of it? I mean, come on, what do I really know?'

She was only the cleverest person I knew. Which was why I'd turned to her in the first place. 'But you believe it, don't you?' I asked her, sniffling back the sobs.

Jess took two long drags on her cigarette, exhaled them just as lengthily. Then she sighed even more lengthily. 'Wish I'd never opened my mouth now,' she said.

'Just tell me the truth, you've never lied to me before, so tell me the truth now. You believe I'm some kind of modern-day Cupid, don't you? And I leave, what was it you called it, The Cupid Effect, wherever I go. You believe that, don't you?' I'd banished the whiny, crying sound from my voice by then, which was good cos it was starting to piss even me off. 'Don't you?'

Jess reluctantly looked at me, her eyes searching my face for some kind of semblance of sanity, or ability to deal with her revelations. She sighed again, obviously finding no such sign of sanity. Not surprising since I felt so on the edge I might lose my grip and fall deep into the pit of insanity. 'Yes sweetie.'

I sagged in my seat, took a sip of the tea. Jess had put sugar in the tea. Good for shock, I guess. I wanted to cry again. This couldn't really be happening. And if it could be happening, then why did it have to be happening to me?

'I don't want to be Cupid,' I said again.

'It's not that bad, is it?' Jess said, stretching out on the sofa. 'Being responsible for people finding their heart's desire, for people falling in love, and for people having sex. That's nice. That's good. Most people depart the earth without ever committing one act of public servitude; you get to do loads.'

True. But . . .

'What about me?' I hit my chest. 'I want my heart's desire and love and . . . and sex! What about me? When do I get all that?'

I sounded selfish. Possibly, maybe, because I was feeling incredibly selfish. Charity begins at home, and so do expectations of love and affection. Jess pulled a slight, 'hard luck' face. Not a full one, not even a quarter one, just a fraction, a hint of a grim smile, eyes slightly sad.

When do I get all that? Never, clearly.

'And anyway, why do I have to be Cupid? How come I don't get to be Venus or Aphrodite?'

Jess looked guiltily into her tea, smoking as though her life depended on it.

'Really, I want to know.'

'Because,' Jess began, 'because . . . people fell in love with Venus and worshipped her . . .'

'But no one noticed the little fat git with wings. He just went about disrupting stuff and being unnoticed.'

'Yooouuuuu, could put it like that.'

I felt my bottom lip go again.

'Put it like this, at least you'll never be short of a wedding invite or two.'

'Does this mean I'm going to be disrupting lives and not getting proper love for the rest of my life?'

'To be honest, Ceri, I don't know. I don't have all the answers. I spent a lot of time on the Internet and in books pulling together what I have told you. The original Cupid did find love, but he loved her from afar for years and then he lost her. It could be different for you. Like I said, I don't know. But it's been like this for at least ten years. I suspect it'll be like that for ages. I think, sweetheart, you've got into a bit of a self-fulfilling prophecy situation, no matter how hard you try, you do it anyway.'

'I don't mean to.'

'I know, that's the irony. You don't mean to, but you can't help it. It's your nature. I mean, didn't people used to call you Auntie Ceri when you were in college? I seem to remember you always being surrounded by people who had problems. You could walk into any room anywhere and within five minutes you'll be talking to the person in the room with the biggest problem or biggest dilemma. You don't mean to do it, you just do it.

Something in you draws out that kind of honesty. And it encourages people to, for better or worse, follow their heart. That's who you are, it's what being modern-day Cupid is all about.'

'Yeah, yeah, I get the idea.'

'Look, somebody's got to do it. I'm sure there's been someone like you for ages. Hey, you could be like Buffy, you know, into every generation, a Cupid is born. She will be the disruptive one.'

I glared at Jess. 'Oh yes, ha, ha, let's all laugh at the funny Ceri who's going to be alone for the rest of her life, shall we. Ha ha. Excuse me while I hold my sides to stop them from splitting at how amusing all this is.'

She hung her head. 'All right, what I was going to say was, somebody's got to do it, my only bit of advice is to go with it.'

'Yeah, course you'd say "go with it". It's all right for you, Mrs Married With Gorgeous Children, I'm the one who gets to, well, not. I'm the one looking at the next forty or fifty years of my life alone. Course you're going to sit there and suggest "going with it".' I put down the tea on the floor by the armchair. I had to get out of there before I started laying into Jess for only telling me what I didn't want to hear. I got up, grabbed my bag and my jacket. 'I need to go for a walk, think things through.'

'All right, love.'

I spun around, my whole body aflame with anger. 'Don't. Call. Me. That.'

CHAPTER 31

CURSED

So, this is it, is it?

This is my talent. My purpose in life. I am here to make other people fall in love, have sex, find their heart's desire. But not me. I don't get any of it.

I sat in Burley Park, on a bench in the middle of the park. The grey concrete path wound around me. The emerald blanket of grass rose and fell in tiny hills and odd-shaped mounds.

I was hunched over, my shoulders tense, my hands pushed deep into my suede jacket pockets. Another few minutes and the jacket would be ruined beyond repair. It wasn't raining, it was pouring. The main reason for me being hunched up. As if that was some protection from the weather. It was merely a physical reflex, though, the rest of me didn't care if I drowned in rain.

I'd sat there for about forever since I'd left Jess's house. Water drizzled down my face, down my neck and inside my clothes, while frizzing my hair.

This is my life, is it? My talent, my gift, my search for the holy grail. My huge, throbbing, pus-filled curse.

This so wasn't fair. I know I'd said this to Jess,

but now it screamed in my brain: WHAT ABOUT ME?! When do I get that love and sex and settled-ness?

It wasn't as though my life was purely focused on finding a man. It wasn't. Part of me expected love. Not a man, but love, companionship, someone to pull around me like a person-shaped duvet at night. Someone to share and share alike with. Love in its purest sense.

It wasn't like I was asking to win a few trillion pounds on the lottery, was it? Or to walk along the Pacific Ocean floor. Or win a gold medal. I just wanted love. I'd waited patiently for years for that. What I got, what I was rewarded with was everyone else's life.

I was modern-day Cupid.

Jess was right, of course. That's what was so awful about it. As soon as she said it, the scales fell from my eyes, the barbed wire screens lifted from my brain.

The world suddenly stopped being like those old-fashioned photos I'd seen of the world – all black and white; monochrome. As all of Jess's words hit home, I stopped seeing the world as three-dimensional. Everything became colour. The world had more substance, it was multi-dimensional. I couldn't simply see things any more, I experienced them with all my senses. Everything had its own frequency that it reverberated on, and now I knew my *raison d'être* I was attuned to these frequencies. Every frequency. Life became more than a three-dimensional experience, it became a multidimensional experience. It was so hard to explain when the only way I had to explain it were words and they and their meanings were firmly lodged in the reality of three dimensions.

I was plugged into the world, for real. And I didn't like it. Not one bit. A little knowledge is a dangerous thing. Whoever coined that term wasn't wrong. Now I knew this, I couldn't unknow it. I couldn't deny it.

Right now, I was so unconfused. This was how it felt when I first put on my accursed glasses. I'd turned to the optician and said, very loudly, 'Oh my God, I can't believe how much I couldn't see before.' And they gave me headaches for ages after I started wearing them because, I guess, my brain was seeing more than it had in a while; too much information was entering my head. I could see far too clearly. And, hey, now I could live too clearly. I had no more confusion. No more veils and fuzziness. No more drifting aimlessly wherever life was going to take me. That was why I felt others' emotions. Why I'd start crying for no reason; why I felt morning sickness when I'd never been pregnant; why I felt everyone else's confusion, hurt, hate, humiliation, joy, love, lust, ecstasy. Because I was cursed to. I was modern-day Cupid.

I'd always felt a tad different to everyone else. It wasn't the feeling that I was unique, tortured, misunderstood; not that no one understood me, it was that I understood everyone else. I knew too much about how everyone else could find what their heart was sickening for; fix their relationship; speak their mind; follow their dream; get a life, etc., etc., etc., even though I had relatively no experience of most of those things myself, I could talk and advise on them as though I'd been there, done that – several times.

I remember when all this started. The first event when I put my big mouth and need to interfere and need to help to proper use.

I'd gone on a walking holiday in the Lake District with a couple of friends. Post O-levels, pre-results, almost my birthday. I was sixteen and the three of us had our reasons for going: mine, to get away from my parents; Kathleen, to do what she wanted; Marian, to walk.

We spent most evenings and lunchtimes in the central lodge, me not drinking, just eating. I'd been dragged out walking a couple of times and it'd tripled my appetite. But, wherever we were, walking, eating, sitting, there also seemed to be this desperately unhappy couple nearby. I say desperately unhappy couple, but it was her who was miserable, under constant fire as she was from her husband. He constantly called her stupid, ugly, fat, pathetic, etc., etc. . . . in a voice that reverberated around the lodge or rang out through the hills. He never seemed to stop criticising her clothes, her walking abilities, the way she ate, the way she breathed at one point.

Everyone focused on their food when he started taking potshots at her in the central lodge. Everyone listened to his abuse; feeling embarrassed for her, feeling embarrassed for themselves but no one wanting to get involved. I wasn't embarrassed, I never felt embarrassment, all I experienced was rage. Deep rage and shame. Every word, every insult went through me as though directed at me. Meant for me. My rage, indignation and humiliation built up, day after day until day four.

By then, I'd forgotten that the rage I felt was irrational considering I'd never had a boyfriend in my life, I'd never experienced this type of constant abuse and, for all I knew, he was right. Maybe he did look at her and feel physically sick because of her body. Or her face. Or the way she breathed.

On that day, I felt how she felt. Not felt for her, felt through her. It was as if she was projecting her emotions straight into my brain and heart and I could feel her hurt, her humiliation. She also loved this man, that was apparent, she had a bond with him. All of this was being broadcast straight into me. I found it harder and harder to push food into my mouth because of what he was saying and the effect it was having on me. The pain, the anger, the resignation.

'Look at you, how am I supposed to even want to touch you when you sit there with that look on your face and all that blubber melting onto your seat and the way you eat, the way you drink. You've

352

got . . .' his staccato voice shot across the room, ricocheting off the embarrassed silence.

Before I knew what was happening, I was on my feet, my friends had faces of horror, Marian went to grab me but it was too late, I'd spun to face the couple. 'Who the hell do you think you are?' I shouted at him.

The pair of them stopped, stared at me in abject shock.

'I asked you a question,' I shouted, 'who do you think you are to sit there talking to anyone, let alone your wife, like that?'

Like the bully he was, rather than say anything to someone who challenged him, he simply sat there and stared at me.

'I mean, we have to sit here, night after night and listen to you abusing someone constantly, and for what? For killing someone? For mutilating someone? No, for her size. For the way she eats. For the expression on her face. How dare you. How *dare* you.

'I mean, you can dish it out, but can you take it?'

He stared at me. No hint whatsoever of pummelling my face into silence. 'I asked you, you can dish it out, but can you take it? Hmmm?'

Miraculously, he just shook his head at me.

'No, thought not. Well, let me tell you, Mr Loud And Rude, you're not Mel Gibson yourself. In fact, you make David Hasselhoff look rather appealing. And, even though your looks aren't all that, you don't even have a nice personality to compensate for it. So, do the world and us a favour and SHUT UP.'

I turned to the woman. 'And you, have you no self-respect? I mean, I can understand that you put up with this in your own home, because at least then you can ignore him, or put rat poison in his food or drop the odd cup of tea in his lap, but in public? How dare you sit there and let him abuse you in front of everybody. I know, I know, you love him, but there's one person you should love more and that's yourself and . . . and, the fact you can sit there and let him abuse you night after night means you need, you need . . . I don't know, you need to think about how much you mean to yourself.'

The silence after my storm frightened me. It was pure silence. Everyone in the room was probably holding their breath cos not even the sound of respiration could be heard.

Then the room suddenly erupted into applause. Everyone around me was clapping and congratulating me for doing what no one else would. I came down from the head rush that had pushed me into action, giddy, unsteady on my feet. And, mortified. Who did I think I was? I was worse than him, at least he knew the person he was insulting, I'd never met them before.

I turned on my heels and marched out of there, shame burning in my ears and on my face. Ironically, I went for a long walk around the lake not far from the hostel.

I was shaking for most of that walk, I still couldn't understand what I'd just done and why. I sat by the edge of the lake, staring into it.

'Hello,' a voice said, some time later.

I turned around. It was the woman. She looked older close up, her blond hair streaked with white, her face lined and her eyes puffy and reddened, probably from crying. She stared at me, I stared at her. She sat down and we sat in silence for a while.

'He wasn't always like that,' she said eventually. Sadness and frustration were like a shroud around her. A shroud that encompassed me.

'Well that's all right then,' I snapped. 'He wasn't always like that so that gives him a good excuse to behave like that now.' This really wasn't me talking.

'It's not like that,' she said.

I gave her a hard look. Shrugged. 'Why do you care what I think, anyway? I'm just some sixteen-year-old, what do I know about life, right?'

'I . . .' she began. Stopped. 'You stood up for me and I feel I owe you an explanation.'

'I also insulted you, or have you conveniently forgotten that?' Why couldn't I shut up? I'd been known to go without speaking for days and now I had a cross between verbal diarrhoea and abusive Tourette's Syndrome.

'Yes, but you were trying to help me.'

'Two wrongs don't make a right. Or make it all right.'

This seemed to go over her head. 'It was like you were reading my mind back in the lodge. Like everything I was thinking was coming out of your mouth. Even down to the David Hasselhoff thing.'

I *knew* that wasn't me speaking, I quite fancied David Hasselhoff in *Knight Rider* at that point, not that I'd *ever* tell anyone that.

'But, you're going to stay with him and carry on letting him treat you like that, aren't you?'

Her face contracted in pain.

I sighed. 'I just said that out loud, didn't I?' I said.

She nodded.

'Sorry,' I mumbled, then stared out across the lake, everything seemed green up here. Green and wet. Haze hung over the lake, moisture oozed out of the air. You could feel the wetness in the atmosphere as you inhaled and exhaled. Except I couldn't because her emotions were choking the life out of me, making it hard to even breathe. I didn't want to be around her much longer, but I couldn't get up and walk away. I'd started this.

'How long have you been married?' I asked.

'Fifteen years,' she said in a small, small voice. She married him a year after I'd been born. I'd barely have been walking when she said 'I do' to him.

Her expression was taut across her face, each facial muscle tensed while she tried to control herself, then she crumpled, giving in to tears.

Now look what you've done. 'I'm really sorry,' I said. 'I didn't mean to upset you.'

'It's not you,' she said through her tears. She wiped her sleeve across her eyes; I would've offered her a tissue but decided she probably didn't want the dried-up snot rag that had been squatting in my jacket pocket since last winter.

'You just . . . when I thought about marriage it wasn't meant to be like this. You don't think it'll turn out like this. And I don't know how to get out. I just don't know.'

I put my arm around her shoulder, it was expected, and who had started her blubbing? *Moi.* She leant in to me and started sobbing for real. I thought I'd seen crying before, but I hadn't. She wailed and talked and explained her predicament. All the while talking like she expected me to have some answers. I had no answers, I was sixteen for heaven's sake. I hadn't kissed a boy, much less gone out with one, got married and worked out how to leave him if he started to destroy my soul.

We sat at the lakeside for a long time. And then she got up, dried her eyes, dried her nose and wandered off into the mist that had settled over the path leading to the lodge. I sat waiting, counting seconds, waiting until she got far enough away so that I could get up and run back to the lodge. It was creepy out there and I'd seen a horror film or two in my time. In fact, by the time I went speed walking back to the dormitory we were staying in, I'd convinced myself a monster lived

357

at the bottom of the lake and Jason from *Friday the 13th* or *Halloween* or whatever was lurking in the bushes with his carving knife and hockey mask. But that was a hyperactive imagination for you.

I never saw her again. The woman. I never knew her name, I just knew her ailment. And, while she constantly came to mind, while I hoped it'd been all right in the end and that she worked out how to pack a bag and walk away for ever, I never did find out what happened.

Things had continued from there. Since that holiday, my life had never been uncomplicated or uncoupled from the intimate lives of others.

I shut the front door a little too loudly as I dripped and squelched into the house. The anger in the slam brought Jake to the living room door.

His eyes doubled in size when he saw me.

'Cezza! Look at the state of you! Are you all right?' He came to me, obviously ready to offer comfort.

'I'm fine,' I snapped. 'Perfectly fine, thank you very much.'

I hadn't forgotten his role in my current predicament. I didn't want his help or affection or a hug. Especially not when I knew how cross he was with me about Ed. I trailed a wet patch up to my bedroom.

I cried as I took off my sodden clothes. Not as big a cry as I did at Jess's place. More a constant cry. For one who didn't cry very often, I was certainly making up for it. I trembled and cried during the whole disrobing and showering and putting on my pyjamas process.

It was like I'd just been chucked by my first love, my big love and my dream love at the same time. Except, this was worse. More painful. This wasn't merely the loss of love, the loss of *grand amour*, this was the loss of the *idea* of love. This was accepting that it'd never happen to me, that I would shuffle off this mortal coil without ever knowing what really being in love feels like. Without knowing I could be myself, my nasty self, my nice self, my manic self, my depressive self, my hopeful self, my totally fucking loony shouldn't someone lock me up self with someone and still find they loved me. Still find they were there in the morning.

Getting to the end of my life and finding it'd never happened would be one thing; knowing at this stage of the game it'd never happen just made me want to take my ball home and never play again.

What was the point? I'd never win. Not when I had this Cupid thing oozing out of my skin.

I remember reading this quote once that went something like: 'A poor person who is unhappy is in a better position than a rich person who is unhappy. Because the poor person has hope. He thinks money would help.' Much like myself. I thought love will help.

★   ★   ★

After two days in bed, feeling soooo sorry for myself I couldn't even bear to put on *Angel* because the pain of knowing he'd never love me was too great, I realised something. All I had to do was break the curse. If I wasn't so loving, so caring, so open to callers twenty-four/seven, how the hell could I be Cupid?

All I had to do was not be Cupid.

So simple, it was scary.

All I really had to do was be cold. Be a cow. Start secreting negative hormones like the rest of the population.

How hard could that be?

CHAPTER 32

NO LIFE CONTACT

Claudine knocked on my office door the very next day. I knew it was her because she'd rung my mobile earlier and left a message asking if I was coming to college. I hadn't called her back. And when she knocked and turned the handle, I froze. Sat very still and held my breath in case she put her ear to the door, listening for signs of life.

The door was locked. I'd come in to surf the Net on my time and college money and prepare for the next day's lecture and tutorials. I had the time to talk to Claudine, but not the inclination.

My time was my own now. It'd do no good to start off on the wrong foot by talking to Claudine. Even though I wanted someone else to run all this Cupid Effect stuff by, I didn't want to be in a position where I might have to listen to any more of their traumas. That was part of the problem, wasn't it? I felt it, I dealt it.

She knocked again for luck, in case I'd fallen asleep and hadn't heard her the first time. This was unnatural, not jumping up and running to the door to open it. Not being ready to listen and offer advice, but I'd get over it. I'd have to. I was doing this for the good of my health and for the good of my love life. It was for their own good, too. I wouldn't always be around, would I? I might go back to London in February when my contract came to an end – who would they whinge at then? Who would they blame their mess on? They had to stand on their own two feet. Accept that what ailed them was of their own doing. I didn't ask them to shag their friends or to hate their students or to give up college.

Yeah, Ceri, say it a few more times and you'll believe it.

Claudine wandered off and I ignored the urge to leap up and sprint after her, check she was all right. I turned to my computer screen, got back to reading movie scripts.

'Hi, Ceri,' Claudine called down the corridor later that week as I left the office.

I'd been doing the locking-the-door thing whenever I was alone in the office, I didn't go to the common room or to the library, not the library in college, anyway. I hid in a variety of pubs within walking distance of the college. Sometimes I'd go to the main university library, careful not to run into Jake or Ed. If I went to a pub down in Horsforth, I made sure it was different to the one I'd been to the day before I wanted to ensure that if someone saw me somewhere one day, they wouldn't be able to 'accidentally' find me there the next day.

It was like being on the run, I felt like a modern-day David Banner at the end of each episode of the *Incredible Hulk*, slinging his bag on his shoulder and wandering off to another town where no one had heard of the Hulk. I also felt like the original *Fugitive*, with one eye over his shoulder on the police and one eye in front, searching for the one-armed man who'd offed his wife. I was constantly moving, constantly aware that I might be spotted by someone who knew me and wanted to talk to me.

At home, so as to avoid Jake and Ed, I hid in my room until they'd gone to sleep then made dinner. I called my family so they wouldn't call me and if one of the lads came knocking, I pretended to be asleep or naked.

It was a lonely experience, I spent a lot of time in my head or with my nose in a book or itching to be doing something that involved other people – but I'd get over it. I had to. This was an extension, I suppose, of the no eye contact thing. This was no life contact.

I didn't realise, though, how much I lived for human contact. I thrived on it. Not the 'please sort out my life' part that seemed to plague my very existence. My new life did nothing to help the loneliness I felt hounded by. Duh. It just accentuated it. The irony of it being, I was avoiding eye contact in the life sense; I was being alone now so I wouldn't be alone for ever. The desired ends would simply have to justify the means.

'Haven't seen you around much,' Claudine continued, although clearly, *clearly* I was getting ready to chew half my body off to get away from her. 'I've called you loads. And emailed you.'

I shifted weight from one foot to the other. 'I know,' I said, stifling the urge to explain and/or apologise for not being her personal, unpaid therapist, while swiftly asking her what the problem was. And, if I needed any more reminding, she, like most people, wouldn't give a monkey's left eyebrow what ailed me.

'Are you OK?' she asked.

'Yup, fine,' I replied.

She looked at me, I looked at her. Silence came to us like a soft falling of snow. Claudine was wondering how big-mouth Ceri had mutated into duo-syllabic woman; I was wondering how I was going to keep it up.

'Have you been avoiding me?' she asked.

'Course not.' *I've been avoiding everyone, you're nothing special in that respect. It's nothing personal.*

Claudine's elfin-cut hair had grown. She seemed older, taller. That was because she was skinnier. Probably not eating properly because of the *ménage à trois* she was embroiled in. A truthful word or two from me could end it. I could say what she needed to hear. It wasn't my place, not now – it never had been. I ached for her though. My heart

364

reached out to her. I wanted to make her safe. I wanted her to eat properly, to sleep properly, to live properly, and if I could help her do that, then . . . but what if she gets to a place like this again and I'm not around? She'll totally fall apart, won't she?

'Claudine, I can't talk right now, I've got to dash,' I forced myself to say. 'Bye.'

'Is it cos I punched Mel?' she said, stepping into my path.

'Sorry?'

'Are you pissed off with me because I punched Mel?'

'Course not,' I replied.

She didn't look convinced.

'Claudine, you can punch whoever you want. Apart from me. If you punch me, I'll kung fu your ass. But I don't mind who you punch.'

'I've missed our chats. Are you sure I haven't done something to upset you?'

I nodded. 'I've been very, very busy. Loads of research to do.'

'If you're sure . . .'

I nodded. 'I'll see ya, bye.' Guilt pounded in my head as I walked away.

From Mel, I got: 'Is it because I said you were quite vaguely attractive?'

'Nope, I'm busy.'

From Ed: 'Is it cos Robyn might be moving in?'

'Nope, I'm busy.'

From Jake: 'Is it cos I had a go at you about Ed?'
  'Nope, I'm busy.'

From Gwen: 'Oh, Ceri, I'm glad I caught you. Demon year group have pushed me too far this time and I'm goi—'
  'You wanna be talking to an exorcist, mate.' Of course, I didn't say that. I just remembered a phone call to my parents I had to return, told her I'd be right back and went off home.

It made me pause and think, though, that they all – apart from Gwen – thought that they had offended me with their small acts. I suppose, if I was in their position, I'd rack my brains for some explanation as to why someone who was available twenty-four/seven had suddenly shut up shop. But, I'd started so I'd finish. It was a lot more difficult than I expected. As hard as breathing without two functioning lungs, as hard as thinking without a brain. Totally unnatural.

CHAPTER 33

SLIP UP

'Hi, it's Ceri, isn't it?'

I kept my head down as I nodded. I so did not want to talk to this person. Of all the people on earth, I did not want to talk to him. I'd spotted him across the bar in Leeds City Centre that I was doing my marking in and hadn't got my stuff together fast enough to make a run for it.

That'll learn me to get everything out on the table. Just have what you need out, the rest of the stuff should be piled up, ready to be hoisted into my arms, so I could peg it at a moment's notice. (Some Fugitive/Incredible Hulk type person I was. I couldn't even get out of a pub in under thirty seconds. Imagine if I really had the police and a reporter after me, I'd be done for.)

'Do you mind if I join you?' he asked, sitting down anyway.

He, who? He whose name was not to be mentioned in our house. He who slept with the fishes (and every other form of aquatic life for all I knew). He who was named Terry at birth but had been renamed The Git by me. Him, Jake's man.

Or not, as the case was. I'd seen pictures of him. I'd even been introduced to him once long ago at a party Jake, Ed and I went to. Now he was sitting opposite me as I said, 'I'm a bit busy right now.' Even though it'd been a week and a bit into my no life contact, I still hadn't managed the art of being out-right rude, but I didn't look at him as I told him I wasn't free to chat.

'Right,' he replied and sat there anyway. 'You're Jake's flat-mate, aren't you?'

'We live in a house,' I replied. I could probably get a bit more frost into my voice, but not much.

The Git laughed.

'Jake talks about you all the time. You and Ed, you're like his family. I guess it comes from him being an only child. You and Ed are like his brother and sister.'

'Really,' I said. Yup, I could crowbar more frost into my voice and there it was – icicles were hanging off that one word.

The Git leant forwards over the table, obscuring my papers with his elbows. The world revolved around him, clearly. I sat back, focused on his bare elbows. I couldn't look him in the face without scowling.

'I'm glad we've met up,' he said.

'No, we didn't meet up, you came over and disturbed me,' I said. 'I'm in the middle of marking.'

'OK, I'm glad I've seen you, then. I'm really worried about Jake.'

I raised my eyes to him then. Oh no! Jake. My heart sprinted, my breath came in short bursts. I'd been shutting him and everyone else out. Had something hideous happened while I was doing that? 'Why, what's happened?'

'I rang him the other day, he sounded really down. I asked him if he was OK and he said he was at college and he'd call me back. And he hasn't. That's just not like him. He always calls me back when he says he will.'

'Do you always call him back when you say you will?' I asked.

He frowned, thought about it. 'No.'

Well then, my face said. I looked back down at the work I was marking, raised my pen.

'No,' he put his hand between my pen and paper, 'but I'm busy. And then I forget. It's not like I do it on purpose. I'm just busy.'

'And Jake isn't?' I asked.

'But Jake's just always been there. For him to not call me back something must've happened. I'm really worried.'

I slammed the pen down, raised my eyes again to him. 'Do you know, Terry, I try not to judge people. Mainly, because of the "let she who is without sin cast the first stone" thing and also because I hate it when people judge me but, BUT, I really think you're the most odious type of person. You're an arrogant, self-serving little prig and I can't even bring myself to think that you're a nice person who does bad things because

369

you're not, are you?' I paused. 'You treat Jake like dirt then you're surprised when he cuts you out of his life. In fact, you have the *audacity* to be hurt.'

'You know nothing about it,' he retorted.

'No, I don't, so why did you come sit over here? Why? Because you want me to do your dirty work for you, so you just wandered over here and decided to charm me so I'd get Jake to talk to you.

'Mate, and I use that word because that's how I speak, not because you are in any way a friend of mine, I've only heard Jake's side of the story, but the fact you've come worming around me just proves what a git you are.

'Jake opened his heart to you. He asked you to tell him how you felt, he wasn't asking you to leave your boyfriend or for you to say you loved him. All he wanted was for you to tell him if you had any feelings for him because you've spent seven years sending him mixed messages, not to mention having sex with him. All he wanted was for you to say something like "I don't think of you in that way" or "I love you like a mate" so he could let go and move on. He did not expect you to sit there and say "I do not love you. I've always known how you felt and I kind of hoped if I ignored it you'd go away. And, by the way, everyone you know has known how you felt and – while they've all been laughing at you – they've tried to convince me to go out with you but y'know, I couldn't face it. Because you know what, you're funny, and gorgeous and clever, but you're missing that certain something that makes you lovable. And, you know all those times I've shagged you, well, it was out of friendship, not cos I've felt anything, despite all those mixed messages I've been sending and how I've reacted in the past when you've gone out with other people. Oh, yes, there was also that night when I told you that if you loved someone, then you should tell them how you feel but when you tell me I just piss on your emotions." So, buddy, do not sit there and tell me I know nothing.

'You've known Jake for so long, you know how sensitive he is, you know how hard it is for him to open up and admit how he feels and you still, *still*, couldn't even afford him the luxury of being patronisingly nice. Anyone who could do that to a friend is a freak.

'Now, please go away and if you can manage it in your egocentric world, stay away from Jake until you find a way to treat him with some respect.'

The Git stared at me and my newly-vented spleen. He'd probably never been told about himself before. Everyone tiptoed around him because he was so gorgeous and did a good impression of being a nice bloke. Everyone around him thought he was a good bloke, a nice lad, really great. The only people who saw the real side of him were the ones who, like Jake, loved him and wanted to be with him. They were the ones who got screwed over because they were stupid enough

371

to fall completely for the nice-guy act. And, well, people like me had to pick up the pieces. Really pick up the pieces. Everyone else just got sick of hearing about it and started to tell the ones like Jake to just put him behind them. To 'get over it'. While I, *I* felt it. I had to feel for Jake and pick up the pieces and want to cry and feel his pain and understand and fret about it. I was the one who got to understand how even when Jake said it was OK he was just putting a brave face on it because he was so humiliated that all his friends knew and had tried to talk The Git into going for it. And all his friends probably sat there discussing it and pitying and wishing he could get a grip. I was the one who knew he was so humiliated because if The Git hadn't said anything, he'd never have been any wiser and in some cases ignorance was bliss; what you didn't know really couldn't upset you.

I glanced up, The Git was still there. 'No, really, I mean it. FUCK! OFF!'

A few people in the pub looked around as he, still wearing that wounded face, got up and walked away. He even left his drink on the table, left a short glass with orange juice and melting ice cubes to dribble condensation on the table as he left the pub.

I watched his back leave the pub. Then it smacked me in the face. Hard. So hard I had to drop my head into my hands.

I've done it again. I've only gone and done it again.

I've gotten involved. I've broken my silence. I've behaved like BLOODY, TWATTING Cupid again.

Oh well, just this one thing couldn't hurt. Could it?

CHAPTER 34

DOWN AND DOWN

'Hi, Ceri, it's Viv. Remember me? I used to be your old boss. Actually, I was your boss and your friend. I know I didn't come to your leaving do, and I know I didn't speak to you during your last month working for me, but we were friends, weren't we?

'Anyway, I was just ringing to see how you are. And to get your advice on something. My husband's sister is going to work abroad and she asked me to go with her. I was wondering what you thought I should do? I mean, you gave up everything to go chase a dream in Leeds and I was wondering if I should too? Anyway, give me a call or email me, I need to hear from you. Bye.'

After the incident with Jake's man, I became hot property. My life became the epitome of 'treat 'em mean, keep 'em keen'. My mobile rang off the hook with people calling me 'for a chat', i.e., to tell me their latest problems. I was literally getting calls back to back.

The people from Leeds realised I'd taken my ball home so didn't bother me as much. It was everyone I'd known in London, everyone from my past stepping into the breach. 'Just ringing to say hi, see how you are'; 'haven't spoken in ages, just wanted to catch up', i.e., I want to tell you my problems. I want advice, I want to share my latest love news with you.

The woman who was living in my flat and whose boyfriend had moved in, rang to tell me they were getting married. Having lived together for, what, four months, they couldn't imagine being apart. They were getting married in December – six months' time – and would I possibly consider

a) being a bridesmaid

b) letting them stay in the flat when I moved back to London

A few days later she rang again to ask me if I'd consider selling my flat to them. They'd pay almost double its worth cos they'd really fallen in love there and wanted to stay. I was still going 'huh?' when my paranoid ex-boss Viv called to ask about her love life.

A day later, Whashisface Tosspot rang out of the blue. I hadn't spoken to him in almost three years, and let's not forget that I didn't say his name out loud so he wouldn't ever call me. But I'd answered my mobile not recognising the number and it was him. He'd simply wanted advice on why his marriage was going wrong. Was it because he'd only known her nine months when they said, 'I do' or was it because I'd cursed his marriage? What should he do?

My first ever boyfriend called to tell me he was getting married, finally, to the woman he left me for ELEVEN years ago. Oh, by the way, his best mate was getting married in Skipton at the end of the month and he'd been told to invite me. On and on, people who I didn't even know had my number were calling me, or emailing me. Or finding me via the college website and dropping me a line. I took to turning off my mobile for hours and hours – only to find my messages backed up to the answermachine's capacity; I only spoke to my family on my home phone and I started to develop a phobia to email.

It was as though something was trying to tell me: 'You think you had it bad before? Well, this is what it could really be like. Count yourself lucky it's not everyone beating a path to your door, all right?' After ten days of this, I conceded. Gave in to it.

I lay in bed one Tuesday night and accepted my fate. Accepted my fate may have been overstating the case. It was more a case of resigning myself to it for the moment, until I could find some kind of get-out clause.

'All right, God, The Universe, Karma, Whoever You are who has placed this upon my head, You win,' I said out loud. 'I will go back to being what I was before. I'm not necessarily saying I believe I'm Cupid, modern-day or otherwise, I'm just saying if it's my purpose in life to fuck up friend-ships; incite people to have sex with their exes;

make young boys get married too young and make older women unhappy with everything, then I'll do it. I've learnt me lesson. No shirking my responsibilities.'

I closed my eyes and tried to sleep.

'Oh, PS, I'm not saying I'll go about my duties happily, though, all right? Just as long as that's clear.'

CHAPTER 35

'I'M BACK, BABY'

I made my reappearance in the canteen the next day. I'd not mustered up the energy to face a Gwen session, so hid out in my office until lunchtime. Screwing up her life, making her unhappy would just have to wait. It was one-fifteen by the time I got to the canteen. I got food, a charming-looking Caesar salad with a side order of chips. (The chips served to remind me that I hadn't been to the gym. At all.)

I took a couple of steps away from the cashier and immediately found myself not only up Shit Creek without a paddle, but also without a boat. On one side of the canteen, in the blue corner was Mel, hunched over a magazine he so wasn't reading; in the red corner sat Claudine, doing the same with a book. It'd got that bad they couldn't even sit together. Both looked up when I left the safety of the company of the cashier and, even without my glasses I saw each of their faces light up.

Mel waved and beckoned me over; Claudine grinned and pulled out the chair beside her. A surge of rage overcame me. I loved neither of them best; I wasn't sure I liked *people* at that point.

378

How dare they? How dare they use me as a tool in their stupid row. And, God forgive me, it was stupid.

I walked between the two warring factions, found the middle ground (a table equidistant to both tables) and placed my tray on it but I didn't sit. I went to Mel, because I'd met him first, 'Come join me,' I ordered. It was a pleasant order, but an order nonetheless.

Mel was overjoyed at being invited to join me at the big table. Who knew eating with me would be so exciting – many men before him would've paid good money not to eat with me. He got up, picked up his tray and magazine, minced over to where my tray was. The campness came from trying, through his walk, to stick his tongue out to Claudine. *Na, na, Ceri loves me more.*

While Mel minced, I sauntered over to Claudine. 'Come join me,' same tone, same order.

'No thanks,' she replied, glaring at Mel.

'It's not an invite,' I explained, 'it's an order.'

Claudine's eyebrows shot up. *You are ordering ME?* those eyebrows said.

'Claudine, you have burdened me with the very minutiae of your love life, the least you owe me is joining me when "invited" (I made the dreaded air quotes) to.

'And you, Melvin Rivers, can sit your butt back down,' I said, very loudly, so it carried and everyone who was dotted around the middle ground and Claudine's corner, heard. Humiliation wasn't out of the question. This Cupid thing had some perks and being outrageous, saying anything, was one of them. The Universe, Fate, God, Karma, Whatever, expected it of me.

'Well?' I said to Claudine.

She sighed, screwed up her face, then reluctantly got up, gathered her tray and book. 'Don't expect me to talk to him,' she warned in a low voice.

They sat as far away from each other as possible, but were still technically sat opposite me. *Had I really done this? Had my Cupid curse really prised these two close people apart?*

In that moment, I felt a flash of power. It passed as quickly as it came, overtaken by annoyance at these two people who, literally, should have known better. Because not even me and my big mouth and my pheromones and other 'qualities' could've torn apart their friendship if they weren't so bloody pathetic. They should know better, they knew they should know better, but insisted on playing games. And, not very good games, either. My six-year-old niece could play mind games better than these two. If I thought for one minute either of them was genuinely attempting to hurt the other one, I wouldn't be so annoyed. Annoyed and frustrated. It was clear, if you thought about it. And, hey Mel, hey Claudine, I'm sure you've done nothing else but think about it. You both know what is ticking away in your hearts and minds, neither of you wants to face it, though. You'd much rather live in discomfort than face the truth.

'OK,' I smiled. 'Dearly beloved, I have brought you together today, because I think you both need to be told what's going on in your minds.'

I paused, struggling to get warmness back into my voice.

'Claudine, news flash, you do not have to be "in love" to "make love". It's all right to have sex with a man and find that afterwards, you don't want to run away with him. Admittedly, your boyfriend might not see it that way, but you did what you did. You can't unsleep with Mel. Pretending it didn't happen won't change things either.

'I'm telling you, categorically, you're not in love with Mel. You may love Mel, but you're not in love with him – I know it's not what you want to hear, but it's the truth. And he certainly doesn't compare to Kevin. If he did, you'd have left Kevin, life or no life. Well, you'd have at least done it more than once.

'So, bloody stop trying to convince yourself that sex equals love. You might be an old romantic, you might *want* to be in love with Mel, because, well, you've known him for years and he's lovely and he's a good friend and he's a great shag, but you don't. Just because all the elements are there, doesn't mean it'll work. You know I'm right, it's already in your mind. Which is why, when I asked you that night at my house why you didn't go round to Mel's and shag him senseless, you were horrified. You wouldn't do that to Kevin, not twice.'

Claudine opened her mouth to speak.

'Shut up. I'm talking.

'Before I realised what I wanted to do with my life was wreck it by coming up here, I read this quote. It went: "Ours is a world where people don't know what they want and are willing to go through hell to get it." That's you, except you do *know* what you want, can't accept that, so are willing to put yourself through all types of hell to get what you think you should want.

'My advice, the last bit of advice you get for free is this: tell Mel you're not in love with him. Once you say it out loud and the sky doesn't come crashing in, you might actually believe it.

'Then, go home, talk to Kevin. Sit him down in a room, look him straight in the eye and talk to him. At the root of all of this is the fact that, despite how beautiful you are, how lovely a person you are, you have low self-esteem. Mel made you feel good, he gave you the attention you craved from Kevin. You needed Mel to tell you you're beautiful and worthy. You probably felt indebted to him for giving you that ego boost when you needed it most. That doesn't mean you have to talk yourself into being in love with him. Tell Kevin you need his attention and his time, roger him senseless, and then start building the next stage of your life together.'

I twisted a fraction in my seat. 'Mel. You are a commitment-phobe. There is nothing wrong with it, some of my best friends are commitment-phobes, you just shouldn't have got married when you did.

'You felt the fear, you did it anyway and you screwed over three perfectly great people in the process.' I raised my fingers.

'Number one: your wife. She never stood a chance because you thought you wanted a mythical person who was gorgeous, fertile, funny, fun, etc., etc., when all you really wanted was a friend. Which, she wasn't. That was her one fatal flaw.

'Number two: Claudine. She was your get-out clause – not just with your wife. I'll bet you've compared every woman you've met to her. And, I'll bet my flat, my savings and my lunch that none of them matched up. They were all in a different league, none of them good enough. When you were looking for a way out of your marriage, Claudine became the reason. Not the fact Fran wasn't the type of woman you wanted in the first place. If you loved Claudine like that, you'd have done something about it. Don't give me that, "you have no idea how it is to love someone from afar" look. I do, I've done it far longer and far more intensely than you could ever do, and you know what? It's bollocks. If you truly love someone, *truly*, you would do something about it. Anything to get them to love you. I learnt that the hard way. You wouldn't wait until you want a reason to get out of your marriage to engineer a one-night stand. To basically do something you felt was so unforgivable that you'd be forced to end your marriage. If you love someone, really love them, you would, at least, have done the whole, sit them down the night before you get married thing and tell them how you feel.

'Much as you love Claudine, she has always been Ms Convenience. And now you're free, she's Ms I Should Want Her. Mel, if you really love her. really want her, then get down on one knee and propose right now. And find out what she says. But you won't cos you're not in love with Claudine, no matter how much you love her.

'The third person you've screwed over is you. You have spent so much time avoiding yourself and your fear of being tied down, you ruined your marriage, almost ruined your friendship with Claudine, got smacked in the face. You're allowed to be friends with a woman without wanting to shag her. You *need* to be friends with women without shagging them. It's a radical, scary concept, but as Mark Twain said, "Courage is the mastery of fear – not the absence of it." Be brave. Accept what happened before Christmas for what it was – a way to get out of your marriage, a drunken fumble, then be friends with Claudine again, instead of a reminder that you had sex. Despite what you've been led to believe, sex isn't the be all and end all, it's just sex. If it was more with Claudine, you would've done it more than once.

'And, once you're friends with Claudine again, try getting on the phone and apologising to your wife. The fact you hardly spoke to her for the last however many months of your marriage should tell you something, namely, you'd both forgotten what it was like to be together as two people rather than as "a couple". Which is the root of your commitment-phobic nightmare – the reason you want a friend, not a wife. You've always thought that once you get settled, fun goes out the window but that doesn't happen with friends. It doesn't have to happen with couples, but you don't know that yet. In time, I reckon you'll sort out your head, you'll get some perspective on the whole thing and will be able to have a settled relationship and not run away from it, but for now, apologise to Fran. It's not her fault you wanted to live in a fun house twenty-four/seven.'

I paused, sagged in my seat, spent. I never thought I'd get tired of hearing myself speak; I'd never thought I'd get tired of talking.

'Now, one final thing. Something aimed at the two of you. In all of this, you seem to have forgotten something very important: you two are friends. Beyond the sex, the marriage break-ups and the face-punching you two are real friends. Nothing should stand in the way of that. So many people are crying out for someone they can trust, for that kind of friendship. You've got it – stop fucking about with it.'

I dropped the leaf of lettuce I'd used as a pointer and got up, picking up my tray as I stood. I didn't hang about to see what they did next. I didn't need to. All those two really needed was someone to say what they didn't want to hear. Voice their inner turmoil.

I took my tray up to my office – my office buddy Sally wasn't in on Wednesday – and I sat at her desk so I could stare out the window as I ate.

Knock! Knock! came two minutes later. I was never going to have lunch, was I?

'Yes?' I called, twisting in my chair to look at the door. I had a crisp piece of iceberg lettuce poised to go into my mouth. I lowered it when Gwen's head popped around the door.

'Hi, Gwen,' I said, steeling myself for a rant. She had over a month's worth to deliver. 'Come in.'

'Just a quick word,' she said, fixing me with her blue eyes. 'There'll be a memo coming around later, but I wanted to tell you in person first.'

'Oh?' I said. The funding to the department's been cut – I was out on my ear.

'What's the problem?'

'No problem,' she said. 'I've resigned.'

She didn't even look serious, much less sound serious. 'Got to go. Bye.'

Oh my giddy aunt, uncle, nieces, nephews and unlikely to be born grandchildren.

CHAPTER 36

THE REAL GWEN

This was something I never thought would happen. Gwen and I sitting in the Fox & Hound, having a drink together. I'd bolted after her to check she was serious. She confirmed she was. Before I knew what I was doing I was saying we should go for a drink round the corner and down the road.

She'd leapt at the offer like a thirsty woman in a desert. I'd forgotten that I was the nearest thing she'd got in college to a best mate. Or a mate.

'What's going on?' I asked her.

I'd got myself a beer and her a brandy. I remember her saying once she liked brandy.

She lit up a cigarette, I held my breath.

'I've resigned,' she squealed. Then she covered her solar plexus with her hand. 'That feels good and scary to say at the same time.'

'Why?'

She shrugged. 'I felt like it.'

'Have you got another job?' This was like pulling teeth.

'No.'

'And you're going in a month?'

'Yes. They want me to do the summer, supervise the exams and whatnot. But I'm going in a month.'

'You've got interviews lined up?'

'No.'

It's all right. Don't panic. She's got a husband, he'll take care of her if she falls on hard times. And you've probably got nothing to do with her screwing up her life by leaving the only paid position she's qualified to do.

'When you wrote to me about a position in the psychology department, did you have other things lined up?'

WHAT THE HELL HAVE I GOT TO DO WITH IT? 'No.'

'But you still took a chance on giving up your life. What if we'd written back saying "no vacancies"? What would you have done?'

'No, you see, I hadn't resigned from my job in London when I wrote to you.'

'Emotionally you had.'

'What?'

'Ceri, you don't really believe we'd have given you an interview on your qualifications and experience if we thought you were committed to your job in London, do you?'

It's not my fault, it's not my fault, la la, it's not my fault.

'The reason I gave you that first interview was because of the passion in your letter. Everyone who read it said your enthusiasm and passion and *joie de vivre* came through in it. That's very, very rare. Almost extinct these days. You put everything into that letter and you couldn't have done that if you were happy with your job.'

'I was still doing it though. Still getting paid. Still paying the mortgage, etc.'

'You had emotionally left. I emotionally left my position here ages ago. And now, I'm physically leaving too.'

'What does your husband say about all this?'

Gwen moved her gaze from me, to the other side of the bar. 'I wonder what it's going to be like, waking up on the day after I finally leave and know that this is the first day of the rest of my life.'

Clearly, transparently, screamingly obviously she didn't want to talk about what her husband said about her decision. When has that ever stopped me wading in mouth first?

'What does your husband think about your decision to quit?'

She replied first with the filthiest look known to womankind. Part of me expected her to jump up onto the rickety table and sing: 'Hey you! Don't rain on my parade!'

Once my face was smeared with her filthy look, she said: 'He's fine with it. Whatever makes me happy makes him happy.'

When I first saw *Cat On A Hot Tin Roof*, I'd never heard the word mendacity before. Immediately after I saw it I heard mendacity everywhere. And now,

I was sitting beside a woman whose very name could be mendacity, she reeked of it so. At the very least her husband didn't approve; at the most, he didn't know. Actually, at the most, he didn't exist.

'I still haven't been around for dinner yet,' I said. 'I'm free most nights for the next couple of weeks, how about we fix a date?'

'Vernon is away,' Gwen said, faster than a speeding bullet. 'Business.'

'For two weeks?'

Gwen sighed the sigh of an annoyed creature. 'Why are we talking about Vernon? It's me who has resigned.'

'You haven't resigned in a vacuum, there are other people who'd be affected, namely your nearest and dearest.'

'Keep talking, Ceri, you've just about disinvited yourself to my leaving do.'

Well slap my face and call me Cupid, Gwen had a nasty streak. She wasn't simply demented and unable to be happy, she had viciousness behind them there squeaky vocal cords.

'I suppose I'm just being selfish. If you leave, who'll – *[suffocate me with smoke/bend my ear by whining alone/make me grateful for my deep voice]* – encourage me? Who'll – *[remind me to avoid pastel flowers/show me how not to teach/make me avoid the common room]* – be my champion in the psychology department?'

Gwen looked away, lit a cigarette, I wondered if she was fighting to put that nastiness back in its

390

box, or if she was formulating a clever way to tell me to fornicate off.

'You'll survive,' she said. *Ah, so we were still being nasty.*

'I guess I'll have to.'

'You haven't done that badly so far. I'll have to do your assessment before I leave, and you haven't done too badly.'

There it was again – praise so faint it was damning. First Mel, now Gwen.

'You're very popular with the students,' she went on. 'Although, that's not always a good thing. You're there to assist their learning, not befriend or entertain them. Students need someone to look up to, to respect, they can't do that if they think of you as nothing more than a buddy.'

'Yeah, you're probably right.'

Gwen looked at me.

'No, really, you're right. I'm a big interfering herd, but I can't help it. I just have this gift for being too nice. You know, when people vent on me, I don't have the gumption to ignore them, or tell them I'm not interested, I just sit there and listen. If some student looks bored, I try to make things more interesting.' I slid down in my seat. 'I wake up every morning saying to myself: "If someone tries to embroil me in their life today, I'm not getting involved. I'm not allowed. Just don't listen; just don't care. Let them go about their screwed up lives without you." And then, someone will sit down beside me, start to unload, and rather than go glassy-eyed and tune out so they don't do it again; rather than get up and walk away. I listen. I care. But you're right, I'll try so much harder next time to be short, uninterested and to be the unfriendly lecturer that everyone respects. Thanks for that reminder.'

Yes, I actually said that. Out loud. She was leaving, I could. Also, I was thinking, *What's the worst that could happen if I said what I thought?* She could glass me was the worst. Seeing as I couldn't imagine that vividly enough, I went ahead and spoke my mind. Jess would've been proud of me. Jess would've glassed me. But that was my best friend for you.

Moreover, I wasn't sat in the Fox & Hound, passively smoking and drinking on an empty stomach for my benefit.

'I, I didn't mean to upset you,' Gwen said, suddenly sounding much more squeaky again.

'You haven't. I'm crap. I needed to be told, didn't I? Cast ye not pearls before swine and all that. I might've gone on through life, being nice to people for the sake of it.'

Gwen now looked suitably shamefaced. I felt no guilt. Why the hell should I?

'I'll get this next round in,' Gwen squeaked, then scuttled off to the bar. Some people just don't know when you're trying to help them.

CHAPTER 37

SAVING ED

Claudine and Mel had been relatively easy to sort out. All they needed was a verbal head banging together. If that hadn't worked, I would've gone in for a bit of literal head banging.

Gwen, on the other hand, was a work in progress. Later, obviously, I'd been visited by the guilt demons for being so sarcastic when she obviously wasn't happy. It was true, no one resigned into a vacuum. And no one upped and resigned because they'd emotionally left. You might want to, you might dream of it, but anyway, blah, blah, work in progress. Another chapter, another time. I'd sort her out later.

It was Ed that I didn't want to encounter.

Robyn was about to move in. Jake had given his consent, all the while glaring at me. Later, when Ed had bounced off to his room to start making space for his new love, Jake had glared at me while offering me a cup of tea.

I'd left it a couple of days after that to broach the subject. In fact, four days. In fact, four days that seemed to be more a week. I was that much of a coward. I didn't want to burst his bubble. It was all right for Jake, he wasn't being asked to go life-destroying.

Ed's hair had grown a bit, taking the harshness off his face. His face was so flushed with joy, his body was back to being clothed in his usual type of attire, the jeans, the heavy metal T-shirt, the lumberjack shirt but this time they all looked cleaned and ironed. You thought you knew someone, but that bendy kid with the blank stare was richer than I'd ever imagined anyone could be. The son of a tinned foods manufacturer, so he was. The irony of that being Ed constantly looked like he needed a good feeding. How the hell would I approach this, anyway? 'Ed, that good-looking woman you're so enamoured with, well, Jake thinks she's after your cash, and well, he might have a point . . .' I mean . . .

Anyway, a week later, I climbed the stairs like a woman approaching the gallows. I wanted him to be happy. Even if for a little while. It was the reminders of those small pearls of happiness we needed to cling to in those times when you were so lonely and hurting you thought it'd never end. Ed might not get this happiness again.

I knocked, turned the doorhandle. 'Ed, you got a minute?' I asked.

'Course,' Ed grinned, pausing in folding up his clothes. 'Come in.'

He indicated to a small clear space on his bed. 'Sit yourself down.'

I sat on his pillow, pulled my bare feet up, moved a little to get my bum into a comfortable position. His room was almost as large as mine. He'd even squeezed a small sofa in the corner, it was like a studio. Nice carpet, pale blue walls, high ceilings. Oh for God's sake Ceri, it's not as if you've never been in here before.

'Hi,' I said. Always the best way to start a difficult conversation.

'What's the matter, Cezza?' Ed said, sitting on top of a pile of clothes. Seeing as he'd seemed to wear the same set of clothes until of late, he had rather a lot of clothes.

'Ed,' I began. 'I know you're totally . . .' *What's the word, infatuated, in love with, brainwashed?* '. . . with Robyn, but I wonder if it's all moving a bit too fast.' That didn't sound too bad, did it?

'Yeah, it is. But I'm happy Ceri.'

Fair enough. I'll be going then.

'I know Jake thinks that,' Ed said. 'He's made no secret of it, but I thought you'd understand.'

'Ed, you're getting married next year. You won't have known her but a year before you make a lifetime commitment. I do understand, but it doesn't stop me worrying.'

'I love her.'

'But why do *you* have to give up college? Why not her?'

Ed got up, went to the window, perched himself on the wide window ledge. 'Jake told you, didn't he?'

'Told me what?'

'I told him to not tell a soul, but he told you how much money my family has. And he thinks Robyn couldn't possibly love me for me being me, it has to be for my money. Well, my family's money, I'm not worthy, I'm not good-looking enough, I'm not funny or witty or clever enough, it has to be my family's money. Is that what you think too?'

'It's crossed my mind, but no, I don't think that. Even if your family were as poor as church mice, I'd still want to know why you have to give up college and her not. You're in this fifty-fifty. Why do you get to make the big sacrifice?'

'Really?'

'Yes, really. I don't think for one minute you're the sort of person who would live off his family money. You'd get bored. You need to be working, Edwardo, you're that kind of lad, so why give up your chosen path?'

Ed stared at the ground, then looked up at me. 'Ceri, I hate college. The only other person I told that to is Robyn. I mean, I really hate college. I was only doing a PhD cos I couldn't think of anything else to do. I finished college, and it made sense to carry on. And now, I've got a reason to give it up.'

'But Robyn shouldn't be your reason.'

'She isn't. I said I've got a reason, I didn't say Robyn was that reason. She loves college, she's staying till the end of the year.'

'And your reason is . . . ?'

'Only Robyn knows. And me, of course.'

'Of course.'

'Robyn and I have this plan. It was my idea, a vague idea, and then I told her and she helped refine it.'

Ed moved off the window sill, went to his desk drawer, pulled it open, pulled out a folder, bulging with papers. He handed me the folder. On the front was scrawled *Ed & Robyn's Top Secret Project*.

I opened the orange folder, flicked through. There was page after page of what looked like a business plan. Letters from banks, info on business loans, specs on office space. 'What is this apart from your Secret Project?' I was too stunned by how much was done to take any info in.

'We're going into business. But not like that. The only part of my college life I like is the teaching part. And I love literature and plays and Robyn's an actress. She knows lots of actors who'll be willing to give up their time for a while. So, well, we're going to set up a touring company. We travel to schools, teach them about putting on plays, how all the boring stuff they read was meant to be done. It'll help get children interested in literature.'

Vague idea indeed.

'We won't make big profits. We'll just charge a fee to cover costs and to allow us to live. Any profits will go back into the business at first. I mean, it's top secret now, but when Robyn finishes college we'll get to it. We've almost got the funding sorted and . . .'

I could warm myself by the fire that burnt in Ed's eyes; I could lift my heart with the passion that fuelled his words. This really was the real deal for Ed.

'And you're going to do all this with Robyn?'

'I told you before it wasn't just a wank thing with Robyn. It's not just a sex thing with her now that I've got her. It's an every thing. Cezza, I don't know if we're all supposed to be with one person all our life; I don't know if we've got soul mates, but I do know Robyn is the only person I want to work towards something with. I'm on this road, she's on it with me. "A life lived in fear is a life half lived." That's what you said.' (I knew that would come back to haunt me at some point.) 'Now that's what I'm seeing through. I might very well hate Robyn after a few years; our business might fall flat on its face, but it might not. And at least I'll know. I'm young enough to start again if it all goes horribly wrong.'

And what do you say to that? Go back on everything I've ever done myself?

'I'll leave you to it, then.' I stood.

'Thanks, Ceri,' Ed said.

'For?'

'Speaking your mind instead of just being nasty to Robyn. I really do love her.'

'Good for you, sweetie.'

'Oh, and I haven't told Robyn about my family's

money. The only person I've told was Jake and now you.'

'Don't worry, I shan't tell another soul. Not even Jess.'

'Thanks.'

No, sweetheart, thank you. For reminding me why I gave up my life down south in the first place. Wasn't it, life's too long not to go for it?

'Mission accomplished,' I said to Jake, when he came back from college later.

'You talked to Ed?' he said, relieved and terrified in one go.

'I did.'

'And he's going to slow down. Not leave college?'

'Jake, he's happy. He's really happy. Leave him to it. If it does go horribly wrong, you'll be the first one he comes to. Unless, of course, you're going to turn your back on him.'

'Course I wouldn't. But Ceri, you do realise that you can't ever leave us now, cos if it does go horribly wrong, you're going to be picking up the pieces too.'

'Yeah, you might have a point there.'

Jake's face came over all mysterious as he said, 'Oh, I got a letter from Terry today. He kind of guessed I wasn't speaking to him or opening his emails, so he wrote to me.'

'And what did it say?'

'Quite a lot. He apologised for what he said that time. He said that he was really ashamed of how much he hurt me. That it didn't occur to him how hard it was for me to say all that and how his panic that I was making demands on him made him say all those awful things. He also explained that he'd flirted with me because he likes me, but thinks we'd make a nightmare couple, which is fair enough really. I just wanted to be treated with a bit of respect. For him to know that because he didn't love me he had no right to ill-treat me or be rude to me, you know?'

I nodded.

'Anyways, the letter went on and on, apologising, not trying to excuse himself and he ended by saying could I ring him and meet him for a drink so he could say all these things face to face.'

'Are you going?'

'I've been.'

'And?'

'And he's nipped down the road to get some milk.'

'Does that mean he's getting another chance?'

'Yes. And you know what, it doesn't matter what you think, or anyone else thinks, it's my life. My emotions. I can give the bastard a second chance if I want to.'

'My work is done, here,' I replied, then leant across the sofa to grab the remote control.

There was a short rap at the front door.

'I just wonder who the woman in the pub who called him an arrogant, self-serving little prig, could've been,' Jake said as he went to answer the door. 'You wouldn't know anything about that would you, Cezza?'

'Why would I?' I replied, innocently.

'Why indeed.'

CHAPTER 38

LOVE IS IN THE AIR

'Champagne, champagne,' Claudine waved two bottles about as she sang her way into the centre of the Senior Common Room. 'I've got champagne. It's even cold,' she said. 'Someone get the plastic cups.'

The Senior Common Room was unusually full. It was nearly the end of term and almost everyone came to college every day because they had things to finish before the summer. All except Gwen, she'd started coming to college less and less. She had that, 'what are they going to do, sack me?' attitude. Whether she had another job seemed to be contentious. Whenever I asked her, she gave me an enigmatic smile Mona Lisa would've been envious of and said she had something sorted out.

Craig furnished the champagne bearer with small white plastic cups. Mel appeared to help Claudine open the bottles.

'What are we celebrating?' Craig asked.

'Oh, just the newest addition to my jewellery collection,' Claudine held out her left hand – flashing her engagement ring. 'Actually, I didn't have a jewellery collection until yesterday,' she confessed.

Everyone crowded around, even the men oohed and awwwed at the gold ring with three sapphires glinting on her hand.

'We're going to get married just before Christmas. It'll be a small service, but we'll have a big party, which I hope all of you will come to.'

The crowd murmured yes as plastic cups with champagne were handed out.

Claudine, looking radiant, grinned from ear to ear. Her skin was back to being vibrant, her cropped black hair was glossy again.

She'd put on enough weight to make her look healthy as well. 'Three weeks ago I was plotting to be single, albeit unintentionally, and last night I got engaged. Who knew things could change so suddenly. Isn't life funny?' Claudine said. 'Cheers.'

'Cheers,' the room replied. People broke off into little groups, started chatting amongst themselves. Most of the women stayed where they were to admire Claudine's ring. I stayed in my seat, I'd look at the ring later. I was happy for her. She deserved this happiness with Kevin, but then, so did I. Not with Kevin, obviously. But with someone. And I wasn't likely to get it, was I?

Moments like this made me feel sorry for myself, again; dragged me back to my 'what about me?' lamentations. Really though, what about me? When would I get a ring on my finger or even a declaration of love? Or have those bouts of lone-liness abated?

I stared forlornly into my plastic cup of light, bubbly liquid.

Never, was the short reply.

'Life *is* funny,' Mel said, flopping beside me. 'I called my wife.'

I looked at Mel. It was because of things like this, people like this that I'd be alone for ever. *Come on, you do care*, a voice inside said. *Pretend all you like that you don't want to know, but you do. You're a nosy cow and you're going to spend the rest of your life doing it. Yer might as well enjoy it.* 'Oh?' I said.

'I told her everything. Everything. She wasn't happy. In fact, she abused me quite a lot. She used language that would make a sailor blush. And she hung up a few times. But, I apologised, for everything and . . . we're having lunch on Saturday. Ostensibly to talk about our divorce. After the abuse, though, we had a laugh for the first time ever. A laugh, like I do with Clau. We could become mates after all.'

I nudged him. 'I knew you could do it.'

'Yeah, just needed that kick up the arse. Clau told me that she and Kevin had a really good chat. She told him that she thought she was heading towards something with me and that she wanted them to sort themselves out before it happened. He took it really well, apparently. So, they've managed to move on and, *voilà*, one engagement later.'

'And you're all right with that?'

'Yep. I am, actually. I thought it'd devastate me, but when she told me, I was so overwhelmed with happiness for her, I realised you were right. I wasn't in love with her. I was in love with the idea of her. Like you said, she needed attention. I needed to talk to Fran.'

I lowered my head onto Mel's shoulder, looked at Claudine being the centre of attention. 'You and me, kidder, we're not so different. We should stick together,' I said to him. Mel tucked a lock of my hair behind my ear. Jake and Ed would have a fit if they saw us. So would Staring Man.

'Can I get a bit of champagne, please,' Trudy asked Craig. I'd begun to think that she didn't exist. I hadn't seen her at all since the loos.

'You're looking unusually chipper these days, Trudy,' Craig said as he filled her plastic cup. 'Anything we should know?'

An audience of expectant faces held their breaths and awaited her response. I stared into my plastic cup and started counting bubbles. I wondered if any of them had actually been on the receiving end of one of her outbursts.

'The reason I look so "chipper" these days, you cheeky *get*, is that somebody inadvertently gave me a reality check. Made me face a lot of things I'd been hiding from.'

That was open.

'And,' Trudy ploughed on. 'I might as well tell you all now, I'm going to have a baby.'

405

Another collective sigh went around the room. This was celebration city today. As everyone crowded around her with questions about due dates and names, I chanced a look at her. Just to see what she looked like when she wasn't shaken up, crying or screaming abuse. Our eyes met, and, before I looked away, her face relaxed into the most beautiful smile, then she mouthed: 'Thank you.'

After time had passed, and people had left the SCR to finish finishing off for the end of term, I caught Craig watching me with my head still on Mel's shoulder, us talking about nothing much. His face showed he was thinking hard, like he did when he 'sat back' in a conversation. Then, he said, very loudly: 'Has anyone noticed the vibe that's been going on around here since Ceri started?'

I stuck two fingers up at him. It was an automatic gesture though. I didn't actually care what he said. I'd be more surprised if he'd said: '*Have you noticed how nothing has changed since Ceri started?*'

'We were all stuck in this rut of normality before, and then Ceri turns up and Claudine's engaged, Gwen's resigned and Trudy's up the duff. And I, well, I am back with my ex-girlfriend. And, all right, most of you have heard me say she was a psycho but once I got to know her, she really wasn't that bad. Or mad.'

'I thought you went out with her for two years,' one of the women admiring Claudine's ring said.

'Exactly. I only started to bother with her when Ceri started. And once I bothered, I found out there was goodness inside her. She's really sweet. I like this vibe around here, though,' Craig said. 'It's like, anything's possible now.'

'I know what you mean,' Claudine said. 'It's like, the sky's the limit.'

'Yeah,' Mel added. 'It's like everything is good underneath even if it's bad on the surface. There are lots of good vibrations.' He sang: 'Good vibrations are all around us.'

'That's, love is all around us, duh brain,' Claudine said.

Craig's mouth dropped open as he swung round to gawp at me . . .

SUMMER HOLIDAYS

CHAPTER 39

THE CUPID EFFECT

Why I had to meet Gwen here, I didn't know. I wasn't a big fan of airports at the best of times. Mostly because you had to travel halfway across town to get to them. It'd taken me ages to get to Leeds Bradford airport by public transport. I'd tried to get Jess to drive me there and she'd told me where to go.

I wandered across the concourse, feeling lost and cross. *Meet me in the main bit*, Gwen had said. I'd not realised there was so much to the main bit. And there was every danger of me making eye contact with someone, seeing as I was looking for her. I was hot and bothered. I should be at home, in bed. I was going to London in two days, I needed all the sleep I could to handle sleeping on my parents' sofa for a while. The offer on my flat had been tempting, but I hadn't accepted it. I'd not known what I was going to do next February when my contract was up so I wasn't going to be selling owt until I decided.

Gwen had made sure I'd travel practically across the world to see her by saying she had my copy

411

of my assessment with her and she'd give it to me if I met her. Crafty old woman.

'Ceri!' a voice squeaked across the concourse. I looked around. No one who looked even vaguely like Gwen stood among the crowd. She waved. I double-took. A woman with long black hair stood where Gwen should have been. She wore a black vest, a denim overshirt and, whoa, shorts! Gwen was wearing shorts. I looked behind me to check this woman wasn't waving at someone else. No one behind me. Which meant, shorts woman was Gwen.

We sat on a bench, her rucksack on the seat between us, Gwen leant on the rucksack as she talked. She'd handed me a white envelope with my name on the front the moment we sat down.

'It's your assessment,' she said. 'Don't open it yet. Wait till I'm gone, then you can't tell me off.'

'So this is your new job?' I asked, prodding the rucksack.

'The Ancient Traveller? Yes.'

'Hey, less of the traveller bit, you, you're only going on holiday,' I joked.

Gwen laughed. 'No, I'm going away for at least a year. And if I come back, I'll be moving to London or Dublin. Or maybe even Paris. But not Leeds. Definitely not Leeds.'

'Don't tell me, you've emotionally left Leeds.'

'By Jove, I think you've finally got it.'

She was all right, Gwen, when she wasn't being

her usual self. And she so wasn't looking her usual self. Shorts. I glanced at her shorts and then her legs. Double-took. Her podgy pins were a patchwork of scars. Some circular, others deep and long. The skin on her legs, which had obviously not seen the light of day in years, were bluish white, making the disfigurements more prominent. *That's* why she wore thick tights no matter what the weather.

My heart raced all of a sudden, sickness washed through my stomach. I wanted to tear my eyes away from her legs, wounded as they were.

Ouch, there it was again. An aching for someone. For Gwen. This really hurt though. My legs began to throb with the agony she'd endured. With whatever it was that caused her scars. I suddenly knew what it felt like to not be able to wear skirts or shorts. How much self-disgust went into bathing every day and seeing your skin marked like that. The non-physical pain of knowing that if you went out without tights everyone would stare at you in horror and fascination. No one would skip over your legs, see it and accept it. There'd be pity or disgust, never indifference. I inhaled deeply. This was part of Gwen's problem. She never felt normal. She couldn't be. I felt that now. I understood that now. Probably why she latched onto me. I didn't know anything about her, so that made me an ideal friend.

'It's going to take getting used to,' Gwen said, raising and straightening her legs, 'showing off my legs. I haven't worn shorts in . . . years. Not since I got married. Actually, about a year after I got married.'

More pain shot through my legs, but this time the pain carried on travelling up to my heart, as everything finally, finally fell into place.

That day in my office when Gwen thought I'd been beaten up flashed through my mind. '*When one of my friends was being physically abused by her husband, it was virtually impossible for her to talk about. She had bruises all over and an excuse to match each one. I don't want you to feel you have to suffer in silence like that. I understand.*' At that time, she saw me in her. She thought I was suffering like she was and had tried to reach out to me. Tried to save me. I might've guessed if I hadn't been so consumed by the Angel/huge bruise on my face thing. Not that I would've been able to do anything. Except, possibly, not be so down on her when she resigned. Not given in to irritation when she 'whinged'. I'd kind of guessed there was something behind her odd behaviour, her inability to be happy or to relax. But I hadn't cared enough to pursue it. Her problems weren't 'sexy', literally, like Mel and Claudine's. How could I do that? I thought I was open to all callers at all hours, but no.

Gwen looked from her legs to my face. 'But it's all right now,' she added, obviously seeing my concern. 'I finally did it. That's why I quit, that's why I'm here.'

414

'Finally did what?' I asked.

'This is my escape, Ceri, from all the things that held me back.'

'Your husband's not going with you?' I asked cautiously. I just wanted to double-check I'd decoded the speak about her legs correctly.

'Vernon's gone on a business trip for a few days. I think he'll be surprised when he comes back to find me gone and our joint savings account and our investment account and the accounts he had in my name a few thousand pounds lighter. In fact, he'll only have £10 left in each of them.'

'Where are you going?' I asked.

'On the third flight out of here. Three's my lucky number, so I'm going to get on the third plane. Which means, I need to be going.'

She stood, hoisted her rucksack onto her back. She was truly transformed. Her black hair flowed down her back, instead of being pulled back into a bun, or straightened to hang around her face like slabs of dead meat. Her body was comfortable. Not slender, not tall, comfortable. At ease. Relaxed. She moved with elegance and ease. As though someone had finally given her permission to enjoy moving in her body. WHAM-BAM! It hit me. No cigarette. That's why she looked different. No cigarette. No look as though gagging for a cigarette. She looked about ten years younger with this comfortable persona.

'I've told the college to offer you a permanent position. They might not, but I've told them. Your research supervisor is very impressed with what you've done so far, she thinks it's PhD material, so you could stay, do a PhD. You'd have to work on getting yourself funding and getting the title right, but you could do it. Although you might not want to stay, but I think you should.'

'I might, I haven't decided what I want to do yet. February is a long time away.'

'I know. But with all the changes in the department, this is probably the time to decide if you want to stay or not.'

'Thanks, I'll think about it.'

'You do that.'

'OK, bye.'

'Bye.' Gwen turned and went to walk away, then she suddenly spun on her trainered feet. 'All this is thanks to you, Ceri. That's why I wanted to see you before I went.'

'No,' I raised my hands, 'do not put any of this on me. Good or bad, do not put it on me.'

'Have it your way. But when you breeze into a place, so openly following your heart by leaving your comfortable life, going back to living like a student and being happy with what you're doing and who you are, please don't be surprised if people copy you. Especially people like me who thought they were stuck as they were for ever.

'When you show people it's possible to live their dreams, don't be surprised if they,' she took my hands, squeezed them, 'thank you.'

Didn't I say not to put it on me?

'I'll email you from wherever I end up,' Gwen called over her shoulder as she headed off towards the bank of check-in desks.

'OK,' I replied, then spun away before I saw which desk she was heading for. It was Gwen's big adventure. I didn't want to impose on it by knowing which place the third flight out of there went to.

To be honest. I had always thought of Gwen as a bit of a cow. A deranged cow who didn't know what made students tick. I thought she was one of those people who would love teaching if it wasn't for the students.

When, really, I had no right to judge her. I had no idea what went on in her life beyond the faculty. Her dress sense shouldn't have mattered. I thought I'd left all that vacuous nonsense in London. Not that I thought I was into it. I used to put down people who found dress sense and labels and looks important. But I noticed when Gwen didn't 'fit in'. I noticed the thick black tights, I scorned her because of her thick black tights. Never knowing that they hid the horrors of her life.

I walked around people, heading out of the airport. The pains in my legs had gone now I wasn't near Gwen. As I moved, I felt something odd about my face. I reached up to check what was wrong, found my fingers resting on my teeth.

All right, despite everything, this kind of thing did make me happy. I did find myself enjoying it.

Other people's joy was heartening. The Cupid Effect meant I'd be alone, without long-term sex and love for the rest of my natural life but, sometimes, other people needed it more than me.

EPILOGUE

JUST IN CASE YOU WERE WONDERING . . .

'All right, that's it,' I mumble, slap my hands on the table. 'I'm sorting this out once and for all.'

Jess reaches out to me, but no, nothing is going to stop me. Jess and I had dropped in to college so I could get some stuff done, we could have some cheap lunch and then we'd head off to Otley for the day. But, as I sat eating with my best mate, I'd glanced up to see *him* again. Staring at me.

'Leave it, Ceri,' Jess says.

'No, he can't go around glaring at people and expect them to put up with it.'

Jess makes one more futile grab for me as I pass her. I storm around tables and chairs and the odd diner and head for his table.

'Excuse me,' I say, standing opposite Staring Man at his table.

He glares up at me, his bronze eyes fixed on my face.

'Why do you keep glaring at me?' I demand. 'What have I done to you?'

He frowns slightly, but manages to keep the glare going.

I fold my arms, rest my weight on one leg and continue in my sternest, non-shouting voice. 'I've hardly spoken to you, but in the past six months you've done nothing but give me evils, why?'

'I haven't,' he replies, and his rich voice weakens my knees as usual.

I pull out a chair and sit down. 'You have.'

'I, er . . .'

'You. Have.'

'I admit I've been staring at you. But not giving you evils.'

'All right, the jury's still out on if you were giving me evils or simply staring, but why? Have I got some sort of growth on my face that only you can see? Do I remind you of someone? Do you hate black people? What?'

Staring Man blushes, searches my face for a moment, blushes some more. 'Well, I like you, don't I?'

'Eh?'

'I think you're beautiful and I'm too shy to just come over and start talking to you, so I stare at you instead.'

'Ah.'

'Besides, I thought you had a thing going with Mel. You left that party together and you were together quite often. Even in the supermarket car park when I thought we'd made a connection over *Star Trek*, you brought up Mel. But I

420

still had hope cos I know Mel hates *Star Trek*. Then, like a moment from my worst nightmare, I hit you in the face with that door and, after that, well . . . it became academic if you were with Mel or not; no matter how charming or funny you try to be, no matter how much you bond over *Star Trek*, no woman's going to go out with you once you've knocked her halfway across a shop floor. So I gave up and went back to staring at you. I didn't mean owt by it. I just like you. A lot.'

'Oh.'

He smiles, and again, the grin softens his chiselled features. He runs a hand through his short, spiked-up black hair. He's about my age, maybe a fraction older, but his face looks like he's lived, like he'd have a story or two to tell. And he likes me.

I relax into the chair, I can't help but smile back. He's very attractive. When I first saw him in the pub, he reminded me of an artistic stroke on a page, didn't he?

'I really didn't mean to glare at you,' he says.

'Hmmm,' I reply with a raised eyebrow.

'How about I apologise by buying you a drink in a public place, lots of people around so you know I'm not some mad staring stalker. Oh, and without any doors to hit you with.'

'It *was* six months of glaring. Really hard glares.'

He laughs. 'How about dinner then? Dinner in a public place, I'm afraid, though, there might be doors involved in a restaurant.'

'I'm willing to risk it if you are,' I laugh and steal a chip from his plate. 'I'll be in college tomorrow afternoon, you can call me to arrange it. We could go down to Town Street or New Roadside.'

'Tomorrow?' he asks.

'Unless you're busy.'

'No, no I'm not. Tomorrow would be great. Fantastic, even.'

'Tomorrow it is then.'

Staring Man grins, really wide. So wide, I have to look away. I haven't had this in a while, someone who thinks I'm beautiful and looks so pleased at the thought of having dinner with me. I'd actually forgotten how it felt to have someone fancy me, not just want to unload onto me. I'm not feeling anything problem-like from him – no need to share; no ulterior motive. He's just looking forward to dinner with me. Wow.

'Your friend's trying to get your attention,' he says, indicating behind me.

'Friend?' I glance over my shoulder. Jess is staring at us, open-mouthed. She thought I was coming over to start a fight, which I was, and now we're grinning at each other and I'm stealing his chips. She's going to faint when I tell her about dinner. Oh, Jess, Otley.

I get up, 'I've got a prior engagement, I'd better be going,' I say. Then I remember. 'Oh, my name's Ceri. Ceri D'Altroy, I'm finally in the college phone book. What's your name? I can't keep calling you Staring Man. Which I only called you

422

in my head and to my friend, over there. But not to anyone . . .' *Ceri, shut up. Now. NOW!* 'Anyway, what's your name?'

He rolls his eyes and sighs silently. 'I've got a bloody stupid name. Blame it on my parents. They wanted a girl, so when they got me, they kept the name but didn't even consider that it'd humiliate me for the rest of my life.'

Ah ha! Someone else who understands the torture of being callously named. Ceresis, indeed. 'Go on . . .'

'It's all rather embarrassing, really. That's why everyone at college calls me Bosley.'

'It can't be that bad,' I say.

'You'd be surprised.'

I frown. 'Oh come on, just tell me what your name is.'

His bronze eyes meet mine as he says: 'Angel.'

271/12